BAIT

INCLUDING PREQUEL STORY - TARGET

LISA PHILLIPS

First Edition March 2014

Published by Lisa Phillips

ISBN: 1495489531

ISBN-13: 978-1495489532

Cover art by Kristine McCord

Photos from Shutterstock

Denver Cityscape - gary yim / Shutterstock.com

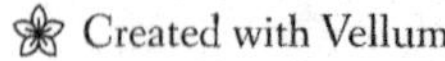

You wouldn't be holding this book if it wasn't for my girls:
Becky Avella, Heather Humrichouse,
Hilarey Johnson and Kristine McCord.
Not only fantastic writers in their own right,
they're also the best critique group in the world.

Thank you doesn't begin to cover it.

ACKNOWLEDGMENTS

In the course of writing this book I had to contact the FBI. It's safe to say they exceeded my expectations in both the time it took them to get back to me (literally, days) and the wealth of information they supplied.

Any errors you may find in this book are due to the fact that story is king,
and honestly, reality isn't always all that awesome anyway.

"If anyone comes to me and does not hate father
and mother and wife and children and brothers and sisters, yes, and
even his own life, he cannot be my disciple."
Luke 14:26

TARGET

DENVER FBI - BOOK 1

ONE

The sweat on Special Agent Liam Conners' forehead froze. A tan colored van was parked between two street lamps, out front of his neighbor's apartment across from the clubhouse. The door to the gym clicked shut behind him and his breath puffed out as a cloud.

The rear of the van was wide open. A five-eleven man in a heavy overcoat, dark pants and black boots stepped off the curb with a bundle over one shoulder. On the man's head was a knit cap, but Liam couldn't see what shade it was, just that the color was bright.

Liam stepped out. It was probably nothing. Why did he tense up at the slightest thing? No wonder he couldn't sleep. He grasped the damp towel around his neck and the door to the gym at his apartment complex clicked behind him, shutting out the light from inside. It was two a.m., but the sweat-session hadn't done anything to settle his nerves. After a long day, the last thing he needed was an equally long night of sleeplessness. And yet here he was.

The van man shifted his weight and dumped what was over his shoulder inside the vehicle. Liam's foot hit the pavement before he even registered that what had been on the man's shoulder was a body.

His neighbor was being abducted.

Liam ran. He might not know her name, but he knew her.

For some reason, in a complex of a hundred or so apartments, she seemed to be there anytime he was coming or going. The woman had dark red hair that would have been called *carrot top* in elementary school, and a slender body. She probably had an amazing smile, but he'd never caught it. She was kind of serious—as in, all the time. In fact, Liam had never even seen her look happy, or anything other than completely neutral.

The back doors of the van slammed shut. Liam's towel went flying as he sprinted across the grass hill in the center island of the complex's main street.

The shorts and t-shirt he wore to work out weren't much protection against the frigid air of February in Colorado, but he barely felt it. Instead his mind washed with the things he'd seen at work, hunting down degenerates and crazies.

Denver wasn't better or worse than any of the cities he'd lived in. Not even D.C., where he'd grown up. And no one, least of all a woman who desperately needed to laugh, should be at the mercy of any of the criminals he'd ever met.

He jumped the curb onto pavement and the man opened the driver's door.

"Freeze!"

Still running, Liam reached for his weapon, which was back in his apartment, along with his badge...and his cell phone. His night-time workouts were the one thing he didn't let work intrude on. Why did he do that?

Nothing deterred the abductor from his task. Not even when a hundred-ninety pounds of frustrated FBI agent bore down on him. He didn't even turn Liam's way; he just climbed in the van.

The door slammed shut, the engine fired and the van sped away. Liam got there in time to grasp the back corner with his fingertips.

Then he was alone in the street outside *her* apartment, sucking in ice-cold air.

The van had no license plate. It turned the corner without slowing down, tilting so it almost went up on two wheels. A Ford; older model with rust on the edges of the doors.

The front door to her apartment was ajar, so Liam went in and called 9-1-1 from there.

When the cop cars pulled up outside and Sergeant Tucker got out of the first one, Liam's shoulder blades loosened. His partner kidded him that one of these days he would wind up permanently shrugging from all the tension. But what did she know? Caisey had more issues than the main character in a Kristine McCord novel.

"Evening, Special Agent Conners." Sergeant Tucker was a late-fifties African- American career cop he'd met before. The other officer behind him headed over to the clubhouse, probably to rouse the management.

Liam held out his hand. "You can just call me Liam, since I'm in my shorts."

"Good deal." Sergeant Tucker smiled. "Now let's get started."

He turned to the front door, but stopped and looked at the cop. "Swing shift or night shift?"

"You're not keeping me from my bed, Conners."

"Good." He should probably explain why he was asking. "It's not that I think you'd do a less-than job if you were at the end of a long shift, but—"

"You have a thing for this girl?"

"What? No." Liam cleared his throat. "No, I don't."

One of the sergeant's eyebrows rose. "Sure?"

"She's my neighbor, but I've never even spoken to her."

Liam ignored the sergeant's measured stare and ran down what had happened. In the end what he had to say didn't amount to much, and so he led the cops inside and they walked through the apartment.

The living room would have been immaculate had there not been a pizza box on the table with two cold slices left uneaten and a bunch of empty beer bottles. The lamps looked expensive and the coffee table was cherry wood and shined, except for the ring where someone had set a cup down without a coaster. The carpet and walls were standard for all the apartments, but her couch was a deep burgundy and as soft to the touch as it looked. The decorations were simple and elegant, much like the woman herself.

He didn't like not knowing her name, so he searched in the kitchen and the second bedroom she used as an office—same as he did—until he found an envelope with her name on it.

Andrea James.

It was a simple name for a classy woman, but he liked it.

Liam flicked further down the stack of mail and found a brown envelope with nothing marked on the front. He turned it over and a photo of Andrea clutching a briefcase, walking outside somewhere, and talking on her cell phone slid onto the mail stack.

Sergeant Tucker stuck his head in the room. "Got something?"

"Surveillance photo. Could be the killer sent it to her."

Liam stared at it and the urge to be certain this whole situation wasn't ten times worse than he thought took over. He strode past the sergeant.

"What is it?"

Liam stopped in the bedroom doorway. On the pillow was a white square of material, and the room still held the faint odor that was the modus operandi of a serial killer. The same killer Liam and his partner and the rest of the task force had been chasing for months.

Chloroform.

He turned to the sergeant. "I need your phone."

CAISEY LYONS SLAMMED the dash of her stupid car on the off-chance reasonable force might jog the heater into pumping out something vaguely warm. But she was already pulling into the apartment complex where Liam lived. She parked and lifted her scarf at the front, so it covered her mouth and nose.

What was it about being woken from a deep sleep that made her freezing every single time? It wasn't even that cold out, just a tad bit chilly, as Grams would say. Caisey's grandma was British, so she came out with all kinds of phrases that made no sense at all, but she insisted on using them anyway—to the point that Caisey had adopted some of them, too.

She used her key to enter Liam's apartment and grabbed his cell phone and the wallet that held his badge from the entry table. *Seriously*. The man had an entry table, for goodness sake. He probably had smoked salmon in his fridge, while hers was full of important things, like chocolate milk and leftover nachos. He probably ate the salmon while he read the girlie- looking paperback that sat next to where he kept his keys.

When she pulled up outside the apartment number he'd given her, Caisey stared for a moment. Not at the cop cars, or the SUV that their boss, Special Agent Burkot, drove. No, she was staring because it was *this* apartment—the one Liam always glanced at when she picked him up.

Caisey showed her badge and gave her name to the officer. Liam was in the second bedroom, where an agent from IT sat at the desk, working on the computer. The officer who'd been questioning Liam closed his notebook and passed her on the way out, giving her a nod.

Her partner perched on the edge of a neatly organized bookcase that came up to his hip, his legs stretched out in front of him. His blue, sweat-wicking t-shirt was damp and he had bleached-white shorts on. His sneakers looked brand new.

By the looks of things, if the apartment resident was here, she'd probably tell her partner to kindly remove his rear from the furniture. Caisey decided the missing woman and Liam might just be soul mates.

Liam ran a hand down his face. He looked seriously worried about this mystery woman he had a crush on.

Caisey opted to defuse the tension. "Only you could manage to have a tan in February. Do not tell me you fake bake."

He looked up. "What?"

"Tanning beds? Ring a bell?"

It worked. The corner of Liam's mouth twitched. "No."

LIAM KNEW what his partner was doing, and he was grateful for it, even if he would never give her the satisfaction of telling her that.

Tanning beds? Her blonde hair was pulled back in a pony-tail like always, and she wore jeans and a Colorado University sweatshirt under her FBI jacket and the black cowboy boots her dad had given her.

"So where are we at?"

Liam held her gaze, thankful for the switch to business talk. "Local police are checking traffic cameras to see if we can find out where he took her. But with no license plate, there's little chance we're going to find her in the city."

He had to face the fact there wasn't much hope of finding the missing woman alive. Instead the likelihood was they'd find her the same way each of the Chloroform Killer's other victims had been found.

Don't think about them.

Liam and Caisey had been on the task force working this case for six months now, although the killer had been active more like eighteen months. After the daughter of Senator Paulson was killed it seemed like everyone was re-tasked.

"Okay. That's good." Caisey turned away.

Liam followed after her, mostly just for something to do. If he stayed, just him and the silent office, he'd think about the other women.

Caisey entered the bedroom, which was as immaculate as the rest of the apartment except for the rumpled comforter and the crime scene techs. A black book lay on the floor beside the night-stand, as though it had been knocked off and landed in disarray.

Caisey motioned to the tech closest to her. "May I?"

She slipped on the glove she was handed and picked it up—a Bible. Andrea read the Bible? Caisey set the book back on the night-stand and they trailed back through to where their boss and two other agents were talking in the kitchen.

Caisey's boot heels clipped the linoleum. "Anything?"

Liam stopped beside her.

Special Agent Burkot, their boss, shook his head. "Must have been something, seeing him take her like that. You okay, Conners?"

Liam gritted his teeth. "I'm fine." So long as he didn't keep thinking on it, at least. Who wanted to drown in the fact that they had failed? Again.

"And the Chloroform Killer to boot? I'd have loved to have been there. With my gun."

The reprimand was there, but no one answered it. Caisey stiffened. Liam didn't need her to defend him, but he knew she wanted to.

"We'll get him." Liam's words were calm and measured, but his body was wound tight.

Burkot zipped up his jacket and looked at Caisey. "I want everyone in the office first thing so we can see where we're at. You'll stay and work with the locals?"

Caisey nodded. The two agents Burkot had been talking with trailed behind him like a Secret Service detail. She turned to Liam. "You want to run home and get changed?"

Liam needed something to keep his thoughts from what was happening to Andrea, and it might as well be getting dressed to work, to chase down the few leads they had and maybe...just maybe have a shot at getting Andrea back.

Despite the odds.

Despite the fact no other victim of the Chloroform Killer had yet survived.

There might not be a whole lot of rational hope, but he wasn't going to look at another dead body of someone he cared about.

Not again.

A police radio murmured and he wondered for the billionth time how they even understood what was being said.

Sergeant Tucker stuck his head in. "One of our patrol officers found the van."

TWO

Liam drove them in his car to the craft store parking lot where the van had been spotted. Fresh clothes felt good, even if he hadn't had time for a shower. Caisey didn't argue, she just grabbed her backpack and tossed it on his backseat.

He climbed out of the SUV and they walked to where the police officers stood by the van. Crime scene techs were already there, squinting and doing that flicking thing with their tiny brushes. If this was the Chloroform Killer's work, they wouldn't find anything. But there was always a chance, and if it meant he might get Andrea back before it was too late...well, then.

Sometimes a slim chance was all you needed.

Liam stopped by the cop, who introduced himself as Officer Todd Barnes. The officer leaned forward on the balls of his feet and rocked back. He never stilled the whole time he told them how he came upon the scene.

Caisey turned to Liam. "Is this the same van?"

He didn't answer his partner's question. Instead, he stepped back and to the side about the same distance he'd been at the apartment complex. Closed his eyes. Opened them. The lights had come on as it drove away, but the shape was the same. No rear license plate.

He looked at Caisey and nodded. "It's the same van."

"So where are they?"

Ms. James was victim number six, and they'd never found a vehicle. Nothing like this had ever happened before, not with any of the other five abductions. Then again, there had never been a witness worth anything before. Why it had to be Liam, and why now, was a mystery. Whatever the reason, he wasn't going to pass up the chance to get a result on this case.

Caisey thanked the officer and motioned to Liam's car. He followed her over. "I'm fine."

She didn't back off. "I think he dumped the van because you saw him. But if he's got a passenger with him, he must have had a vehicle here. It's not that easy to haul a hundred- plus pounds any distance, not without being seen. Again."

"So he planned to switch vehicles?" Liam looked around, high on the parking lot street-lights for surveillance cameras. "Maybe he does that every time."

"Whether he does or not, I doubt he'll be back. And there's no way he would have left it here if it would lead back to him."

"You think they won't find anything?"

Caisey folded her arms. "I think we don't have a lick of evidence except the chloroform-soaked cloths, and not one of those has ever had anything on it except generic soap and the chemical."

Liam clenched his jaw.

"We should see if the Sergeant got anything from the cameras. Maybe the guy slipped up and glanced the wrong way, or we can get a shot of the vehicle he's driving." Caisey scratched her hairline where a strand of her ponytail had come loose, and talked as they made their way to the building. "I wonder if he uses a different van for each girl, or if he just dumped it since you saw him."

They went into the store, which was shut down for the night. Caisey led the way to the back like she knew where she was going, which she might. That was just her way. "Ever been in here before?"

"Grams needed more wool for a scarf she was knitting. I clocked two kids stealing paints for a school project, so I wound up in the security office giving them the talk."

Liam smiled. He'd seen her do it before, several times. She wasn't a tall woman— barely five-three—but with the badge and gun on display, Caisey probably looked nine feet tall to a teenager who just got busted by an FBI agent.

Sergeant Tucker was already with the security guard, who brought up one of the camera feeds. They watched the van park twenty minutes after Liam chased it leaving his apartment complex. The picture was of the wrong side, though. Liam could only see the front passenger door and not in a way they could get a look inside.

The driver's door opened, but the dim light on a black and white picture didn't give them much, especially when he hauled the body off-screen.

"You have any other cameras that will give us another angle?"

The security guard shook his head. "This is the only one that works."

Caisey glanced at him. "We confirmed it was him. We've never found a van before...maybe it will give us something."

He knew she didn't believe it, but Liam said, "I hope so."

He hadn't put much stock in hope, not for a long time. He didn't want to think the worst, but Andrea James didn't have anything left to put her faith in. Not anymore, and not if they couldn't find something that might lead them to her.

And it was all Liam's fault.

Caisey grabbed his arm and pulled him into the hall. "This isn't your fault."

He almost smiled. "Why would you think that?"

His partner rolled her eyes. "Puh-lease. We've worked together for three years. Tell me you're not wondering what might have happened if you'd been thirty-seconds earlier out of the gym."

Liam folded his arms. "It's better than resigning myself to the fact that she was as good as dead already and there was nothing I could've done."

"I'm sorry you couldn't help her." Caisey paused a beat. "I'm sorry that of all the people in the city it had to be her that he picked as his next victim."

"I am too."

Caisey hesitated. "But maybe..."

"Don't say it."

"It's just...I don't know. Maybe it's a blessing you don't really know her."

Liam looked at the ceiling for a moment. "Sure, if she hadn't just been *abducted by a serial killer*."

"Okay, yeesh. So this isn't about it being Andrea of all people. It's really just because you were there, and powerless to do something?"

"My neighborhood. My neighbor. It shouldn't make a difference who it was." Even though it kind of did. "She's still a human being who deserves our best effort."

"Agreed." But Caisey clearly didn't buy it, mostly because he wasn't selling. She just wanted to know exactly how torn up he was about Andrea—he knew that much about his partner after three years.

"We're not going to find her."

"We might."

He gritted his teeth. "Not before it's too late. If he knows we're on his tail he's just going to fast-track it. There won't be ten days before he's done. Not if there's a chance he could get caught."

Caisey glanced aside for a moment. When she looked back at him there was a spark in her eyes. "Unless he thinks there isn't a chance."

Yeah, because Liam really needed to entertain the idea of Andrea James going through what the other victims had.

"Let's just go, okay? It's not like we're going to find her standing around here."

LIAM SNAPPED UP THE PHONE. "CONNERS."

"It's Grams, ducky. Is Caisey about?"

He slumped back in his chair and transferred the call to Caisey's extension. Her elderly grandmother dialed the wrong number and got his desk enough that it didn't even bother him anymore, even if it was barely seven a.m.

While Caisey chatted with her Grams, Liam ran a hand down his face. His eyes were hot and gritty and the coffee in the office was like drinking molasses. He preferred it light and vanilla flavored, but no one else seemed to appreciate his good taste.

He clicked on the file and looked—again—at Andrea James. She didn't even smile for her driver's license photo.

"You're staring at her."

Liam gritted his teeth. Caisey couldn't see the screen on his monitor from where she sat. "I'm working." Liam glared at his partner. "Or is that a federal crime now, too?"

Her eyes narrowed. "I'm going to let that slide because you're stressed out. But I'd like to point out at this juncture that, given your involvement, your guilt is now driving your need to solve this case."

She didn't know the half of it. This wasn't the first time Liam could've stopped someone from dying. That time hadn't turned out well either, and now Liam would have two deaths on his conscience.

His face hurt from clenching his jaw all night. He'd been inches from her when he'd touched the van's back light and it meant absolutely nothing. And if Andrea's disappearance tracked the way all the others had, they wouldn't find anything. In a couple of weeks her body would be discovered and the hunt for the Chloroform Killer would continue.

And he'd never even spoken to her.

He'd never even approached her and struck up a conversation, let alone asked her out. He could've done it a hundred times, but something always held him back. They might have had something great. True, it could just as easily have gone nowhere, but he'd never even tried. All because he was too busy.

Liam tossed his pen on the desk. "What do we have?"

"Fingerprints in the van."

"Which won't belong to the killer."

"Surveillance video."

"Which told us basically nothing."

"What about her apartment? Email, phone records. The photo." Caisey looked at the papers on her desk. "The technicians who went through her apartment are getting me a timeline of his contact with Ms. James."

Liam's stomach turned over. Nothing this guy had done yet had ever left a trail. Victims were often stalked, but rarely did he make direct contact before he abducted them, so far as the evidence indicated at least. Email and phone records in each case hadn't turned up anything.

The photo at Andrea's apartment was new.

"Look, we work this like we work everything. One piece of evidence at a time until we find something we can run with."

Was she trying to placate him? Liam didn't suppose it would affect the outcome whether she was or not.

Caisey stood. "You want more coffee." Revulsion churned through him and must have shown on his face, because she laughed. "Never mind."

Liam checked his email, but there was nothing new. Any test results would take longer than a few hours to get back to them, but the clock was ticking on Andrea James' life. And he was still sitting here.

Caisey set her mug down, steam curling up from the coffee. Between the two of them they should be able to find something. Or, that should be the case. But with a whole team of agents and months of work they still didn't have a clue who the Chloroform Killer was. Or why he only targeted women in their twenties, with no other discernable correlations.

Before yesterday, Liam had been able to affect at least a semblance of distance between him and the victims—*I don't like that word.* It hardly seemed right to call someone helpless who was going through something that forced you to be strong even when you were broken.

Now things were unavoidably personal, and Liam didn't want to admit he was having trouble staying detached. Empathy did not help you catch a serial killer. In this job, you had to leave it at home.

His phone rang; the number for the local police department.

"Conners."

"It's Sergeant Tucker. Ms. James' next of kin just got back to me. I hope you're up for a road trip."

THREE

The road trip turned out to be a twenty-minute drive down to Castlewood, a suburb of Denver. Caisey still insisted on stopping for Starbucks on the way, like she hadn't had four cups of coffee already. Since they were both coasting on little more than fumes, Liam didn't gripe too much. It wouldn't be long before they'd have to re-charge.

The address the Sergeant had given him was a mansion. He hadn't known what to expect of Mr. and Mrs. James when they arrived. Especially given the police had informed them already that their daughter was missing—suspected of having been abducted by a known serial killer. But this wasn't it.

"Thank you." Liam nodded to the butler, or waiter, or whoever the guy was with the pressed suit who set the china cup on the table.

Caisey sat beside him, perched on the edge of the silk-covered settee like she was worried she'd get dirt on the furniture. Given how much she was shifting around, the damage was likely already done.

Mr. James had one leg of his Armani suit crossed over the other, his armchair a perfect match for the sitting room decor. His dark brown hair didn't have a strand of gray, despite his drivers' license putting him at sixty-five. His attention was on his iPad, and had been since they'd entered the residence.

It was Mrs. James who'd answered the door, in a floor-length white gown she may or may not have been wearing all night given that it was rumpled and she smelled like gin. Her nose was permanently scrunched—likely to the dismay of her plastic surgeon—in what appeared to be a concerted attempt to remain upright. She also didn't speak until she sat, given it probably took all of her concentration to ambulate from the front door to the receiving room.

Liam glanced between them. "When was the last time you spoke with your daughter?"

"A few weeks, maybe?" Mrs. James looked at her husband. "What do you think, darling?"

"What?" Mr. James glanced up and his wife repeated the question. He looked at Liam. "Andrea and I had dinner two weeks ago."

"Dinner, where? And why didn't I know about this?"

Caisey shifted again. Liam wanted to kick her like two kids under the table at Thanksgiving, but that never went unnoticed. So these people cared more about their own squabble than the fact that their daughter had been abducted by a serial killer—it wasn't up to Liam and Caisey to give them a lesson in familial love.

Liam took a sip of his tea. Caisey had left hers untouched, but only because she drank exactly one kind and this wasn't it. Liam gave them a couple of minutes to have their muttered squabble, which quickly dissolved into tutting and a curled lip from Mrs. James.

When he figured they'd had enough time, Liam broke into their stalemate. "When you spoke with your daughter, Mr. James, did she give any indication she felt she was being followed, or watched?"

"Of course not. No. Andrea would have told me if she thought she was in danger."

Was that the truth? It could be that the man was just adept at compartmentalizing his life to the point he seemed permanently detached. Liam turned to the wife. "And you, Mrs. James? Did your daughter give you any indication she felt threatened the last time you spoke with her?"

She perked up and shot him a weathered beauty-queen smile. "I'm not sure I can remember." Mr. James snorted; his attention once again on his iPad. The woman's smile fractured at the edges, but she persisted. "It was a few weeks ago."

"You and Andrea aren't close?" Caisey's opinion was present in her voice. She didn't tend to warm toward people who ignored their families—Liam knew some of that long story—and she didn't particularly like rich people either. No wonder it had taken her so long to warm up to him being her partner.

Mrs. James kept her attention on Liam. Was her perfect posture just for his benefit? "My daughter is a complicated woman. She inherited that, among several other things, from her father. We have not always seen eye to eye, but we do talk. At least as much as her schedule allows." She shot her husband a glance. "Although apparently it does allow for dinner engagements."

Mr. James sighed. "I was downtown. It was spur of the moment, not that I am required to explain myself to you. Andrea and I enjoy spending time together. We had sushi. You were busy, if I recall."

Mrs. James' reaction indicated she might well have been indisposed. Liam figured drunk off her posterior was probably it.

"Are you aware of anyone in Andrea's life who might have a reason to harm her?" It tasted bitter, saying her name, but warmth still flared in his chest.

The couple looked at each other, sharing something for the first time since Liam and Caisey arrived. Liam glanced from one to the other. "Mr. James? Mrs. James?"

Mrs. James smoothed the wrinkles in her dress.

Mr. James set his iPad on the coffee table and folded his arms. "There is no one in the world who would want to harm Andrea."

"Why would they?" Mrs. James shrugged one delicate shoulder. "Andrea is the best person we know." Her smile cracked and tears filled her eyes. "Who would want to hurt her?"

"Now, dear." Mr. James reached over and patted her on the knee, but held himself back. "I'm sure this is all some misunderstanding. Andrea will be fine."

Liam pressed his lips together.

"That's really what you think?" Caisey shifted; her back straight for once, instead of slouched. "Your daughter was abducted by a known serial killer, and we have exactly nine days before her body will be discarded for someone to find."

Liam didn't need that visual, but there it was. He'd been to each of the crime scenes so far. He wasn't looking forward to going to this one. Not when he knew what Andrea was like whole.

Like his sister.

Caisey sighed, her ire apparently burned out. "I'm sorry we have to be the ones to tell you this. I'm sure the police explained everything that is going on. And I'm sorry for your loss, but she is lost. There is little hope that your daughter will be found alive."

Caisey took a breath. "The likelihood is that your daughter knew this man. And unless you can think of someone in her life who might have done this, or anything she said to you that might indicate she was aware she was being targeted, then I'm afraid we shouldn't take any more time here that could be better spent following up on leads elsewhere."

And that was putting it nicely. Liam was kind of proud of his partner, since her tendency was to be a whole lot more blunt than that speech. She'd actually been sort of eloquent—for Caisey.

They stood and Liam buttoned his suit jacket. Mr. James' attention caught on the pin on Liam's lapel. "Harvard, eh?"

Liam shook his hand. "Yes, sir. You'll call us if you think of anything further?"

When he got a nod, Liam handed over his card, which Mr. James slid into the pocket of his pants. He followed Caisey down the hall to where the waiter/butler guy held the door open for them, chewing his lip. Liam stopped.

The butler glanced at the sitting room Andrea's parents had stayed in, and then whispered, "Find her. Please?"

Liam couldn't offer platitudes that would bring up the bile lodged in his throat. He held the guy's gaze and nodded, which seemed to satisfy him, and handed over another of his business cards.

Liam started the car and immediately punched the off button

for the radio. He didn't like Caisey's country hits at the best of times, and definitely not now.

She crossed her arms and huffed. "Can you believe those people? Not a tear or a single sniffle in the place and their daughter's as good as dead."

Liam's stomach churned. "Thanks."

"I'm serious. I wouldn't have believed it if I hadn't seen it right in front of my face."

"Isn't it you always telling me not to be surprised when people aren't inherently good? We're all selfish sinners, or whatnot?"

Liam didn't agree, since there was no way everyone in the world was bad. His sister had been the best person he knew until she took her own life. There was no way Bethany could be called evil like some of the people they met.

Caisey glanced over. "Fine. Throw my words back in my face. But you'd think parents who just found out what they did would be a little more upset. I mean, how many times did we interview someone who could barely talk they were crying so hard?"

"People don't process their grief in the same way."

"People don't all have feelings in the same way either."

Liam nudged her with his elbow. "Yeah, you would know."

"Yes I would." Caisey chuckled. "That whole thing was pretty funny in a tragic, I- want-to-cry-now, kind of way. You know, if I was the kind of person who actually cried."

Liam drove toward the office. It was after lunch, but he didn't expect to be hungry for about a month.

Caisey shifted in her seat. "They were definitely hiding something."

Liam pulled into a parking space outside the Denver FBI office. "You think everyone is hiding something."

"They are."

"Even you?"

Caisey's chin lifted a fraction. "Uh, yeah."

"What are you hiding?"

"I think it would be more interesting to know what you're hiding."

Liam brushed it off. "I'm not hiding anything."

"Nice try. For the record, I don't buy it."

"Maybe you should try looking on the bright side?"

He might not be able to manage it right now, but one of them looking up couldn't hurt.

Caisey pushed the door open. "Please. An optimist would assume everything is going to work out and Andrea James is going to turn up without a scratch on her. I've read all the reports, just like you. That's impossible. It's just not—"

Liam stopped when Caisey did and followed her gaze to the woman waiting at the security checkpoint—a redhead without a smile on her face. In fact, she looked kind of mad.

What on earth?

Andrea James strode toward them, stopped and put one hand on the hip of her slim- cut business suit. "Am I to take it from the looks on your faces that you two are the ones responsible for the mess in my apartment?"

Liam blinked. She really was here. That meant...

"And what's this insane story about me having been abducted by a serial killer?"

Liam's body came unstuck. He moved toward her and Andrea's eyes widened, but he didn't stop.

He wrapped her up in his arms and hugged her.

FOUR

Andrea's first reaction was to push him away, but the feeling of someone bigger and stronger with their arms around her penetrated before she could stop it. Not that it was him, of course. Just that it had been so long since anyone hugged her.

Years even.

Her arms came up and she gave him a gentle squeeze. The FBI agent must have taken that for a sign, because he let her go and stepped back. A chill crept in and Andrea pulled her wool overcoat tighter around her. His cheeks were flushed. Had she ever seen a man blush?

She held her hand out. "I'm Andrea James."

It was the woman beside him who slapped her hand into Andrea's and said, "Caisey Lyons. This is my partner, Special Agent Liam Conners. He was the one who witnessed your abduction."

Agent Conners—Liam—shook his head and glanced around the crowded lobby, most of whom were staring at them. "We should do this upstairs."

Andrea followed them to the elevator, a visitor's badge hanging from a lanyard around her neck. Their security measures were extensive, but she got why they were necessary. The whole office was imposing. It was good she'd never broken the law. FBI agents were intimidating, even if they didn't keep their guns on display like cops.

The Special Agents led her to a conference room and the female one said, "Coffee?"

Andrea nodded. "Please. Just cream."

The woman strode out like she was supremely confident of who she was. Andrea had never been that sure of anything. Then she realized she was alone in the room with the FBI agent who hugged her hello.

She caught his gaze and stared right back. His jaw was square and his blonde hair had been cut recently. The suit he wore was expensive and he had a Harvard pin on his lapel, even though he'd probably graduated at least ten years ago.

He was the kind of guy who regularly broke hearts while he had an on-again-off-again girlfriend who was a yoga instructor. The kind of guy whose hair never got mussed and never looked like crap, even when he was tired or sick. But she'd definitely seen him somewhere before.

Andrea tipped her head to the side. "Why do you look familiar?"

Agent Conners' lips curled up at the edges. "We live in the same apartment complex. That's how I came to believe I witnessed you being abducted. He took a woman out of your apartment."

"Are you sure?"

He smiled. "Am I sure a woman was abducted, or am I sure it was your apartment?"

"My apartment."

"The door was open."

Andrea didn't want to assume, but there was only one person who could have been at her place "It wasn't a break-in, a woman was in there?"

"It's difficult to say, since whoever abducted this woman would have had to break in." He seemed to measure his words carefully, in order to allow her time to absorb it all.

"You've been out of town?"

Andrea nodded. "I was in Chicago, visiting our headquarters. I work for Samuels-Kelper. I'm a CPA, and we had some problems with a client that had to be worked through in person. It was all wrapped up late yesterday evening, so I slept the night at my hotel and then flew back this morning. I got home a little while ago to find the police tape and an Officer guarding my front door. I had to show ID just to get into my home."

Her apartment had looked like they'd managed to touch everything she owned. The bathroom and kitchen were a mess and her bed even looked slept in.

"You have your ticket, or a receipt?"

Andrea pulled the paperwork from her briefcase and slid it across the table. It grated on her that she had to justify herself to them, but that was their job. Dotting I's and crossing T's and all that. Fine, if it helped people, and they caught criminals. But did she have to be okay with it when it was happening to her?

Special Agent Conners gave the itinerary a once-over and handed it back. "Most of this is just procedure, but I'd like to say I am really glad you're okay."

"Me too." Andrea half-smiled, because what else did you do? Who wouldn't be glad they hadn't been abducted by a serial killer? Even though she was ticked the police had gone through her belongings, she understood now why they hadn't felt the need to inform her first.

"Whoever was abducted from your apartment spent time there. Ate there, slept there. Do you have a roommate, or significant other?"

"No. There's no one."

"Is there someone with a key, who might have stayed over while you were gone?"

"Oh." Andrea's thoughts tumbled over each other like a wave. "She knew I was gone, though I don't know how. Or maybe she came over to crash and stayed because I was gone. She does that sometimes. Brings her laundry and has dinner with me, or orders...pizza."

That was why the empty pizza box had been on the coffee table when Andrea hadn't had a slice in years. "Sometimes I give her a little cash, but never too much. I know what she does with it, I'm not ignorant. I know I'm enabling her but what else do you do?"

"She?"

But if Keira had come over, that meant she was the one who'd been abducted.

Andrea rummaged for her cell phone, found the contact for the house phone number where Keira usually stayed and dialed. Liam was talking, asking her something. Andrea squeezed her eyes shut and listened to it ring.

"Yeah." It was a man's voice.

"I'm looking for Keira."

"Ain't no Keira here."

Andrea bit her lip. "Sunny?"

"Haven't seen her." He hung up.

The phone slipped from Andrea's hand and fell to the floor. Liam crouched beside her and retrieved it. He set the phone on the table. Andrea squeezed her fingers together, but they wouldn't stop shaking.

"Ms. James?"

"Her name is Keira. She's my sister."

~

LIAM PULLED HIS CHAIR CLOSER. Andrea James looked like she was about to lose what little control she was holding onto. "Tell me about your sister."

Caisey strode into the room, her mouth open about to say something. She stopped and swallowed whatever it was. His partner's entire manner changed as she stepped quietly around Andrea, set the cup down in front of her and took her seat.

Andrea clenched her fingers together in her lap. "She stays with me, sometimes, like I said. Our parents disowned her. They threw away every picture of her. They won't say her name or even acknowledge her existence."

Caisey got out a notepad and started scribbling.

Liam kept his focus on Andrea. "Is it possible she was the one at your apartment?"

"I'd say it's very possible she was who you saw being abducted. If the guy who just answered the phone isn't out of it, then she's not at the place she usually stays, not that that's abnormal. But if she isn't there and she's not at my apartment, there aren't many places she'll be for long and nowhere else she would sleep. She's paranoid about where she sleeps."

"How old is Keira?"

"Twenty-nine."

Liam had seen Andrea's date of birth, but he still said, "Older or younger than you?" She needed the space to focus on ordinary details while it sank in.

"Two years younger."

Liam held Andrea's dark gaze with his. "How long has she been an addict?"

Surprise flared and she said, "A long time. Nearly six years, maybe. Since Brad died and she lost the baby. She was always wild, but not like this."

Liam squeezed her hand. "We need to talk about the Chloroform Killer now." When she nodded, he continued. "Have you had any reason to think you were being watched or followed recently?"

There was a slim chance the sister was the target and the crime had taken place at Andrea's because that was where Keira James went. But given the surveillance photo he'd found in Andrea's mail, he was leaning more to the idea that she was the target. That meant the killer had made a mistake and grabbed the wrong sister.

How closely did they favor each other, if it truly was a case of mistaken identity? Otherwise it was a crazy thing, given how closely Andrea had escaped. If her sister really was the victim, there would be a whole lot of survivor's guilt to work through.

Andrea stood, shifting fast enough she looked antsy as she backed up, her eyes wide. "You think he was after me, not Keira?"

"We have to look at all the possibilities."

She walked to the window and turned back to Liam and Caisey.

"There have been some weird things. Emails with a picture of me doing something, like someone was following me and watching me."

"And in your regular mail?"

"Not that I'm aware of. Was there?"

Liam nodded. "One."

"This is unreal." She ran a hand down her face, her shoulders slumped. "Was it really the Chloroform Killer? The police officer said that, but I thought he might just be guessing."

"The evidence certainly points to it being him, yes." The square of material with chloroform left on each of the victim's pillows wasn't something that had been made public. "Did you tell anyone about the emails, or file a report with the police?"

"I just thought they were a nuisance. I told the IT guy at work and then I deleted them and didn't think about it. I've been really busy at work. There wasn't time to deal with some weirdo stalker."

"You didn't think it was worth your safety?"

"It would have been worth Keira's, but I didn't know she was going to be abducted, did I?"

Liam sucked in a breath. She was always so staid; the rush of energy in her anger was like a sign of life. "We're not blaming you, and this isn't your fault. I don't really get why you didn't want to make an issue of it, but I need as much information as I can if we're going to catch this guy."

"And find Sunny."

"Sunny?"

"My sister."

"Keira's name is Sunny?"

Andrea sighed. "When she was disowned and cut off, she decided to change her name. She figured if they didn't want her, then she didn't want anything to do with them either. Not even their name. I helped her do it, so now she's legally Sunny Chapman. It's her fiancé Brad's last name. They were going to get married, since they'd gotten pregnant. Keira figured that would have been her name anyway."

Liam nodded.

You need to find her."

He didn't want to lie. And since he'd come to terms with the fact it was Andrea he wasn't going to be able to get back, didn't that mean he knew, at least to some degree, how she felt?

"We'll do our best. There's a window of time in which she's likely to...remain alive. If we can figure out who he is before then, it's possible we might be able to find her. But I'm not going to lie to you, Andrea. You need to prepare yourself for the worst. Your sister might not get out of this alive."

Andrea sank into a chair on the other side of Caisey, across the table from him. So much for remaining close, so he could reassure her. Apparently she didn't want anything to do with his comfort. It stung, but he wasn't going to leave her in the lurch.

Her eyes swam with emotion. Andrea tucked hair behind her ear and looked away. She didn't want him to see her upset? Or had she been conditioned not to show emotion?

"I have to go home. I'm exhausted." She labored to her feet and said, "Maybe you could keep me updated?"

She really thought he was just going to let her go, so she could have her meltdown in private?

Caisey held out her hand, stopping Andrea's progress. "We actually need you to stay here for the time being."

"What? Why can't I go?"

"We need to update our boss and find out what he wants to do with regards to your protection."

"But I'm not the one in danger."

Liam said, "If you were the target, he may realize his mistake and come for you again."

Andrea's eyes widened. "What?"

"You could be in serious danger, Andrea."

FIVE

Liam stood with Caisey in their boss's office. Special Agent Burkot was a former Marine and he'd never seen the guy drink anything other than coffee—even at the office Christmas party. Burkot's suit came from the same tailor Liam used, the one he'd found tucked away on a side street on one of his runs through lower downtown Denver.

Burkot peered at them with his "thinking" stare that meant he was assessing the situation and working through all the variables in his head. "What about her apartment?"

Caisey said, "Should be cleared by the end of today."

Burkot's desk was clear, but the walls were covered with pictures of his kids' college graduations, his wife, him shaking hands with President Bush (both of them), and two flags—a US flag and the flag for the Marine Corps. He clicked the mouse on his computer, likely looking through the case file. Liam had added his write-up from the interview with Andrea, but that was only minutes before they'd come in here. He didn't like making Andrea stay in the conference room, but they couldn't just let her go home and leave her vulnerable to being abducted.

Burkot looked at Liam. "You think the Chloroform Killer will come after her again, looking to rectify his mistake?"

"It's enough of a possibility that I don't want to risk her being unprotected when it happens. There isn't any solid indication, but he's never abducted the wrong woman before, so far as we know. It's unprecedented, and the best chance we've got of catching the guy if he does show up."

"Okay." Burkot folded his arms. "The two of you sit on this woman, twenty- four/seven. Speak to the manager at the apartment complex and get a place where a team can set up with full view of Ms. James' front door. You have fourteen days. If he doesn't show up, if the sister's body has been found by then, we'll scale it back."

"Yes, sir."

"But I want to know for sure if the sister is who he took. I don't want any more surprises."

Caisey nodded. "Yes, sir."

Liam had no idea how they were going to ascertain that it'd been Kiera, short of the tests coming back to confirm it was her in the apartment. But it looked like they'd be doing interviews with friends and roommates for the rest of the day.

"He shows up, you take this guy down." "Yes, sir."

They filed out and headed for their desks.

Caisey glanced at him. "You really think he's going to realize his mistake and try to abduct Andrea again?"

"I don't know, honestly. It could get ugly, fast, when he realizes Kiera isn't the woman he thought he was getting."

"And then he'll be twice as determined to get Andrea."

"Which is why we have to protect her. She doesn't need to be caught up in all this."

"Does anyone?" Caisey stopped and turned to him. "It's not just about protecting her. This is our chance to catch him."

"I know. That's why we'll have a team on surveillance."

"But they won't be in the apartment. We will. We're the ones who can get him."

"Sure, but—"

"Do you know how many agents would kill for the chance to take down a serial killer attempting to kidnap his victim?"

Liam lifted his chin, not liking where this was going. It wasn't like he didn't want to catch the guy. He just didn't like the idea of baiting a trap for a psychopath. There was no way that would end well. "I was there, remember? I'm the one who let him get away."

"Well, then, don't let him get away this time." Caisey's face was flushed with excitement. She didn't get out much. "This is our chance to become legends."

Liam wouldn't mind the notoriety that came with an arrest like that, but he'd much rather the guy never murdered anyone in the first place. "Maybe I don't want to be a legend."

Her face screwed up, like a three-year-old about to throw a tantrum.

"I'm just saying I like where I'm at. Don't you?" It was a struggle, but Liam kept a straight face. Caisey never reacted well to neediness. There was no way he was going to pass up an opportunity to tease her. "What, you don't like being partners anymore? You want to move on?"

"No, of course not. I—" Her eyes narrowed. "Oh, you're such a jerk." Caisey stormed to her desk, looking back over her shoulder. "I'm going to take this guy down, you'll see."

Liam grinned to her back while she swiped up her mug and stomped to the coffee pot. Good for her. He could be proud, even while he understood the majority of her drive came from the fact that Caisey was a "legacy" agent. Her father had been a Special Agent, too. He'd been killed in the line of duty, but not before he got to hand Caisey her badge at her Quantico graduation.

Liam's father was a retired Major General whose only emotion was a severe displeasure that his son had not gone into the Army, but to law school and then the FBI. But the Army would never have settled Liam. It would never have given him the chance to put to rest the powerlessness he'd felt when he found his sister's body. Catching murderers was what did that. Putting in jail the same kind of people who'd twisted his sister's mind into believing she was better off dead. There was just one problem.

It wasn't helping as much as it used to.

~

ANDREA SHIFTED ASIDE the blinds and stared out the window at downtown Denver. In her other hand she held her cell phone, pressed to her ear, while her mom went on and on. *And on.*

"I'm so glad, darling. So glad you're okay. Just so relieved to hear your voice."

"I know, Mom."

"You can't know, not until you have babies of your own." Her mom's breath shuddered as she sucked back tears. "I'm so relieved."

Andrea pressed her lips together. It was just after lunch, but still her mom was two drinks past sauced. A beautiful woman, a trophy wife with nothing to do all day but down glass after glass and wonder why she'd never done anything valuable with her life. Never mind that she'd raised two girls, or all the charity work she used to do. Andrea's mother had given up her dream job in order to get married and had mentioned that fact to whoever would listen practically every single day of her life.

Andrea enjoyed her job, most days. She didn't intend to get married and wind up resenting everything and everyone around her for all the changes it made. That was no way to live life. Kids should be loved simply because they were. And if a parent wasn't going to treat them as precious, then what business did they have even having kids in the first place? Andrea wasn't willing to risk resenting anything about having a husband or kids even for one second. Not when she'd seen what drinking too much would turn her into.

Or losing control, the way Kiera had.

Andrea's life was closely ordered between work and the peaceful solitude of her home life. She didn't need anything messing that up.

A rustle came through the phone line. Andrea could hear her mom still talking, but her voice was muffled. *She's passing out.*

Andrea sighed and hung up the phone. She found her dad's number in her contact list and dialed.

"Andrea?"

"Hi, Dad."

"Thank goodness you're okay. I was so worried."

Andrea felt her lips curl into a small smile. Despite the distance between them, she still felt closer to her father than anyone else in her family. Which wasn't saying much. "Thanks, Dad."

"So it was all a mistake? You weren't really abducted then." He sighed. "That's such a relief."

Andrea touched the window with her fingertips. "Actually, someone was abducted. She was at my apartment while I was away on business."

Silence stretched out into a full minute.

"You told me you never saw her. You said you don't have any part in her life, just like we decided."

"I never said that." Andrea swallowed, feeling her throat close up. "I told you I couldn't cut her out of my life like that. Not after what happened to Brad and the baby."

He scoffed. "If there even was a baby."

"Dad—"

"You know what she put us through. We can't just brush that off, Andrea. It doesn't work that way. She has to earn our trust back."

"And how is she supposed to do that, when neither of you will even speak to her?"

"I offered to get her into a program."

"She wasn't ready."

"Then she won't ever be. And if she's not willing to change, there's nothing I can do to help her."

Andrea's eyes filled with tears and the city blurred in front of her. "There's nothing any of us can do. Not now. Because Kiera—"

He gasped. "I told you not to say her name to me!"

"Kiera was at my house, Dad. She's the one who was abducted instead of me, I'm sure of it. All because she looks like me and she was staying there while I was gone. And it wasn't her fault. She didn't ask for this."

"It's for the best."

"How can you say that? That man is going to kill her, Dad."

"Then she'll be at peace."

Andrea tried to speak, but could only choke.

"She brought this on herself. It's only fitting this happened, given the lifestyle she lives."

"Are you even listening?" Andrea gasped for air. "The FBI thinks he was after me. If it's anyone's fault, it's mine."

"No, you didn't do this. Darling, don't worry. Everything is going to turn out like it's supposed to. Isn't that what you're always saying? God's will and all that?"

"This isn't His will. God wouldn't do this. He wouldn't want this for Kiera."

Tears streamed down Andrea's face. She could hear her dad speaking, but the words were lost in the muddle of her own gasps and choking attempts to pull in air.

Her sister was going to die and she was the only person in the world who cared. Kiera's pain, and her attempts to cover the agony with her addictions, might have put strain on their relationship, but that didn't mean Andrea didn't love her.

The phone was pulled from her fingers. Andrea spun around to Liam, his eyes shifting as he took in what was probably a pretty bedraggled appearance. He stepped forward, like he wanted to hug her again, but Andrea couldn't handle it if he did that. She was barely holding it together as it was. If she was given someone to lean on, she would lose it completely.

She put her hand out and the warmth of his chest hit her palm.

"Andrea—"

"Don't." She shook her head and let her hand drop back to her side. "Please. Don't touch me."

She backed up, stumbling as she rounded the table and sat on the far end with her back to him. The door didn't open or close. He was still there, listening to her cry broken, ugly sobs as she succumbed to the horrible reality that she was the only person in her family who had a heart; or a conscience. How was she going to do this all by herself?

Kiera was gone. Kiera who loved with everything she possessed, so fiercely that when it ended she was destroyed. Andrea couldn't fall into that trap. She sucked in a breath, knowing she couldn't let herself end up that same way.

She had to hold it together

SIX

Liam set his backpack down by the front door of Andrea's apartment, got out his tablet and put it on the coffee table. Andrea had disappeared into her bedroom to unpack her suitcase.

The quiet was eerie, so he flipped on the TV and found a news channel but lowered the volume so it was just background noise while he got to work cleaning up the mess.

Hopefully Andrea would do more than just unpack. If he thought she would do it, he would have told her to take a bath and a nap. After the crying jag she had in the conference room she'd looked like she needed about a week's worth of sleep. He knew how that felt, but everyone had their own way of dealing with trauma. Sometimes you retreated into solitude, and sometimes you went out and partied too hard, drinking your way into oblivion because nothing else erased the image of your sister lying in the bathtub in a pool of blood.

There was an electric kettle in the kitchen, so Liam filled it and found the tea Andrea kept, which supposedly helped you sleep. He grabbed a washcloth from the sink and wiped down the kitchen and was almost done when Andrea brushed past him in her slippers. Her hair was down and wet and she'd changed into sweatpants and an oversized *Denver University* sweatshirt.

He stood, completely still.

Andrea put the tea bag in the cup and poured water over it before she turned around. "Thanks." She gave him a small smile. "I didn't realize I wanted tea until I heard the kettle boiling." Her smile faltered. "What?"

Liam didn't say anything. How did he tell her that her presence felt so comfortable it was like they'd been sharing a kitchen for years?

When she brushed past him, he'd actually relaxed for the first time in what would be twenty years next month. Was it the sweats? It couldn't be simply being with Andrea in her kitchen.

Liam cleared his throat. "Caisey should be here soon with the food."

Andrea turned back to her tea and Liam felt a rush of disappointment. Did she really expect him to open up the first time they were really alone? Maybe Andrea was the kind of honest person who simply expected everyone else to be completely honest also. He didn't mind that, but sometimes it paid to wait until later.

Liam slipped back into the living room for his tablet, not just because her tea smelled weird. He unlocked the screen and opened the file of his notes. Andrea was at her little circular dining table so he sat on the other chair. "You feel up to going over some things?"

She shrugged one shoulder.

"Tell me about the emails."

Andrea got up and came back with her phone, which she switched back on. "You had it turned off?"

"I didn't want work to call, or anyone else. I like quiet while I'm at home."

"Sorry."

"It's fine." She glanced up at him for a second, enough time for him to ascertain it wasn't fine. "I'll just do the "do not disturb" thing." She tapped and scrolled through her email and then slid the phone around so he could see. "This is the only one I hadn't deleted yet."

There was no subject and no text, just a generic email address and a photo of Andrea getting gas. "I thought the FBI was looking into my email. Isn't that why they have my computer?"

Liam looked up, his jaw locked. "It is, but I like to get as much information as I can also. Computers can tell us a lot, but I'd rather get your impression."

She looked much younger than early thirties, with no makeup on and both hands around her mug like she was cold. He wanted to set up a barricade on her doorstep and be the line of defense between her and all the ugly, painful things in the world. If she would let him.

"For example, what does this email say to you?"

"I'm watching you." She paused a moment. "A hello from someone who ordinarily wouldn't speak to you."

Liam wasn't surprised often, but he liked that Andrea had the power to do that. "Did you think about reporting it to the police?"

"I told the IT guy at work, like I said, since it's my work email. He tried to look into it, but couldn't find out anything about who sent it. He recommended I make a report with the police."

"So why didn't you?"

She sipped her tea and set the mug back down. "Work sort of blew up, I got really busy and there just wasn't time to go into a police station and fill out a bunch of paperwork for something that could turn out to be harmless." She sighed. "I was going to go for sure if it got worse. I didn't know he would try and abduct me."

Liam wanted to tell her that her sister would be fine. It was on the tip of his tongue to say it, but he'd known it was false hope when he was sure Andrea had been taken. Was it so wrong to be glad she was okay? She probably wouldn't think so, given it was her sister who was missing, but Liam couldn't help being relieved she was here to sit with him, even if he was working and she was distraught.

He needed to keep his distance. This was work, and he needed to treat it as such. At least until the investigation was over and Andrea was in the clear. Then, who knew what could happen? Liam wanted her in his life. If nothing else, thinking she'd been abducted by the Chloroform Killer made him realize how much time he'd wasted so far.

His cell vibrated. Liam pulled it from his pocket and saw it was Caisey. "Conners."

"I'm outside. Get the door, I don't have a free hand."

He was up and moving toward the front door. "What all did you get?"

"Just a couple of bits since you guys will be stuck indoors in the evenings for a few days at least."

He opened the door and she handed him two grocery sacks, clicked her Bluetooth and took it off her ear. "You always go all British when you're trying to explain your way out of something you did."

Caisey's eyes widened, but she tried to look innocent. "Who me?"

Liam followed her to the kitchen, laughing.

"Hey, Andrea. How are you doing?" Caisey set the bags on the counter and started unpacking.

Andrea got up to help. "I'm holding on."

"Liam is good for that."

Andrea blinked, but recovered fast and said, "Did Liam just say you were British a minute ago?"

"Only a quarter. My Grams was a nurse during World War Two and she met my grandfather in France. He was an American soldier. She's lived with us since I was tiny, and we still live in the same house now. My dad was an FBI agent too, so she pretty much raised me. I went to kindergarten calling a sweater a jumper and chips, crisps." Caisey grinned. "Some of it still pops out every now and again."

"That's cool." The first smile he'd ever seen from Andrea, and she gave it to his partner.

Liam didn't want to be mad, but that was what happened. Plus, it took him six months to learn all that about Caisey and Andrea had just found it out in thirty seconds. What was it with women that they just shared like that?

Caisey went back to pulling stuff out of the bags. White paper sacks, cardboard cartons, little tubs and finally two pints of ice cream and a bottle of Liam's favorite soda he never bought because it had way too much sugar and caffeine in it.

His stomach rumbled.

Caisey shot him a grin. "Fried chicken, potato wedges, coleslaw. I got you a bag of salad too."

Then he realized she hadn't taken her coat off yet. "You're not staying?"

"There's a football game at the high school. So I'm going to go watch Jake do his trumpet thing in the marching band. I'll be back later. A lot later."

"Oh, okay."

"Plus, they do this hotdog with grilled onions that's really good."

Andrea turned away to get out plates, so Liam followed Caisey back to the front door. When they got out of earshot, he said, "I can't believe you'd stoop so low as to use your godson as an excuse and leave me here."

"You don't need me being a third wheel." She grinned. "I'm giving you alone time, and the chance that maybe one of us could be something other than desperate and single. You should be thanking me."

"It's not appropriate. And I was never desperate."

"You won't be, if you get in there."

She wasn't even going to respond to the question of it being appropriate? "I can't believe you just said that."

"There's a sappy movie in the bag too, maybe she'll let you comfort her."

"You need to stop talking."

"I'm going to do one better, I'm going to go." She opened the front door, a satisfied smile on her face like the time she'd spent all morning calling in to a radio station and finally won rodeo tickets. "I'll be back at bedtime with my PJs to relieve you."

"Okay."

"Be nice, yeah?" Caisey glanced down the hall behind him. "I know you don't want to mislead her, but you can't just be silent. If she's looking at you, but she's not saying anything, that means you need to talk. Got it?"

"I can't believe you're giving me advice." Liam pushed the door, but she held it open. "Go already. You'll miss the game."

"There isn't a game, it's not until tomorrow. I'm going back to the office to look over the files and see if I can figure out where he might dump Kiera's body. I just didn't want to bring all that here."

Liam nodded. "Okay, good. Andrea doesn't need to see the photos."

Caisey waved him away. "Now go, before your dinner gets cold."

"Sure, mom."

"What can I say? Jenna's parenting rubs off on me. Besides, you should try it.

Sometimes it even works."

Liam laughed. Caisey's best friend and her son didn't just live with her and her Grams, they kept her grounded. "Goodbye, Caisey."

"Remember, be nice."

He shut the door. Caisey had some crazy ideas, thinking she needed to remind him to be nice of all things. He was a perfectly nice person; he just didn't know why women couldn't tell you what they needed. They just figured you'd understand intuitively why they were shutting you out.

It was why he'd given up on second dates a while back. Meeting people was easy enough, but Liam didn't have time for a heavy relationship that he'd have to give a ton of time and attention to. Not in the middle of a serial killer investigation.

The microwave beeped, and Andrea pulled out a steaming plate. She handed it to him.

Liam smiled. "Smells good."

"You want to eat on the couch? There was a movie in the bag."

"Sure. What movie is it?"

"Dirty Dancing."

Liam got a look at her, wide eyed with her lips twitching. "We don't have to watch it."

Andrea smiled. "I'm game if you are."

SEVEN

Caisey grasped around in the direction of the coffee table and found her phone. She swiped to take the call and put it to her ear, all without opening her eyes. "Yeah." Her voice was like Barry White, so she cleared her throat. "Lyons."

"It's Burkot. We got a body, found an hour ago. Preliminaries indicate its Kiera James."

Caisey rubbed the grit from her eyes and tried to focus on Andrea's living room. "Text me the address."

"Stern and Wing are on their way to relieve you. They'll cover Ms. James until you and Liam are done at the scene."

Which meant they would also be the ones drafted to tell Andrea her sister was dead for sure. Was it wrong to want the body to be some nameless, faceless person? Anonymity didn't make it better that someone was dead, but it would hurt Andrea less. Caisey hung up and sat up. Life was like a runaway freight train sometimes. It didn't matter how fast you ran down the track, trying to get ahead of it. Eventually it hit you.

"Is something wrong?"

Caisey shifted and looked over the back of the couch. "Liam and I have something to do this morning. Two other agents are coming to take you to work."

Andrea cinched her robe tighter around her. "Is it Kiera?"

"As soon as I know for sure, I'll tell you."

"I'll make the coffee. You'll want a cup to take with you, its cold out."

Caisey watched her head for the kitchen. It was either deep denial or unrelenting strength that allowed Andrea to focus on what Caisey needed when Kiera might be dead. Between Andrea and Caisey's Grams it felt like everyone had overcome something in their lives. How had they managed to hold on to hope? And their sanity. Even Jenna, who lived with Caisey along with her son—Caisey's godson—held down a great job at a spa and raised her son alone. Support system or no, Jenna was still a single mom and yet she'd never once complained.

How did they all do it?

Caisey hit the bathroom to change into fresh clothes and just got done brushing her teeth when the doorbell rang.

Andrea moved to answer it, so Caisey tugged on her arm. "Let me get it." She stopped two feet back from the door, hand on her weapon. "Who is it?"

"Who do you think it is?"

She rolled her eyes and opened the door to Liam, who handed her a half-gallon of chocolate milk on his way in. "Andrea only has half and half."

Caisey shuddered and shut the door. Coffee wasn't coffee without chocolate in it.

ANDREA HELD her coffee to her lips, her cheeks warm. Liam stared at her a lot, like he was doing right now, in the kitchen. As though she didn't all the way make sense to him. And why was that? Not that she was complaining, he wasn't hard to look at.

"Have you ever taken a yoga class?"

He did read women's fiction. She'd found that out last night. Now she wanted to know if she was right about his on-again-off-again thing with a yoga instructor. It had happened way too many times for her to assume he wasn't already involved with someone way more interesting—and flexible—than her.

His lips twitched. "Uh, no. Why?"

"Nothing." Andrea shook her head. "Never mind."

His eyes were shadowed in the harsh light of her kitchen. "You sleep okay?"

Andrea hadn't particularly, but she said, "Sure."

Liam frowned, but Andrea didn't want to know if he didn't believe her because she looked awful or she had a crease down her cheek or something else equally embarrassing. Being caught up in this with these two FBI agents, she'd realized at two a.m. that they carried the weight of what they did.

They actually felt Andrea's grief. Not the same way she did, but they felt it all the same.

Realizing that had led to a division of her fear over what was happening to Kiera, and the relief that she didn't have to go through this alone.

In the end, she'd lain in bed with the notes app on her phone open. Trying to quantify precisely how their presence lessened her anguish should have been a whole lot easier. Solvable. It hadn't worked. It never did, even though she'd tried many times to calculate as an equation what was only human. That was always the point where Andrea dug out her Bible—when life got so confusing she couldn't reason her way out of it.

She'd slept better after reading for a while.

Liam's suit was neat, his hair damp and his cologne made her want to lean closer and get a big whiff. But...that would be weird, so Andrea said, "How about you? Did you sleep okay?"

Their evening had been fun, sitting close on the couch and sharing ice cream grins in the awkward moments of the movie. She'd almost managed to forget that a serial killer might come after her again. And if Kiera was really gone, Andrea didn't know if she could survive if Liam disappeared from her life too. That was why she couldn't let him in beyond protecting her.

So when he just nodded, she headed for her bedroom to get dressed. When she came back out in a skirt suit, heels, straightened hair and light makeup, there were two FBI agents in the kitchen. Both older, one had gray hair and a belly and the other was a lean, Asian female.

Liam motioned to the gray-haired guy first. "This is Agent Stern and Agent Wing.

They'll escort you to work."

"Sounds good." Andrea grabbed her briefcase from the hall closet. How was she going to explain the presence of two FBI agents to her co-workers? At least she had the car ride to work to figure that out. She slipped her coat on.

"You're not going to eat breakfast?"

Andrea straightened. "I usually grab a bagel on the way."

Liam shook his head. "No extra stops. Go straight to work and if you need lunch then order it in. Better yet, Caisey and I should be done by then. We'll bring lunch with us."

Because she needed a side of fries with the news her sister was dead? Liam must have read something on her face, because he took her elbow and steered her into the living room. Andrea set her briefcase down and folded her arms.

"As much as possible, you need to make it as hard as you can for this guy to catch you alone. If he's going to come after you we'll have the chance to stop him then, but not if he gets to you before we even know. So you don't go anywhere without Stern and Wing, you don't change from your most basic itinerary. No trips or stop-offs." Liam pushed out a breath.

Was he as worried about the Chloroform Killer coming back as she was? He seemed almost scared at the idea she might be the next victim.

"Did you get all that, or do you need me to go over it again?"

Andrea sighed. He'd been waiting for her to respond. "I'm not an idiot. I understand what protection means, and I'm not going to jeopardize your investigation." Her thoughts lit on something else he'd said and she lifted her chin. "I won't ruin your chance to catch this guy."

Liam's eyes narrowed. "That's not what this is about."

"It is some, isn't it? I'm not naïve, I know the chance to maybe catch him is worth you sticking around here."

"I would still be here, even if you weren't in danger."

"Why?"

Liam's mouth opened, but he didn't say anything.

"Never mind." Andrea grabbed her briefcase, but Liam stalled her with a hand on hers, over the handle.

"There are rules."

"Okay."

"But when this is wrapped up, I'm not going to disappear. I was...hoping we could be friends, at least. Then after you're in the clear, maybe we could go out for dinner?"

Andrea liked the idea of a reprieve—at least until the killer was caught, or she wasn't in danger anymore. But she didn't want to lead him on. "I'm not sure that's a good idea."

"Why not?"

Andrea tugged her hand from his fingers and took a step back. "It just isn't."

She wouldn't mind the friends-thing, but if Liam really liked her then he would always be wondering why they couldn't be more than that. And if life had taught Andrea anything, it was that she had to keep everything straight and un-emotional, because there was nothing worse than drowning in your own emotion.

Her worry over Kiera was strong enough it was taking every ounce of determination to hold on and keep everything together. If she took on Liam's emotion too, she would crumple under the weight of it.

~

"MAYBE IT WAS JUST that your timing was off?"

Liam's lip curled at his partner's words, but he kept walking. Eyes on the ground he searched for anything the killer might have dropped, stepped on...sneezed on. He hadn't even looked at the body yet, that was a job for the Medical Examiner.

"I don't want to talk about this." His voice was gruff, but it was more because he couldn't seem to get over his reaction to seeing a girl, dead. Any girl; it didn't matter. They all looked the same in his head, only he'd see them lying in the bathtub instead of on the ground in a copse of pine trees behind an upscale neighborhood.

"Just give her some time, that's all I'm saying." Caisey's voice tracked with him, but in a wider circle. "Andrea's going through a lot, and she's doing great. But if you come on all strong—"

"That isn't what happened."

"Maybe she thought it was. You don't know, maybe your dinner and movie last night was the highlight of her dating life for the last five years."

Liam nearly rolled his eyes. "It wasn't a date. And just because you haven't gone on one in five years either, doesn't mean Andrea has a scant love life."

"Yeah, but we're not all Mr. Sociable like you."

He snorted. "I haven't been on a date in six months."

"Six months, ooh. I'm surprised you haven't shriveled up from a lack of perky conversation with co-eds trying to convince you they're twenty-six so you'll give them a shot at your lusciousness."

Liam stopped and looked up at her. The woman was nuts. "Did you hit your head?"

"Are you thinking about your sister?"

"No, I'm—" She was trying to distract him. Right. "Next time pick a different topic other than my lusciousness."

The ME's aid barked a laugh. Liam shot the guy a look and he shut up pretty quick, and then he turned back to his pain-in-the-rear partner. "Let's just get on with this so we can figure out how to soften the blow for Andrea, okay?"

Caisey looked over his shoulder to where Kiera James was sprawled out on dirt and pine needles behind him. The Chloroform Killer had not been kind, Liam had seen enough to know that much. This kill lacked any semblance of his usual control. Her eyes darkened. "I'd suggest telling her and her parents at the same time, but I think that'll make it worse."

Liam agreed. "We should wrap this up and get over to her office.

I don't like leaving her for this long, even if she is with Stern and Wing."

Caisey nodded slowly. "Yeah, plus if you're gone too long she might forget about your lusciousness."

Liam reeled back with this cell phone in his hand and pretended to throw it at her. When she flinched like he might actually do it, he smiled. "You know nothing can happen while she's under our protection. It's not appropriate."

"Yeah, but where's the fun in that?"

Liam frowned. "Not everything has to be fun. Some things are just...stuff. Life, you know?"

Caisey's lip curled. "Sounds boring."

"Good point," Liam said. "I've seen you bored and it isn't pretty."

EIGHT

Liam wanted TO hold her hand, but he held himself back. "It's not going to look like her, so don't expect that. All I need is for you to tell me, yes or no, if it's Kiera."

Andrea nodded, a jerky motion that he'd seen before when a person was barely hanging on.

"Ready?"

It was a stupid question, but no one wanted to be bombarded with the visual of their dead loved one. When she'd taken a full breath in and let it out, Andrea said, "I'm ready."

The Medical Examiner pulled back the white sheet. Kiera's hair had been cleaned, her face now free of the blood and dirt that had been there when she was found. Her skin was pale white, showcasing the cloud of freckles across the bridge of her nose and her cheekbones.

Andrea's whole body shuddered. Liam caught her and she fell against him, but not with all of her weight. Even now she held herself up, self-contained in a way he didn't know whether to be proud of, or fear for when she was going to break.

"It's her."

~

"ARE you sure you want to do this?" Andrea was in the backseat of Liam's car instead of the front seat, where both Liam and Caisey were waiting for her to decide. How was it they were so finely tuned to her emotional state?

She didn't want to do this, but she was going to.

Her phone, tucked away in her briefcase, beeped twice. But emails could wait. As could the two voicemails she'd gotten from missed calls while she was identifying Kiera's body.

She blinked away that mental picture, hoping she would never see it again and stared out the window. The house she and Kiera had grown up in looked the same. Why had she expected it to look different? Kiera was dead, and yet the impact would barely make a ripple in any of their lives. That was what got to Andrea the most—that Sunny could move on, for all intents and purposes, unchanged.

While she was...stuck.

"Andrea?"

"I'm sure."

She got out of Liam's expensive SUV. She'd overheard two of the HR guys at work talking about that model once, so she knew it wasn't quite her annual income, but it was pretty close. She preferred her little two-seater car. At least until she picked up Kiera from a club about a month ago when she needed a ride and Kiera puked in it. Now there was the faint odor of up-chuck every time the heater warmed up.

Andrea stopped on the concrete step that was flanked by two bushes. The door was within reach, but she didn't knock. She stared at the door handle and sucked in deep breaths, not naïve enough to think her parents were going to be overwhelmed by grief. There would be some kind of reaction; she just had no idea what it was going to be.

Caisey laid a hand on her shoulder. "You don't have to do this today."

"If I don't, I won't want to come tomorrow."

"Ah, I see you're a, "rip the Band-Aid off", kind of girl."

Andrea didn't get the chance to knock before the door opened and Morton stood there, skinny as always in a suit that would put most male models to shame except that his thinning hair was combed over and his cheeks were permanently flushed.

"Andrea." The butler's smile shone in his eyes.

"Hello, Morton." If it was anyone else, Andrea would have hugged him and he'd have hugged her back, but as it was, neither of them was big on touching. Instead, Andrea held out her hand they settled on a long grasp. Why did that mean more to her than any familial embrace she'd ever had?

Kiera had hugged him, once, back when her head barely reached his chest. He'd been so caught off guard he fell back and they both landed sprawled on the carpet. The memory brought a smile to Andrea's face.

"You should come in." Morton stepped back and held the door open.

"How are things?" He knew she meant her parents.

"As per usual."

Great.

Andrea strode through the lobby to the reception room where her mother kept the largest supply of spirits in the house. She heard Morton greet Liam and Caisey, and a low whisper she took to mean they were telling Morton about Kiera. Morton sucked in a breath which broke in the middle, and then his dress shoes clipped the tile floor as he retreated to his wing.

The curtains were drawn in the reception room. Andrea strode to the windows and pulled the heavy drapes back.

Liam and Caisey stopped just inside the doorway, but Andrea knew the moment they saw her mother draped across the settee with a bottle hanging from one hand. Caisey apparently didn't feel the need to hide her wince.

"Mom." Andrea crossed to her, set the bottle on the table and tugged her mom upright. "Mom."

She didn't wonder that her voice was stern. Andrea was past being concerned about how people would view her because of her family. Her only sister was dead. And after the morning she'd had, she didn't feel the need to be the bandage that held them all together.

Andrea sat on the coffee table, while her mom blinked and struggled to focus.

Finally her gaze settled on Andrea. "What is it?"

The slur in her mom's voice made her want to cringe, but Andrea kept herself straight and emotionless. "They found Kiera."

Something flashed in her mother's eyes, the last vestiges of a mother's love for her wayward daughter. "And?"

"She's dead mom. The killer should have taken me, but he got Kiera by mistake and now she's gone."

Andrea had to say it out loud. Not that it was her mistake, or that she'd asked for it, but she was an integral part of what had happened. Kiera was dead because of her and it was important that she acknowledge her culpability.

Her mom slumped back on the couch. "Well."

The news washed over her mom, but there was nothing Andrea could do to help. It wasn't worth trying to comfort her with a touch, or even a hug, so Andrea just sat there beside her.

When her mom's eyes fluttered closed, Andrea wondered if the period of lucidity had been real. When she woke up later, would she even remember? Andrea never felt the need to escape to the point she was unaware, but both her mom and her sister had. What flaw did they share that they succumbed to it? Andrea simply closed herself off to the pain and buried herself in work, like her father.

The study door was closed, but she didn't bother knocking. Her father spun from the window, an empty glass in his hand. Maybe there wasn't such a big difference after all. How long would it be before Andrea was tempted to drown her sorrows in a bottle? Would she be strong enough to stand on her own? Her steps faltered and she stopped two feet from her father.

His eyes were dark, almost hard. "She's gone?"

"Kiera has been gone for a long time, Dad. But yes, Sunny is dead." It felt better to say it like that, to acknowledge that the person Kiera had made herself into was the person who had passed away.

His lip curled at the mention of Sunny, but they'd never even seen her since they severed all contact. Kiera had cut and streaked her hair and the short, sleek look resembled Andrea's hair more than her former style. She'd been flattered at first, especially when Kiera told her she'd done it to try and borrow confidence from Andrea. Now that she knew it contributed to Kiera's death, Andrea had to bite her lip because her eyes started to burn.

She sucked in a breath. "I wanted to be here, to be the one to tell you both. I've done that now."

Her dad stepped forward, sweeping her into a hug. "I'm so glad it was all a mistake. When the agents told us you'd been abducted, I didn't want to believe it." He gave her a squeeze that was a little too tight and then released her. "I'm glad you're okay, Andrea."

He looked happy, as though released from what had weighed him down. Andrea opened her mouth, but bit back the words. What good would it do? They had considered Kiera dead for a long time. But still...

"I'm not okay, Dad. Kiera's dead, and not because she put herself in a bad situation. She was safe at my apartment eating pizza, for goodness' sake. She should have been fine, not the victim of a—"

Her voice broke. She turned from her dad to Liam, who had crossed the room. He didn't say anything, just put a hand on the small of her back and led her out while she struggled to breathe. Her face itched and when she scratched at it, she was crying.

In the hall, Andrea bent forward with her hands on her thighs and sucked in air. Liam rubbed up and down her back, but she didn't think anything would cut through the chill of the fact that she was alone.

Her parents were too wrapped up in themselves to worry about growing their relationship as a family. Kiera might have been self-destructive and generally a wreck, but Andrea had needed her sister almost as much as Kiera needed her.

And now Sunny was gone.

A tissue was pressed into her hand. Andrea wiped her face and straightened. Both Liam and Caisey stood in front of her, but it was Liam who motioned to the front door. "Let's get some air."

"We should just leave." Andrea took a breath. "I've said what I came here to say. It's done now."

His eyes softened, where Caisey looked like she wanted to

punch someone. They made a good pair, opposites working together and balancing each other out.

Andrea wondered if they'd ever been more than partners, but figured if they had there was no way it would have ended without completely destroying their working relationship. They were both way too strong-willed to part amicably.

When she was settled in the back of the car, Caisey looked back from the front seat. She'd argued, wanting Andrea to sit up there. But being by Liam would be a bad idea when her emotions were this close to the surface.

Caisey's eyes were soft. "You need anything?"

Andrea thought for a moment. Was it too early to ask?

"Just say it." Caisey smiled. "How bad could it be?"

"I need the key. Kiera's key. It would have been on a gold chain around her neck."

Caisey's face flashed with surprise. "I'll see what I can do."

Andrea turned to the window. She stared at the sidewalk and the trees as they blurred past, but all she saw was Kiera's face. Pale. Lifeless.

Emotion burst from her throat again. Andrea leaned forward and put her forehead on her knees. She needed Kiera's key. She needed to see her sister happy again, even if it was only in the pictures she kept in storage. Otherwise, all she would ever remember is what Sunny did to herself and the part Andrea had played in her sister's death.

Her phone rang, but she left it in her briefcase. The real world could wait until later. This place was a whole lot more scary and exhausting, a place where she needed constant protection from FBI agents, but at least she didn't feel like the robot she usually was.

It rang again.

Andrea pulled it out to look at the screen. The number was blocked. Who would bother to restrict their number? Unless they didn't want to be found.

She swiped the screen. "Hello?"

"Think you're so smart, don't you? Well, you're not." His voice sounded like pure evil, and nothing else. Nothing at all. "I can hear you laughing from here."

Andrea's body jerked. Liam slammed on the brakes and pulled to the side of the street. "Give me the phone."

She looked up at Liam but didn't move.

"Who was that?" The Chloroform Killer sounded ready to snap. "It doesn't matter. I'm coming for you. No one makes a fool out of me."

The line went dead.

NINE

Liam was so mad he had to fold his arms to contain the urge to do something he shouldn't. "When I tell you to give me the phone, you give me the phone."

Caisey stepped between them. They'd made it back to Andrea's apartment, but only because it was closest to where they'd been when the call came in. "Let her be."

Liam didn't need to be told she was having a rough time. It was plain on Andrea's face that she was about to bolt somewhere she could lose it in private. "What were you thinking?"

Andrea's face was completely red. "I was thinking he killed my sister! If I want the chance to talk to him, that's up to me."

"Liam—"

"No, Case." He pinned his partner down with a stare he knew was hard because he saw her flinch. "She doesn't get it. You don't understand a guy like that."

Andrea said, "He's angry he got Keira and not me."

"And now he's going to come after you again, try and finish what he started."

"Good!"

Liam snapped. "No. It's not good. How can you say that?"

"You don't want to arrest him? Now that Kiera's gone are you going to leave me here, a sitting duck, waiting for him to come back and abduct me this time?"

"Of course not."

"Then what's the problem? You think I don't want the chance to look my sister's killer in the eye, even though it scares the ever loving crap out of me? I want to kill him right back for what he did to her."

"You think I'm going to let him get within ten feet of you?" Liam jerked his head, side- to-side. "There's no way."

Caisey turned so her back was to him. "He's right, Andrea. There's no way that's going to happen."

Andrea looked around Caisey, at him. "Neither of you can control the future. You can only put up safeguards. If he tries to take me again, you might not be able to stop it."

"You want to die?" Liam pushed Caisey aside and moved in close. "You want to go through what Kiera went through?" He swallowed the sick feeling.

Maybe his boss would let him put her on a plane to Australia. But that wasn't likely, not if they wanted to catch the Chloroform Killer. If he lost Andrea it would be so much worse than some nameless, faceless victim he didn't know.

"I'm not just going to sit here."

"You will if I tell you to. I'm in charge, and don't forget that. I'm the thing that's standing between you and an insane serial murderer who wants to kill you."

The noise that burst from Andrea's throat was a mix of grief and frustration. She spun around and strode from the room. A second later her bedroom door slammed.

"Good going, champ."

Liam's head whipped around to his partner.

Caisey's eyes widened and she lifted her hands. "My bad. Yell all you want. But maybe this will penetrate, and I pray it does." She pointed at the door Andrea had slammed. "That girl has nothing but her grief and helplessness. If she needs to get angry and rage about how she's going to kill the killer the first chance she gets, then who cares? She needs to get it out, to feel like she has some control over all this. It doesn't mean either of us will ever let that happen."

Liam pressed his fingers against his eyes. "I don't want her to do something stupid."

"You really think she would? Andrea James is probably the most level-headed woman either of us has ever met."

"Or it's just a front. You saw her family."

"Yeah, that was a train wreck." Caisey shook her head. "I thought my lot were dysfunctional, but Andrea's family takes the biscuit. The mom's on another planet and the dad is seriously disconnected. Andrea's holding herself separate from the whole world, avoiding relationships and living her narrow life of work and a boring apartment just so she's not like them. I'm thinking Kiera was the only honest one among them. At least she knew she had problems."

Liam sighed. "So what do we do?"

"Apart from everything we're already doing? I already emailed Burkot about the trace on her phone. I'm waiting to hear back if we got anything."

"So we just hang around for him to make his approach?"

"I hope it takes weeks. Andrea's couch is way more comfortable than my old mattress."

Liam didn't respond to that. "Did you ask about the key Andrea mentioned?"

"I asked for the list of Kiera's personal effects. If the necklace was there, we should be able to get it to Andrea. Although we'll need to see what the key is for, first."

Liam nodded. When was his brain going to start catching up? "I'm going to run home, take some time. I'll relieve you before dinner so you can go home to eat."

Caisey nodded, like she knew why he wanted some time to himself. Liam didn't request concessions much, so she'd know when he did that it was important. "Sounds good."

Liam grabbed his backpack and opted to walk through the complex toward his apartment. He needed to clear his head, get a little distance from a frustrating woman who was tying him up in knots with her reactions to everything. He felt like crying and laughing at the same time. Crying for Andrea, growing up in that crypt of a house raised by the walking dead, her only solace a troubled sister bent on self-destruction. Laughing for the sake of helping her heal, watching her find strength in fighting for her own life and the legacy of her sister.

Liam's phone rang, the screen flashing with the five stars of his father's rank. "Hi, Dad."

"Liam," he yelled. "My plane just landed. I have some business in town, how about dinner?"

Liam dropped onto his corduroy couch and closed his eyes. Why did his dad feel the need to bellow like he was commanding troops? Of course, Liam was going to drop everything on a whim. "I'm busy, Dad."

"Bah. Too busy to see your old man?"

"I'm going to be working tonight." It wouldn't feel like work, eating dinner with Andrea and spending the evening with her. But he had to remember it was.

There was silence on the line. A measured, weighty quiet that Liam was familiar with. "Maybe we could have lunch tomorrow?"

The old man sighed. "No can do. I'll be in meetings all day. I'm staying downtown. They're putting me up in some swanky hotel. Come by for dinner tomorrow, you can say hi to everyone."

"Everyone who?"

"I brought my staff, didn't I? They're all excited to meet my son, the Special Agent. Especially Elaine. She's my new assistant, you know. Graduated Harvard same as you."

"I'm not being set up, Dad. So don't even bother."

"What, you're not dating someone are you?"

Liam squeezed the bridge of his nose. "Technically no, but that doesn't mean I want to meet someone who lives in D.C. Or that I'm even in the market for a long-distance relationship."

"Well, come by anyway."

"Dad." He drew out the word, registering his displeasure. Why did he feel fifteen every time he spoke to his father? He was a grown man. When would that ever change between them?

"Suck it up, son. I'll see you at six."

~

CAISEY WAITED thirty minutes after the shower shut off before knocking on Andrea's bedroom door. Not everyone got ready as fast as she did, but then she only pulled her hair back and didn't usually bother with much makeup beyond mascara and lip balm.

Andrea opened the door a crack.

"Liam went home for a while, so it's just me. Do you need anything?"

She sighed. "A new life? A different family?"

Caisey gave her a small smile. She wasn't too good at empathy, but even she knew a soft touch was what Andrea needed, not yelling at her and telling her what to do. Sometimes Liam was such a man. "I have tea bags. You want a cup?"

"That sounds great."

Caisey boiled the kettle and added sugar to Andrea's mug. She only had skim milk in her fridge, so that would have to do. Caisey preferred full fat, because life was way too short to worry about calories. She just ran enough miles to break even.

Andrea came out, walking slowly like it hurt to move. Caisey had felt that way after her dad was killed. Shot in the line of duty, there wasn't a more noble way a Special Agent could go out. Even if it sucked, they had to die at all. Senseless death was so much worse.

She set Andrea's mug in front of her. Andrea frowned. "This is tea?"

"Yep."

"With milk?"

Caisey sighed. "It's not that herbal crap, if that's what you're asking. I buy these pyramid shaped tea bags from the specialty store. Try it, it's really good. A proper English cup of tea."

Andrea smiled, but it didn't brighten her eyes any. "Thanks."

"No problem. It's not much, just tea." What more could she do? She wasn't really good at this part of her job. Caisey was better at running down leads and getting answers when people underestimated the short blond chick, never imagining she was packing a gun and a badge.

On the fridge behind Andrea was a collection of papers. A weights and measures conversion chart, a menu for the local Greek restaurant and a magnet with a Bible verse on it.

She looked at Andrea. "You're a Christian?"

Andrea nodded. "Not a very good one."

Caisey smiled. "Me either. I go to church, but there seems to be a disconnect between my life and how it is for other people who go there. The super-spiritual types, you know?"

"I had a friend in college who went to all the meetings and Bible studies. I like the sentiment, peace and joy. Freedom. I just never seemed to be able to get it to sink in enough that I actually felt free."

"And then in the unlikeliest of places, you meet someone who feels exactly the way you do." Caisey paused. Andrea's face said she knew what Caisey meant. "Who else could that be, but God? I don't believe in coincidences, or magic, or destiny, or any of that. Life is just too...raw."

Andrea took a sip of her tea and placed the cup back down. "I can't live with no hope, that's all I know. There has to be something good and it isn't us. We're too capable of awful, ugly things to be the source of goodness in the world. There has to be something more under the surface that we're not seeing. Otherwise, what's the point? There's no way all of our trying to do good and pay it forward, or whatever, outweighs the atrocity even one single person is capable of."

Caisey studied her face, marveling that someone who had never seen half of what she'd seen could understand that there was no way the good in the world outweighed the bad. Unless there really was a fundamental good behind everything. Otherwise, they were all lost, waiting for something more, something that would explain the whole confusing, ugly beauty of the world. Which made no sense, but it was what it was.

Caisey didn't get it any more than that. If there was something more to fall back on, something bigger than people or even the heights of goodness or even true love that so often failed, then it meant that—even for a second—she could let go and trust more than just herself. It had saved her life more times than she could count.

Andrea took a deep breath and sighed. "Let's talk about something else."

Caisey was willing to concede that, even if she was having an existential moment. People didn't always appreciate it. "Sure. What do you want to talk about?"

"Why don't you tell me about Liam?"

Caisey grinned. "Boy, do I have a story for you."

TEN

Liam heard the laughter before he even opened the front door. He juggled the sacks of Chinese food and got the door unlocked without dropping wonton soup all over Andrea's entry mat. When he got to the living room, Caisey and Andrea were both doubled over laughing. Andrea sat up and swiped a tear from her cheek.

Liam couldn't move. He stood there while she laughed—her face completely open for the first time. She was beautiful.

"Liam." Andrea shot to her feet, an endearing blush staining her cheeks.

He cleared his throat and glanced at Caisey, only to find she was giving him a look. Liam turned and strode to the kitchen. The last thing he needed was his partner giving him grief about Andrea. She knew it wasn't appropriate when this was their assignment, so why did she persist in throwing them together? If she didn't push, maybe he'd be able to spend time with Andrea without actually thinking about how soft her lips might be.

"I'm going to head out."

Liam glanced back over his shoulder. "Fine." He needed a quiet evening, and the only person he wanted to spend it with was Andrea.

"Later."

He listened to Caisey leave and dished out the food.

"Can I help?" Andrea's cheeks were still stained with pink.

"I got it. Where do you want to eat?"

"The table is good." She pulled open a drawer and got out two place mats. When they sat, Andrea kept her hands in her lap and looked up at him. "Do you mind if I say grace?"

Liam didn't begrudge her something that simple. His mom always prayed over her food, and he actually sort of liked it. "Sure."

He listened to her voice as she spoke. The gentle words rose in cadence as she gained a rhythm that was like the chorus of a familiar song. She asked for protection for all of them and that the killer would be brought to justice. When she finished, she opened her eyes and gave him a small smile. "Thanks."

"No problem." He picked up his fork but didn't take a bite. "You believe that God can do all that?"

"Sure, I do. He's God, isn't He?"

"But...does He really care that much? I'd think He'd be busy with all the famine and war, stuff like that."

Andrea took a bite of her food, chewing while she looked aside for a minute. "Jesus said God is like a shepherd who leaves his ninety-nine sheep to go search for the one lost one. He doesn't just stick with the flock and write off His losses like we'd do, thinking at least He still has the majority. God pursues that one sheep and carries it home."

Liam didn't know what to say. He'd never heard that before, or even considered that God cared about individual people. He'd figured it was more of Him generally caring for humanity—the greater good in spite of earthquakes and floods and such.

She smiled. "Thank you for asking me if He cares. I needed to remember that."

"You're welcome." He returned her smile and opened his mouth to say something when a phone rang. Liam pulled his cell out, but no one was calling.

Andrea had hers in her hand. "It's the office."

She went to get up, but he put his hand on her arm. He'd rather she was close by than risk not being near her if something happened, especially when it was only for the sake of politeness.

She sat. "Hello?" A frown creased her forehead. "No, that's not right...I know. Yes, thank you. I appreciate you calling...I'll be there as soon as I can." She hung up. "My office was broken into. The security guard thought I might have left it unlocked, but I'm sure I locked my door when we left after lunch."

"You did." He worked his mouth back and forth. "Did they call the police?"

"I have to go and look at it so I can tell them if there's anything missing."

"Okay. Grab your coat and I'll call Caisey."

Andrea hesitated. "Do you think it's him?"

"Whether it is, or not, either way we need to know."

CAISEY SET her fork down and sat back in her chair. Grams' smaller portion of dinner was gone, and Jake was already texting. Jenna was still taking her ridiculously dainty bites. "Are you going to be done some time this year?"

Jenna didn't react. She was used to Caisey's moods. Anyone would be after more than twenty years of best friendship. Jenna cut a tiny piece of potato into two miniscule pieces, put it in her mouth excruciatingly slowly and gave Caisey a sugar smile. "What was that?"

Caisey growled. "I would like to get up from this table sometime this year, that's what. Are you going to be finished before we're fifty?"

"Or before I'm one hundred."

Caisey shot Grams a smile. The apple didn't fall far from that tree.

Jenna rolled her eyes. "Gang up on me, why don't y'all."

Caisey gagged.

Grams shook her head. "We don't use that word, dear. You know that."

Jenna took a dainty sip of water. "Just because y'all don't say y'all, doesn't mean I can't say y'all as much as I want to."

Caisey grabbed her plate and Grams' and took them to the kitchen. Who said she had to wait around? Jake trailed in with his dishes and she bumped his shoulder at the sink. "Doing okay, kid?"

He bumped hers back. "Sure."

"Need anything?"

He shook his head. "Don't worry. You're not slacking on your godmother duties."

"Good."

And then Caisey was alone in the quiet kitchen, listening to the animated conversation still going on between Jenna and Grams at the dining table.

Home was a pocket of safety. But one day the evil in the world would cross their doorstep. Despite her daily fight against it, there was nothing Caisey could do. She didn't want crime to touch her family, but it could. She knew that as well as anyone. She did her job, but was it enough? As soon as one conviction was brought down, another criminal rose up. It was relentless.

Wasn't there something she could do, something to stem the tide of evil and protect her family? Caisey braced her hands on the counter and hung her head, praying if there was something that she would know what it was.

There was nothing worse than feeling inconsequential.

"Caisey, your phone is ringing."

LIAM LED Andrea past the officers and into the building where she worked. The security guard's jowls were red and his hairline was damp with sweat. He hefted himself over to them and stuck out his hand. "I'm really sorry about this, Ms. James. I know this is a hard time for you. I'm sorry about your sister. Really sorry."

Andrea gave him a pleasant smile and squeezed his hand. "Thank you, Steven."

It took a considerable amount of pulling, but she extricated her hand from his. Liam gave the guy a look, letting the security guard know he hadn't missed it. Liam produced his badge. "Special Agent Conners."

The guard's eyes widened and then maxed out. "Uh...um."

Liam led Andrea down the hall to the elevator where she leaned back against the mirrored wall and folded her arms. "That was rude."

"That guy has a crush on you."

"That doesn't mean I should be rude to him. Steven is nice."

"Maybe."

Liam didn't know why she didn't put her accountant brain to the task and come up with the fact a serial killer was stalking her. What if it was Steven? She didn't know what the killer looked like. Liam had seen the Chloroform Killer and there was no way Steven was him. But still, the thought should at least cross her mind.

Instead, she smiled. "So cynical."

Liam shrugged. "It's better than being dead."

Andrea's lips pressed together.

He blew out a breath. "I'm sorry. I shouldn't have said that."

She looked aside. "Thank you for apologizing."

The lights on the fifteenth floor were all on and a crowd of police officers and FBI agents moved in and out of the rooms. Andrea's office was at the end of the hall, full of the same team of technicians who had swabbed, tested and catalogued her apartment. She pushed out a long breath.

"You okay?"

Instead of answering, Andrea stepped over the debris that looked like papers, what had been a glass-topped coffee table, and pieces of stuffing from her chairs. She moved to the desk and looked around. "This is just mean."

"Is there anyone you can think of who might have done this?"

"You mean someone this angry at me?" She motioned to the room. "There's only one person I can think of."

Yeah, there was only one person Liam could think of, too.

"Knock, knock." Caisey strode in and stopped short. "Whoa, I wasn't expecting this."

"Me either." Still, he shot his partner a look and then glanced back at their charge. "Are you okay, Andrea?"

"I had my laptop at home with me, so I don't think this is about work. I challenge anyone to get through the security features on the desktop computer. I was told it's better than what the military has."

"Why do you need all that?"

Andrea turned to Caisey. "We deal with a number of sizeable, international companies. And those are the ones I'm allowed to tell you about."

Liam didn't want to be so superficial he was impressed by the scope of her work, but the truth was he was proud of who Andrea had made herself to be, especially given her sister's emotional issues and their family dynamic. Andrea had climbed a steep ladder and claimed a successful life of her own.

Sergeant Tucker came in, nodded to Liam and Caisey and turned his attention to Andrea. "How are you holding up, Ms. James?"

She gave him a small smile that cracked at the edges. "It doesn't look like anything is missing, just tossed around."

He nodded and handed her his card. "I'm sure the FBI is taking excellent care of you, but don't hesitate to let me know if you need anything."

"Sure, thank you, Sergeant." Andrea tucked the card in her pocket and pulled her coat tighter around her, as though warding off a chill. "Can we get out of here?"

Caisey moved to her and swept Andrea along with the force of her presence, herding her out the door. "Sure we can. How about we go somewhere and get a hot chocolate? You're probably ready for a break and I know this great little bookstore with a café that puts those huge marshmallows on top *and* whipped cream."

Andrea moved with her, toward Liam. "That actually sounds great."

Liam decided he wouldn't mind one of those, either. For the sake of work, of course. Andrea's mental and emotional stability wasn't part of their assignment, but no one wanted to guard someone who was losing it. The more focused and together Andrea was, the easier this would be. And if it made his heart warm to help her, then so be it.

His phone rang. "Conners."

"It's Agent Wing. You should get back here, the Chloroform Killer is in her apartment."

ELEVEN

Andrea shifted from one foot to another. Why couldn't they just let her in there? It was her apartment.

Finally, Caisey came out and strode over to Liam's car, sliding her gun into the holder on her hip and clipping the strap down. She opened the rear door. "It's clear. And there's something you should see."

Andrea climbed out and glanced at the agent who'd been guarding her in the car. The older man nodded. Her apartment was full of cops, but still managed to be cold like the time the heater broke, making her shiver. Her eyes burned with the need to blink, but she had to know what he'd touched. Or left for her.

"It's on the coffee table."

The thing she needed to see was a white box, small enough it was probably meant to hold a bracelet, or some other token of affection. Andrea shuddered. Why was he fixating on her? There was nothing special about her at all. It made no sense.

Andrea reached for the lid. Her stomach clenched but she wasn't one to drag out something like this.

Caisey's hand grabbed her wrist and at least two cops yelled. Andrea straightened. "I was just going to open it. Isn't that why I'm here?" Why were they all staring at her?

Beyond Caisey, Liam's eyes softened. "You're not wearing gloves and its evidence, that's all." The tension seemed to bleed from his shoulders. A police officer gave Liam some latex gloves and he took the lid from the box.

Curled up inside was the thin gold chain of Kiera's necklace, the gold darkened with something that—when not dried—was probably bright red liquid.

Andrea's eyes burned again, and she blinked but they filled with tears until moisture spilled out and ran down her cheeks. How could he know she wanted Kiera's necklace?

She brushed past the outstretched hands and fled to her office. Andrea rounded the desk and sank to the floor beside the chair, her breath coming heavy.

She pulled up her knees and wrapped her arms around them, squeezing like she could expunge the pain by sheer force of will. Grief swelled in her like a wave until she was crying out.

"Andrea." His voice was hard, but when she looked up she saw the fear in Liam's eyes. "Andrea." Her name was a groan, and he handed her a wad of tissue. He sat on the carpet next to her and pulled her to him.

LIAM STROKED her back because that was all he could think of. What else would help? As much as he hated it, the reality was that nothing he said or did could take this pain away from her.

Eventually her sobs tapered off to shaky breaths and she started to pull away. Liam let her go, but rubbed from her shoulders to her elbows and back, trying to stop her shudders.

Andrea pushed hair from her face. "Sorry. I'll be fine now, if you want to go do your thing." She rubbed her cheeks.

"You think I'm going to just leave you in here?"

She frowned.

"I do need you to tell me about the necklace."

She looked away, smoothing down the edges of her clothing. "It was Kiera's. The necklace she always wore. The one I asked you for."

He nodded. "And the key?"

"It's for a storage unit. Kiera had stuff, photos and some furniture. Things from her life with Brad that she didn't want to throw away, or risk getting lost or damaged since she was always moving from place to place. I convinced her to let me rent her a small unit where she could keep those mementos so they would always be safe."

"That was very...pragmatic of you." At any other moment he would have laughed. It was seriously cute how responsible she was. Liam was sick to death of flighty women who never took anything seriously. "Thank you for telling me that."

"I'll be okay now."

He nodded, not that he'd thought otherwise. "I'm glad."

Andrea was way too used to relying only on herself and he knew now that a measure of her strength came from her faith. He wanted to think it was because of his presence. But he wasn't going to kid himself that he'd made that much of an impact on her in only the few short days they'd known each other.

Her nose crinkled. "I just figured you'd have stuff to do, with the box, and the other cops."

"Caisey can handle it. She'll give me all the time I need while I'm giving you the time you need."

"I don't really need...uh, you, uh...anymore. But thanks. I really am good now."

She didn't need him?

Her eyes widened. "I don't mean I don't need you. The killer is still after me, obviously. That's not what I meant. I just..."

"It's okay, Andrea." But his body had gone solid and he dropped his hands. If she wanted to be self-sufficient, he had to let her do that. "I'll let you get cleaned up and then we can figure out what we're going to do next."

Liam forced himself to walk away. If Andrea wanted to do this on her own, that was fine. If she wanted him to protect her but not get involved with her personally, fine. He understood overbearing parents who didn't understand you, and self-destructive siblings. It turned out they had more in common than he'd even thought possible. But if Andrea couldn't see that, then he wasn't going to wait around for her to figure it out.

~

CAISEY SAW the look on his face, but just couldn't joke him out of this. Andrea was breaking his heart, and if Caisey didn't like her so much then she'd want to punch her. Still, maybe Liam needed this. Maybe it would be good for him. He'd been so controlled for so long he needed shaking up, and what better way to do that than a relationship? The best ones always flipped you upside down and tied you in knots so you barely knew what was going on.

She should know.

But that was a long time ago. Long enough that it well and truly qualified as ancient history.

"So what's up with the necklace?"

Liam rubbed a hand down his face, his go-to action for frustrated and tired. "It's Kiera's."

"So he's toying with her, or reaching out in his way. It could be an apology, if that was likely, just as much as it could be meant to mess with her head." Caisey paused. "You think the break-in at her office was a distraction?"

"But we still had a team watching the apartment."

"He doesn't know that. And it's not like he got caught. They barely knew he was here before they saw he'd come and gone already. Or he's so cocky the team on surveillance didn't bother him in the slightest."

She wanted to shoot Wing and Stern a dirty look for being incompetent, but she tried not to act like that in public. Would she have done better if it had been her watching the apartment? They were good agents, but that didn't change the fact none of this was right. She'd rather be irrationally indignant than a staunch realist. That was just sad.

Liam was worried. "You think he's going to try again to make contact with Andrea?"

Caisey bit her lip. "Nothing about this is your typical serial-murderer scenario. I mean, he was obviously angry to discover it was Kiera, what with the way he disposed of her. Now he's back to making contact. So is he going to try again? Does this come to a head when he abducts Andrea for real this time?"

"I won't let that happen."

"What else would make him stop? I don't think he'll just give up and move on to someone else."

"We're going to stop him. That's how."

"Liam—"

"I know what you're going to say, and yes, this is personal. But I'm not going to let him terrorize someone else the way he's done to Andrea and Kiera and the other victims." He folded his arms. "There's just no way. This has to stop."

What would she do if the Chloroform Killer turned his attention to her? Would she deal with it with the same strength Andrea was? Caisey liked to think she was strong, but how would she know unless it actually happened?

ANDREA FOLDED her pajama pants and tucked them into the little roll-on suitcase she traveled with. Her nose was all stopped up and her head was pounding, so she took the usual mix of over-the-counter meds she fell back on when she got a sinus headache, and simply carried on. She heard someone at the door to her bedroom, but she didn't look up, just closed the suitcase lid and zipped it.

"Going somewhere?"

Andrea set the suitcase on the floor and pulled up the handle. "You think I'm going to stay here? A serial killer was in my home."

He stood like he was braced for her to hurl something at him. Why did he think he needed to protect himself from her? Andrea was the one who kept getting hurt. Liam was one of the best things in her life right now. There was nothing typical about whatever was between them, but he'd said he hoped it might grow to something more after the danger was over. Maybe that wasn't such a bad idea. She needed something good to look forward to.

But that was before. Was he just planning on doing his job and letting her walk away now? Was she supposed to want him to be there more? She liked the feel of him comforting her. She just wished it wasn't so embarrassing. She wasn't a shallow person, and didn't much worry about what she looked like, but Andrea didn't like people thinking bad about her. Or that she was needy, like her mom. Did Liam want a woman who needed saving? Maybe that was what had drawn him to her, the fact she was in trouble.

As much as she didn't want to go home, about the safest place she could think of was her parents' house and their security fence.

She straightened her spine. "I'd like to go to my parents' home for a while. I think it might be the best thing for all of us." Except, she really meant it was the best thing for her. After all, she was the one being targeted. Wasn't she allowed to be a little bit selfish, given the circumstances?

Liam's lips pressed into a thin line. "We'll have to make arrangements. If you're going to stay with your parents there needs to be room for Caisey and I. Space for a team to watch the property. We're not going to just let you go without protection."

She wasn't an idiot. "You think I don't know that? You want to catch him, and I'll screw up your case if he gets me. If he kills me, like he killed Kiera—" Her voice broke.

Why was this so hard?

Liam's arms wrapped around her, the heat inescapable as his hand moved up her back to her neck.

"I'm sorry."

But his hand drifted up, and then his fingers got lost in her hair. Andrea barely drew a breath before his lips were on hers. For a full minute she couldn't even think. There was nothing in the world that had ever felt like this and she wanted to submerge herself in it.

Liam pulled back and she went with him. Andrea opened her eyes and saw his face.

Oh, no. He was—

"I shouldn't have done that."

How on earth could he be sorry for that? Andrea lifted her chin. "That was the best kiss I've ever had."

Liam's head jerked. So he hadn't expected her to say that. Well, that wasn't her problem now, was it? His lips twitched. "It was, wasn't it?"

"So what are you going to do about it?"

TWELVE

So the timing was awful, Andrea wasn't going to pass up something that felt like that. She'd lived her life for too long by the tenet, "if it feels good, it's probably wrong". It was time for her to have a full life of her own for once.

"Okay, then." Liam huffed out a laugh. "But that doesn't change the fact I'm here to do a job. I need you to let me concentrate on the case and keeping you safe from the Chloroform Killer. When that's done, maybe we could go to dinner?"

"I'd like that."

He glanced down at her suitcase for a second. "Are you sure you want to go to your parents'?"

"They have a security system."

"You'll be putting them in danger." She wanted to argue, but he held up his hands. "I'm not saying you have to stay here, but we can find somewhere else that's secure."

"But you'd rather I didn't go anywhere, because the Chloroform Killer will have to find us, wherever we go?"

"I'm not worried about him finding us, or about waiting around while he does. I don't like the idea of him being near you...at all." Liam sighed. "But we are already set up here."

Andrea let go of her suitcase handle and sank onto the end of the bed. "I don't know if I can be here. He was in my apartment."

Liam crouched in front of her. "You're not going to be alone. We're going to protect you."

"I know you will. It's just..." She shuddered.

"As soon as this is over, you can move." "Get a new place?"

"If that's what you want."

"I always planned to buy a house, eventually." What would it be like to actually have her own little back yard? She could plant flowers and grow tomatoes. "Maybe now I will."

"I have an app on my tablet that will show you what's for sale. We could look at it later, if you want."

It was nice of him to want to distract her, to keep her mind off the horrible tragedy that was her life right now. Even if there was little chance it would help. "I'd like that."

"Don't worry about the Chloroform Killer, okay? Caisey and I aren't going to let anything happen to you."

Andrea followed him out into her living room, now free of all the people who'd been there. "You can't know that. You can't predict the future any more than I can."

"You think I'm lying?"

"No. I know you have no intention of letting me get hurt. I'm okay with that." It wasn't like she particularly wanted to get hurt. "But you can't control everything. You can't guarantee everything is going to be fine."

Liam looked at her, his face hard and his eyes stormy.

"What is it?"

"I won't let anything happen to you."

"Liam—"

"No. Just...hear me out, okay?"

Andrea nodded.

"When you showed up at the office, I was glad it wasn't you who'd been abducted. I'm sorry about your sister. I'm so sorry she was killed..." He shook his head. "This isn't the time for this."

Andrea laid a hand on his arm. "It's okay. Tell me."

"My sister killed herself." He swallowed. "I was fifteen. She slit her wrists in the bathtub. I saw the water under the door, it was pink. That's why I went in. It was—" His voice broke. "I was glad when it turned out it wasn't you in that van." He looked at her. "I was really glad."

"I was, too." That might make her a horrible person, or more like her father than she cared to admit, but Andrea was happy to be alive.

"After she died, I pretty much went off the rails. Drinking, partying with my friends. High school is a blur, but I remember my pickup truck was blue." He blew out a breath. "If something happened to you, I don't know how I'd deal. Not now that I've gotten to know you a little."

Liam didn't want her to be another woman he cared for, dead. Andrea might not have a problem with that sentiment, but if he was going to convince himself everything would be fine then what would happen if she was hurt—or killed?

The thought of him checking out like Kiera, or winding up like her dad was the last thing she wanted to contemplate.

Did she want another person like that in her life? She needed someone safe, not another powder keg waiting to erupt.

And after the danger was gone, when she was just boring, ordinary Andrea with a dull job and a duller existence...what then? A guy like Liam wouldn't want to stick around when there was nothing else to take care of.

"I'm not your sister, Liam. I'm not going to die." Okay, so she was going to die sometime. But for right now, he needed to know she wouldn't do anything to put her safety in jeopardy.

Liam rubbed his eyes. "I'm sorry. You don't need this, today of all days. I shouldn't be dumping my drama on you."

Andrea took hold of his elbows and leaned in. "Its okay." She liked how determined he was, even if he couldn't know the outcome. Time would tell if they were suited to each other. She had to guard her heart or she'd wind up in love with him before she knew it.

Liam pulled back, shaking off whatever he'd been thinking. He smiled, but it wasn't convincing. "Let's clean this place up. You can unpack and we'll see what's for dinner. Sound good?"

"Sure."

~

CAISEY SHOWED up ten minutes after Liam sent the text. Andrea was cleaning up the kitchen, but after his emotional meltdown, Liam needed space. And air. Caisey had better not make a big deal about this.

When he opened the front door she took one look at his face, grabbed his arm and pulled him outside. "What is up with you?"

"I just need some time. Are you going to give it to me, or are you going to make this as difficult as possible?"

Caisey shut her mouth.

He blew out a breath. "Sorry."

"Go." She stepped around him. "I'll tell Andrea there was a change in plans. We'll see you later. Or tomorrow."

"Case—"

She shut the front door.

Liam didn't go back inside for his coat. As he walked home, he sent a text to the surveillance team and found out Caisey had already informed them of the rotation. His apartment was dark, so he flipped the switch for the two living room lamps and sank onto his couch.

He knew Andrea wasn't Bethany. He knew that. And yet, if he found her covered in blood it wasn't going to hurt the same way it had with his sister—it was going to kill him. That was why he couldn't let it get to that point, because he might have been broken before, when Bethany died. But if something happened to Andrea, Liam would be destroyed.

He shot up from the couch to pace the space between the coffee table and the TV.

It didn't make any sense. He barely knew her, so why did he care so much? What was it about Andrea that had caught his attention so thoroughly? Maybe he shouldn't be asking that, just accepting the fact he'd found someone he wanted to spend time with and who seemed to like him enough to say yes to dinner. Maybe that was the secret—you just shut up and said thank you and got on with making your life the best it could be.

Liam pulled out his phone. His dad was in town, and he'd wanted them to visit together. He dialed before he thought about it too much.

"Liam!"

He winced and pulled the phone from his ear. "Can I talk to you? I know you have dinners and such, but can you make some time for me?"

"I can get away. If I don't and your mother finds out, I'll never hear the end of it."

Half an hour later, Liam pulled up outside at the lobby of a hotel downtown and gave the valet his keys. His father was in an armchair in the lobby with an empty cup on the table beside him and the Wall Street Journal open. Liam knew it was him, just by the shine on his shoes.

"Hey."

The newspaper lowered. The old man's face was older, even though it hadn't been more than a few months since Liam went home for thanksgiving. "You look like crap."

"Thanks, Dad." He slumped into the chair beside his father, for once seeing the man and not the rank he wore like it was a limb. *Thank God.*

A perky waitress Liam would have looked twice at only a week ago bounced over with a refill for his dad. He was here, he might as well drink a cup while they got through the small talk to the real reason he'd called his dad away from his entourage.

His father's head was back behind the paper. "Why don't you just cut to the chase?"

Liam smiled. His dad was two inches taller than him, and working on his old-man belly if the empty plate of crumbs was anything to go by, but aside from the physical resemblance they were very different. It was probably why they had such a hard time communicating.

Liam took a sip of coffee and set his cup back down. "Who says there's anything to talk about? Maybe I just wanted to see you."

Newspaper rustled. "I thought you were busy tonight."

Liam leaned back far enough to see a smirk on his dad's face. He grabbed the newspaper from his dad's hands and set it on the table.

"This is about a woman." His dad's eyes narrowed, but he was still smiling. "It has to be. Well, who is she?"

"Her name is Andrea."

"And?"

"She's an accountant."

"Good Lord."

Liam laughed. "She happens to be very nice. And beautiful. It's a long, complicated story."

His dad shook his head. "No, it isn't."

"Excuse me?"

"Love. It's never complicated. Either she's the one, or she's not. Finito."

Liam pressed his lips together.

"Well?"

"She is."

"Did you tell her that?"

"Uh, no."

His dad nodded. "There's your problem."

Liam got up. "This probably wasn't a good idea. I do have a lot of work."

"Sit down, son."

Liam stilled, and then sat.

"I told your mother I knew she was the one the first time I saw her."

"Did you?" Liam had never heard that story.

"No. I was dating Sally Turnell at the time. But later, after the bloom of the Sally Turnell rose lost its luster, I saw your mother for the gem that she was."

They'd been together forever, as far as either of them ever said. "When was that?"

His dad sniffed. "End of third grade."

Liam laughed. "My deal might be different. Neither Andrea nor I are grade school kids."

"Young people these days. They're always making everything so complicated."

"It's connected to a work thing—"

"Chloroform Killer?"

"How do you know that?" His dad shrugged.

"Anyway, while I'm keeping her safe it's not okay for us to be romantically involved, but things keep happening." Liam sighed. "She's a Christian, too. Prays before she eats, believes God will take care of her."

"Sounds like your mother."

"Does mom still go to church every Sunday?"

His dad nodded. "Bible study with the ladies on a Thursday morning."

Liam didn't want to ask, but he did. "So why didn't it help Bethany?" He didn't like how small his voice sounded, but it was past time for them to talk about this. "All Mom's religion and it didn't stop Bethany from killing herself."

"Your sister was eighteen. She was hurting. So much pain...and she made a choice to end it. As much as it kills me that she did, your sister took the power back. Maybe, for Bethany, suicide wasn't cowardice." His dad cleared his throat. "I was gone, but I knew she was spiraling. Your mom told me you were the one to find her."

Liam nodded. He couldn't speak.

"This woman, Andrea, you can do your best but people's lives are their own. Your sister was loved and she knew that, but there was something inside her that couldn't live with what happened to her."

Liam looked down at his clenched fingers. "I have to help her. I want us to have a future, a chance to see what we can build. But we can't do that if Andrea is the next victim."

"So don't let her be." His dad shifted in the chair so he was facing Liam. "Your job to take care of her won't end with this threat. It stays with you for the rest of your life when you sign up for the job of husband, and, God willing, you add kids to that scenario. It's your role. It's not bad, Liam. Don't think that. You didn't fail to protect Bethany. You were a kid yourself and all the treatment in the world didn't stop her from purging that pain the only way she knew how. You didn't do anything wrong."

THIRTEEN

Andrea scrolled through listings of houses, but the rush of buying a place all her own had lost its luster pretty fast. She sighed and set the laptop on the table.

Caisey glanced over from her side of the couch. "You want to watch a movie? I can see what's on TV."

"You don't have to entertain me. I don't mind just hanging out." Andrea smiled. "Truth is, the last few days have been the busiest in the last few years."

Caisey grinned. "I figured as much. Are we overloading you?"

"It's not bad, even given the circumstances. Maybe I'll miss it when you're gone."

"Liam will still be around, won't he? And I'm sure we'll see each other if you and my partner have a thing."

If that was even going to happen. "Sure, maybe."

"Liam didn't tell you what he wants yet?"

"Why does it have to be about what he wants?"

Caisey chuckled. "Sort of helps if the guy is on board, too. You know?"

"I'm guessing there's something deeper behind that. A little personal experience?"

"There was a guy." Caisey shifted. "It was a long time ago, and he hasn't been back since."

"I'm sorry."

"You know what? So am I." Caisey stood. "Don't worry about it." She picked up both of their empty glasses. "You want a refill?"

Andrea nodded. She wasn't particularly thirsty, but Caisey seemed to need a moment by herself. It was easy to see the woman as impervious to just about anything, but apparently Caisey wasn't tough all the way to her core. There was hurt there that Andrea didn't think had anything to do with some long-ago guy.

The commercial break ended and a local news program started. Kiera's picture flashed on the screen and Andrea sucked in a breath, choking. "Ca-Caisey!"

The Special Agent ran in, her gun drawn. "What?"

Andrea grabbed the remote and turned up the volume.

"...latest victim. Our sources have confirmed that the death of local woman Kiera James was the work of the Chloroform Killer, an active serial killer whose first murder took place nearly twenty-two months ago. Ms. James was his sixth victim. We also have indications that the FBI is currently protecting an unnamed woman, although that has not been confirmed at this time."

"How do they know this?" Andrea turned to Caisey, whose mouth was pressed into a thin line as she shook her head.

"Someone's going to get my boot in their backside for leaking this."

"Our source has also indicated to us that it is common for the Chloroform Killer to contact his victims, prior to abducting and killing them. He appears to take pictures of his intended victims, which he then sends to them via email and regular mail in order to taunt them. We also have information that indicates phone calls were made to the victims by the killer."

Andrea covered her mouth.

"If you have been the recipient of anything that could be from the Chloroform Killer, please call this number. We will put you in direct contact with police and federal agents working this case."

Caisey shifted. "Yeah, and get an exclusive in the process."

"So far the police have no leads as to the identity of this elusive murderer. If you feel like you are in danger, please take necessary steps to ensure your safety."

The newscaster took a breath and immediately launched into the next story, like that whole segment hadn't even happened.

Andrea twisted on the couch. Caisey lifted one finger, eyes on her phone. "In a minute." She pressed a series of buttons. "Heads are gonna roll for this, believe you me."

Andrea did believe her.

She put the phone to her ear. "No, I don't believe this. What are we going to do?" She paused. "Seriously. This chick needs a lesson in what's for public consumption and what most definitely is not. Inciting panic for no reason other than so she can get an exclusive on the Chloroform Killer? I need to head down to the news station and have a word with this girl." Caisey looked at the ceiling. "I know that...I am."

Andrea couldn't help it, she smiled.

The Special Agent sighed. "Yeah, yeah. Fine. But I better not bump into this Barbie- doll newswoman or I'm liable to speak my mind." Her lips twitched. "Later."

"What did Liam say?"

Caisey stowed her phone in the back pocket of her jeans. "That was my boss."

"You talk to your boss like that?"

Her head tiled to the side. "Like what?"

Andrea bit back what she'd been intending to say. "Never mind."

She wouldn't ever talk to her superior that way. Although, her boss barely stepped foot in the office; he did most of his work from the country club where he settled things over eighteen holes with CFOs of fortune five-hundred companies, and then let Andrea worry about the paperwork.

"So what do we do now?"

Caisey flipped off the TV. "Not a lot we can do, aside from what we're already doing. Protect you and wait for him to make his move. Carry on with life as best you can and stay safe. The Medical Examiner will release Kiera's body and you'll be able to make whatever arrangements you need to make with regards to burial or cremation."

Andrea nodded. "That would be good."

"I'll be here to help if you need it. I remember how hard it was after my dad died, having to make all those decisions that seemed more important than anything else ever had been." She gave Andrea a small smile. "Half of me didn't want to think about it at all, but I knew I had to. Then it was over, and I kind of felt ridiculous for making it a big deal. Like he wouldn't have liked it if I got a black casket instead of a brown one, you know?"

"I do. I'd like to bury Kiera alongside Brad, but I'll have to look into that. See if it's even possible. I guess his parents would know."

"I'll get you their information. You can decide if you want to make the call, or if you want me to do it."

Andrea smoothed the creases from her pants.

"One thing at a time."

She looked up. "Can we get out of here?"

"Where do you want to go?"

Did she even know? Andrea thought about it, but could only come up with one thing. "What about going to my office? It'd be nice to clean up before tomorrow morning."

"If you'd said anywhere else, I'd have said no. But your office is doable." Caisey pulled her phone out again. "Sit tight for a minute and I'll make the arrangements."

BRENDA PETERSON SET her remote down. In the dark silence of her apartment, she perched on the edge of her couch. Icy fingers crept up her spine, even though she was alone, until she shuddered to ward off the cold.

Could the news report be right? Did the Chloroform Killer actually contact his victims before he abducted...*Don't think about that.*

She moved on wooden legs to the computer and opened her

email program. Although she'd wished it gone over and over again all day, the message was still there.

She clicked and the image loaded. A picture of her exiting Macy's inside the mall just days ago.

She picked up the handset of her landline and stared at the number buttons. There was no way she'd call the news station—not if this was for real. If it really was life or death, Brenda was going straight to the top of the food chain.

She set the phone down and went back to the computer, where she pulled up the search engine and typed, *Denver FBI*.

JUST AFTER NINE a.m. the next day, Liam directed the woman to sit on the same chair Andrea had in the conference room.

"I appreciate your time." The pink cheeks on her round, pixie face bulged in a smile, while the rest of her was pear-shaped in the same way Caisey was. Curved, but still lean. Short. Their blond hair was a similar style, too. "I honestly don't know what to make of this. If the news report hadn't said all that about emails and phone calls, I might have left it. Thought nothing of it."

Liam picked up his pen. "Brenda Peterson, right? Is that S-E-N or S-O-N?"

She clutched her giant white faux-leather purse on her lap. "With an "O"."

"And you're an accountant?"

She nodded. There seemed to be a lot of that going around, but did it mean something to the killer?

"When did the contact start?"

"About a week and a half ago."

Andrea's emails and phone calls had been a week before that, which meant either the killer courted his victims simultaneously, or he chose more than one and picked depending on their reactions.

"Do you think it's him?"

Liam set his pen down and linked his fingers on the table. "Our computer technicians are taking a deeper look. They'll confirm whether the emails originated from the same account as the emails received by the other victims, or as far as we can tell. We haven't been able to trace it beyond the location where the internet connection was made, and he's been using different locations each time. But if there's enough of a correlation then we'll be able to confirm it."

"So I just go home and wait for you to call?"

"Honestly, if he's watching then he may now divert his attention from you altogether since you've brought this to our attention. Or..."

"I might have made things a lot worse."

"It's possible. I'm not going to lie."

Brenda Peterson's eyes filled with unshed tears. "Of course." She sucked in a breath. "What do I do?"

Liam leaned forward. "Let us take care of this. I'll speak to my boss. We'll arrange for protection for you."

"Like that other woman on the news?"

Liam's stomach roiled, thinking about Andrea. Her cover had effectively been blown regardless of the fact the media hadn't leaked her identity. But then, the killer already knew they were protecting her. Still, the last thing they needed was the media, and anyone interested, sticking their nose in Andrea's life trying to find out what was going on.

"You let me worry about her. I'll get someone reassigned and we'll make sure you're safe."

Liam left her with a fresh cup of tea and strode to Burkot's office. He knocked, but didn't wait. Burkot looked up. "It's legit?"

"That hasn't been confirmed yet, but my gut says, yes."

"Does she really look like Agent Lyons?"

"Yes, but don't tell Caisey. She'll get mad if she finds out she's not as original as she thinks she is."

FOURTEEN

"Ready to go?" Liam's presence filled the doorway to Andrea's office more effectively than his lean physique.

She glanced back at her computer. Best not to think about that too much, otherwise she'd end up all hot and bothered, which wasn't totally helpful when you'd decided to save that stuff for after marriage. "Sure, I can wrap this up."

It was after eight, and even though there wasn't much waiting for her at home...except more waiting, it was still better than keeping everyone out late just because she didn't want to leave.

Why couldn't the Chloroform Killer make his move already? Enough toying with her. Andrea was ready to throw down, which even she could admit was hilarious, since she'd never learned how to fight and hadn't thrown a punch in her life. Not even in a gym class, because you actually had to *go* to the gym to take a gym class.

Liam wandered over and sat on the edge of her desk, by her right elbow.

She looked up at him.

"Don't mind me. I'm good whenever you're ready."

Yeah, because it was so easy to concentrate on quarterly earnings reports when his leg was right by her arm. Apparently, he'd decided to forget about the whole *professional distance* thing. Where was all the awkwardness from yesterday? "How was your evening last night?"

"Good." He smiled. "I spoke to my dad, about my sister."

"You did?"

"I realized I was still looking at it like I was fifteen and powerless. He gave me a different perspective." He paused. "I should call my mom, too. Talk to her. She's a Christian, like you."

At least he wasn't totally unfamiliar with what that meant, if his mom had been a believer for any length of time. Everyone was different and everyone understood faith from their own perspective, but the basic tenets were the same, no matter which denomination you belonged to.

"But you've never made that decision for yourself?"

Liam shrugged one shoulder. "I was always busy. But my mom will tell me about what she's learning when we talk, you know? So it feels familiar, even though I know you're supposed to pray and take it on board in your own life and all that. I like my life; I didn't really want to change how I do everything."

"And you still feel that way?"

"I'm not sure. One person in my life who believed was fine, then there was Caisey, but she doesn't bring faith into her work much. Although sometimes it's just there because it's part of who she is. Meeting you and finding another person I respect who holds it to be true...that's a little less avoidable." He studied her for a moment. "Is this a deal breaker for you?"

She didn't want to say yes, even if his being a Christian would be the best way to begin a relationship—on the same page about fundamental things like life and marriage. But she didn't want him to believe just because it was important to her. He needed to discover what was truth for himself, like she had in college when her roommate had told her about church and Jesus. It had taken a few weeks, reading a lot, and asking some questions, but Andrea had finally accepted Christianity was the truth for herself.

Liam needed to do the same. On his own terms.

"Now might be a good time for you to look into that. I'm here if you want to ask any questions, and I'm not going to write you off if you decide you don't agree with me. But I do think relationships should have shared values. It makes you stronger when you can stand firm on the same things."

She'd seen it at church, and in friends who did activities as couples. Who wouldn't want that?

"Agreed." He gave a gentle squeeze to her elbow. "All right then, I'll do that."

The lights flickered and went out.

"Stay in your chair. You hear anything you don't like you get under the desk, get your phone and call 9-1-1."

Liam stepped to the door, his shoes completely silent on the floor.

CAISEY GRABBED two paper towels and dried off her hands. The harsh glare of the bathroom's fluorescents didn't do her any favors. She looked like she needed a week's worth of sleep. Or more than just another swipe of mascara and some more lip balm. When the case was over she'd have to raid Jenna's exploding makeup case and borrow something her friend wasn't going to miss anyway. It was one of the benefits of having her as a roommate.

And anytime Jenna needed a pair of black ankle socks—or a pistol—she knew where to come.

The lights shut off.

Caisey pushed out a breath through pursed lips, breaking the silence. She didn't move, just pulled out her phone and turned on the flashlight that activated the camera's flash.

The lock on the door turned.

Caisey went to the handle, but it wouldn't turn. She pulled at the door, jiggled the handle again, and then gave it a swift kick with the toe of her boot.

Liam answered before her end even rang. "Conners."

"He's here?"

"No sign yet. I already called it in."

Caisey gritted her teeth. "I'm locked in the bathroom."

"Down from the elevators?"

"Yup." If she tried hard enough, she could break the door down. Maybe.

"Sit tight. I don't want to get that far from Andrea. The rest of the team will be here shortly."

While her partner took on the Chloroform Killer all by himself?

Caisey shoved at the door. "Liam..."

But he'd already hung up.

ANDREA DIDN'T WAIT for the Chloroform Killer to show up. She crawled under the desk and sat by the space heater she used to warm up her feet in the mornings, before the coffee was done brewing.

Why had she made them all stay late? They could have been home. Not safe, but at least not here. Why hadn't she listened to her own good sense? Now Liam was out there, facing down the killer. He was an FBI agent, but that didn't mean she wasn't sick at the thought of something happening to him.

God, keep him safe.

A creak.

The door was opened.

The wood dragged across the floor and Andrea froze; her whole body solid. She didn't breathe for fear the Chloroform Killer would hear her. This was the monster who had killed Kiera. He'd taken an already broken woman and totally destroyed her. What was he going to do to Andrea?

Liam wouldn't let that happen. He couldn't. He'd promised her that she would be safe and she'd believed him. The kind of man he was would shift the axis of the world to keep his promises. That was why she had every intention of holding on to him now that she'd found him.

In the dark, curled up under the desk, Andrea tracked his footsteps. He moved with no light as though he knew intimately the layout of her office.

God, please...

What was she going to ask? She couldn't even think, let alone form a silent prayer that was her only hope that she and Liam, and Caisey, would get out of this alive.

"Hello, Andrea."

~

LIAM HEARD the scream and raced back to Andrea's office. He scanned the room with his flashlight and weapon both aimed.

Empty.

He could hear Caisey banging on the bathroom door and yelling. The closest exit was to the left, the stairs at the end of the hall opposite the bathroom. If she wasn't hurt, she was going to have to wait until he found Andrea.

Liam raced to the stair exit. The door was ajar, dim light coming from the stairwell. Emergency lighting.

A black form disappeared through the door and it clicked shut. Liam slammed into it at full speed, hitting the handle with his hand and turning into the stairwell landing, lifting up his gun as he swept the space.

Two steps down and descending, Andrea was over his shoulder.

"FBI, freeze!"

The Chloroform Killer dropped Andrea on the concrete stairs and ran. Liam fired off three shots. The guy's body jerked, but he kept going.

He stopped by Andrea and pulled out his phone, dialing his boss.

"Burkot."

"He's in the stairwell, heading down."

"We're still half a mile away. There was an accident on Broadway. We won't make it in time, you have to get him."

"He's gone. I'll never catch up and I'm not leaving Andrea."

Burkot hung up.

Blood streamed from Andrea's temple. Head wounds always looked worse than they were, but tell that to his heart. It felt like it was going to explode out of his chest.

God, don't let her die.

He'd always known there was a God, but never acknowledged Him much before now. But if it meant the difference between Andrea living or dying, he wasn't going to risk not playing all the cards he had to play. And imploring a higher being was one of them.

I'll follow You. Just don't let anything happen to her.

It was lame to make that bargain, like God was so petty he'd save her just because Liam agreed to trust in Him.

But he didn't have anything else God might actually want.

CAISEY LIFTED her chin and looked over Burkot's shoulder. She agreed with his description of the night's events and the Chloroform Killer's escape, but tried not to use that particular word to describe anything, let alone the colossal mess they'd made of the case.

Liam was at the hospital with Andrea, who'd been admitted for observation even though the tests they'd done on her head all came back fine.

Caisey had been locked in the bathroom, the entire time. How dumb was she? A serial killer came after her friend, her charge, and her partner had to face him alone. Caisey had been taken out of the equation by something so stupid as being locked in the bathroom.

"Let me fix this."

His eyebrow lifted. "And how exactly do you intend to do that, Special Agent Lyons?"

Since Liam told her about Brenda Peterson and their resemblance, the idea had been forming. Could she really pull this off? If she didn't try, she'd never live down the stigma of being the agent in the bathroom. It was already all over the office and nearly everyone had commented on it.

But this could change all that. She could get back in good standing. Make her dad proud. Finally do something that would end this and bring the Chloroform Killer to justice.

Caisey sucked in a breath and said, "I have an idea.

BAIT

DENVER FBI - BOOK 2

ONE

Caisey lyons lived someone else's life for three days before she got abducted. In the early hours she heard his footsteps in the hall. Her eyes flew open, but she didn't move. The temperature in the room cut through the blanket and the thin white nightgown that belonged to a stranger. Three days of walking around someone else's house, passing the time until he would come.

The bedroom door eased open.

Caisey kept her eyes shut and prayed the darkness would hide the fact she was awake. She wrestled away the revulsion with deep breaths and fought for calm. No one else on the FBI task force fit the victim's description. Now instead of a badge and gun, she had a tracking device injected below the skin and a team of agents on stand-by. She wished she could struggle, give him a taste of his own violence. But that wasn't the plan. His death would find justice for each of the victims, all the more significant since this case had touched Caisey and her partner Liam's lives personally. This was for Andrea's sister.

All Caisey had to do was stay alive.

Soft footsteps crossed the carpet to her. A shell jacket rustled and a sickly-sweet smell filled the air. Caisey knew it was coming before the cloth was placed over her nose. The ice cold liquid touched her face and she sucked in a breath that smelled and tasted...wrong. One hand closed over her mouth and nose and another wrapped around the back of her head.

It was like being shut in a tomb.

Caisey squirmed to get a grip on him. Her hands and arms went from tingly to numb and something broke inside her. A rushing sound filled her ears. Would she end up laid out on a metal table for the Medical Examiner? What if the signal malfunctioned? What if the agents watching didn't see him take her out of the apartment?

She tried to breathe...but there was only darkness.

~

Three days earlier

CAISEY STARED AT THE CLOSET, trying to decide what to pack.

"What are you doing in my room?"

She spun from the business-wear to her best friend and tried not to look pathetic. "I need to borrow something."

Jenna strode over, her gray pencil skirt and sling-backs contrasting with the pink ends of her blond hair. "You mean more stylish? Or just not your usual jeans and boots, and boots and jeans, and more jeans?"

If only the worst thing about this assignment was that she'd have to wear uncomfortable clothes. Caisey pointed to a pair of silver heels with tiny straps. "Can't chase a perp down in those things, I'd break my ankle."

Jenna laughed. "You'd break your ankle walking downstairs in them. Just like—"

"Yeah, yeah." Caisey sighed, remembering the disaster that was Prom.

"What is this assignment anyway?"

"I have to—" get kidnapped. "Pretend to be someone."

"Someone classy?"

Caisey slung her arm around Jenna's shoulder with every intention of getting her back for that comment, but it turned into a side hug. She left her arm there, soaking in the comfort of decades of friendship that felt more like family than much of the family either of them ever had.

Her temples throbbed a rhumba beat and she closed her hands into fists to keep from massaging them.

Jenna frowned. "This is about that serial killer, isn't it?"

Caisey smiled and shook her head. "Why couldn't you be just another dumb blonde?"

"You mean an idiot who wouldn't be smart enough to worry about you?"

Something like that. "Call Liam if you have any problems while I'm gone, okay? I'll be out of contact."

Jenna swished hangers to the side. "Switch your usual black or gray fitted t-shirt for a light blue blouse. Black slacks because you don't want to be uncomfortable in a skirt. Also, you don't want anything tight in case you have to kick someone."

"Right." Caisey grabbed the bundle. "Thanks Jenna."

"Yup."

There was something in the tone that made Caisey turn back with her armful of clothes. "Spill it."

Jenna made a frustrated noise. "I can't keep anything from you."

"Quit stalling and tell me."

Jenna rolled her eyes. Her blonde bangs lay perfectly across her forehead. Caisey had grown hers out because she couldn't figure out how to get them to do that. "Don't be mad. I did it for your own good."

"What did you—?"

Jenna's face had guilt written all over it. "I may have...sort of... signed you up for a dating service."

"What?"

"Just think about it while you're gone, and maybe check out your profile. I said good things about you, made you sound like a catch." She held out both hands. "Which you totally are."

"Jenna—" Caisey drew the word out, her jaw tight.

"You should at least try it out. I mean, when was the last time you went on a date?"

Caisey smiled sweetly. "When was the last time you went on a date?"

"I date. I also have a teenage son. The two don't exactly mix."

"Ha. Like the right guy is going to care. Jake is great."

"I know." Jenna shot her a look. "But you have no excuse whatsoever. Nothing but a memory."

"Hey—"

Jenna clutched Caisey's elbows. "I just don't want you to waste your life on that one perfect guy. Your one perfect date before he disappeared forever. Jerk."

She had tried to get past it, to feel those sparks with someone—anyone—else but it never happened. All these years and no one had ever measured up to that date where dinner turned into a walk and the walk turned into talking all night about nothing and everything. Laughing together. That one great kiss.

And then nada. Not even a phone call.

Jenna's eyes softened. "It's time we both moved on to bigger and better things. Let the past be the past. Please. Let him go."

Caisey slung her arm around Jenna's neck and kissed her temple, then walked the length of the upstairs hall to her bedroom. She didn't want to be a source of pity for her friend, which meant that as much as she might not like the idea, she'd have to look into this dating site when she got back.

Caisey got dressed and stuffed a change of clothes into her gym bag. She left the bag by the front door and walked through the living room to the hall off the kitchen.

Grams sat in her armchair with a tray across her lap. "The answer is Canberra, you imbecile!"

The chair enveloped her small frame. Her plate had only crumbs and a blob of yolk from the soft boiled egg and toast she had every morning. Caisey picked up the tray and went into Grams' tiny kitchen.

Grams' aide was elbow-deep in soapy water, and gave her a smile. "Morning."

"Morning, Sara." Caisey slipped the plate and silverware into the water.

She went back to Grams and sat on the end of the loveseat. "Hi."

Grams' wrinkled lips twitched. "Good morning."

"I don't know how long I'll be gone. If you need anything, any of you, you can call Liam. You have his number, right?"

Grams lifted the china cup from the end table, looked inside and frowned. "Why is it always gone when you want a bit more?"

Caisey rose and took it from her. "I think I have time for a cup of tea before I go. You?"

"I'd love one." Grams looked up, a smile in her eyes. "Only, don't skimp on the sugar like you did last time, hmm?"

~

Present

CAISEY WOKE up to a dark space that wasn't much wider than her elbows. She kicked up her legs and hit the roof about a foot above where she lay. It was taller than a coffin, which was something at least. But it wouldn't open, no matter how hard she kicked and shoved.

What else could it be?

The whole thing was moving, like she was in the back of a vehicle driving who-knew- where. Stashed in a deep freezer or some other airtight container where he could probably hear her thrashing around. Which begged the question, did he know about the tracking device?

Caisey prayed the team would find her soon, because it was getting hard to breathe.

~

Three days ago

CAISEY CLIMBED in Special Agent Liam Conner's SUV and slammed the door against the February air. The inside was immaculate, as usual, and it stank like he'd polished the dash. Again.

Her partner huffed out a sigh, but not so big that it mussed his perfect hair. "I don't like this."

Caisey pulled out her BlackBerry and read the text from her boss. Did Liam think she was going to change her mind? "Brenda already called in sick. She's ready to make the switch."

"Are you listening?" Liam pulled the car away from the curb in front of her house.

Caisey looked back at the two-story house. The siding needed to be painted. Her dad's old Chevy truck was parked on the gravel beside the driveway, ready for when they decided Jake was allowed to drive. Most of her life had happened in this house, except those first few years with her mom before her dad brought her back to Denver. Then there was her time in Quantico, and four years spent at the FBI office in Salt Lake which consisted of traipsing around Idaho and Montana, up to the top of her boots in mountain man extremists. At least they let her wear her jeans so she blended in. She'd just ignored the license plates and pretended it was Colorado.

"I said—"

Caisey turned to her partner. "I heard you."

"I know you want to do this, I just don't like the idea of you being abducted. Like, at all."

I've done it before.

The words were on the tip of her tongue to say. She'd have told him why she was uniquely qualified to get kidnapped, but if she'd done that there was no way he would let her go. Now she would have another stash of memories to add to the archived file in her brain. That was how the shrink told her to think about it. As an inaccessible store of memories that were closed off from her everyday experience. Otherwise they could jump up at any moment.

But all that was need-to-know, so Caisey crossed her arms and for the first time in her life kept a secret from her partner.

She didn't need to mention the victims to him. They both knew each of them by name, and the last murder was the younger sister of Liam's girlfriend. "I'm not going to let her death mean nothing."

"We could have found someone else to pose as a potential victim. I don't like that it has to be you."

Caisey looked at him and his neat blonde hair, Ivy League silk tie and polished black shoes. Liam had found Andrea, he was happy and in that first blush of new love—just in a totally manly kind of way that didn't involve roses and candlelight. Knowing Liam it was probably the opera, or some crap like that.

Caisey was more of a rodeo type of girl.

Then there was his newfound faith. Caisey hadn't been part of his conversion, which grated her. Wasn't she supposed to be a bold witness for Christ? Now Liam was all fired up and praying about everything. When was the last time her faith had been exciting?

God, help me keep them safe.

Part of her wished for a cozy life of her own, but that wasn't real. Safety was an illusion, a wishful thought that brought easy smiles and peaceful childhood dreams. She knew what was real.

Liam drove up to the rear of the apartment building where Brenda Peterson lived. He put the SUV in park and turned to her. "You'll be careful?"

Caisey rolled her eyes. "Seriously?"

"Just say it."

She held up her hand to swear her oath. "I will be totally careful while I'm being abducted by a serial killer."

"Thank you. How's your leg?"

She rubbed her thigh where the sub-dermal tracker had been injected. "Just don't press any buttons on the computer and accidentally delete the transmitter's signal, okay? I need you to be able to find me."

"I would not—"

"You are the single most technologically accident prone person I've ever met. Why do you think you manage to get your phone stuck on Spanish at least once a month?"

His eyes narrowed. "I thought it was Jake messing with me."

It was Jenna's son, but Caisey wasn't going to tell him that. She put her BlackBerry in the glove box, pulled out her sidearm, unloaded it and put it with her phone. She added her badge ID to the immaculate storage space. Yeesh, there was even a dryer sheet in there.

"And your backup weapon?"

Caisey blanked her face. "What backup?"

"Please." He motioned with his fingers. "Hand it over."

She pouted and pulled at the Velcro securing the small caliber weapon to her leg. She slapped it in his palm. "Satisfied?"

"It's not like you can shoot him."

"I know that."

"We need him alive so he can tell us where the missing girls are."

"I said, I know." Caisey blew out a breath. "That doesn't mean I wouldn't have felt better at least."

"You don't need it."

She grasped the handle of her bag, her other hand on the lever to open the door. "Wish me luck?"

He grinned. "I can do better than that."

His hand circled the back of her neck and squeezed, imparting his strength to her jumbled up stomach. And then he prayed for God's protection over her and the agents providing backup.

Caisey climbed out. "Don't shoot your foot off while I'm gone."

~

Present

CAISEY'S HEAD SWAM. She tried to breathe but there was no air. Her chest heaved as she sucked in gulp after gulp of nothing. She needed to get out of there, but she was at the mercy of a killer.

God, don't let me die.

She should have brought her gun.

TWO

Special agent liam Conners looked at the clock on the dash for the four hundred twenty-seventh time as they raced along the highway between Denver and Idaho Springs in a convoy of unmarked SUVs. The signal disappeared as soon as Caisey was put inside, but the helicopter still had eyes on the white van.

He gritted his teeth and looked out the passenger window at the dark night.

"I just can't relax." Andrea's soft voice warmed his ear.

Liam shifted the BlackBerry. "I know. Stay with the officers. Be safe, okay? As soon as I know anything, you'll know too."

Andrea had almost been abducted herself. She knew the risk Caisey was taking, and had focused on that instead of grief over her sister. He'd rather be there with Andrea, but then who would make sure Caisey was safe? His girlfriend had been the Chloroform Killer's intended target—that's how they met, when the killer took her sister by mistake. Now his partner was in the middle of it and there was nothing he could do.

"Bring her home."

"Sure, Andrea. I'll get her." He hung up.

That wasn't all Liam was going to get. He glanced over at Special Agent Burkot, the head of the team, who was driving the vehicle. Balding and in his fifties, Liam's boss clung to the remnants of his physique from his glory days at Notre Dame. Burkot had the job Liam wanted in seven years. He knew he'd be able to do it after Burkot retired; they were both cut from the same piece of Italian weave, extra-fine wool.

One missing girl was enough for a manhunt, let alone multiple women dead and more whose bodies had still not been recovered. It didn't matter if Caisey was one of them. Right now she was an abductee.

The tech in the backseat said, "Half a mile up there's a right turn, a dirt road that leads to an old abandoned mine."

Burkot made the turn and they were on dirt road. The crack of the radio in Liam's ear preceded the helicopter co-pilot announcing that a van was parked outside the mine.

Something wasn't sitting right with Liam. This whole thing was a bad idea, though he was the only one who thought that. Still...

"If he knew about the tracker, surely he knew we would be following too. And yet we've had the van in sight this whole time."

Burkot nodded. "We saw him put her in there. He's probably convinced himself there's no way we're going to catch him."

Liam figured the same thing, with the killer likely being highly intelligent. Enough he could have slipped into assuming he was uncatchable. "What is going on?" He whispered it more to himself than his boss. He'd half assumed the helicopter would lose the van on a back road and—as much as it made him sick—find Caisey's body somewhere days from now. Outwitted. Again.

Did the killer really want this to end so badly that he would lead the FBI right to him?

It didn't make any sense, though it was possible.

Burkot grunted. "Make sure the team is ready. I want to move as soon as we hit the ground."

Liam got on the phone and checked in with the other vehicles. His phone buzzed with an incoming call before he'd even hung up. He hit the button again, "Conners."

"Hello, dear."

"Grams." He smiled. Technically she wasn't his Grams, but Caisey's. Either way, she was still family. "You need something?"

"Is Caisey finished with her assignment?" Elenor Lyons' accent was strong as the day she left the United Kingdom with Caisey's grandfather, a U.S. serviceman she'd met in France. "Tomorrow is Saturday morning pancakes. I hope she doesn't get too busy she has to miss it."

"You really think she would?" Liam smiled. "She'll be there. You know Caisey, she'd quit the FBI before she missed Jenna's pancakes."

"I just had a funny feeling all evening. Unsettled. Like something might happen to Caisey. Perhaps I should pray. It is that sort of middle-of-the-night nudge."

"That's a good idea, Grams. Maybe it's exactly what Caisey needs right now."

There was a moment's pause. "Is she not safe?"

Liam looked out the window. "Just pray, okay?"

The tech in the backseat let out a yelp. Liam looked up and saw the fork in the road ahead of them. Burkot swung the steering wheel to the right. Haines squealed and the sound slid across the backseat. Liam gripped the dash and they took a turn that bent the road nearly ninety degrees. Two wheels left the ground. His breath evaporated, but he didn't chance a look at his boss.

The road straightened and they all exhaled, even Burkot.

Liam turned to the backseat. "Where now, Haines?"

"The trail dead-ends in a quarter mile at an old abandoned mine. Hasn't been used for years. Like a hundred-fifty."

"Good place to go unnoticed."

Burkot did a chin lift, his eyes on the road. "How deep is it?"

"We don't know." The tech sounded mad, probably because he didn't have a good answer for their boss. "This mine isn't listed anywhere, no maps, no records. Nothing. The UAV transmitted some pictures so we've seen the entrance. All we know right now is it's old."

"Great." Liam had hoped for detailed schematics, but apparently that wasn't meant to be.

God, I have to get her back.

He really didn't want to have to tell Andrea that Caisey wasn't coming back. Then he'd have to tell Caisey's Grams, her best friend and her godson the same thing.

"We're approaching the perimeter."

Burkot pulled the SUV to the side and parked. The other vehicles did the same behind them. Men and women piled out, donned bullet-proof vests and readied their weapons—SWAT and half their team, since no one was about to stay home when one of their own was being abducted by a killer.

Liam snapped the condition lever on his MP5 from 'safe' to 'burst' and gathered in a huddle with Burkot and the tech, Haines. The tech sat in the open door of their SUV, tapping buttons on his laptop.

"Well?"

The tech looked up at Burkot and Liam and flinched. "We know which mine, since the van is parked outside. The tracking device pinged for the thirty seconds it took to get her out of the van and inside, then it disappeared." He took a breath. "The mine is shielding the signal like one great big Faraday cage."

Burkot said, "How big?"

Haines' face was pained. "All these mines are alike. It's going to be a maze down there, miles and miles of switch-backs and blind corners. He could have her anywhere."

Liam's gut clenched. "Then we should get started."

WHEN CAISEY WOKE up it was colder than a fridge, but she wasn't in that box anymore. The air was thin, but at least there actually was air to breathe. Her whole body ached like she'd run ten miles in frozen rain. The floor under her bare feet was like a tomb of rock and her hands were bound behind her, tight against the arms of the metal chair.

She was tied to a chair. Again.

Sure, this time she volunteered, but wasn't once in a lifetime enough for that blessed experience? Not that she thought the Chloroform Killer would beat the crap out of her to prove a point. That wasn't his thing. Caisey lifted her feet and tucked her knees to her chest. She was still wearing Brenda Peterson's ugly white nightgown so nothing freaky had happened while she was unconscious which was very good. Very, very, very—

Okay, focus.

Clay-brown walls were jagged from being chipped away at. A mine? It was lit by the white glow of halogen lights strung along the ceiling. The space was a sizeable cavern but in what mountain? There were plenty of old abandoned mines outside Denver.

She tried to pull on her arms, but the restraints didn't give. Not in the slightest. Her mouth was taped, so she couldn't scream. She strained her ears and listened to him tinker with things that clanged together. Caisey didn't let her mind go there. Instead she thought of the deaths they had investigated. One had an allergic reaction to the chloroform. Her body was found disposed of, but not like the others.

Whatever this guy had planned, he hadn't been satisfied with the murders he'd already committed and Caisey had no desire to become his next victim. She closed her eyes and pictured her partner, his hands holding her elbows in the briefing room. Just a couple of days, he'd said, and then she would be back at home and this would all be a memory.

Any time now would be good, God. I'm not telling you what to do or anything, but feel free to send Conners and Burkot and everyone in to get me....Any time now.

Caisey flexed her toes and tried to get some feeling back in them. She stretched out her legs, wondering why he hadn't tied those to the chair too. If they weren't so numb, she would be able to affect a decent amount of damage to someone who came close enough to—

First there was just the impression of someone beside her.

She looked up.

A knit cap covered his face with three holes cut out so she could see the set of his thin lips, and his silver eyes that seemed to stab at her like daggers. Light skinned Caucasian. Lean. His eyes weren't lined, but she didn't think he was particularly young either. He didn't look like much of anything. It was no wonder he'd gone unnoticed for so long.

This was the guy who was going to kill her? His eyes meandered over her face and then his lip curled as though this entire scenario was abhorrent to him.

He must know by now that she wasn't his intended victim, if he hadn't known all along. Every muscle in her body braced while she waited for him to come close enough that she could seize the moment. He was going to explode. The profiler had concluded as much. Used to control, to order, he would likely have an adverse reaction to being deceived.

Liam had turned to her in the middle of the briefing. "When he realizes you're not Brenda Peterson, he'll go nuts."

"Thanks for the translation, but I got that."

It'd been easy to dismiss the cons of doing this and focus on the end result. Face to face with the Chloroform Killer, it was a little different. Where was Liam, anyway? In short order she would either be dead or busy, so she wouldn't likely get this chance again.

Caisey lifted her chin. "Can I help you?"

His eyes flashed. Determination and...nerves? "Actually, Special Agent Lyons, it's me who's going to help you."

A cold wet cloth covered her nose and everything went cloudy. She kicked her legs but it was just like before. One disgusting breath and then...nothing.

THREE

By the time Caisey could bring herself to shake the fog in her brain she was on the floor. Cold had completely numbed her cheek that was pressed against the ground and she was beyond the shivers. The lack of sensation was the only thing she could feel.

The Chloroform Killer stood at a card table with his back to her. His elbow jerked back and forth, like he was writing something.

Caisey blinked and tried to think. This was what he wanted for her? The other women hadn't been killed like this...he knew who she was.

Her thoughts sputtered like boiling water.

The Doc who did all their profiling hadn't been able to figure out a solid motive beyond the usual childhood trauma, or psychosis. So much of what they knew was nothing more than educated supposition. But it all pointed to one thing...hurt.

An ice cold tear leaked from the corner of her eye and ran toward her ear.

What broke a man so completely that he chose to do something like this? He turned; a paper in one hand and a knife in the other.

"You're awake." His lip curled.

Caisey's eyes shifted from his face to the paper to the knife as he stepped forward.

"In that case, this will likely hurt."

~

LIAM LED the way through the mine with Burkot on his six, guns angled down as they speed- walked the dirt packed floor of tunnels interspersed with cavernous rooms. The shuffle of boots behind him meant the team kept pace as the well-worn path twisted and turned, descending beneath the mountain. The air grew colder. Liam wasn't about to slow down, not when seconds counted and minutes meant life or death for Caisey. A rock tumbled down the path ahead and pinged all the way to the bottom.

Liam broke into a run. Every step reverberated through the mountain, but he ran faster. They needed to get out before the ceiling came down on top of all of them. Faster. Toward his partner. Toward the light.

He burst into an open room lit by construction lanterns.

Caisey was on the floor with a knife handle sticking out of her right leg. Precisely where the sub-dermal tracker had been injected. Red-soaked paper was pinned in place by the blade. Her chest rose and fell in spasms as she tried to breathe. He knelt beside her and touched the sides of her face so she focused on him.

"Hurts."

"I need a medic!" But they were already coming in, shifting him aside to see the wound.

He focused on her again. Her eyes were cloudy and her hands were freezing.

"You with me?"

She blinked.

"Why are you wearing this ugly thing anyway?"

"Sup-posed...be in character." Her words were slow and slurred, but the corner of her mouth creased up. "Did it work?" She blinked again. "Did you get him?"

Liam looked around the cavern and back at her, praying she couldn't read it on his face. Where did he go? "Let's just worry about you right now."

She exhaled and her grip on his hand relaxed, apparently satisfied with his non- answer. "Can I have a cup of tea now?"

He chuckled and took the blanket that was handed to him, covering her upper body and arms. The other agent frowned. "Why is she talking like that?"

"Her Grandma is British. Apparently when she's drugged she gets an accent." He looked down at her again. "Perhaps a side trip to the hospital first. But I'll make sure you get some tea."

~

CAISEY WOKE up to itchy blankets heavy enough to suffocate her and a dull ache in her leg. Her gun and badge were on the table above her feet and she knew immediately Liam had put them there. The small TV in the cabinet was tuned to kid's cartoons with the volume low. Liam's black loafers were stacked on the rail of the bed. Caisey wiggled her toes. She had socks on again and she wasn't wearing that nightgown anymore. Even a hospital gown was better than that thing.

The pain was being pushed to the back corner of her brain by whatever was dripping through the tube to her elbow. Caisey sent the memories there too, so she could pretend it was a scary dream.

She kicked Liam's foot with her good leg, but it was more like a gentle nudge. "What day is it?" Her mouth tasted like the skin of an unripe peach.

Liam looked up from his phone and frowned at her.

"I didn't hit my head. I just don't remember."

He didn't look convinced. "Saturday."

"What time?"

He glanced at the clock. It was on the wall two feet from the TV. "Six-twenty."

If she got out of there in the next hour she'd be home in time for Jenna's Saturday morning pancakes. At least that's what she told herself, but since when had hospitals ever done anything quickly? She'd probably still be here next Thursday.

"Are you going to sit there or are you going to get me some water? I'm dying of thirst."

Liam rolled his eyes and handed her a cup with a straw. "Only because the nurse said it's okay. I'm trying to tell myself it's just because you were abducted. Too bad you're like this all the time."

She frowned at him. "So what's the deal with my leg?"

He huffed like a teenager. "Sixteen stitches and you slept through the whole thing. I told the doctor you need to be home or you'll be a nightmare. She said if you wake up and you're clear of the drugs you can go, but you'll have crutches for a while and she wants you on bed rest until Monday. She also gave me a referral for a physiotherapist."

"So let's get going." She pushed up, waylaid by the tube in her arm. *Ouch.* "I'm gonna need my clothes." She'd figure out some way of pulling the pants up over the bandage.

"As you wish, my lady."

"Don't get smart with me. I still want to know where my tea is."

"I went to your house and got a tea bag and everything. You're the one who conked out and let it go cold."

"So nuke it."

He sucked a breath through his nose.

She pushed back the covers. "Give it to me. I'll do it myself."

"Get back in bed."

The door opened and Burkot strode in. "You're awake." He dumped her gym bag on the end of the bed. "The killer is in the wind. Any idea as to his identity?"

"Silver eyes and I can give you a basic height and weight, clothes, but that's all. He was wearing a mask." She squeezed the edge of the blankets. "What about the note?"

Burkot's face was grim. "You cannot catch me. You cannot find me. I find your attempts humorous but you are wasting my time. If this happens again I will not be so merciful."

Caisey winced.

"That was good work, by the way."

She smoothed the wrinkles in the blanket. "Thank you, sir."

"Now don't come back for two weeks."

Her head shot up. "What?"

"Sick leave. I'm authorizing it, you're taking it. No one is arguing. Spend time with your family. Take a vacation. Come back with a tan. I don't care."

Liam snorted. Caisey shot him a look, "Do we have the killer's identity yet?"

"We're going through the van and the scene. I'll know more later but it won't much change what happened or what's going to happen to him. Still—" Burkot blew out a breath and she knew why.

They hadn't caught him. They still didn't know who he was.

The door clicked shut. Caisey whipped her head around and pinned her partner down with a stare. "What wasn't he saying?"

Liam's jaw clenched. "The shrink is outside. Burkot wants you to talk to her before you go home."

"Okay."

His head jerked. "You're fine with it?"

"What am I, stupid? I just got abducted by a serial killer. I mean, it was on purpose, but still. Who else am I going to talk about it to? My family?" Caisey sucked in deep breaths to try and calm down.

"You'll see the shrink?"

She blew out a breath.

"But you hate the shrink."

"I hate being psychoanalyzed, like my brain is a puzzle that anyone could figure out. So I'll talk about how I felt when my dad died and how my mom abandoned me at a truck stop outside Sturgis. It won't take that long and then I can get back to work."

Liam stared at her. "You mean vacation."

"Did Burkot really think I'd go nuts about seeing the shrink?"

He didn't move.

"Come on, I'm not that bad."

Liam patted the gym bag and headed for the door. "Get dressed. I'll send the shrink in."

Caisey pulled her yoga pants on, not liking the niggling dissatisfaction that would probably linger for the next two weeks. It made her want to do something other than go home and sit around for a fortnight. Burkot had been satisfied with her work. What more did she need?

Still, the sensation persisted, even when the nurse disconnected the IV. Past when Doctor Amanda came in with two coffees and made Caisey tell her exactly what happened.

She hadn't wanted to think about it at all, but knew if she didn't say it out loud it would manifest itself in nightmares. Caisey knew as much from experience so she didn't argue. But it wasn't fun.

When they were done, Liam came back in pushing a wheelchair but she didn't look him in the eye. He needed to know she was strong. Caisey wasn't sure why that was important, but it was. Her partner needed to see her as capable and not the victim.

She looked up and Liam gave her a small smile. "Come on. I'll drive you home."

~

LIAM DROVE through downtown to her neighborhood. Caisey watched as offices and hotels rose and fell as they passed. The city was sunshine and busy people on the surface, but she knew what lurked underneath. What was hidden from most people was the evil that chomped its teeth on the innocent. Growing up here she'd only seen the shiny outer shell. Even as the daughter of a cop, she'd still been guarded from what lurked in the shadows. Until the day she met it face to face.

After that there was nothing she wanted more than to be FBI. She'd spent just enough time working out of Salt Lake to figure out the kind of special agent she was, apart from her dad's legacy with the Bureau. But the Denver she returned to was not the same city she remembered. This Denver was populated by crazies, murderers, rapists, liars and thieves. Then there were the people who worked to barricade regular folks from the tide of crime and evil that threatened to flood their cozy lives.

But at what price?

He pulled his SUV into her driveway. He put the car in park, but didn't switch off the engine. Caisey frowned. "Aren't you coming in?"

"I'm going home to sleep and then I'm going back to the office to type up my notes."

"Okay."

He held her gaze. "You'll call me?"

She nodded.

"For anything?"

"I will." She held his eyes until he knew she meant it. It didn't matter whether she was bored of inactivity or it was two a.m. and she awoken in a sweat, tangled in the blanket.

She'd call.

"Are you going to sit there with one foot out the car all day?"

FOUR

One week later

"Jacob samuel cartwright get your backside in gear or you're going to miss the bus!"

"I'm coming!"

Caisey flipped back the covers and grabbed her University of Denver sweatshirt. Her leg hurt like it was being poked with something sharp, but she'd quit the heavy drugs after the first few days. Too many injuries lead to bigger problems when you got hooked on narcotics. Caisey didn't want to go there. Ever. She wanted her job back.

She hobbled down the stairs and reached the front door just as her sixteen-year-old godson was pulling on his gloves for school.

He looked up and grinned, his backpack over one shoulder. "Nice bed hair."

Caisey put her hand on her hip, taking the weight off her leg. "And what's this thing you're doing with yours? Looks like you were mauled by a wild raccoon."

Jake opened his mouth to fling back a retort.

"Children, play nice." Jenna came out of the kitchen, her eyes on her son. "Have a good day at school." She handed Jake a hot cup.

Caisey grinned. "Yeah, don't do anything I wouldn't do."

Jake snorted. "Later."

The door shut and Jenna turned to her. "Why do you two have to bicker like that all the time?"

"He started it."

"You're such a child."

"And you've been my best friend since sixth grade. What does that say about you?" Caisey swept past Jenna into the kitchen. The coffee pot was warm, but empty. "Did Jake drink all the coffee again?"

"I gave him the last of it. It's cold outside and I didn't want him to catch a chill."

"You're such a mom." Caisey put the empty carafe in the sink and turned on the water.

"And you've been my best friend for two and a half decades. What does that say about you?"

Caisey laughed. She got coffee grounds on the counter, but when she saw the pot start to sputter she sighed.

"I heard you down here in the middle of the night."

"I needed a drink of water." To wash away a bad dream. "Did I wake you?"

Jenna's brown eyes darkened. "Do I look like I care that you woke me up? I care that I had to text Andrea, only to find out you were abducted." Her voice got louder and louder until she was practically shouting.

"Keep it down." Caisey hissed the words. "Grams will hear you."

Jenna waved her hand. "She has all her friends over for Bible study. The door is closed."

"She does?"

"They meet here every Monday."

Caisey frowned. "Why didn't I know that?"

"Probably because you either run or you hit the gym at oh-good-grief-a.m. and you're out the door for work before seven thirty. Don't think we aren't going to discuss this."

"Do not use the 'mom' tone on me. I'm not your teenager. It was a good idea. It worked. The end."

"And your leg?"

Caisey shrugged. "I got stabbed."

"I don't believe this! What kind of job are you doing that you get kidnapped and your partner lets you get hurt?"

"Jenna, yikes—"

"Do not give me the brush off. This is me you're talking to, Caisey."

"It was a delicate situation." Caisey got a mug down. "I'm fine."

"You better be."

Caisey dipped her chin. They were the same height, but Jenna had freckles on her tiny nose and ate spinach with everything. If Caisey was as brave as her, she'd have her hair cut in that cute bob and get the ends dyed pink like Jenna's.

"My leg is sore and other than needing to take a couple of painkillers every few hours, I'm fine."

"You weren't going to tell me any of this, were you?"

"Nope."

Jenna sighed. "Are you really okay?"

Caisey nodded. "Promise."

"Good, because replacing a best friend of two and a half decades would be a pain in the-you-know-where."

"So you're saying I'm irreplaceable?"

"I didn't say I wouldn't do it, I just said it would be difficult."

Caisey grinned. "You have work today?"

Jenna got a mug from the cupboard. "First client is at ten and then I have a full roster of acrylics and facials until four thirty. It's not taking down serial killers but it's mine. Jake has band after school so we decided on pizza. Plain cheese for Grams."

Caisey got the chocolate milk from the fridge and splashed some into both cups. "I'll be here. Why don't I cook something?"

A nervous noise emerged from Jenna's throat. "We'll get pizza."

~

AFTER SHE FORCED down a slice of toast, Caisey poured herself more coffee and hobbled to the other end of the house with her cell in her pocket. Someone at work might have a question about one of her open cases.

She hoped.

The twittering of little old ladies got louder as Caisey walked the hall lined with pictures of Grams and Grandpa. Her favorite was their wedding picture, where Grams wore her British nurse's uniform and Grandpa Thomas his US Army uniform outside the little church in Dover where they were married.

Caisey peered around the doorframe. They were all tiny and wrinkly, with bright eyes and easy smiles, except one.

Sarah, who was maybe in her forties, sniffed and pressed a balled up tissue to her nose. "I hate him so much for doing this to me."

Grams reached over and touched the woman's knee. Sarah was in her forties, but Grams said everyone under seventy was a baby. "I was a nurse in France during World War Two, you know that."

Sarah nodded.

"What you don't know is that a group of German soldiers attacked me." Several of the ladies gasped. "My Thomas was the one who found me. As I healed, that despair turned to anger and anger turned to hate until I was consumed with it."

"What did you do?"

Grams exhaled. "My Thomas took me to church. Threw me on his shoulder and carried me through the door kicking and screaming. I'm glad he did." She chuckled. "I thought I deserved justice, like I'd earned the right to it. As though I had more of a right than anyone else back then to feel hard done by."

Caisey leaned her head back against the wall and looked at the ceiling. The line where it met the wall was blurred. Didn't matter how many times she heard the story, it always cut right to her heart. She blinked and a tear ran down her face.

The doorbell rang.

Caisey wiped the tear away and limped over to answer it.

The man at the door had a white minister's collar above the

buttons of his wool coat and his dark hair was capped with a brown Fedora. There was no smile. Average height. Average features. Meant to blend in and go unnoticed.

"Help you?"

He nodded. "I'm looking for Samuel Lyons. He's a Special Agent with the FBI. I'm told he used to live here."

"He did."

"I would have gone to the Denver office, but this is a personal matter."

Caisey winced. "He's—" kind of, sort of, "—dead." She swallowed. "And you are?" "Oh...Patrick South, I'm the prison chaplain at Florence."

The Federal Penitentiary?

"I'm Samuel's daughter. He died four years ago."

"I'm very sorry for your loss." He didn't look sorry. He looked inconvenienced.

"What's this about?"

Patrick the Chaplain reached in his pocket. Caisey's hand planted on her hip, where her sidearm would have been—if she was at work. Right now it was in her bedroom and she was on the doorstep in her socks.

He produced an envelope. "Under the circumstances I was given permission to hand- deliver this."

Caisey read the name of the sender. Toben Carlen. Even written in ink it brought a rush of heat that lit up the world like a flash of lightning. Seeing the name made everything a little righter and cleaner than it had been that morning, knowing he was behind bars all this time right where he should be.

The letter was addressed to Gabe Carlen, a name that birthed an altogether different reaction in Caisey.

It was the case that made her father's career.

And killed him.

She looked up. "You should come inside."

Patrick the Chaplain perched on the edge of the couch. Caisey didn't offer him a drink. She just sat so the coffee table her father had built was between them. He'd said woodworking cleared his mind of the things he saw every day as an FBI agent. Caisey hadn't figured out what she needed to do for that and she'd been an agent nearly eight years.

She tapped the letter against her good knee, trying to ignore her leg. "Tell me about him."

Patrick blew out a breath. Apparently prison inmates were a comfortable topic. "He's a troubled man, that's always been the case. Although lately he's begun to change. Whether or not it is genuine remains to be seen. Toben has much cause to regret, if the things he's told me are true. But he wishes to make amends."

Caisey swallowed. She needed to see what he wanted. "Why come looking for my father to deliver Toben's letter?"

The chaplain shrugged. "He felt it was a natural place to start. Though Toben evidently did not know your father was no longer of this earth."

"Shot in the line of duty."

"Was he a man of faith?"

Caisey hitched one shoulder. "You could say that." She wasn't going to go there. Not with a stranger. "What does Toben want?"

"To make amends with his son. And if there was anyone who might know Gabe's whereabouts, Toben assures me it would be your father."

Caisey worked her mouth. "Why now?"

There was a moment of quiet, then, "He was recently diagnosed with terminal lung cancer."

"Facing his own mortality, he suddenly gets religion and needs to right every wrong?" Caisey stood. "Thank you for coming. I'll take care of this."

By burning the letter.

"Ms. Lyons—"

"It's Special Agent Lyons." She lifted her chin. "And even if I had the first clue how to find this—" She glanced down at the addressee's name like she didn't know who he was. "— Gabe, person. What makes you think I would destroy his peace of mind and whatever life he's built for himself just because dear old dad had a change of heart?"

"Surely with your resources—"

"That's not going to happen."

The chaplain sighed. "I will admit that often in these situations the conversion is...less than genuine. But I don't believe that to be the case here."

"Do you believe it strongly enough to risk a man's life?" Caisey's nails dug into her palms. "This case destroyed my father. If staying out of it now means that I fail to respect the wishes of a permanent resident of Florence Maximum Security Penitentiary, then so be it. I've got a family to protect."

"Forgiveness isn't something we can do in and of ourselves, Special Agent Lyons. It is a divine gift and an act of faith." His eyes flicked back and forth across her face. "Did you know your name, Lyons, refers to a fierce and brave warrior? A defender of those unable to defend their own. Be careful that you do not protect them so thoroughly that they never learn courage for themselves."

Caisey walked to the door and held it open. "I'd like to say it's been a pleasure, but..."

"Of course." The chaplain replaced his fedora. "Good day, Ms. Lyons."

Caisey closed the door behind him and rested her forehead against the wood.

Would it really be such a big deal if she went into work? She could do some paperwork. The house was too eerie during the day, like it had been back when she'd come home from school and there was no one home yet. Before Jenna's parents kicked her out and she came to live with them.

"You all right there, ducky?"

Caisey backed away from the door. "Yeah, Grams."

Elenor Lyons was five feet on her tiptoes. Her white hair was tied back and she wore a pair of gray slacks with a crease ironed down the front topped with a peach colored sweater set and a flowery scarf.

"You looked wistful for a moment."

Caisey shrugged, glad Grams hadn't seen the complete and utter dread she felt at being home for another week with nothing to do.

"What's that you've got there?" Grams motioned to the letter.

"Nothing really."

Grams snagged it and read. "Who's Toben Carlen?"

"No one."

"And there's a lot more to that story, but you can't tell me." Grams smiled. "Let's take the family out for dinner."

"So long as it's not an early bird special." Caisey mock-shivered. "Old people freak me out."

Grams laughed. "Me too, ducky."

FIVE

Caisey wiped barbeque sauce from her fingers and set the napkin on her empty plate. Liam had tagged along to dinner, bringing his girlfriend Andrea with him. It was hard to believe it was only a few weeks since they first met, when Liam had seen Andrea's sister being abducted. They'd been through a lot, but come out of it with a relationship that had a strong foundation of shared faith and weathering the stress that brought them together.

Caisey caught Andrea's gaze across the table and said, "How are your parents doing?"

Andrea winced. "Not great. They weren't that close with Sunny, but since her body was found it brought all the old stuff back up. I should have helped her more, got her into rehab or something."

Liam squeezed her shoulder, his thumb tracing the tendon in Andrea's neck. She smiled at him. At the other end of the table, Grams had ear-bud headphones in and was laughing at something on Jake's phone.

Caisey took a deep breath and smiled at the picture her partner and his girlfriend made. "Are they talking to anyone?"

"I had hoped to get them into some kind of counseling." Andrea sighed. "I know they need help, but they won't talk to me."

Liam drew her close. "It'll take time."

"I know."

"That's what I figure too." Caisey didn't want to admit the abduction had scarred her, but she didn't mind sharing some of what the shrink had told her. "Not that it's helpful when you're in the middle of it."

Time dissipated the effects of most things, or so she'd learned. And yet the slightest thing could bring it all rushing back—the smell of dirt, or a man's cologne—to the place where Caisey could feel the slam of fists and the fire of pain in her ribs and her face.

Now it was the pain that came when she moved her leg too fast.

Jenna leaned close. "Are you okay?"

Caisey looked at the table at large and the assessing eyes that preferred to see strength in her, not weakness. "Jenna and I joined a dating service."

Noise erupted. Except for Jake who looked like he was about to throw up.

Caisey grinned. "Although I'm holding out for a couple of Bronco's players so we can double date, I'll be scouring the hordes of men that no doubt flock to us when they hear we're on the market."

Grams clasped her hands in front of her, a smile on her face. "We can triple date!"

Liam shot a horrified look at Andrea.

Jake's eyes were so wide it looked like they were in danger of falling out of his head. "I don't want to know. Don't tell me anything. I don't want to hear any of it."

Caisey smirked. "Wh-y." The word was high-pitched and three seconds long. "You could join us. We'll make it a family event, that way we can see who you're spending time with and you can check out who's got their eye on your mom. Sounds perfect if you ask me."

Jake clapped his hands over his ears. "La la la la la la, I'm not listening to you talk about my mom man-hunting."

"Jake!"

Caisey laughed. "Well, at least the kid isn't emotionally scarred by the thought of sharing your attention. Or, he's not emotionally scarred by that, at least."

Jake scooped up a glob of ketchup on his spoon and prepared to flick it at Caisey. Jenna sighed. "What is it about the two of you that brings out the inner twelve-year-old in each other?"

Liam waved to the waitress. "Can we have the check, please?"

Jenna got Andrea's attention off Liam and said, "You guys should come back to ours for dessert."

It was after eight by the time Caisey pulled onto the driveway. Grams was in the back with Jake, head back eyes closed and mouth open. Jenna was in the front passenger seat texting on her phone.

"Andrea said they'll be here in a minute."

Caisey parked the car. "Just don't let Liam make the coffee. He likes it weak."

Jenna gagged. "That's gross."

They piled out and Jenna went to Grams' door to help her out. Even if they hung out in the living room Grams wouldn't hear them if she was in her bedroom sleeping. Just so long as it didn't get wild like the time Caisey was fifteen and her dad was gone on an assignment in Nevada for the week. Grams had marched out of her room and announced the party was over. No one messed with the crazy old British lady with wild hair and a peach bathrobe.

Liam pulled his SUV on the drive beside her Toyota. Caisey got two steps from the car and saw the open front door.

She bent like she needed to tie her shoe and pulled the gun from her ankle holster. The front door might be open but the alarm wasn't beeping and the local police hadn't been summoned by the security company. Either it hadn't been set, or it had been disconnected by whoever broke in.

"Liam." She called his name over the roof of the car.

He sauntered over. "You really need an upgrade in the car department." He reached up and back over his shoulder, bleeping his car locks with a click of the remote button. "That thing is seriously boring."

Caisey glanced at the front door. She looked back and saw his eyes flare. She kept her voice even so no one knew anything was wrong. "I'm not buying a new car just because you think mine ruins your street cred. If I want a wild ride I go in Jenna's Mustang. Why do you think we won't let Jake drive until he's seventeen?"

Jenna's hands went to her hips. "You said we were waiting until he was responsible. You didn't say it was because I'm some crazy driver. Which I am not."

Liam gave Caisey a short nod and turned to Andrea. "Take Grams, Jenna and Jake back to your place." He handed over his car keys. "Go. Now."

~

CAISEY SWEPT through her bedroom and the bathroom and left the shower curtain pulled back when she came out. "Clear in there too."

Her leg hurt like nobody's business and she really needed to take more Ibuprofen, but that would have to wait. She'd wanted to be off the crutches and was willing to be on her feet less to make it happen but it'd been a long day. She needed to get this done because it was time to lie down.

Liam stood beside her bed, his brow creased as he took in the room. "Did Jenna decorate in here?"

"No. I did." Caisey put her free hand on her hip. "What's wrong with it?" "Nothing. It's just...very...uh, purple."

"I happen to like purple."

His lip twitched. "I guess so."

"What now?"

Liam rolled his eyes, but he was smiling. "So nothing was disturbed?"

"Not that I can see." Caisey scratched her hair. "Front door ajar, alarm disconnected. Maybe when the perp left, they didn't check it was shut. Or they were in a hurry."

"They?"

Caisey shrugged. "But why break in and let us know you did if you aren't going to take anything?"

"You guys didn't leave it open?"

She shook her head. "I checked it myself."

"Looking for something. Didn't find it." Liam's face was set. "Sending you a message, maybe? We can get to you."

"But why?"

"You tell me."

Caisey trailed him down the stairs. "There's nothing obvious I can think of, just the prison chaplain who visited earlier. He was looking for my dad, had a letter for Gabe Carlen."

Liam frowned. "As in, the Toben Carlen case?"

Caisey nodded. "Gabe agreed to testify against his father. Dad hoped to get the uncle too, but the charges were dropped for lack of evidence. The uncle went back to work running guns, drugs, women. Toben went to jail and Gabe disappeared. Probably witness protection, but I was seventeen."

And at the time, Caisey had been in no condition to be inquisitive about her dad's work. Not when knowing would put her in more danger than not knowing ever did.

Liam's lips were a thin line. "I hate coincidences."

"Me too, but there's not much I can do. Except—"

Caisey could have kicked herself. She went back upstairs and pulled open the top drawer of her dresser where she'd stashed the letter. Liam was still at the bottom of the stairs when she sat on the top step, trying to hide the wince from both her leg and the situation. "The letter the chaplain gave me is gone."

"So the uncle has either you or the prison on radar? I'd guess both. Chaplain visits you. Ping. He has someone break in to get the letter. What did it say?"

"I didn't read it."

"Do you know where Gabe Carlen is?"

"He's been missing for years."

"The uncle probably still wants revenge."

Caisey shrugged. "I'd have thought he'd be busy, what with his gun-running, drug- dealing, flesh-peddling organization still in full swing. But what do I know?"

"Getting that close to being brought down, he probably still hates his nephew enough to use resources keeping tabs on people who might lead him to Gabe."

"But I don't know where Gabe is. It was years ago."

The questions persisted, even after Grams, Jenna and Jake came home. After Liam was done on the phone with the security company making sure her system was still working fine. After Caisey had taken painkillers. And a bath, where she had to keep her leg out of the water the whole time. Which kind of defeated the purpose, but she didn't care. Then she stretched out in bed and stared at the ceiling.

Why did his name have to come up again after all these years? Gabe had disappeared from her life and she'd made peace with that even if she didn't understand why he'd never contacted her. It might carry a risk, but she would do everything she could so the person she cared about knew she had never forgotten them—which proved her theory that he hadn't thought as much of their one date as she had. But that didn't make sense at all. The signs had been there.

Or she thought they had.

Evidently Gabe had just been passing the time until he testified against his father. Blowing off steam, hanging out doing something normal before his whole life changed. She'd wanted to ask her father if Gabe had mentioned her at all after he left, but she'd never been able to muster the courage.

Then Gabe's uncle had her kidnapped, and there was nothing more to say.

SIX

The front door of Gabe's bookstore flew open. The bell above the door clanged back and forth and got jammed when the door shut behind her. "I got an A!"

Emma ran to the counter, waving papers above her head and trailing snow across the floor tiles that he would have to mop up before he left. Gabe closed the research book he'd been reading. "Congratulations."

"I had no idea. I mean I knew it was good and stuff but I never thought I would get an A. Thank you so much for helping me, Mr. Thompson."

"You're welcome."

Her head tipped to one side, her teenage face frowning. "I was failing this class and I just got, like, the best grade ever. You should be excited."

"I am excited."

"You don't look so good. Are you getting sick? Am I going to catch it?"

Gabe rubbed the heel of his hand against the side of his head. "I'm not getting sick. I just got up early."

"Did you have a nightmare? Do you have like—" she leaned in and whispered "— PTSD?"

"I do not have Post Traumatic Stress Disorder."

She worked her mouth like she didn't believe him at all. "Whatever you say, Mr. Thompson."

"You should probably get on to your dad's office, Emma. He'll be wondering where you are."

She started to chew on her lip. "Mr. Thompson?"

"What is it, Emma?"

"You're a man...I mean, it's obvious you're a man but what I mean is, when a guy says he likes you, but the—"

Gabe cleared his throat. "Is this really something you want to talk to me about?"

"It's just...look at the way Becka, you know, from the diner, looks at you. She wipes down the counter without actually looking at it because she's too busy staring at you." A dreamy look washed over Emma's face. "One time she knocked over the salt and the lid came off and salt went all over the counter. Mal was ticked."

"Yes, well." He looked down at the textbook and the picture of an Iron Age soldier on the front, wondering how fast this conversation could be over with. "What do you need to ask me?"

"When a guy obviously likes you, I mean, not just likes, but seriously actually likes you like forever marriage kind of likes you maybe even loves you..."

Gabe blinked. It was like a completely different language, except he spoke and read several ancient languages and it wasn't any of them.

"And he wants to take you out, but he doesn't want to come and talk to your dad first, like to ask if it's okay because he wants you to do the asking...is that weird?"

Yes, she was actually asking him for relationship advice.

"If this guy isn't willing to talk to your dad then you need to seriously consider if he's going to be it for you. You want to be with someone who doesn't even have the guts to look your dad in the eye?" She blinked, but Gabe kept talking. "The right guy is going to be someone who gets your dad the way you do, someone who see's past the gruff to the kind of man he's trying to be, even if he doesn't always do a great job of being a human as well as a lawyer. That's the man for you, someone who'll be part of your family. Not who'll take you away from your world like being together means you have to separate yourself from who you were."

Emma smiled shook her head. "I think that's the most words I've ever heard you say at one time."

Gabe smiled. "Maybe you've been a good influence on me."

"But what if I tell him what you said, and he doesn't agree?"

"That alone tells you what you need to know."

She walked to the door. "You know, I keep telling people you're not what everyone thinks but they never listen."

Gabe's chest shook with silent laughter. "Good job on your paper, Emma."

A smile stretched her mouth and shone in her eyes. She shut the door behind her but the light of her lingered in the late afternoon sun that shone through the front windows, though it was barely thirty degrees outside. Not much more than that inside.

He'd seen that light before, on the face of another girl what seemed like a lifetime ago now. That Gabe had had family and a future. This Gabe ran a musty bookstore that barely made enough to cover the rent and utilities on the Main Street store-front. Not that he even needed that income, but it was nice to see paper copies of novels with his penname on display in the front window.

The sound of an incoming call cut through the quiet. Gabe crossed the room, flipped the sign to CLOSED and locked the door. He lifted the lid of his laptop, clicked to answer the call and settled back on his stool.

"Man, you look as bad as I feel."

Gabe crossed his arms. "Thanks, Mitch. That's really nice. What time is it there?"

The camera flickered and Mitch's image came on screen. "It's like one thirty in the morning."

Gabe stared. "What is that thing on your head?"

Mitch's grin filled his whole face. "It's a fez."

"Seriously?"

Mitch laughed. "You do a good impression of a grumpy old man, but you forget how well I know you. Down deep you have a marshmallow center you don't want anyone to see."

Gabe didn't say anything for a minute. He just sat with one eyebrow up long enough for Mitch to get the message.

"Right. Anyway, the reason I called is because we found something today I thought you'd like to look at."

"What is it?"

Mitch grinned. "A letter. I'm emailing you the picture now."

Gabe minimized the call window and went to his inbox. "It's not there yet."

"I'm sending it now, hang on a minute. You know how bad the internet connection is here."

He refreshed it and an email from Mitch appeared. "Got it." He downloaded the image and scanned the Arabic text like a former captive with his first cheeseburger. Plot ideas weaved like a spider web from the words. Gabe grinned.

"I'll leave you alone with your contraband."

Gabe laughed.

"I have to sleep or I'll be worthless tomorrow."

"Thanks for this."

Mitch nodded. "Sure. Soon, okay?"

Gabe lifted his chin to his friend. Mitch had ended their calls that way every time— once a week for seventeen years. The seventeen years since they last saw each other, as classmates in Ancient History, though Gabe had been the teacher's assistant.

Sighing, he readied the store for the next day, locked up the cash he kept on hand and put the books he would need tonight in his backpack, along with a print out of the picture Mitch had sent. He pulled a wool hat down over his ears, which pushed hair into his eyes. He really needed a haircut.

Gabe locked up the store and walked down Main Street in Buckshot, Colorado. Past the bar with a row of Harley Davidson's parked outside and the hardware store, around the corner to the diner. It was just past five but the diner was nearly full. Gabe's usual table was free of people and the kid who bussed dirty dishes was clearing it off.

He nodded to a couple of people he'd only seen around—he didn't know their names—and when the table was wiped clean he said a quick, "Thanks," to the kid and slid in.

"That's cool. What is it?"

Becka's honey voice washed over him and Gabe glanced up from the printout. "It's a letter."

Her brow furrowed behind the red-framed glasses she wore. "Well aren't you full of surprises?"

Gabe swallowed. She had no idea.

Becka tapped her pen on the side of her notepad. "I just assumed you were reading the newspaper. Did you hear they tried to catch that serial killer over in Idaho Springs?"

Gabe shook his head. "Recently?" He'd seen something online about the Chloroform Killer when he last checked the news website he preferred, but didn't know this.

"Like last weekend or something. An FBI agent from Denver pretended to be one of the victims and he abducted her. They tried to catch him and he got away. Can you believe that? It's like a movie or something, not real life." Becka shuddered. "I'm still going to carry my gun, though. You never know who's lurking these days."

He smiled. Now that Emma had told him how Becka felt he looked at her and tried to see past the yellow waitress uniform. She was probably mid-twenties, a little young for him but pleasant in pretty much every other way. Gabe wasn't the tallest man in the world so any woman had to be in the low five feet so they didn't tower over him. "How are you, Becka?"

"Uh..." She blinked. "Fine, I guess. Sorry I went on and on about that. Did you want to order? I can make you some green tea."

"That sounds great. How about dinner some time?"

She blinked and then laughed. "You're sitting here right now. You need a menu?"

"No. That's not what I meant." Gabe sighed. "I'm not very good at this. I meant do you want to have dinner with me some time?"

She blushed. "Oh. Well, yes. Actually, I'd like that a lot."

"Good. Tomorrow?"

"I'm working tomorrow, but I can do Thursday."

"Thursday sounds good."

She took a step back and bumped into a couple walking by her. "Oops. Sorry. I'll um...go get your tea then."

"I'll have the veggie burger."

"The veggie burger." Becka smoothed down the side of her short red hair, now matched by the shade of her cheeks. "Right."

Gabe nodded and looked down at the picture again. This was good. Moving on and building a life in this town didn't just mean running a business. It could mean having relationships, and even a family one day. Well, maybe he wouldn't go that far. Families were a minefield he wasn't sure he wanted to go traipsing around in.

A blonde woman walked past the front window. Her mouth stretched into a smile directed at the man she was walking with and he was jarred back to that night years ago. The face was different, but Gabe still saw her on that one perfect date that lasted until the next morning in a diner not much different than this one, eating pancakes. Before his life ended.

When his meal came, Gabe bowed his head and closed his eyes.

It's been years since I left Denver. Why do I still feel tied to her?

He didn't even want to think her name.

~

THE CHLOROFORM KILLER blew on his icy fingers and watched the girl strut down the sidewalk, flashing her smile at every person she passed like she was in a fashion parade or on a red carpet. She turned the corner and he started up the vehicle.

It wouldn't be long now.

~

GABE ROLLED over to look at his alarm clock and sighed. He tossed the blanket back and added another log to the stove. Shadows of the past danced in the corners of the room. Menacing specters that laughed at the man he was, the man he'd always thought he should have been. Emma hadn't been entirely wrong about PTSD, though he wasn't about to search out a doctor for a diagnosis. Didn't everyone have something that kept them up at night? Maybe it wasn't that he relived the day he watched someone die, but that didn't make it easier to deal with. Gabe wouldn't wish his demons on anyone else.

The flames crackled and spat. He stayed there, crouched in front of it and let the heat warm his body. He might have turned his past into fuel for the novels he wrote, but his books were also about apologizing. He'd hoped it would help ease some of—

There was an almighty crash out in the living area. Gabe stood up as booted feet thumped across the rug and back onto wood. The bedroom door flung open, hit the wall, and two big men with guns rushed in. Gabe was grabbed and tossed on the floor, but caught a glimpse of the bigger man's hat.

"Sheriff?" The word cut off when his cheek hit the floor. Gabe's hands were wrenched back, causing his spine to bow. Ice cold cuffs clicked around his wrists.

"I ain't the sheriff right now, boy." The bedroom light flicked on and hot breath blew across the side of his face. "Where is she?"

Gabe tried to breathe, but only managed half a lungful. "Who?"

"I said, where is she?"

"I heard you. I just don't know what you're talking about." Gabe was lifted up and dropped. His chest thumped the floor, but he managed to keep his chin from slamming the wood.

"Cut the crap, Thompson, and tell me where my niece is!"

Gabe tried to roll on the floor enough to see the Sheriff's face. "Why would I know where Emma is?"

"She was at your store today."

"That was hours ago." Gabe tried to suck in another breath while the muscles his shoulders shook. "I helped her with her history assignment."

There was silence. Then, "You helped her with her history assignment." Like the idea of Gabe being useful was akin to believing aliens built the pyramids.

Gabe was hauled to his feet—which hurt a lot—and shoved to sit on the bed. The sheriff towered over him; his gun put away, hands folded across his chest. Over six foot, Frank Allens didn't hesitate to use his size as a weapon. His head was covered with a hat with flaps that hung down to cover his ears, his eyes were so dark they were almost black and the lines around his face bespoke a permanent frown.

Gabe mostly tried to give him slack. Being the uncle to a girl with looks like Emma's—and who apparently had a secret boyfriend—likely wasn't easy. Was that why the sheriff always assumed the worst? Having a cheerleader for a niece that every boy in the county had eyes for would probably make Gabe hostile too.

Behind Sheriff Allens was Deputy Bud Paulson. In his twenties, Bud would have fit the role of bumbling sidekick were it not for the fact that in high school he'd achieved some kind of football record for running a lot, or something. His hair was crusted with frozen styling product and his nose rivaled Rudolph's.

A teenage girl might find a twenty-something, good looking, former football star an attractive prospect, right? Gabe scrutinized the kid's face, but since he wasn't so in touch with his inner teenage girl—perish the thought—he called it at a maybe.

"Talk."

Gabe glanced at the sheriff. Not happy. Right.

"Emma was assigned a paper on the historical validity of the Trojan war for her AP history class. She came into the store asking for books on ancient history and I pointed her to an online resource. It's an author's website where he puts up all his research information, but fictionalizes it so it's fun to read. There's tons of info on what it means, and links to other websites where you can do further research—"

The sheriff cleared his throat.

"She asked me if I'd look over her paper after she finished it. It was really quite good."

The sheriff's eyes narrowed.

Gabe sighed and carried on. "Today she stopped by to tell me she got an A."

Bud huffed. "Of course she did. She's smart."

The sheriff turned back to look at Bud. The kid was redder now.

Apparently he'd suddenly decided not to add anything else to the conversation.

"Can we take these cuffs off?"

"No." The sheriff sniffed. "Then what happened?"

"We talked for a minute and she left to walk over to her dad's office."

"Time?"

"Four thirty-five."

"You're sure?"

Gabe nodded. "I got a call right after."

The sheriff stared at him for a minute. "We'll need to verify this call of yours, and I'll need your alibi for the rest of the day if you hope to prove you didn't dally with my niece."

An alibi? "What happened?"

"Emma never showed up at my brother's office."

"Did you try to call her?"

The sheriff's mouth twisted. "The only thing you need to worry about right now is you."

Gabe opened his mouth, and then closed it again. "The call came on my computer."

"A phone call?"

Gabe half-shrugged. "A video call."

The sheriff's eyes narrowed. "We'll need access to your computer, and who knows what we're going to find."

And have some sheriff's office tech person rummaging through the files on Gabe's computer? No way.

"You think you're going to stop us?" The sheriff sneered. "You're coming back to the station." He grabbed Gabe's elbow and yanked him to his feet.

Gabe glanced between the two men. "Why? I'm sorry she's missing, but I don't know where Emma is."

"A single man who lives alone in a mountain town, never talks to anyone—except my niece apparently—and runs a bookstore that acts more like a lending library? Nothing about you makes sense, and until I know you ain't a killer, you're coming with us."

"Surely it'd be a waste of time to arrest me when you could be out there finding her."

Bud chimed in. "You're not under arrest, we just have more questions."

"I don't even know anything."

Gabe looked left and then right like a spectator at a tennis game. Neither man acknowledged him. Instead they walked him through the cabin and Gabe halted at the door long enough to slip his feet into shoes before he was pulled outside, where they marched down the salted steps and crunched in the snow to the Jeep with flashing lights illuminating the clearing in flashes of red and blue. The frozen air cut through his t-shirt and pajama pants like they weren't even there. Thick redwood trees surrounded Gabe's home like an army of giants that hemmed him in on all sides.

All these years trying to live under the radar and now he was the prime suspect in the disappearance of a sweet young girl.

God let this all be a mistake, let Emma be safe.

SEVEN

The couple on screen kissed each other with all the pent up tension of the first hour and a half of the movie. Caisey rolled her eyes and beside her on the couch, Jenna laughed.

"I would have picked your type of movie, but I figured you didn't want to watch a show where half the people in the movie were dead by the end."

Caisey didn't mind conceding that point. "True."

There was enough death playing on repeat in her head, and not just when she dreamed. Those scenes featured the Chloroform Killer and she was the one dying, then it changed and Gabe's uncle stood over her.

Caisey looked at Jenna. In the dark living room her face was lit by the light from the TV. Jenna's jaw flexed but her eyes stayed on the movie. "I worry about you, you know?"

"I'll be okay."

"Don't—"

Caisey reached over and squeezed Jenna's hand. "I'm not dismissing it, or diminishing it. I'm saying it'll take time, but I'll be fine."

"Did you talk to the shrink again yet?"

"I made an appointment for next week."

Not that Caisey particularly wanted to talk to Doctor Amanda about how she was doing. What helped last time was the major distraction of Jake's birth. It'd been hard to get depressed at two a.m. holding a squalling little body in her arms with no clue how to make him quiet down.

"Listen I'm sorry I signed you up for that dating service. It's probably the last thing you need right now."

Caisey nudged Jenna's shoulder. "I might have...logged on. Just to check it out."

The regret on Jenna's face morphed as her eyes widened and she smiled. "And?"

"You didn't do a horrible job of it."

"Using British phrasing doesn't make it less obvious that you're hedging, you know. You liked it."

Caisey smiled. "Yeah, okay. I liked it. You did pretty good making me sound cool, working in federal law enforcement, and not like a desperate sad case who hasn't had a decent date in ten years."

"We should form a club."

Caisey arched a brow. "Desperate thirty-something sad-cases-R-us?"

Jenna smiled. "Something like that."

"I looked at your profile too."

"And?"

"I didn't change too much."

Jenna's jaw dropped. "What did you put?"

"Just more about how awesome you are being a businesswoman and the mom of a great kid. That type of thing." She nudged Jenna's shoulder. "Where was that picture of me from?"

"Jake's last birthday when we all went to Caliente for dinner. I love that it's not posed. It's totally natural with your eyes bright and laughing at something Grams said. I wanted a picture of you in a dress, but since that would mean the moon had spun out of its orbit and crashed into the sun thereby ending life as we know it, I had to make do."

"Why didn't you tell me that shirt was so sparkly?"

Jenna's lips twitched. "It was better that you didn't know it shimmered like that when the light hit it a certain way. It's a great top for you."

"I did look pretty good."

Jenna's head tipped back and she laughed full out.

"What?"

"Sometimes it's like you crack open and a little bit of *girl* spills out."

Caisey grabbed a pillow and slammed it into Jenna's face. "Take that back!"

Jenna put her hands up, laughing again. The sound of it swept through Caisey like warm caramel.

"How old are the two of you?" Jake stood in the doorway in black sweat pants with a white stripe down the side of the leg and a t-shirt that showed off his man-boy muscles. His face was all smooth skin and big brown eyes. It was no wonder his cell phone constantly beeped. "Can you keep it down? I'm trying to write my English paper."

Caisey snorted. "Don't ask your mom for help. She got a C in that class."

Jenna gasped. "So did you. We worked on that paper together."

"Grams already helped me." Jake held up Caisey's cell phone. "This was ringing, like five times. You might wanna check your messages or whatever."

Caisey got up and took it from him. The kid might act put out, but he'd still brought her BlackBerry downstairs to her. He was the only one who hadn't thought it necessary to have a talk with her about her going undercover. Probably because he knew family was everything. And you did everything to keep them safe.

"Sorry we were loud."

He shrugged. "I'm gonna get back to it."

Caisey nodded. "Goodnight"

Jake rolled his eyes, tagged her shoulders with one arm and leaned down to kiss her forehead. He looked at Jenna. "Night, Mom."

"Goodnight, honey."

Caisey watched him leave; struck at his action because it was the same thing she did with Jenna. She'd done the side-hug/forehead-kiss to Jake back when he was little enough he didn't mind displays of affection. Apparently it sank in.

The phone rang. She looked down and saw it was Liam. "Hey, partner. What's up?"

"Where've you been? I've been calling you for half an hour."

"I was watching a movie with Jenna, I didn't hear the phone."

"We think the Chloroform Killer struck again."

Her whole body went solid. "What?"

Jenna came to stand beside her. "What is it?"

Caisey held up one finger to her friend and asked Liam, "What happened?"

"We got a hit from a report of an abduction in a small town about three hours west of here. A teenage girl is missing and there's a folded cloth on her pillow. We think its chloroform."

Caisey sucked in a breath and blew it out slowly, focusing on the texture of the carpet under her bare feet.

She wasn't in that mine, she was home.

"Everyone is being called in. Burkot is sending Tanners and his team and I'm going with them. Local law enforcement has a suspect in custody."

Caisey was already halfway up the stairs, ignoring the ache in her leg. That was just because it was late. "So they have him?"

She heard Jenna follow her up, but ignored it. There was no way it was all over this easily. If they had a suspect and he was the one who abducted this missing girl, it likely wasn't their guy. Probably just a copycat.

"That's what we're going to find out."

"I should come in."

"No." Liam's voice was hard, like when he tensed his jaw. "You're still on vacation. Burkot's orders, remember?"

She didn't much care that he was frustrated. "Every pair of hands is going to help, like you said. I'm the one who let him get away. If he's killed again, it's on me."

There was a pause and she imagined he was digesting her guilt.

Thankfully he didn't comment on it. Instead he said, "Case, you're injured."

"I'm not going to go chase through the backwoods of Colorado after him. But I can sit at my desk and type."

Liam sighed, long and loud. "You can make the coffee."

~

THE CHLOROFORM KILLER, that's what they called him. Someone to be feared. Not even the Federal Bureau of Investigation could outwit him, no sir. Power coursed through his veins, heightening his already significant intelligence. He was unstoppable, or so each of his previous subjects could testify.

He picked up the hatchet he had purchased after his dagger was disposed of so judiciously. That little tidbit would keep the not-so-special agents running in circles for weeks.

The laughter that spilled from his mouth was high pitched.

Whimpering behind him made his head snap around. This one had turned out to be pitiful. All he could think about was the special agent he had taken. She would not have acted like this. He should have killed her; it would have been a sweet victory.

Now all he had was regret.

And dissatisfaction.

~

DESPITE THE FACT it was after eleven at night, Caisey arrived to find the office lit up and everyone at their desk. Phones all around the room rang while agents talked and typed. Their profiler stood in front of the boards on the wall to the right. To the left was a wall of windows and Burkot's office was at the far end. It could have been any other office, except for the fact there were at least two dozen firearms in this one room. Those who'd been there all day wore suits that were now rumpled and their eyes tired, and everyone else—including Caisey—was in jeans.

Caisey put her coat on the back of her chair but didn't bother to turn on her computer. Liam's desk was opposite hers. He was on the phone, making furious notes on the pad in front of him. When he saw her, she pointed to the profiler. Liam's eyes flicked to the Doc and he nodded.

Caisey poured two cups of coffee. She held one in front of the profiler's face until he blinked and looked at her. His gray hair had undertaken a coup and emerged victorious over the dark color it used to be, and coupled with the bushy beard it made him look more like an old prospector than a doctor of psychology. And if he stared at her much longer, she was going to shift her stance and he'd know he was making her nervous.

"Doc."

"Agent Lyons, how are you?"

"Same old." Liar, liar...

The board on the wall was covered with papers. She stepped closer to study what they knew—which wasn't a whole lot beneath the supposition—and took a sip of coffee. It was thick like treacle which meant Liam hadn't made it, not that anyone in the office would let him. They knew better.

"We still don't know who he is."

It wasn't a question, because Caisey knew the answer full well. Her foray into the world of undercover operations hadn't yielded much beyond a vague description, a dagger no one could place...and a van they could add to the one impounded when Andrea's sister was abducted. She stared at the picture of the vehicle she'd been transported in and the deep freezer that had been in the back. "Fingerprints?"

"Just the partial from the door handle. We had the test rushed, but still no results in IAFIS. No ID on him. The van was registered to an old lady in Kansas."

"Any connection?"

"Not that we can see, except she used to run a flower shop and used the van for deliveries."

"Stolen?"

He nodded. "Wasn't reported since the old lady died of a heart attack six months ago."

"Of course she did." The death of an old lady was a sad thing, but it was also a little coincidental in this case.

"It's being looked into by the local Kansas office."

Caisey sighed, unable to shake the image of the Chloroform Killer looking her up and down while she was tied to a chair. She'd had enough of that to last a lifetime. "So basically we have nothing?"

The Doc took a sip of his coffee. "It's never nothing. But it certainly isn't a lot at this point. Still, we drew him out once not knowing who he was, thanks to you."

Caisey met his eyes, saw the admiration there. The tension in her shoulders eased and she nodded.

"Lyons!"

She jumped and swung around. Burkot was in the door of his office. "Get in here."

"Thank you for the coffee."

"You're welcome, Doc."

Caisey wound between desks, ignoring the smirks and jibes all the way to Burkot's office. It was tough not to feel like you were being summoned to see the principal. Not that she'd done that in school. Uh...much.

She stopped in the doorway. "What's up boss?"

"Shut the door."

Caisey sat in one of the two chairs pulled up to the desk. An American flag had hung on the wall behind his desk for as long as she'd been here, beside another flag for the Marine Corps.

Burkot shuffled some papers aside and looked up at her. "You know I worked with your father?"

Caisey bit her lip to keep from frowning and nodded. Where was this going?

"If he was still alive he'd have my hide for letting you in here when you're supposed to be healing."

"My leg is a lot better."

"And that was the only thing injured during your assignment?"

She didn't answer because it wasn't a question.

Burkot stared at her for a moment and then sighed. "You are not here. Until the shrink okay's it, you're not cleared for work anyway.

You can observe, you can assist. The minute you dip one toe into the operation to re-acquire the UNSUB you're going home."

Caisey shut her mouth, not entirely sure how she felt about that. "Yes, sir."

Burkot dismissed her.

Caisey slumped into the chair at her desk and closed her eyes. The hum of conversation and ringing phones was like a sedative. She should record it and listen to it on her iPod when she couldn't sleep.

Her phone rang. The number was blocked, which usually meant an informant. "Lyons."

There was silence for a second, and then, "Special Agent Caisey Ann Lyons?"

Her stomach flipped over. Hearing her mom's name in the middle of hers was like a sucker punch. Double whammy since it was the voice from the mine. She shot up out of her chair and clicked her fingers until she got Liam's attention. "Why don't you start by telling me your name?"

The room fizzed into action and the hum of adrenaline rushed through the air like a living thing.

"I thought you guys did all those tests, you know, like DNA and stuff. You don't have my spit in a tube somewhere?" The voice was sardonic.

Caisey pulled over a notepad and clicked her pen. "Maybe you could tell me what you want."

"So you can distract me long enough for a computer to ascertain my location? Credit me with more intelligence than that."

Caisey sat back in her chair. "Well then why did you call me?"

"I thought we should talk or something. You know, get to know each other."

"And why is that?"

There was a long pause, and then he spoke.

"Because I want you to find me, Caisey."

EIGHT

Caisey blotted the water from her face with a paper towel. So much for sleep. Hopefully she'd be able to head home later for a nap, though she wasn't sure she'd be able to rest when her brain wouldn't quit. All she could think of were those beady eyes staring at her...and his voice.

I want you to find me.

Caisey rubbed her temple. It had been over a week since the last time she'd done any work, why was she so tired? Nothing about this particularly invigorated her, not when she was being baited. And not when Grams, Jenna and Jake would be in the middle of it. She needed to deal with this in a way that meant it didn't come home with her, a way that meant they'd be safe. Protected.

She tossed the soggy paper towel in the trash and turned, sucked in a breath and caught herself before she shrieked.

Doctor Amanda's lips curled up at the sides. "Don't look so happy to see me."

"You scared the crap out of me. Don't you know better than to sneak up on people who carry guns?"

Amanda assessed her, as though she read a bunch of psychological mumbo jumbo into every single thing Caisey said. "Feel like going somewhere to talk?"

Not really. Then again, if she went with Amanda, she might be able to persuade the shrink to let her go back to work. Not fully, but she could do desk work until her leg healed.

She weighed the pros and cons until Amanda started laughing. "Wow, Special Agent Lyons. Is the prospect of talking to me really that scary?" She paused. "Okay, scratch that. Is the prospect of telling me the truth really that bad?"

Caisey allowed herself the luxury of a small smile. Amanda wasn't all bad. It was just that her occupation put Caisey in the position of being required to be vulnerable, which she had never liked. Her dad had been enough of a man not to want displays of emotion. Grams would have accepted it from her, but it made Caisey feel uncomfortable.

Still, she needed to be able to work more than she needed to hoard her emotional state. "Why not."

They walked down to Amanda's office, where Caisey scanned the psycho-babble books on her bookshelf. She straightened a photo frame of Amanda and her husband and smelled the candle to see what scent it was.

"Sleeping okay?"

Caisey shrugged one shoulder, but didn't turn.

"I'd suggest a sleep aid, but I know you'd never take it."

Caisey walked over and sat on one end of Amanda's brown leather couch. Her leg hurt, but rubbing it wouldn't help plus it was a huge tell. Instead, she kicked off her boots and stacked her feet on the coffee table with her good leg on bottom. "You probably see that a lot."

"Sure I do." Amanda sat. "But it's not a crime to admit you need help. Looking less than strong doesn't make you less human."

That depended on your point of view.

"Since I'm fine," Caisey pointed out. "It's kind of a moot point."

"Naturally," Amanda conceded with a wave of her hand. "How's your leg?"

Caisey laughed but the humor dissipated fast. "It really hurts."

"And yet your brain is still on the job."

"That's a good way of putting it." She never had figured out how to switch off her mind. Now that she'd met the killer face to face she saw his eyes everywhere. "The results were supposed to outweigh the mental stress. That's what we all decided. I didn't think there would be much correlation between this abduction and what happened to me years ago, but when I dream one bleeds into the other."

Amanda nodded. "There is still so much of the brain we don't understand. But the similarities in the two events, however minimal, have invited your mind to associate them." She paused. "Is it possible you haven't fully dealt with the past? Maybe there is more you need to work through before you can put it to rest."

"Do we ever totally put anything to rest? I mean, we say it's in the past or whatever, but it isn't like it's forgotten."

"True." Amanda studied her. "What I'd like to know is whether you are simply processing what happened, or is all this a result of the fact that the killer got away and you were left with little as far as quantifiable results?"

Caisey thought for a minute. "Both, maybe. We knew there would be residual effects, flashbacks to this abduction and possibly the one before, symptoms of Post-Traumatic Stress, insomnia. If I wasn't okay with that, I wouldn't have agreed to do it."

"It's a little different being told about those things than actually experiencing them, don't you think?"

"I guess."

"And yet I think you suffer willingly, knowing at least it's you and not someone else. Someone who might not handle it as capably as you, or that you'll admit."

Caisey shot her a look. "Because I think I'm the best or something?"

"No. It's more sacrificial than that. But it is not always the wisest course of action."

"Since when is sacrifice bad?"

Amanda shifted on the couch. "What most would assume is bravado, is actually something far richer. I think you enjoy being the martyr."

"Seriously? You believe that?" Caisey got up, ignoring the stab of pain in her thigh.

"Your reaction implies you might even believe it too. Or at least you've entertained the possibility."

Caisey wanted to fling the door open and stomp away, but that would mean Amanda had won. "So you're saying I'll willingly go undercover just to save someone else from having to do it? Well too bad, because we didn't fool him one bit. He played us. And now it looks like he's abducted another girl. We have nothing and he still holds all the cards."

"And that's what you hate the most, isn't it? That feeling of powerlessness. Because while you were abducted by a known killer, you had a tracking device and a team of people to back you up. You considered yourself to be in control even despite what was happening. Then when there was a moment in there somewhere when you felt genuine fear because you weren't in control. The team lost your signal, it took too long to find you, you were injured, and the killer got away." Amanda paused. "Whose fault is that?"

"No one's. That's just how it played out. I knew the variables. I knew I could be killed, the plan wasn't fool-proof. Too bad we were the fools."

"And yet you still volunteered." Amanda uncrossed her legs and stood. "And now he wants you to come after him."

Caisey shrugged. "I'd be well within my rights to kill him if the situation arose."

"I believe you. I also believe you would come in the next day and quit." Amanda's eyes softened. "Tell me. Do you enjoy being an FBI agent?"

"What does enjoying have to do with it?"

"Having a calling is very noble, but any job should have good days. Not just mediocre ones interspersed with particularly bad days. Have you ever even had a good day on this job?"

Caisey closed her mouth. What did she say to that? No job was perfect. Hers was more stressful than most, especially given what was happening but it would get better as time went on. Wouldn't it?

"I've wondered why you'd choose it in the first place, if not for your father being an agent. Living as a legacy is a powerful motivator. Especially when you've experienced first- hand the damage that can be done to someone innocent caught in the crossfire. You're trying to live up to a legendary agent shot in the line of duty. But that doesn't mean you have to live your life on the edge of death every minute for the sake of keeping everyone safe. Eventually you're going to have to let go."

~

CAISEY LOOKED up from her computer when Burkot approached her desk. "I'm only clearing out my inbox."

"Good. When you're done, head home." Sometimes her boss reminded her of her dad, especially when he sat on the corner of her desk like that. "Let everyone know to be careful. It wouldn't hurt for your Grams and everyone to keep an eye out. Stay safe. We don't need anyone caught in the middle if this guy sets his sights on you."

And wasn't that the understatement of the century. "Will do, sir. What about the missing girl?"

"The team is headed to Buckshot this afternoon."

Buckshot? That was where the girl had gone missing? "My dad had cabin there."

"Of course he did." Burkot sighed. "Have you thought about taking a vacation? Pack everyone up and head to a beach for a couple of weeks until your leg is healed and this guy is caught?"

Caisey bit her lip. Getting out of town wasn't a wholly bad idea, but if the killer decided to pursue her, she wasn't going to take her family. She would go alone...and armed. And come back when the guy was caught, only she'd be the one doing the catching.

She nodded to Burkot. "I'll think about it."

"You're a lot like him, you know?"

She waited.

"Your dad."

Caisey smiled, praying silently they weren't about to have this conversation.

"Never backed down from anything. Stubborn enough he'd

chase down an angle no one else thought was worth a second look and then he would wind up breaking open the whole case. Happened more than once, though we only worked together directly for a short while there at the end."

"I remember." She did, because years ago his need to get to the bottom of everything nearly got her killed.

Burkot stared at her for a moment and then turned to the room at large. "Okay, people. Let's get this done!"

While Burkot strode off to his office, Liam sat at his desk and grinned. "Another rousing speech?"

Caisey smiled. "Something like that."

His eyes narrowed. "What is that look? I've seen it before and it never means anything good. What are you thinking?"

She felt her smile drop.

"What did Burkot say to you?"

"He suggested I take a vacation." Caisey sighed. "Actually, it sounds like a good idea."

"I thought you already were on vacation."

Caisey closed her eyes. Her shoulders shook and her mouth curled up with the surge of amusement that came out of nowhere. Nothing about this was funny.

"You might want to start with a nap. You look punch-drunk tired."

"Yeah." She opened her eyes. "We get anything on the trace from the phone call?"

Liam shook his head. "He used a computer to make the call and the signal goes all over the place. Should keep the techs busy for a while."

"Great." She sighed again and fished around in her desk drawer for her keys. "You know what? A nap sounds good." She stood up and shrugged on her coat. "Call me later if we learn anything else and keep me posted."

"Are you sure you're okay?"

She nodded. Fatigue wasn't something she needed to feign. What would Liam say when he found out what she was going to do?

As long as nothing happened to him or Andrea, or Grams, Jenna or Jake...then who cared?

It had been years since she'd visited her dad's old hunting cabin. If she happened to meet some locals and find out more about the man their sheriff had arrested it would simply be coincidental. She needed to clear out the cabin anyway, maybe talk to someone about renting it out, or selling it. The place was probably falling down by now but it might be good to be in a place where she could feel close to her dad. Get some perspective.

If it served the dual purpose of being a landing spot where the team could fuel up with food and coffee and get some sleep, that was fine. She'd be saving money they could spend elsewhere in catching this killer.

What could it hurt?

NINE

Jenna stared at the name written in the two o'clock slot for a haircut. It had to be someone else, or did her mom not know Jenna managed the place?

"Everything okay?"

Jenna fixed a smile at the receptionist. "Sure, Pam. Everything's great."

The reception area of her spa was all white, except for the mural of pink lilies that stretched around the walls and crisscrossed each other. It wrapped around the lettering Jenna had stenciled on the wall behind the front desk herself. Jake had assured her it looked totally girly, which was what she was going for.

She looked up from the appointment book and saw Caisey in the front window of her spa, holding up a white paper bag. Jenna looked at the clock on the wall, sure enough it was lunchtime. Caisey didn't like the smell of hair products, but Jenna loved the way it permeated the place. The warm scent was more than just her work; it was the smell of the life she'd made for herself.

She left her receptionist, the exceptionally perky Pam, and walked around the circular front counter to meet Caisey in the middle of the white tiled floor. Her friend's eyes were lined with fatigue.

"You should be at home sleeping."

Caisey shrugged and looked around, avoiding Jenna's eyes. "Figured you'd be hungry."

The spa phone rang. Pam snapped it up and gave the standard greeting with honest warmth. Jenna studied her friend and then looked down at the bag. If it was two salads, Caisey had done something she thought she needed to make up for by eating healthy. Barbeque chicken sandwiches and fries meant she was in the mood to celebrate and Chinese food meant someone had died. Caisey never shared actual details of cases, which was fine with Jenna since it was mostly gross, but she had learned to tell by the food.

"What'd you bring?"

"A humongous burrito. Wanna share?"

This was a new one. "Let's go to my office."

Jenna spun on her heel and led the way down the hall, past the salon, the massage rooms and the lounge where manicures and pedicures were done. The sight of women with their heads back and their eyes closed listening to soothing music that played through the overhead speakers had the same effect on Jenna. Satisfaction. It had taken a number of years after Jake was born, juggling classes with Caisey's, but she eventually qualified as a beauty technician. The day Samuel Lyons introduced her to an old friend of his who owned a spa and was about to retire, Jenna had grasped the woman's hand and sucked back tears.

Blubbering was never a good first impression.

Four years after that Jenna became the owner and manager of Spa Yourself Beautiful, with a full roster of clients and carte blanche to change anything she wanted. It was a lot of work, managing stylists who wore drama like a diva in a fur coat, but she loved being the boss.

Behind the door that had her name in gold lettering was a small office. The couch was white suede with a cluster of pink throw pillows at each end and a glass vase full of fresh calla lilies on the table. The desk was antique and she had one of those computers that was a huge widescreen monitor with everything built into it. Jenna loved it.

She sat on the couch and slipped off her heels while Caisey slumped down on the other end and laid her head back.

Jenna laughed and grabbed the bag. "I said you should be sleeping." She tore the burrito in two, pressed the bag flat on her lap and laid her half on it. "So what's going on, anyway?"

Caisey didn't move, or open her eyes. "I'm going on vacation."

Jenna coughed. She wiped her mouth with a napkin. "To get abducted by a serial killer again?"

Caisey flinched.

"Please tell me that's not what you're doing." Jenna hated that her voice was small. She sucked in a long breath and blew it out. Her friend had a dangerous job. She knew that, but it didn't mean she didn't worry Caisey would go too far one day and wind up with a worse injury than a limp she was trying to hide.

Caisey opened her eyes, dark and full of a pain she didn't let anyone except Jenna see. Certainly no one she worked with.

"Where are you going?"

Caisey hesitated.

"You really think I'm going to tell anyone? How long have we been friends?"

"No I don't think you would, but you still can't say."

"At least one person should know where you're going." Jenna voiced the foremost question in her mind. "Why can't you tell Liam?"

Caisey shrugged again. "I'm gonna use the rest of my vacation time to head up to Dad's old hunting cabin."

"But that's in the middle of nowhere."

Caisey's mouth curled up at one side. "I remember. That was a fun trip."

"Borrowing your dad's car to go hide out in the woods at sixteen, huddled in front of a fire drinking way too much soda so we were sugared up and wired from the caffeine, telling ghost stories all night until we were screaming that some crazy axe murderer was going to knock the door down and get us?" Jenna laughed. "Sure, it was super fun."

"How come we never do that stuff anymore?"

"Oh I don't know." Jenna tapped her finger on her chin. "Maybe because I have a kid, we have a mortgage and we're supposed to be adults?"

"Right." Caisey sighed and her smile dropped. "I'll probably be gone before you get home tonight."

Jenna bit her lip. "Are you going to eat your burrito?"

"I'm not really hungry."

Jenna stood up and held out a hand. Caisey didn't go for too much frou-frou stuff, she was way too down to earth for that, but Jenna knew plenty about how to get a woman to feel better. "Come on. I'll give you a trim. Give yourself some time to relax before you go."

Caisey frowned, but she still took Jenna's hand. The salon had two stylists currently on staff that were both occupied with clients, and a younger girl who worked part time sweeping floors when she wasn't in class. As soon as she graduated, Jenna intended to hire her full time.

She settled the cape around Caisey's shoulders, opting to spray her hair with water. She wasn't going to push it and try to get her to shampoo. She would know that meant more than a little off the ends. Jenna got to work, neatening up the cut and adding some layers to the body of Caisey's thick blonde hair.

Maybe she could get Caisey's cut done before the two o'clock appointment arrived. Why did her mom have to show her face now? Maybe she wouldn't even recognize Jenna. She'd never been in the spa before. Maybe she heard about it and decided to check it out. Get her hair colored. Was she still a redhead? It was hard to remember her aside from the last time; the day she found out Jenna was pregnant with Jake. She would never forget her mom, red faced and screaming like a banshee, telling her to get her stuff and get out of the house. According to her mom, the Cartwright's were not a family who sinned. At least, not so that anyone could see.

Jenna's dad had been at work so she'd been packed and gone before he got home. He'd called Caisey's house later that night, but Jenna refused to talk with him. She hadn't wanted a repeat of the conversation with her mother.

"Isn't this place just darling?"

Jenna froze.

A redhead settled herself into the chair beside the one Caisey was in. A cape was swept over her shoulders and the stylist asked her what kind of cut she wanted.

Jenna walked around Caisey's chair and separated the front of her hair, combing it through before she cut Caisey some bangs. The shorter hair fell against Caisey's eyebrow.

"What did you—"

Jenna moved so Caisey could see herself in the mirror.

"Jenna that looks awesome."

She caught her friend's gaze in the mirror, held her friend's eyes and then flicked them to the side. Caisey shifted in her chair. Her eyes darted to the mirror beside her and then her face shot back around, eyes wide. Jenna bit her lip and nodded.

Nancy Cartwright told the stylist she wanted honey highlights and a re-style into a sleek bob to accentuate her cheekbones. Caisey's body jerked. She was laughing? Jenna's eyes flicked to the woman whose body had nurtured her for nine months. If her cheekbones were any more accentuated she'd be able to cut paper with them.

Nancy Cartwright gasped. Jenna stepped back, half aware Caisey had ripped off the cape and stood. Not behind her, taking her back; Caisey moved so her right shoulder was in front of Jenna.

"Jennifer."

The stylist glanced between them, probably wondering why Jenna looked about to revisit with her burrito. A glance in the mirror told her that her face was green. Her stomach jumped off the high dive and she felt like she was going into premature menopause. Was the air conditioning broken?

The room went quiet. Jenna swallowed, trying to get her lunch to go down. "Mother."

"Wassup, Mrs. C."

Jenna jabbed Caisey with her finger, but got ignored.

Her mother's eyes flickered and took in Caisey. The corners of her mouth curled up in a sneer. "Caisey Lyons."

"It's FBI Special Agent Caisey Lyons, actually."

Her mother made a noise in her throat like that wasn't too impressive. "You always were a tomboy."

Caisey turned her head back to Jenna. "You're done with my hair, right?"

"Y-yes." She cleared her throat and tried again. "Yes."

Caisey turned back to Jenna's mother and the stylist. "I'm sure... Tina here, does a fine job or Jenna wouldn't have hired her, but Jenna really is the master." She glanced at the mirror and grinned. "I mean look at me, she made me a girlie girl."

Jenna nearly groaned. Caisey meant well, but sometimes her incessant need to defend everyone went over the line. She grabbed Caisey's hand and yanked on it. "It was lovely to see you, Mother. But I'm afraid I don't have time to chat. I have a spa to run."

Her mother's eyes gleamed. "Yes, we do what we must to get by."

Like live large off your husband's money? Spend all day getting your hair and nails done, mud wraps and facials and lunch with the girls at the country club? Then parading your family into church on a Sunday dressed to the nines just to make everyone else feel bad?

Caisey's back went straight. "Yeah, especially when you get pregnant and your mom throws you out on the street and the baby's father turns his back on you so you have nowhere else to go except to rely on the charity of people who would, in fact, like nothing more than to have someone they love become a permanent part of their family. To watch that baby be born—well, that wasn't so much fun. It was kind of gross actually. But seeing that little life grow, and take his first steps, and snuggle up to you when he's tired. Watching him go out and explore what it means to live in this world knowing at home there's a family who loves him one hundred and fifty percent. No exceptions or reservations."

Caisey sucked in a breath. "I'd ask if you know what I mean, but I know you don't. All you understand is what it's like to have a shallow existence and live every day knowing you have a daughter and grandson who have lived happy, blessed lives because they refuse to acknowledge you exist."

Jenna gritted her teeth. "Case."

"I did not come here to listen to this...abuse." Nancy Cartwright stood up on her four inch heels and ripped off the salon cape. "This is unconscionable. You can bet I will be telling the ladies at the club never to come here."

"Fine."

"Case—" Jenna's voice was a warning. Both of them stood still while Nancy teetered to the hall and disappeared.

Jenna put her hand on her hip. "Did you have to do that?"

"You wanted her to say that stuff to you? Make you feel small, like you're still governed by her opinion?"

"No, but you could have at least waited until after she handed over her credit card before you did your big, "you're missing their lives" speech." Jenna sighed. "Her money's as green as yours."

Caisey's eyes were apologetic, but she smiled. "I thought I got best friend's discount or something."

Jenna shoved Caisey's shoulder. "Get out of here. I have to fix all this with the other customers you treated to your show."

Caisey took a step back, ready to leave. "See you soon."

Their earlier conversation came back to her. Jenna rushed over and gave her a tight hug. "If I don't see you before you leave, be careful."

When she pulled back, Caisey looked at the mirror again. "You didn't do a horrible job of it."

TEN

Caisey stopped at the door to Gram's living room later that afternoon. The TV was tuned to a decades old British show that featured a group of old men who spent episodes walking around their country village and getting up to mischief. They reminded Caisey of how precocious Jake had been at grade school age. Grams sat in her armchair, her chin dipped as she snored lightly. The air in here was warmer than the rest of the house, since Grams ran her floor heater all day.

Caisey saw the open Bible on the coffee table, but didn't look to see what verse of Luke Grams had highlighted. Instead she eased down onto the couch, trying to be as quiet as possible. There was something about being here that made what constricted her chest ease. It felt more like home than her bedroom, probably because it wasn't just her in here. Living in an apartment alone in Utah had been torture, when here she had the richness of annoying, in-your-face family.

She toed off her brown boots—the ones with the orange design stitched on the sides—stretched out and closed her eyes. Why had Jenna been so ticked that Caisey stood up for her, anyway?

She got that customers were important. The spa kept Jake in winter coats and jeans that didn't show his ankles. Jenna's salary paid the utilities too, while Caisey took care of the mortgage. It was a good system, but her mom was in the running for Worst Mom of All Time, so what was the big deal about one sale? Caisey sighed and squirmed deeper into the ancient couch. At least they were good now. Jenna never would have hugged her if they weren't.

She should tell Liam her travel plans, but it could turn out to be just a vacation where she provided support for the team. There was only a slim chance the killer would make his move in Buckshot when he could be anywhere by now and may not have even taken the missing girl anyway. But if he had and he did come for her, Caisey was going to take care of this in a way that meant no one else got hurt—especially not Grams, or Jenna or Jake, Liam or Andrea.

She could still feel the thud of a man's fist hit the bones of her face, her ribs. There was no way she would let anyone hurt her family. She wouldn't fail. She couldn't. It was enough that Jenna knew where she was going.

Caisey's eyes flicked open, pulling her mind from the depths of the impromptu nap. Grams stood over her. She set a full mug down on the coffee table and sat. "All right, ducky?"

"Sure, why wouldn't I be?"

Grams stared at her. "Maybe because you were stabbed in the leg two weeks ago?"

Caisey swallowed. "I'm trying not to take anything for it."

"It's not a wonder. Your dad never liked painkillers either and I've never liked them."

"Guess it's genetic."

Grams made a non-committal sound. "Wouldn't be the only thing."

Caisey waited.

"Your father was stubborn right down to the marrow in his bones. Never let anything go. Never let anyone get away if he thought there was more to be done."

"I know that."

"You also know what it did to him to see a case go the wrong way. To see someone hurt when he should have protected them. A handful of the people he arrested wound up walking free. Your dad would come in here, fuming, pace the room and when he settled he'd lift you out of your crib in the corner and sleep on that couch with you on his chest."

Caisey squeezed her eyes shut.

"After he got you back from your mom he'd always check on you when he got home. He'd come in with that look, like he'd seen something he needed to erase from his mind. Didn't matter what time it was, he would kiss your cheek and touch his hand to the side of your neck to feel your pulse under his fingertips."

Caisey's chest felt like an elephant had taken up residence there, pushing her heart to her throat and tears to her eyes. "But he—" Her voice broke.

"It as good as killed him, what they did to you."

She clenched her teeth. "I know." Too little, too late. "He said he was sorry, but it didn't erase what happened."

"He failed you. He didn't protect you."

A tear slipped down Caisey's cheek. "You have to forgive him."

"I have."

"Because he took Jenna in when she needed a family? There was no way he was going to say no to you given the state you were in. If Jake's big wide eyes were staring up at you, rimmed in bruises and asking you for the impossible, are you telling me you wouldn't do anything and everything you could to get it for him?"

Caisey swiped her cheeks, stood and grabbed her boots. "I have something to take care of, I should be back in a few days."

Grams studied her face. "You are driven by your need to not fail to protect this family. I can see it in your eyes, because I saw the same thing in your father."

"You make it sound like it's a bad thing."

Grams pressed her lips together. "All things in moderation."

"I'll see you soon."

"Don't do anything I wouldn't do."

Caisey crossed the room and kissed Grams on the cheek. "I'm sorry. I am trying."

Grams started to chuckle.

"What?"

"I said the same thing to your grandfather." She touched Caisey's cheek. "No one is expecting miracles. But answer me one thing?"

Caisey nodded.

"If your dad's job as an agent meant you got hurt, why would you decide to do the same thing? Aren't you worried something could happen to me, or Jake, or Jenna because you're an FBI agent?"

"I won't let it."

"You can't control what happens, Caisey. It isn't up to you."

She straightened and took a step back, her boots swinging in her grasp and looked at the empty cup on the table beside Grams. "Maybe not, but I'm going to do everything in my power to level the playing field. I became an agent because it's what I was born to do. Dad might have failed once, but every other day of my life until the day he died he was right there one hundred percent. I forget sometimes, when the memories try and suck me under. I'm glad you reminded me. He always did the right thing and that's what I'm going to do, too."

She'd known it already, on some level, but saying it out loud clarified it in a way that was inescapable. "Goodnight, Grams."

"I love you, dear."

"I know you do."

~

CAISEY WAS LOADING the backpack stuffed with extra shirts and jeans in the back of her car, wondering if she needed to bring extra blankets when her phone rang.

"Lyons."

"Going somewhere without me?"

"Conners." She sighed and glanced up and down the dark street looking for his car. Liam was parked two houses down, smoke pumping from his exhaust. He flicked his lights on. "You know you're supposed to shut the engine off when you're on a stakeout."

"It's cold out here."

His engine revved and he parked blocking her drive.

"Smooth."

He walked over with a grin on his face, tucking his phone back in his pocket. "Andrea seems to think so." His eyes narrowed. "So where're you going?"

"My dad's old hunting cabin."

"I don't like it."

"Then you're not going to like this, either. It's in Buckshot."

Liam actually growled. She must be rubbing off on him.

"You don't have to like it, but I'd rather you supported me since I'm going to do this either way."

He shook his head. "Charming."

"What?" Caisey lifted her chin. "If you want me to beg you to agree with me, or not do anything until you approve of it, you picked the wrong partner."

"You think I picked you?"

"I'm just saying."

Liam folded his arms too and stood toe to toe with her. "I'll just follow you."

"You could."

"It just so happens I already have a bag packed in my trunk. I'm supposed to head to Buckshot today with the team and I could stand to get a head start. Maybe I'll confirm it's not our guy and they won't need to make the trip."

Caisey pushed out an exaggerated sigh. "Fine, you can come. I guess."

JENNA SET her coffee down and lifted the ringing phone, her finger hovering over the answer button. She knew the number well, but hadn't dialed it in years or seen it on her display. She used to sit on the carpet floor of his office with her toy ponies while he made calls. When she got older they went out once a month to dinner, just the two of them.

"You gonna answer that?"

She jerked so hard she dropped the phone. Jake swiped it up and looked at the screen, so Jenna made a grab for it. "Give me that."

He didn't. "Who was calling?"

"No one."

"Seriously?" Jake unlocked it and pressed buttons, probably going to her call history. "You'd never let me get away with that."

"Which is why I'm the mom and you're the son." Jenna held out her hand. "Now give me my phone." He didn't respond. His eyes widened at whatever was on the screen. "Jake." He bit his lip, what was that about? "Other children listen to their parents. Sometimes they even do what they're told."

He looked up and smiled. "I obey when it's important."

"This is important."

"Who was calling?"

Jenna stared back at him. He'd never asked before, not once in all these years. Like there was some unspoken rule that they never talk about it. And yet, she did see the questions in his eyes when he thought no one was looking.

She took a deep breath. "It was my dad." He waited for her to continue, but she didn't know where to start.

Jake sighed and turned away. "Fine, don't tell me. It's not like I want to know who I am and the people I come from or anything."

Jenna caught up to him at the kitchen door. "It's not like that. This is hard for me."

"You think I don't know that? You've had years to tell me, but you haven't said word one about it. So either it's so bad you can't even say, or you don't think I need to know. Well I do. I need to know, Mom. I need you to tell me."

"Okay." She almost closed her eyes, face to face with the passion she'd fallen in love with in his father—a passion that was going to change the world. "Let's sit." She led him to the kitchen table and he waited while she composed herself. "I haven't spoken to my parents since the day they kicked me out."

"I know about that. It's why Caisey got Uncle Samuel and Grams to take you in."

Jenna nodded. She told him about her mom's visit to the spa and with a roll of her eyes, how Caisey stood up for her.

"Good. If I was there I'd have given her an earful too. I can't believe they kicked you out just because you got pregnant."

Jenna laid her hand over his. "I made peace with it a long time ago. And honestly I'd do it all again so you could grow up in this house instead of the mausoleum I grew up in."

"So why did he call you now? Maybe he wanted to apologize or something."

"I doubt it. He's never called me before. Then I run into mom and all of a sudden he feels bad?" Jenna shrugged. "Does it matter?"

"I guess not."

Jenna studied him. "Have you ever Googled them? Tried to find out who your dad is?" The reaction was immediate; flushed cheeks and eyes that flicked to the side. "What do you know?"

He pulled his hand out from under hers. "That your dad is Congressman Alan Cartwright. He's retired now, but still does charity work and plays golf."

Jenna swallowed. "What about your dad?"

"I have no idea who he was. I asked Caisey, but she got mad at me for bringing it up." His jaw flexed. "What happened?"

The knot in Jenna's stomach had grown. Some days the stain of betrayal was a speck she could almost forget about. Right now what was there felt more like a whole bottle of red wine splashed on a wedding dress.

"His name is Nicholas Arturo."

Jake sat completely still.

"I can see him in the shape of your face."

Jake swallowed. "Where is he?"

ELEVEN

Jenna took a deep breath through the tears that threatened to spill down her cheeks. If she let the dam burst the flood would consume her. She had to remember what Caisey's dad told her so many times. Words she soaked up like they were life. Nic was the one who lost out. He was the one who missed knowing Jake, watching him grow into the mature—most of the time—and smart young man before her.

"I thought it was better to tell my parents first. I don't know why I was that stupid. After that all exploded and I came here, I called Nic. His voice sounded funny like he was really upset. He said he didn't want to see me ever again and I hadn't even told him about the baby—" Her voice broke. "I went over to his house to try and talk to him but his dad totally freaked out. Called me a bunch of horrible names and threatened to set his dogs on me."

Jake leaned back in his seat. "Jerk."

"We were kids. I've had a lot of years to come to the conclusion that he must have known about you. He was probably just scared. Maybe it is true that we were too young to be serious about each other."

"Scared is fine. But so scared you wimp out on the people who need you most?" Jake's lip curled. "I don't wanna know a man who does that." He stood and his chair scraped back on the floor. "Don't call your dad back, okay? Not if it's going to upset you this much. It's not worth it."

Jenna stood too. "If you're thinking we've done okay without them, you aren't wrong. But you need to be careful. If you hate them because they were too selfish to care about us then that only hurts you, not them. Trust me when I tell you that holding onto bitterness makes you an ugly person. You have to let it go."

Jake nodded. "I will."

"I mean it, Jake. You're entitled to feel what you feel, but when you're done processing it you need to set it aside and get on with your life."

Jake came over and hugged her neck the same way Caisey did, but Jenna saw Nic's shoulders and heard his stride as she listened to him climb the stairs two at a time. It had taken years and Grams' help. Eventually she'd been able to work more on what the future could be. At least that was better than spending all her time thinking about why the past made the present less than perfect.

Jake deserved to know there were people in the world who should have loved him but chose not to be in his life. At least that's what Caisey told her. Caisey never spoke of her mom, but she'd left —abandoning Caisey—when Caisey was a toddler. Caisey always said that everyone's family was messed up and you either let it define you or rose in spite of it.

Thinking about life all those years ago, when she first moved into this house, always put Jenna in a melancholy mood. She'd spent the first weekend here lying on the couch watching movies, using up three rolls of toilet paper crying. Caisey had sat beside her with two black eyes, bruises on her jaw, and one arm tight around her waist every time she moved. When Jenna asked her what happened, she'd told her not to worry about it. Jenna did have a lot to deal with back then, but Caisey could have let her in.

It made her wonder what else her friend was holding back.

~

CAISEY GRABBED her phone from the cup holder and called Liam. She'd done the three hour drive west out Denver, got off the freeway and went another forty minutes north, all from memory. The sunrise had lit her rearview mirror, the warmth of the day chasing her like she was trying to remain in darkness.

When Liam answered, Christian rock music was blaring from his radio, but he turned it down. "Feel like turning back?"

"No. Where are you? I haven't seen you in an hour." Through the whole drive she'd spotted Liam's SUV maybe once.

"I just passed the town limits."

"Already?" Caisey was still half an hour out. She'd only been to her dad's cabin a handful of times, until her vocal stance on killing something related to Bambi was enough for her dad to leave her at home. She glanced again at the rusty Camry two cars behind the old seventies RV that was behind her. "I think I have a tail. I was going to have you check it out."

"I'll turn around."

"No, don't bother. It's probably nothing."

"If it was nothing, then you wouldn't have mentioned it."

"I'll catch up. See you soon."

"Case—"

She hung up.

When she flew past the sign for Buckshot, Colorado population 3045, she couldn't help the eye roll. Born and raised a city girl, she'd get bored inside of ten minutes in a town like this.

At the north end of town where this pocket of civilization tapered off she took a left onto a dirt track that snaked up the side of a mountain. No one pulled off after her.

The wheels juddered over crusted dirt and her engine fought its way up the incline, which wasn't even that steep. Maybe Liam was right about getting a new car. She could pull off a cute little Jeep.

The cabin was nestled in a crowd of tall pines that covered the tile roof with rusty needles. Caisey sat in the car, staring at the wood structure. If she sat there long enough, surely she'd see her dad stride around the side carrying an armful of logs for the stove.

The light in her door window darkened and she looked over...

and nearly jumped out of her skin. She grabbed the handle and opened the door.

Liam jumped back. "Careful. You almost hit me in the face."

"It serves you right for scaring the crap out of me." She climbed out. "Any news on the team, or the missing girl?"

Liam fell into step beside her. "The town has search teams out looking for her. There's a lot of ground to cover, but I'm told they're not going to admit defeat." He paused a beat. "Simmons is coming up with the team later."

"Really?"

"Didn't you used to date him?"

She shrugged and tried the cabin door. "He asked me."

"And?"

"It was a few years ago. He made it clear he was interested, but..." She shrugged again.

"No spark?"

"No spark."

He grinned. "Andrea and I got a lotta spark."

"And we're done talking about this."

The door was locked, so she pulled out her dad's old key. She wiggled it and tried to finesse the lock until Liam pushed her aside and took over. After a minute of jiggling, he sighed. "You got another key? This one isn't it."

"That's the only one I have."

Caisey's boots crunched leaves and twigs as she walked around the cabin to the back door. She dumped out a metal bucket full of water for a stool, reached up and gripped the window ledge. There was an almighty crash at the front of the cabin. Caisey's fingers slipped and she fell backwards, hit the ground and landed on a rock in the center of her back. She sucked in a breath through her nose, groaned it out and blinked up at the sky. "Ouch."

The back door opened and Liam stuck his head out. "What are you on the ground for?"

Caisey hoisted herself up on her good leg and brushed off the seat of her jeans. "Did you just break the front door down?"

"Let's not get caught up in the details. You should come look at this."

Caisey rolled her eyes. Why did Andrea put up with him?

The hall had a bedroom on one side and a bathroom on the other. The bathroom had a toothbrush, a razor, and shaving cream on the counter and soap scum in the sink, and the bedroom a worn rug that hadn't been there before, under the queen bed. Neither had the curtains, which she pulled back to let in the light. The bed had a denim comforter pushed back, like someone got out of bed and left it like that.

It couldn't have been her dad; he'd been dead four years. She hadn't been here since he was killed, couldn't spare the time to come when he didn't leave anything between his trips worth retrieving. Only there was a conspicuous lack of four years' worth of dust.

Someone was living here.

Caisey's boots clipped the bare wood to the front room. Liam was in the kitchen. She looked over the living room and small breakfast table. The first thing she thought was, *books*. They were everywhere, on the tables and shelves, stacked in towers by the short bookcase. She picked up the nearest one, *The Empire of the Hittites*, and tossed it back on the table. There was a computer on the roll top desk in the corner.

"So much for the plan."

She caught Liam's wry grin and returned it. "Yeah. Can't really clear out someone else's belongings and sell the place from under them. Well, I could, but my dad might have sold the place and not told me. So who's been living here? Looks settled enough to have been for a while now. Did my dad know about this?"

Liam's face turned assessing. "One person, most likely a man."

"History buff, maybe a teacher. The computer will tell us more." Caisey hit the power button on the tower.

"Is there any way to check if your dad sold the place?"

"His papers were all still in the file. According to what I have it was never sold, so I'm legally the owner. Property taxes and all."

Liam leaned back against the counter. "So do we just sit and wait until whoever it is comes back?"

Caisey shrugged. "I'd like to meet him. But other than that

there's not much point in me being here. I should let you go help with the search."

A car pulled up outside. The engine shut off and a door opened, but didn't close. "This is the Buckshot Sheriff's Department. Come out with your hands up!"

Caisey looked at Liam, who'd pulled his gun out, too. She went to the door, which had been broken off its hinges and now leaned against the frame so it mostly covered the door. "We're federal agents and we're coming out!" She muscled the door aside and shot Liam a look.

"What? The hinges weren't as good as I thought they'd be. I was only trying to pop the lock."

"Right." She stepped out into the sunlight, one palm raised and her gun angled down.

Liam stepped out beside her. His free hand was up, but not as high as hers. The uniformed sheriff straightened from his defensive position behind the car door and eyed them. He was aiming an honest to goodness six-shooter in their direction.

Liam stopped. "You want to lower your gun?"

"Why don't you show me some ID first." His eyes were shadowed by a cowboy hat, but there was suspicion in the set of his mouth and his jaw was covered with day-old red stubble.

"Back pocket."

"Why don't you pull it out, nice and slow-like?"

Liam held it up. "I'm Special Agent Conners. This is my partner, Special Agent Lyons. And you are?"

Caisey stuck the wallet that held her badge ID in her back pocket.

"Frank Allens." He holstered his six-shooter, shut the car door and ambled over to them. "Been the sheriff round here gone twenty years now."

He held out his hand to Liam and then eyed Caisey up and down. His scowl morphed into a look she'd seen on many a good-ol-boy. The members of that particular club didn't believe a woman could be a decent police officer. She found they'd only grudgingly accepted the reality of females in law enforcement.

"What can I do you for?"

Caisey motioned behind her. "This was my dad's hunting cabin."

"That's right, Samuel Lyons. He was a special F-Bee-Eye agent too, wasn't he? Killed in the line of duty a few years back, I heard. Shame. That man could skin a buck quicker than anyone." He shook his head like he was discarding the detritus of happier times and glanced between them. "So you're here to see Gabe then?"

Caisey turned to Liam. *Gabe?*

It was Liam who asked the sheriff, "Is that the guy who lives here now?"

"Moved in a bunch of years back and your dad never came after that, figured he sold the place to Gabe though I don't know why. Weird, the way that man keeps to himself. Runs a bookstore. Barely talks to anyone. Loner, you know? Makes you wonder what they're up to."

Caisey kept her mouth shut. Could he really be talking about the same Gabe, her one perfect date who never called? And why did it feel like the sheriff was holding something back?

She knew Gabe's uncle wouldn't rest until he found Gabe. Because he told her, right before he nearly broke her jaw. She'd always assumed Gabe disappeared into Witness Protection. Had her dad stashed him in his hunting cabin? Going by the same first name all these years was either the stupidest plan in the world, or so simple it was genius.

Liam did a chin lift. "You got a last name on this guy?"

"Thompson. Gabe Thompson." The sheriff scratched his chin.

Caisey's gaze darted to Liam again, who lifted his chin in a motion barely visible. He'd seen it too; the sheriff had scratches on his knuckles. Who had he been fighting with?

"It just so happens I have the guy in for questioning right now." The brim of the sheriff's hat lifted, revealing narrow, ink-black eyes. "Interesting coincidence, two FBI agents turning up the day after my niece goes missing. I mean, I appreciate the, all-hands- on-deck attitude but this is local business."

TWELVE

"Your niece is missing? That sure is an interesting coincidence, but I'm actually on vacation right now." She chuckled, hoping it didn't sound too flat. They would get more out of a belligerent sheriff who didn't think they wanted to take over his case. Later, if Liam and the team confirmed the girl's disappearance was the work of the Chloroform Killer, he could tell the sheriff who they were. "What makes you think this Gabe guy is involved?"

The sheriff sniffed. "He was the last one to see her alive."

"So you're thinking homicide?"

"Can't be sure until we find her." The old man cleared his throat and a dour mood descended like a sudden rain storm five seconds after nothing but clear skies.

Liam stepped closer. "Are you sure you don't want any help? We're here and all."

"No, no." The sheriff took a couple of steps back. "Like I said, this is local business." He waved and headed for his vehicle. "You folks take care."

"Sheriff!" Casey trotted down the steps and caught up to him by his SUV. "You mind if I stop by your office? I'd like to talk to Gabe Thompson, see if he knows why my dad gave up his cabin."

He surveyed her face. "My people have more important things

to take care of right now than entertaining special agents on vacation."

"And I'd really like to ask why you appear to be investigating your own niece's disappearance instead of calling in the State Patrol to take over, but I'm not."

The sheriff wrung his hands together. There was a long silence and then he said, "You can have five minutes."

He got in his patrol car. Caisey watched him drive away and turned to Liam. "Okay, so...that was weird."

"No kidding. His niece is missing and he has a possible suspect in custody. He came here for some reason, but didn't go inside. And he doesn't want help because we're from out of town."

"Doesn't mean he isn't going to get help, whether he wants it or not."

Liam grinned. "I knew there was a reason you're my partner."

"So here's the plan—"

"How come you get to make the plan? You're on vacation."

Caisey rolled her eyes. "Because."

"Let me guess, you wanna go see if this Gabe guy is the same man your dad knew?"

"Right."

"And you want me to ask around about the missing girl and find out what's going on?"

Caisey grinned. "However did you guess that?"

"And the cabin?"

"Chances are Gabe Thompson bought it fair and legal." She frowned. "What are you going to do about the front door? You bashed it in."

"I didn't mean to."

Caisey laughed. "I'm sorry, your honor. I didn't mean to stab her six times, I was really mad and she just sort of...fell on the knife."

"Don't remind me. That case was awful."

"You're the one who volunteered us."

"I'll fix the door, okay? You'd better go or you'll be late for your date."

"What date?"

Liam didn't say anything. The look on his face was enough. "It might not be him."

"But if it is then this is huge, right?"

Caisey put one hand on her hip. "What exactly do you think you know?"

"Jenna sort of, might have, mentioned something to Andrea about a long lost love of yours. Some perfect date where you talked all night and it was magical and you just knew— "

She held up one hand. "Enough. It wasn't like that. You make it sound hokey. It wasn't. It was..."

Liam pushed her hand away. "It was what?"

Caisey chewed her lip.

"You love him."

"I do not."

"Do too."

"We're not having this conversation."

Liam trailed behind her, all the way to her car door. "Seriously? It was one date, how can you fall in love with someone in one night?"

Caisey spun back. "I don't know, okay?"

"You didn't...uh...you know?"

"No. It was a date."

"How can you be sure it was the Gabe who testified for your dad?"

"His picture was in the newspaper." She paused. "I can't explain it. I just know it happened, okay?"

"Sparks?"

She sighed.

Liam tipped his head back and laughed at full volume.

Caisey swung her car door open and was disappointed he got out of the way before it collided with him.

"I can't believe it." He laughed some more. "You're a romantic."

Casey rolled the window down. "Goodbye, Liam. I hope you get mauled by a wild boar while I'm gone."

~

CAISEY DROVE down the hill with a grin stretching her cheeks. When she hit the main road she checked her phone for messages before pulling onto the blacktop.

What would she do if it really was Gabe, her Gabe? She'd existed so long on a memory, what if she'd been wrong? The whole idea of sparks was ridiculous, like they even meant anything. Sure, part of her didn't mind holding onto something magical that was just hers. Grams had made sure Caisey never lost hold of that sense of wonder she said was inside everyone, but fanciful wasn't going to help her. It would just complicate everything.

She had plenty to fill her life—personal and professional—without getting involved with someone on the basis of a seventeen-year-old attraction that was apparently one-sided anyway.

The sheriff's office was a single level building with low windows on the outside wall, which meant it probably had a basement of cells. Two county vehicles were parked adjacent to the building. Caisey pulled up beside an all-black Harley that belonged out front of a biker bar, or a custom motorcycle shop. Inside held the vague scent of cigarette smoke underlain with burned coffee and body odor.

Behind the yellowed Formica counter was a guy whose head almost grazed the ceiling. Six-foot-five at least, his chin had more hair than his head. He was at least fifty and his shirt sleeves were rolled back to reveal sleeves of tattoos. Since he had on jeans and a tan shirt, she figured he was probably a civilian employee of the county.

"Hey."

He looked up from a motorcycle magazine.

Caisey smiled. "That your Dyna Glide outside?"

"Sure is."

"It's sweet."

He grinned and lifted his chin. "Help you?"

Caisey flashed her badge. "Special Agent Caisey Lyons, but this isn't official business."

He flipped the magazine closed. "Big Al."

"Nice to meet you, Big Al." She didn't shake his hand, just gave it a solid squeeze and released.

"You here about Emily?"

"Is that the sheriff's niece who went missing?"

"Yeah." Big Al shook his head. "Weird, you know?"

"The sheriff said I could get a minute with Gabe Thompson. Sheriff Allens said he was here."

"You think he had something to do with Emma?"

"Do you?"

Big Al blew out a breath and rested his elbows on the counter. "Seems like a solid guy. I ain't never seen him at the tavern and his car is outside the little church up the street every Sunday morning, even when I'm out with the snowplow. But you never know, right? Isn't it always the quiet ones?"

He lifted the end of the counter and let her through. The main room held four desks and at the back wall was an office with the Sheriff's name stenciled on the glass. The blinds were shut. Big Al's computer screen showed four windows—camera feeds of the cells. One occupied, three empty.

Caisey motioned to his cup. "Got any more of that coffee?"

"Sure, darlin'."

A woman in a black Harley tank top and skinny jeans sat at the desk in the far corner. While Big Al filled a cup from the coffee pot on the opposite wall, Caisey watched the woman talk into her headset. She waved her hand, complete with long red nails. "Are you serious, girl? I can't believe he'd do that. Not again. Sure enough, I'll get someone out to you a-sap."

She pressed a button on the mic in front of her. "Bud, hon, this is dispatch. Got an idiot ex-husband causing a disturbance at sixty-seven Alto Street."

Big Al stepped in front of Caisey. "That's my old lady, Babs. Got a job here about three seconds after I did, thinks it'll save me getting into trouble if she's here to keep an eye on me." His chuckle sounded like a bear clearing its throat.

Caisey smiled. "Cells are downstairs?" Big Al nodded. "Let the sheriff know I'm headed down there."

"Sure thing, darlin'. Take care."

"I always do."

Caisey took the coffee to the door at the back. The steps were concrete and her boot heels echoed. She turned the corner at the bottom and saw a row of four cells lit by fluorescents. They were all empty except for a guy at the end, stretched out on his back on the cot with his hands under his head, elbows out. A pair of glasses sat folded on his chest and goose-bumps covered his forearms. She'd been right about the t-shirt and pajama pants she saw on the surveillance.

"Here—"

His eyes flew open.

"Hot coffee."

He snagged his glasses and slipped them on. His eyes widened. "You."

"Seriously this cup is hot."

He came over, his eyes on her the whole time he took those measured steps, like he had all the time in the world and wanted to savor it.

Caisey dropped her hands and clenched and unclenched her fingers. "Gabe Carlen."

"You know?"

"Thompson now, right?"

"That's right." Both hands on the mug, he sipped. The steam fogged up his glasses. He was about four inches taller than her, which put him at average height for a man, but that was being generous. "Caisey Lyons." He grinned. "It's been a while."

It took everything she had, even biting the inside of her cheeks, but she held back the smile. "Special Agent Caisey Lyons."

She'd been seventeen and him twenty-one when they went on the date to end all other dates. Though she'd told him she was older. A week later, after he hadn't called or returned her calls, his uncle abducted her.

"Are you here to arrest me?"

"Do you need arresting?"

His smile was easy and softened the fatigue in his eyes. "A trick question. Clever."

"I thought so."

"I'd rather get dressed and get breakfast."

"It's after lunch."

His eyebrows lifted. "No kidding?"

Caisey nodded. "I take it the accommodations at Chateau Buckshot aren't up to par?"

"You could say that." The smile in his eyes darkened. "Seriously though, they said questioning. Am I being arrested?"

"I'll find out what's going on and get someone to rustle you up some food."

"I really sorry something happened to Emma, but I had nothing to do with it."

Caisey took a step back. Evidence didn't lie and while she was as sure as she could be that Gabe wasn't lying, she still wasn't going to do anything that could blow back on her professionally. "I'll be back, okay?"

Gabe took another sip and nodded. "I'd appreciate that. Oh, and Caisey?"

She lifted her chin.

He grinned. "It's really nice to see you again."

Caisey climbed the concrete stairs and sighed.

Stupid sparks.

SHERIFF ALLENS LOWERED the volume on the surveillance and picked up his phone. As soon as he heard Special Agent Lyons say the name Gabe Carlen, he put it all together. While it rang, he picked at a strip of the plastic on the surface of his desk that had somehow come loose. One of the drawers didn't shut, and no one knew where the key was for the other. He'd purchased the safe in the corner with his own money, but years ago. No doubt it needed replacing. The only thing that was top of the line around here was surveillance—on the office and at his home.

"Yes?"

"It's Frank Allens."

There was a click and the phone rang once, which was surprising given how long it had been since he'd made a call like this.

"Arturo." This voice was older, rich and cultured but with an undertone of ruthlessness that wasn't to be ignored.

"It's Frank Allens."

"Well, well, well. It's been a while. What brought you crawling back now?"

Frank sneered. He wasn't going to apologize, that was for sure. "Got a man down in my cells by the name of Gabe Carlen. Figured you might want to know."

"He's been living in your town this whole time?" The voice was low and lethal, like it had been the night Holden Arturo found out Frank had been sleeping with his wife.

"I'm trying to do you a favor here. You could at least be grateful."

"Grateful to you?" Holden snorted. "All those years in hick-ville must have rotted your brain. Or were you always this stupid? You think I don't already know where my nephew is? I've been on Caisey Lyon's trail since she left Denver and the stupid girl led me right to his doorstep. So don't act like this is some grand gesture you're going to use to crawl your way out of the sewer. You might have been a police chief once, but that was a long time ago."

Frank slammed the phone down. He should have known Holden would be on top of all this. No plan had ever gone off without something interfering—he rubbed his leg where the bullet from Samuel Lyons' gun had torn through the muscle.

How could he have known that Thompson was, in fact, Gabe Carlen?

Now he would just have to take care of this himself. There was no other way to fix it. He was always the one who got his hands dirty, who put his life and career on the line to pay back one stupid mistake he should never have made in the first place. Holden had been right about one thing. Frank would crawl out of the hole he'd fallen into. He was going to make sure Gabe went to jail for Emma's murder and everyone believed him to be the Chloroform Killer. That was the only way Frank was going to get his old life back.

His stomach churned, making him reach for the antacids in his drawer.

No wonder he'd snapped before.

Women were nothing but a slow-acting poison, infecting you before you even knew it. His wife had been exactly like that.

Boots clomped outside his door. "Hey, Big Al, can I borrow this?" The reply was muffled. "Sure, darlin'."

Frank gritted his teeth. *Special Agent Lyons.* She was twisting his staff to her side already.

The plan had been a long time coming. Frank had to wait for the right time and he'd been so sure this was it. Now because of one little girl with a gun all of it was going to crap, just like the last time. The memory of it soured his stomach further. Families everywhere, ruining his life—one family tied him up in their war and the other showed up to stick their nose in everything he tried to do to get out of it.

The pencil in his hand snapped in two. His computer chimed again, and he clicked the icon at the bottom. Someone was at his house. He grabbed his jacket off the coat tree and stopped at the door. She was nowhere to be seen, so he strode through the office. "I'm out."

Big Al didn't look up from his magazine. "Sure, boss."

Frank hit the front door with a sneer on his face. She wasn't going to best him.

THIRTEEN

Caisey watched the sheriff leave, exited the women's bathroom and grabbed the nearest desk phone.

"Conners."

She slumped into a chair. "At least one of us has phone signal."

"Not much of one. What's up?"

"The sheriff just left. Where are you?"

Wind buffeted the phone on his end. A car door slammed and the line went quiet. "I talked to the old biddy at the library and got the sheriff's address. I checked out the house, but there's nothing to see other than a whole lot of mess. His cleaning lady is probably on vacation."

"You didn't get in?"

"The guy has motion sensors on all the windows."

"Maybe that's where he went all of a sudden."

It would certainly explain his hasty exit if he knew Liam was snooping around his house. The sheriff was either up to something or he snuck out to get lunch, but Caisey doubted it was the latter. They really needed someone to tail him. She'd have to ask the state police to send officers, since it was bad form for a man's deputies to be assigned to spy on their superior. The FBI team who would arrive later didn't need their focus distracted by a possibly crooked sheriff when they were on the trail of the Chloroform Killer.

"I'll stick around, see if he shows up."

"Keep me posted."

"Do the same, yeah?"

She was about to hang up when she heard him yelling.

"Is it the guy? Is it that Gabe dude?"

"Goodbye Liam." Caisey hung up and lifted her head. Babs' eyes were on her, as were a wide-set dark pair belonging to the biker in the room. "Big Al."

"Yo, darlin'."

"Call the state police. Find out who's in charge and apprise them of the situation, if you would."

"Sure thing." But Big Al didn't pick up the phone.

Babs put her headset down and Caisey waited while they crowded around the desk where she sat.

"Okay, what can you tell me?"

Big Al sniffed. "The sheriff's always been like that, like he's got a whole lot he doesn't want you to know. Kept himself closed off after his wife disappeared—"

"I heard she ran off with the bank manager from the credit union down in Rifle." Babs' face was weathered with more years than Caisey suspected she'd lived. "Couldn't never find out where the rumor came from neither, except that Frank told Pete—he's the bartender at the tavern, Pete's—that his old lady was some kind of cougar, you know?" She shook the cloud of red curls that surrounded her face. "I never believed it."

Caisey blinked.

"I'm Babs, by the way. I hail from Alabama." She curled her long fingers around Big Al's bicep, as though accustomed to the need to stake her claim.

"Nice to meet you." Caisey scratched the back of her neck. "So tell me, why on earth is he the sheriff?"

Big Al shrugged. "No one ever runs against him. Steve Tinner tried, but then backed out last minute before the election. Left town soon after."

"And it's just Allens and the other deputy, Bud?"

Babs shook her head again. "We got a Deputy Samantha Kurter, former Marine and not the washed up kind, you know? More like the kill-you-if-you-look-at-her-wrong kind. She got exiled to the night shift, since she and ol' Frank don't exactly see eye-to-eye. The other deputy is Jed Wilson, works weekends only but he's not worth two nickels. Most folks, if they ain't bleeding to death themselves—just the other guy—they'll call the state patrol on the weekend."

"Right." Caisey motioned to the basement door. "If you'll get me the key, I'll let out Mr. Thompson and I really need you to make that call."

"Whatever you need, darlin'. I'm just glad someone else finally saw what's goin' on around here. Things haven't been right with the sheriff for a long time, we just can't prove it."

Caisey pulled up her email on her phone and wrote a note to Liam, copying in Burkot. Hopefully there was enough signal for it to send.

By the time Big Al had a response to his call in to the state patrol, Caisey had Gabe across the desk from her and writing out his statement.

"I talked to Captain Stenton's secretary. He's in a meeting and would like regular updates. Basically, he'll send someone when we find a body but he isn't too fussed about a runaway teenager. They're sure you can handle it."

"Thank you, Big Al."

Good to know she could count on the state police. Caisey sighed.

The dull murmur of a migraine teased the edges of her senses. She closed her eyes and took a deep breath. There was no way she was going to get sucked into this. She and Liam could end up here for weeks looking for a girl who probably jumped at the chance to get away from an overbearing family—at best. The only problem was the worst case scenario. Caisey had seen the aftermath of that one way too many times to be comfortable letting things just play out.

She looked at Gabe, whose eyes were wide. Across the room

Babs was filing her nails with her head cocked, one ear trained on their conversation. Caisey sighed and rubbed her leg.

"Did you get hurt?"

"It's not a big deal." Not next to the fact that her back felt like there was a huge bruise where she'd fallen on the rock behind the cabin. She eyed Gabe's paper. "Are you done?"

He set his pen down. "I'm not sure there's much to say. She left my shop and I didn't see her after that."

"Who was she close to?"

"I have no idea."

"Babs?"

She snapped up the phone. "I'll find out."

Caisey looked back at Gabe. It was kind of nice, sitting with him. She could almost pretend they were across the table from each other having coffee, or eating dinner. Except she sucked at small talk and quiet made her antsy.

"So...an FBI agent?"

"And you run a bookstore."

He nodded and her eyes fixed on the square line of his jaw and the short dark stubble. "Among other things."

"You like it here?" Living in *my* cabin. Now might not be the time to have that conversation.

His lips curled up at the corners. "Sure, Buckshot's grown on me. I like your dad's place, and the people are nice. The church isn't so big you get lost in the crowd and Tim's a great pastor. It took a while, but it's home now. You?"

Caisey shrugged. "It seems nice enough here. I just never figured Dad's cabin was good for anything more than a weekend."

He shook his head. "That's not what I meant, but you're right. It wasn't. I had to get a new stove and put in a composting toilet. I'm many things, but a guy who uses an outhouse is not one of them."

Caisey saw the gleam in his eyes and chuckled. "It did seem like you made it into a home. And you've heard nothing from your uncle all these years?"

"Not a word."

"Good. Let's pray it stays that way."

Because a serial killer at large and a possibly crazy sheriff she could handle. But Gabe's uncle on a rampage too?

No thanks.

~

LIAM'S PHONE VIBRATED. He covered the pocket with his hand, eyes on the sheriff's house. He didn't like missing calls from Andrea. Tax season was her busiest time of year, which meant she was only calling because she had a minute to talk. By the time he called her back, she'd be busy again.

The air held a chill even though it was the warmest part of the day. He'd lived in Denver for going on five years and he still wasn't used to how different the air was compared to the east coast.

The sheriff's house was a farm on the south side of town that looked rundown, like a foreclosure that had been neglected once the owners gave up on their dream of a forever house. It would give the sheriff a fifteen-minute drive into work, maybe less. But it still felt like the middle of nowhere. Especially since Liam had parked a mile away and traversed through mud and brush to this spot.

A car door slammed. From his cover of dense trees, Liam watched the sheriff dart into the house. The old man's focus never wavered. Liam understood that level of dedication, the only problem being that he had the sneaking suspicion it was directed against him and Caisey. What was the guy up to?

The sheriff seemed to be not the least bit concerned that his teenage niece had disappeared. But was it because he already knew exactly what happened to her, or was he about to try and solve it himself? The alternative was he didn't care at all. But his actions said he cared a lot...about something.

A career lawman wasn't going to let it be known that he'd done harm to his niece, if that's what happened. But since Liam and Caisey had shown up, he was either content that nothing would come to light or not hiding anything.

While Caisey loved the pure rush of justice, the take-down, Liam lived for the puzzle of people and why they did the things they did. His obsessive need for answers could be considered unhealthy, but he was channeling it. Was it a vice when you had to do it for work?

He could walk away if he wanted to. Okay, maybe not, but it wasn't like he was drinking again. This was different. Transferring to Colorado had been the best thing for him. The move set him up to get right with God, which turned out to be the most "right" thing in the world next to meeting Andrea. He never would have believed that if it hadn't happened to him.

The sheriff came back out of the house, one hand pulling the front door shut behind him. But he was evidently so focused he didn't realize the door didn't quite closed. The look in his eyes said he was about to commit murder.

Liam shifted to get his muscles moving, ready in case he needed to run to his car and pursue the sheriff...although the open front door looked mighty tempting. What would he find in there? If the sheriff did kill his niece, he would likely not be stupid enough to leave the body in his house.

The cruiser's engine revved and gravel sprayed out the back as he sped away. Liam selected the last number Caisey called from and listened to it ring.

First the Chloroform Killer, and now a sheriff up to something, too?

What a mess they'd walked into. *God, don't let this get worse.* The Chloroform Killer needed to be locked up, not who-knew-where. Everything they knew about serial killers, everything that was understood about who they were and how they operated had gone out the window on this one. Not that a person couldn't defy what was known, but it made it harder to predict their next move.

Harder to catch.

FOURTEEN

"So you think Emma took off with this new guy of hers?"

Gabe turned away from the passenger window. "That would be my guess. I mean, she said he wasn't so hot on her dad, but that just makes me wonder if he didn't manage to convince her to leave with him."

Her brown eyes were focused on the road. "Makes sense, kids in love thinking its forever and running away together." She pulled her phone out of the cup holder and glanced at the display.

Everything she did was precise. Like she was supremely confident in who she was and what she was capable of. One hand on the wheel and the other in her lap, Caisey kept everything about her easy and natural.

All he had to do was show her the call history from Mitch and he'd be able to prove he was occupied when Emma disappeared. It grated that he had to verify his innocence at all, like some kind of criminal who needed to justify himself. But now he'd seen Caisey, it was worth it. He didn't know what brought her to Buckshot in the first place, and since he got to see the woman she had become he didn't much care.

All those years ago she'd been beautiful. Now she was even more so with the mantle of confidence she wore. The years had grown her from fresh beauty to adult gorgeous. And though some people might see her self-confidence as off-putting, or overbearing, Gabe thought it made her look capable—like she was fully prepared to take on the world for you.

There had to be someone in her life. There was no way she was single. Not that it affected him any, since he probably wouldn't see her again after she dropped him home and checked his computer. He would go on his date with Becka, back to his quiet life of pretending he wasn't much of anything.

When they got there he saw the front door of the cabin had been completely knocked off its hinges. Although the person responsible had been kind enough to prop it against the frame. It didn't look too much like you could just walk in.

He glanced at Caisey, who walked up the porch steps beside him. "You know who did this?"

"Liam will either fix it, or he'll pay for the damages."

Gabe's eyes widened. "You're not even going to try and defend him?"

"Like mention how you could have been dead inside, or any of the other hundred scenarios I've seen?" She swallowed. "I don't think he meant to break the whole door."

Charming. Gabe moved the door to the side, pleased to see not too many leaves had blown in from outside. He waved in the direction of the computer. "I'll fire it up and you can check the call history."

He remembered her Grams was British. There wasn't much she'd told him that night that he didn't remember, or that he hadn't played over and over in his head. "Do you want to put on the kettle? You kind of look wiped."

"Sure." She strode to the kitchen, her boot heels clicking on the linoleum floor. She banged cupboard doors and two mugs slammed on the counter.

Gabe winced, hoping she wasn't going to break something. It would be a pain to drive all the way to Rifle to replace his kettle. He pressed the power button on his computer's tower.

More cupboard doors slammed. "You don't have a coffee maker, or even instant." She sounded aghast. Gabe looked over and sure enough, it was like she couldn't even fathom the concept. "What is this?"

He looked at the box of teabags she held up. "Green tea."

"Is it any good?" She tossed it on the counter. "Never mind. I'll grab the stash of PG Tips teabags from my car."

She stomped out, and he glanced around. Everything in his cabin looked like someone had rummaged through it. Books were askew, though the furniture seemed to be unscathed. Had she and her partner been searching for something? He walked down the hall to the bedroom and muttered when he saw what it looked like. In his defense, the Sheriff and Deputy Paulson had hauled him out of bed.

Gabe closed the door and changed out of his pajamas into jeans and a clean shirt. He would've liked to take a shower, but that could wait until Special Agent Lyons left.

The name reminded him of her dad. Samuel Lyons had been a friend and mentor to Gabe when he needed a good man in his life. Gabe had even reached the point he considered Samuel a father-figure. Between his dad and his uncle, Gabe grew up with plenty of men in his life. Too bad they were all mob-connected, gun-running, drug-dealing criminals who wouldn't think twice before they put one between your eyes.

He'd never quite figured out how a bookworm fit in with them. His mom was sweet, but not that smart, and his sister married her made-man husband at eighteen. That union had connected them all with a powerful Italian family, much to the delight of everyone.

Six months later Andre, his nephew, had been born. Who knew how many children Marianne had now? And the only person he missed more than a blond girl whose dad he respected, was his cousin Nic. Gabe prayed every day of his life that Nic hadn't been pulled into that life, and every day he had to force himself not to pick up the phone and dial his cousin's number.

Missing them was hard, but being dead wouldn't be fun either.

"Gabe!"

He opened the door to his bedroom. "What?"

"Your computer is ringing."

He trotted out and saw Mitch's profile picture. He clicked to answer the call. "Hey, bud."

"Dude, you will not believe what we just found."

The picture flickered and Mitch's face filled the screen.

The smile on his friend's face was infectious. "That's great, but—"

"Seriously you're going to freak out and I'm not even kidding. We were on the south side of the dig and Elanya was working on the wall I was telling you about—"

Caisey put her hand on Gabe's shoulder and leaned down so the camera could see her face too. "Hi."

Mitch's mouth hung open.

"This is Caisey."

She pulled something from her back pocket and stuck it in front of the camera. "Special Agent Caisey Lyons, FBI. Can you tell me if you were talking with Gabe Carlen yesterday at approximately four-thirty here?"

Mitch just stared.

Caisey frowned. "Wouldn't that be middle of the night for you?"

"He had—"

She put her palm in Gabe's face, cutting off what he'd been about to say. "I need him to answer the question." She tipped her head toward the kitchen. "In fact, why don't you go make the tea? I take milk, but no sugar."

Mitch started laughing. Gabe shot him a glare and pushed the chair back. "He's all yours."

CAISEY WATCHED him stride away to the kitchen and then looked back at the man on screen. Mitch's grin was wide, making her lips twitch. She swiped up some headphones from the desk drawer and plugged them straight into the speakers.

"Like I said, I'm a special agent with the FBI. This isn't official, you'll need to do this again with someone from the sheriff's office most likely, but Gabe was brought in for questioning here in—"

The guy slapped his hands over his ears. "No no no no..."

"What?"

"Don't tell me where he is." He let his hands drop. "I'm Mitch Landers. Gabe and I work together, but it's important you don't tell me where he lives so I don't inadvertently put him in danger."

Caisey gave herself a second to compute that. Good friends were hard to come by and she was glad Gabe hadn't been totally alone all this time. "Very well. A local girl went missing. Gabe was questioned regarding her disappearance, which was around the time he says you two were talking yesterday."

"I called late because I was too excited to wait until today. I emailed him a picture too, so the time should be on the call history and in his email."

"Should be easy enough to verify. Thank you, Mr. Landers."

Mitch nodded. "You can't really think he had anything to do with a missing girl, though. That's crazy."

"It's just procedure."

"Gabe isn't like that."

She knew that, she just couldn't say it. "You've known him long?"

Mitch smiled. "Since Mr. Peterson's history class in seventh grade. I moved to Denver after my dad got stationed there. We moved again when I was in high school, but Gabe and I never lost touch and we met up again in college. I actually haven't seen him since then, though we've been working together for years."

Caisey settled back in the chair. "Doing what?" This was about the investigation, not finding out what kind of man Gabe was. *Keep telling yourself that.*

Mitch hesitated. "You don't know about Gabe?"

"Are you going to tell me, or do I have to guess?"

"Are you familiar with Carl Gabriel?"

"The author?"

Mitch nodded; a gleam in his eyes.

"Huh." Caisey glanced back to where Gabe was layering cheese and what looked like ham into two sandwiches. "You don't say."

Evidently, aside from running a bookstore Gabe also wrote

historical adventure novels. She'd liked the movie they made of *The Seventh Kingdom* and Jake had raved about Carl Gabriel's website and how it had a lot of cool stuff on it, but she'd never checked it out.

"Thanks, Mitch. I appreciate your time."

"Yeah, no worries." He gave her a small smile. "Tell Gabe I'll email him."

Caisey ended the call and turned the chair so she could watch Gabe. He made sandwiches like it was a delicate scientific experiment, and he wasn't skimping on the meat.

He looked up. "You like soy turkey, right?"

She swallowed, but the bad taste didn't go away.

"Everything copacetic?"

"The sheriff will need to see the time stamps, but I'm pretty satisfied at this point." She glanced around. "Do you have a land line?" They had to deliver pizza out here, though she might die of hunger before she got cell signal. Not to mention she needed to eat so she could take more painkillers.

"I only have the internet connection that goes through the satellite dish. Can't get much more than that up here." He walked over and handed her a plate.

"Thanks."

He studied her. "You really do look tired."

"It's been a long couple of weeks."

Gabe perched on the arm of the recliner.

Caisey turned back to the computer, opened his browser and searched for anything about the Chloroform Killer. The top link was a news story. When the page loaded, she saw the headline. The sandwich got stuck and she tried to breathe, not choke and not spit it out.

Gabe rushed over with a glass of water. "Are you okay?"

Caisey scrolled down the news article. *Still at large.*

"Is that you?"

She set her sandwich on the plate and took two steps away from the computer.

"This says you're the agent who got abducted." Gabe scrolled down the article. "It says he's still at large and probably looking for you. For revenge, Caisey."

She was going to kill whoever leaked this. Wring their scrawny neck and leave an impression of her boot in their face.

"Caisey."

She spun around, hands fisted by her sides. "What!"

"You were abducted by the Chloroform Killer?"

She didn't confirm, or deny.

"On purpose?" His voice rose. "Are you crazy?"

She gritted her teeth. "Why are you mad at me? I don't have to justify myself and I don't have to explain anything to you." One date didn't give him the right to get mad when she put her life in danger. Admittedly that was nearly every day in her job, but she wasn't stupid and they were calculated risks.

"You don't have to...are you serious? What would your dad say if he knew you put yourself in a situation like that?"

"I would think he'd say, *Great idea, Caisey. Way to get the guy.* But we'll never know because he's dead now, isn't he." She looked away and blinked.

"I'm sorry, I—"

"Do not tell me you're sorry. You don't know anything about it."

"You're right. But..." Gabe sighed. "He was a good man who helped me. I'd be dead if it wasn't for him."

"Good for you."

"Caisey—"

"Can we not talk about this?" She reached for her coat. "I'm going. Have a nice life, I guess."

"Case, don't go. Don't leave it like this."

"Leave what like this? There's nothing here." She motioned between them. "I have to go. Coming here was pointless."

He caught up to her at the door, his hand on her elbow. "I finally see you after years and this is what happens? I don't want it to be like this. It feels wrong."

He wasn't far from the truth. Everything about this was wrong. "I shouldn't have come here."

"Don't say that. Case..." He sighed. "It seems so lame to ask for your number. Should I?"

Caisey bit her lip. Did she want to walk away after all these years of holding on to her dream man? But that was the problem, dreams didn't jive with a reality in which he never called. That was why they were dreams. She looked away from the dark brown depths of his eyes that threatened to draw her in and hold on. As if he didn't already have enough power over her. "What's the point?"

Brakes screeched and a car pulled up outside in a cloud of dust.

Caisey peered out the slit between the door and the frame. Instinct made her push Gabe to the side of the door before the man outside emerged from his car. Sheriff Frank Allens pumped the shotgun and lifted it.

Caisey was halfway across the room, hauling Gabe by his arm when the first shot splintered the broken front door, showering the room.

FIFTEEN

Caisey slammed into the back door but it didn't open. Her mind blanked as dust and splinters of the cabin rained down like a blizzard. The sheriff was shooting at them. Her fingers flexed on the grip of her gun and she glanced back to see the sheriff kick the remnants of the door away and enter the cabin, but he didn't see them. His feral eyes darted around as he wielded the shotgun over his head and then started smashing. The coffee table, the lamp. He pulled down the bookcase and kicked the couch over.

Gabe yanked the lock and they rushed outside where she shoved him sideways out of the line of sight. The sheriff yelled and cursed, his boots darting from one end of the wood floor to the other as he raced around. Another gun blast echoed through the clearing behind the cabin. Gabe ducked and yelped, his eyes wide.

Caisey didn't move as she breathed...in...out. Feet solid, finger on the trigger ready to shoot a fellow cop. It was like the world slowed down. She could smell the needles that had settled in the clearing like a carpet. A dirty cop, even if it was just a smudge it didn't much matter, he was still a cop. All she had was suspicion and no evidence. Except that he was trying to kill them.

Glass shattered.

"If he's broken my computer I'm going to—" The shotgun went off again and they both flinched.

"Let's move out. He hasn't found us yet, he's too busy doing damage. We should be able to get away."

Together they ran for the trees, and Caisey angled right to head in a big circle back to her car. They needed to get off the mountain while the sheriff was busy destroying her dad's cabin and Gabe's stuff. All she needed to do was get to a public place where she could find Liam and get out of Buckshot, Colorado, the preferred home of crazies everywhere. Gabe could get on with his life and she could forget she ever thought coming here would be a good idea. The whole day had been unreal and this just capped it like a nightmare case that got thrown out in court.

An engine revved—less power and a throatier pitch than a car engine. She glanced back over her shoulder, but there were just trees. Still, the sound echoed through the clearing.

Gabe turned. "You are not serious."

Caisey glanced at him, her gun angled toward the ground. "What is it?"

The engine was gunned and the sound grew louder as it neared the trees. Gabe had to shout over the sound. "He found the keys to my ATV. I'm going to kill him if he wrecks it. It's brand new."

Caisey grabbed his arm again and they ran between trees. She was practically pushing him along, one hand on the chords of his back. Over fallen tree trunks with no path to follow, they stumbled and ran. Keep Gabe safe. Get to safety through miles of forest she was unfamiliar with. Ignore how much her leg hurt.

Sweat on her forehead chilled in the mountain air. Gabe twisted to the right and she was forced to follow or abandon him and end up lost. "Where are you leading us?"

"Away from the crazy sheriff." His breath was coming fast, just like hers. He wasn't as bulky as Liam but leaner and more toned, apparently from drinking tea and eating soy turkey of all things. He hadn't been a health nut years ago. Did he run too? It didn't seem like they shared much else in common.

Quit getting distracted.

Caisey glanced around. "Head back to the car."

"So he can shoot us? No way. We're going to the river. We can follow it back into town."

"You know I have a gun, right?"

"You wanna go back and shoot him? Be my guest. But I won't stick around to get shot too."

"You think he's going to shoot me? I can take him out before he even gets in range."

Gabe glanced back at her, his face twisted in a frown. "But he has a shotgun."

"That's exactly what I'm saying." She hissed the words. "Now can we please stop giving away our position by shouting at each other?"

The ATV was gaining. Its engine screamed, climbing the hill behind them. She liked the idea of high ground and scanned the area for somewhere to set up a covered position. There was nothing around them but trees, though she heard water running nearby. Weren't you always supposed to make for a river when you wanted to get out of the wilderness? That led you to a road, or something.

"We need to go east more." His words wouldn't penetrate. Was he still talking about the river?

The ATV engine revved. The trees broke and Gabe pulled up short in the clearing. Caisey bumped into him and his arms shot out to keep her from pushing them both forward—she looked around him—off a cliff?

"Are you kidding me?"

Caisey nearly pushed him over the edge, she was so mad. It was a dead end, which was what they were going to be in a minute. She couldn't see the bottom, and still knew she wasn't going over the edge. No way. This wasn't it for her. It couldn't be. She wouldn't let—

The ATV emerged from the trees behind them. Caisey spun. Gabe's hands settled on her waist and he pulled her close so he was tucked with his chest against her back. If she moved back at all, he'd be over the edge of the cliff.

This was crazy, but she kind of liked that what happened to one, happened to both of them. And there was no time to mull over how nice it felt, sort of right that they stood like that. Destiny wasn't going to matter much when they were dead.

Thanks a lot for leading us here, Gabe.

She looked down the length of her gun at the sheriff, finger on the trigger ready to squeeze. His hat was missing, hair mussed, and eyes wild. No shotgun.

"Did you kill Emma?" Caisey sucked in a breath. "Did you kill your niece?"

The ATV engine revved. The sheriff grinned. "Arturo's plan is fine. Mine's better."

Gabe's uncle?

Mud sprayed out the back as he gunned it forward. Caisey sidestepped to get out of his way, praying they could get clear of his aim. Gabe matched every step until they were practically running, but there wasn't enough space to make a break. He was too close. The ATV angled toward them.

He was going to hit them.

They were going to go over.

She fired two shots into the sheriff's coat at point blank range. The force jerked both her and Gabe back, but the ATV kept coming.

Gabe's arms tightened and then they were falling.

GABE HAULED Caisey up by her underarms, climbed the bank of the river, and laid her on the grass. He sat beside her and hung his head, sucking in cold air to get his breath back. The weight of the river soaking his clothes made him want to sink into the earth. He was so tired.

Water rushed by them. The torrent had swept them downstream before Gabe could even gather his thoughts enough to grab Caisey and try to make it to shore. The struggle for land had drained the strength from his muscles so that he shivered, dripping onto the dirt.

Caisey hadn't moved or even stirred. Had she swallowed water...or hit her head? She was breathing, but her skin was cold, as cold as he felt—like the water had cut through to his marrow. Gabe hauled her onto his lap, desperate for warmth. He ran his fingers over her head and brushed wet hair away. She was still out.

All around them were trees—the river and acres of pines that covered the mountains and stretched up on either side of the water like a giant 'V'. Gabe held her in his arms and looked up at the blue sky while his muscles shook. The sun shone enough to warm his skin, but it wasn't more than forty-five degrees. How long would they last out here, soaking wet?

The sheriff was dead. All he had to worry about was getting them out of there, as if that wasn't enough by itself.

God, I don't even know if I have the energy to walk.

He shifted her and got his feet under him. With Caisey draped in his arms, Gabe kept his focus on putting one foot in front of the other. And again. And again. So long as he followed the path by the river they would eventually get somewhere. They were alive. What more did they need? Well, probably medical attention and blankets. A latte would be nice, and a veggie burger.

A squirrel skittered through the undergrowth to his left and up a tree trunk. The sound was like the clatter of pans in a silent kitchen. Gabe blinked at the disturbance and started walking again. His head swam. Caisey needed to wake up. He wouldn't be able to carry her much longer. Wouldn't be...

Couldn't...

He stumbled and went down on one knee. Pain shot up to his hip and he cried out. Caisey moaned, her head rolled, and she muttered something. The words smoothed from their jumble and she murmured about a blade. She shifted on his knee and started to push away from him. Gabe tightened his hold, but it only made her push harder until she was struggling to get free.

"Caisey, what?"

Her eyes flew open and she screamed. The sound echoed around the canyon until he thought she might set off a landslide.

Gabe set her down fast—probably too fast—and scrambled away. She sucked in a breath and the screaming stopped.

Before she could start again, he lifted his hands. "It's okay, you're okay. Caisey, you're fine." He took a breath to get himself to stop talking.

Caisey reached for the holster on her hip but it was empty. Her eyes were still wide and bright, like she wasn't thinking clearly. Well, neither was he. All he could think about was getting out of there.

"Caisey, it's me. Gabe." He crawled to her and reached out, but she flinched. "It's okay. I'm not going to hurt you. You're safe."

Her lip quivered and tears filled her eyes. Before Gabe could do anything, she took a deep breath and burst into sobs so fierce they shuddered through her. Once again he gathered her to him, stroked her back and tried to figure out what to say.

It took a while, but eventually she calmed down.

She rubbed her leg, as though massaging a knot in the muscle. Did she pull it?

"I-I shot...the sheriff."

Gabe couldn't help it. He had no idea why it was funny, but he started laughing. "But you didn't shoot the deputy?"

"What?" She leaned back and looked up at him. "Why are you laughing at me?"

"It's a song."

She shoved his shoulder and scooted off his lap. "Is this really the time to start joking, when I'm upset? And...and I was being serious."

She'd spoken so fast he couldn't even process her words. "Why is your accent all weird?"

Caisey rolled her eyes and winced. "Ouch. I must have bumped my head." She reached up and touched her temple. Apparently she wasn't going to explain why she suddenly sounded British. It took him a moment for his brain to catch up, but he remembered about her Grams.

Gabe reached over and picked out the bit of leaf that was stuck in her hair. "I'm surprised you can be coherent, actually. Do you feel okay?"

"I'm soaking wet in the middle of nowhere and you're asking me if I feel okay? Maybe you're the one who hit your head."

Gabe took a cleansing breath. "We should get moving if you think you're up to it."

Caisey wobbled to her feet. "Lead the way, my man. And I shall follow thee, wherever thou shall goest—"

She cleared her throat. "Sorry. I think my brain might be rebooting."

He glanced over at her. She was still pale, which couldn't be good when you were blushing. Gabe took her hand and they walked together along the bank of the river. "Headache?"

She scrunched up her nose, which he took to mean she did. He'd wanted her to stay in Buckshot longer so they could have more time together, but not this way. Now the sheriff was dead, Emma was still missing and they were miles from a phone.

Gabe scanned the steep ravine walls and tried to get his bearings. He needed to get them out of there, but had to admit that holding her hand was nice, even if her fingers were like ice. Walking by her was nice too, as was being the man who would get her back safely to her family.

It was a dream to want her to stay, but just for a little while he was content to pretend they were somewhere else. She was undoubtedly spoken for, but Gabe was going to give himself this gift before he had to watch her walk away. They could be anyone, or just a couple out hiking. Bound together by more than one date and seventeen years of nothing but the dream of a memory.

Caisey blinked up at the sky. "I'm hungry. What time is it?"

SIXTEEN

"Buckshot sheriff's office." The voice was gruff, more like a bartender than a police receptionist.

"This is Special Agent Liam Conners. I'm looking for my partner, Special Agent Lyons."

"Liam, you say? I'm Big Al."

Liam scanned the trees, the house. "Is Caisey there?"

"She left to take Gabe home. He was going to show her his computer so he can prove he did nothing to poor Emma, Lord help her."

"Thanks, Big Al. If you hear from her, tell her the Sheriff left his house. It's possible he's headed her way."

"Will do."

Liam hung up and called Caisey again, just for good measure. No answer, probably poor signal, so he drove toward Gabe's cabin... Caisey's dad's cabin. He didn't know what to call it. Probably Gabe's, since Samuel was gone and the other man had been living there for years.

He was at the bottom of the mountain on the north side of town, about to take the turn that led up to the cabin when his phone rang again. It wasn't Andrea. He really needed to call her.

"Special Agent Conners."

"Yeah, it's Big Al again. Listen, no one else is responding and we got a call-in. I wouldn't bother you, but it sounds like it might have to do with Emma."

Liam pulled over to the roadside, but left the engine running. "What is it?"

"A hiker called in just after you. He's up by Lyre's Bluff and he found something. Babs said he was screaming and carrying on, something about a dead girl in the bushes."

"Give me an address, I'll check it out." Liam entered the details into his GPS. "You said no one else is responding?"

"Sheriff's off the radar, Bud was issuing a traffic ticket over on the other side of town. Said it was too far to drive over when it's probably just a prank."

"Right." Liam supposed dead bodies didn't turn up in small towns very often, but that didn't mean a call about one should be dismissed. "I'll take it."

"I'll pray it's not Emily."

"Thanks, Big Al."

Except if it wasn't Emily then that meant someone else was dead. The thought carried him through the turns to the base of a hiking trail.

At the post marker was an older man who looked like he could pull off a marathon at any time. No taller than Liam, he had muscle but not bulk. He had on the fitted pants and shirt runners wore that wicked away sweat and muddy trail running shoes. An orange beanie was rolled up at the bottom to sit above his ears so that gray hair peeked out underneath.

"You're the one who called the sheriff's department."

The man rolled his dull blue eyes, dark enough they might even be gray like his hair. "For all the good it did. Who're you?"

"Special Agent Liam Conners, FBI."

His eyes widened. "I take it back. Someone isn't messing around." He stuck his hand out. "Charles Timson."

Liam nodded. "Walk me to where you found the body."

The hike was a mile and pure uphill. Liam was sweating by the time they got there, having maintained the older man's punishing pace while asking him questions about what happened as they walked.

Local man, retired, a widower who ran marathons for a Denver children's hospital. Didn't know the sheriff's niece was missing and wouldn't be able to point her out if he saw her in town. They stopped a ways away, but Liam saw the female hand—fingernails tipped with pink polish—up to the elbow stuck out between two bushes. Liam got out his phone.

He really did not like dead bodies.

JENNA WAS STILL DRESSED in her skirt and blouse from work. She pushed open the double doors of the Westman building on South Street just after eight; an hour before she had to pick up Jake from youth group.

Her father's office was on the fourth floor, west corner. She'd checked online, but made a point not to look at his picture or the nice things people who didn't know him had to say. Her heels clicked the marble floor of the lobby, lit by the glow of yellow bulbs instead of those white fluorescents that were so garish. The plants were plastic, and the counter was a speckled slab of granite that blended with the color scheme and accented nothing.

She squeezed the strap of her purse and tried to smile. The security guard glanced up from his e-reader and barely nodded, even though Jenna could have been anyone. She strode to the elevator and jabbed the button. Sixteen years and all of a sudden he called? Where did he get off, barging into her life? Like throwing her out didn't mean anything, and he could just sweep it all under the rug with a conversation.

Well, Jake didn't need that in his life. And Jenna was going to make sure her dad understood that.

The elevator took forever to get to the fourth floor. She stood in the middle, tapped her foot and didn't look at her reflection in the window. Who wanted to know what those extra fifteen pounds looked like? Of course, her mom had seen it. Jenna knew when she looked her up and down and her lip curled. No one needed to be told over and over they were doing everything wrong. Where was the fun in being beauty pageant stick-thin, anyway? She kind of liked the extra volume Jake had blessed her with. Caisey said it made her look human.

The elevator door opened. Jenna adjusted the strap of her purse on her shoulder. The carpet muffled her heels all the way to the corner office at the end of the hall, and the whole place smelled like potpourri. No one was around, probably because it was late and they likely enjoyed her father's company about as much as Jenna did.

The memory of sitting on his office floor playing with her ponies popped back into her head.

Jenna blew out a breath. Anger might be justified, but maybe she really needed to get over this and stop being the hurt little girl who wanted her daddy. Life had dealt her that card, and then she'd watched it go up in flames. In the end it was Caisey's dad, Samuel, who told her father that he was never to call again.

And yet her heart couldn't release the image of when her dad stopped talking to the man in her office and turned to her. She was maybe six or seven, and for the first time in her life she'd seen her dad afraid. For her or for him, it didn't matter. Suddenly he was human. She remembered the plastic horse fell from her hand and hit her leg. The man must have been someone serious to make her dad afraid. But when she asked him, he told her not to worry about it. He'd never figured out that Jenna worried about everything.

The door at the end of the hall was open, making the light slash across the carpet. She could do this. She could stand on her own two feet. Jake might have been right that calling her dad back wasn't going to do any good. But looking him in the eye and telling him what she thought of him contacting her out of the blue—that meant something to her. Almost as much as how proud of her Caisey would be when she told her.

"You haven't mentioned it yet?"

Her father's voice, the voice of former Congressman Alan Cartwright, made Jenna's heel catch on the carpet. Okay, so maybe this wasn't going to be as easy as she thought. But she was still going to do it, even if it meant interrupting his conversation.

"Everything is in place. As soon as I explain, he'll come on board quickly and there will be no time for your vacillations. There's nothing to worry about, Alan. Stress isn't good for your heart."

Jenna couldn't place the voice...but she'd heard it before. She paused in the hallway.

"Interesting how that could be construed as a threat, Holden. One I do not appreciate coming from the likes of you."

Holden? It seemed that, after so many years, her father had found his courage in the face of the man who made him afraid.

The familiar voice chuckled, low and deep. "The likes of me... that is rich, especially since there is little difference between us, Congressman, to distinguish us on judgment day. But that is for then, and for right now all you must do is precisely what I have told you. Do you understand?"

There was a brief silence, broken by the tinkle of ice against a glass.

"I understand."

"I will leave you to it then." The familiar voice paused. "I'm trusting in your part."

"In my name, you mean." Her dad's voice wavered at the end.

"That is true. Your assistance in this matter will be invaluable. I cannot set my son on the right path otherwise. His co-operation will ensure our success, both mine and yours." He chuckled again. "Heaven forbid you hide in this office the rest of your days, wasting your life on philanthropy until you've used up all your resources for the sake of avoiding your wife's company."

He stepped out of the office and Jenna swallowed a gasp.

Nic's father.

Apparently even after all these years he was still plaguing their family. Making her father do something he wasn't happy about and insulting him. The man's silver eyes narrowed the way they had when he faced off with her on his doorstep. Right before he threatened to set his dogs on her. When he walked away, it was with a low chuckle that said he didn't think much of her father...or her. Did he even know who she was?

Jenna straightened her shoulders and knocked on her father's door. When she peered in, he was sipping the dregs of a short glass that now held only ice cubes. He placed the crystal cup on a coaster and stared at her with eyes that shimmered, unfocused. His shirt was rumpled, the sleeves rolled back with no consideration for neatness. His red silk tie had been loosened and his hair bore more gray than in the picture she'd seen in the paper five years ago when he announced his retirement. And yet, here he was.

"Hello, Dad."

His lips curved up, then fell back to despondency. "I'm hallucinating."

"If you were, I'd think you could imagine something better to think about than me showing up in your office."

"Not that's what I want to see the most."

Jenna's grip on the strap of her purse tightened. "I live four miles from here and you've had seventeen years. Why call now? Was it because Mom came into my spa and made a scene?" She took a breath. "Did you call out of guilt, or because you agree with her?"

Her dad sighed, a long sound that seemed to bleed years of weariness from his shoulders. "Agree with her...yes, I can see how you might think that."

"Might?"

"Too much time has passed. You think I'm going to fall on your feet and plead, explain how I never agreed with her to begin with? You've always reacted quickly, just like your mother. The two of you were a powder keg of emotions that exploded whenever and wherever you disagreed. A restaurant, a charity function."

Jenna could have thrown up right there. "I'm nothing like her. I can't believe you of all people could say that about me. I always tried to measure up to her standards and it was never good enough."

"So you found it necessary to do the worst possible thing you could think of and show the world exactly what kind of girl you are."

He might have said the words, but Jenna heard her mother's voice. Despite any feelings to the contrary, years of indoctrination had apparently brought him around to her mother's way of thinking. It really was a shame that her father couldn't seem to think for himself. They might have been able to salvage something of the relationship they had shared years ago.

"Jenna. I'm sorry—"

"No, you're not."

Her phone rang. She dug it from her purse as she walked down the hall, away from the man who was supposed to have taken care of her. No wonder she hadn't been able to get Nic to stay and support her through having Jake if this was the legacy she knew.

Her son's number flashed on screen.

"Hey, honey."

"Mom, you'll never guess who showed up at youth group. We're all going to the coffee shop on Third. Can I go, Mom? Please?"

Jenna grinned. "What's her name?"

There was an outburst of rustling. Jenna pulled the phone from her ear until Jake was done doing...whatever it was he was doing. Then he whispered, "Her name is Natalia, mom. She's in my English class and I wanted to invite her a bunch of times, and then tonight she showed up. How awesome is that?"

"Pretty awesome." Jenna punched the elevator button, giving one last glance to the office at the end of the hall. "Listen, just call me when you're done and I'll come get you. Okay?"

"Thanks mom you're the best."

Jenna hung up the phone, smiling for the first time all day. She would have to make sure to arrive at the coffee shop early and get a look at this Natalia, see for herself who had caught her son's eye. Maybe between them they could heal the next generation. Someone had to have the chance to live a full and happy life with the person they loved.

Because it certainly hadn't happened to Jenna.

SEVENTEEN

Liam kept his eyes on the ground as he walked in circles that got wider the further he was from the body. He was sure now this wasn't the work of the Chloroform Killer. There were too many tiny details that didn't add up to a controlled execution. For starters, the victim had defensive wounds on her hands and forearms. Still, someone had gone to a lot of trouble to make it look like the real deal and it would seem they knew several details that had been in the files only, never released to public knowledge.

In the past hour he'd added to his list of dislikes. The first was dead bodies. Particularly ones that looked way too much like finding his sister in the bath. He didn't need extra help to remind him of that day when he was fifteen and found his eighteen year old sister had killed herself and flooded the bathroom with red water.

Number two was bugs. It didn't matter what kind, not when you had to collect them as samples so some lab person could give you back a piece of paper that told you what you already knew: she'd been dead awhile.

He sighed and kept walking, eyes on the ground while Canadian geese flew overhead. *Thank you, Lord.* Life continued on, just like his after he found his sister. Her death rocked the foundation of his family. Liam had made his own way since then, until his father contacted him during Andrea's ordeal and they finally got a start repairing their relationship.

Liam's boots sank into the damp earth, the booties covering his shoes now coated with mud. At least he'd left his dress shoes in the car. Not that he'd forget after the first time when Caisey out right laughed at the dirt covering his loafers. It didn't matter that he'd never been an outdoors type of guy. What was her problem with tennis, anyway?

After the hiker who found the girl's body had stopped sputtering, Liam got more details. The older man had been released a couple of hours ago after two Buckshot police officers arrived, walking away saying something about his RV being unattended.

One officer held the log book at the fork in the path where the hiker got lost and the other had taken yet more pictures, assisting Liam in collecting evidence. Not that there was much to find when all that was out here was dirt and trees. Leaves and twigs. Not much could explain why a beautiful teen girl was lying discarded in the brush like something less than precious.

The sun cast long shadows between the branches. Liam flipped on his flashlight. The county's Medical Examiner was with the body, making observations and doing all that poking and prodding stuff that turned Liam's stomach. He kept walking, circling the area around the body until he found black material—a backpack—and crouched in the underbrush.

The marker had been placed, the photos taken and the sketch noted, and he was just about to take a look at what he'd found, when his phone rang.

"Conners."

"It's Burkot. The state patrol officers are on their way to you. Should be there in a few hours."

Liam squeezed the back of his neck. "I thought I'd be here for weeks working this case."

Burkot chuckled. "It's who you know."

"The Governor?"

"That and the Lieutenant Colonel of that region of State Patrol plays golf with my brother. You're welcome, by the way."

Liam blew out a breath. "Just so long as someone comes to take over this investigation from me, because there's no way the sheriff can oversee this when it's his niece." He wasn't going to add that the deputies were also suspect since they worked for the sheriff. Not when they were within earshot.

"You're sure it's the sheriff's niece, then?"

Liam scratched the back of his neck. "The officers made a visual identification of the body as Emma Allens."

"Cause of death?"

"Multiple wounds on her chest consistent with a blade, defensive wounds on her wrists and arms and she looks like she's been beaten. We're working this as a murder until the ME confirms it." Liam rubbed a hand down his face. "Any update on the Chloroform Killer?"

"The team has been re-tasked to other leads. Your job is this dead girl until the troopers take over, and then you and Special Agent Lyons need to get on home."

Liam squeezed his hand into a fist. "If I can find her."

"What was that?"

"Nothing, sir. I'll keep you posted." He'd tell Burkot when there was something to tell. They didn't need a manhunt for Caisey if nothing was wrong.

Liam hung up and dialed Caisey again. No answer. Again.

He didn't want to believe anything bad had happened, not so soon after she'd been abducted, and especially not when her coming here should have been uneventful. The idea that the Chloroform Killer could have got his hands on her again made him want to rage, but that wouldn't help. Not to mention he'd probably step on something important.

Liam called the Buckshot police department and Big Al answered. Liam looked at the smoky colored sky and shook his head. "You're still there? I thought you'd be long gone by now."

"I would be, but all these people showed up. All hopping about Emma's body having been found, aren't they? Wanting to come up and see for themselves. But I'm keeping them here working on stuff like you said."

"I appreciate that. Listen, have you heard from my partner? I can't get through to her cell phone from here and it's been hours."

"You know—" Big Al paused. "Now that you mention it, I haven't seen her. She never came back after she took Gabe Thompson to his cabin. I wonder what happened."

Liam wasn't getting a good feeling about this at all. *God, where is she?* "And the Sheriff?

Have you seen him?"

"Not since he was here with Agent Lyons earlier."

"Right." Liam wanted to kick the nearest tree. He couldn't leave the scene until the body had been removed and all the evidence was collected. Caisey had better not be in trouble or he was going to get seriously ticked off. "If either of them show up...call me."

"Will do, boss."

"Don't call me boss." Liam hung up and pulled the backpack from the undergrowth. The ME had Emma Allens in a body bag and the sound of that heavy zipper being pulled up was like a gavel, or a gong that marked the period at the end of a person's life. Here in the forest, the noise was deafening.

Liam straightened and called across the clearing. "Can I get an evidence bag big enough for this?"

Officer Samantha Kurter, the former marine, looked where his flashlight pointed and saw what he'd seen. "Yes, sir."

"Don't call me sir." Liam rolled his shoulders, trying to stretch out the tension of being on his feet and staring at the ground for hours. He needed to call Andrea back. At this rate, by the time he returned the call she'd be busy again. He glanced at his watch. *Or sleeping.*

Officer Kurter picked her way to him with a brown bag and a thermos. She was big boned, but wore it in a way that made her look strong and not just solid. She was not someone you picked a fight with. Or hit on. You were probably liable to get punched in both cases.

After the backpack was sealed in the bag, she held out the thermos. "Why don't you take this to the trail? It's cream of chicken soup."

"Thanks. I was expecting coffee, but this is great."

Officer Kurter shrugged. "It's an old habit, since caffeine doesn't do me any favors."

"You don't happen to have a grilled cheese sandwich to go with it?"

"You wish."

"Yes, I do." Liam said grace over a cup of soup on a mountainside in backwoods Colorado. It wasn't steak and a cloth napkin, but that was the job.

He went by Gabe's cabin on the way back to the sheriff's office, but the place was dark. The door was open and everything had been tossed. What on earth had happened there? Caisey was MIA and a shotgun blast had hit more than one spot in Gabe's house. He called Big Al and had an officer dispatched to the scene. He needed to find his partner and Gabe.

It was after ten when he pulled up outside the sheriff's office. His limbs felt like mush, but he dragged his butt inside. Big Al took one look at him and poured him a cup of coffee. Liam took a sip. It was hot enough to burn his tongue and strong enough he'd be wide awake in thirty seconds. "Agent Lyons hasn't been here?"

Big Al folded his massive arms across his chest, stretching his faded Harley t-shirt. "Nope."

"Spread the word to all the officers you have working. I want a call the minute anyone sees either Agent Lyons or Gabe Thompson."

"You think something happened?"

Liam set the mug on the nearest desk, aware he was the center of attention. "I also want a location on Agent Lyons' cell phone. Find Thompson's cell number too, because I want the same on that."

"You think something happened."

Liam didn't miss a beat. "I also want to know where Sheriff Allens is."

The last time Liam saw the man he'd been leaving his house with a shotgun and now Caisey was missing? Liam didn't like this at all. What had the sheriff done?

"But—" A male officer stepped forward.

Liam lifted his hand. "Regardless of his standing in this town, until further notice Frank Allens is a suspect in the murder of his niece and I want him brought in."

The phone rang and Big Al crossed to the front desk to answer it. Liam sucked down the rest of his coffee and glanced at the door. Caisey had been gone for hours.

He didn't like this. He didn't like it at all.

"I've got them."

Liam looked up. Big Al was grinning. "Steve, the tow truck driver from the garage, was on his way back from dropping someone home who got too sloshed at Pete's bar. Says he was flagged down two miles outside of town by Thompson and Agent Lyons. They're soaking wet, but he's bringing them in right now."

CAISEY WAS in the big chair behind Sheriff Allens' desk, eating one of the cheeseburgers someone had picked up from Pete's bar for everyone. The bread was a little stale, but the thickness of the patty and the amount of cheese made up for it.

"Hungry much?"

"You should be thankful Pete's kitchen was still open or I'd be gnawing on your hand."

Liam sighed. "Thanks, I'm done with my burger now."

"Hand it over then." Not that she would eat it, or that he would give it up, but she wasn't going to let an opportunity for extended banter pass by unacknowledged. Batting retorts back and forth with Liam chased away the shadows. Caisey ignored the look on her partner's face and took another bite. For the first time that day she actually felt warm, even if Officer Kurter's workout clothes were for someone nearly a foot taller than Caisey.

"Are you ready?"

Caisey nodded.

"Here—" Liam set Caisey's over-the-counter pain meds on the sheriff's desk between them. "Since you have something in your stomach now, and I know you won't take the hard stuff."

"Thanks."

"How bad is your leg hurting?"

Caisey leaned back in the chair and closed her eyes. She wasn't going to tell him her head hurt now, too. "Worse than a black eye, not as bad as being stabbed in the first place."

"Sure about that? A quick trip to the medical center probably isn't a bad idea."

"I'll see how the night goes."

Liam tugged the desk phone around. He hit speakerphone and dialed the number so fast Caisey's ears blurred the beeps together into a muddle.

"Burkot."

"Yes, sir. I'm here with Special Agent Lyons."

"Go ahead."

Caisey took a deep breath. "I accompanied Gabe Thompson back to his residence, my father's cabin. There I conversed with a friend of his via Skype. The friend—Mitch something, I'll have to check on that—confirmed he had spoken with Gabe at the time Emma Allens disappeared. And I checked the call log on his Skype. Four-fifteen to four fifty- five."

Liam shifted in his chair. "The Medical Examiner put the time of death as between four p.m. and six p.m. which doesn't completely absolve Mr. Thompson. It's still possible that Gabe caught up with Emma, killed her and disposed of her body in the woods. There are officers processing the mess at the cabin as we speak."

He nodded to Caisey and she told them about the sheriff's arrival and his pursuit of her and Gabe. When she described how she'd used deadly force, her voice broke. Then she told them about falling over the edge of the ravine, regaining consciousness on the bank of the river, and how she and Gabe walked six miles to find a road. Liam's face paled. Burkot must have heard the regret in her voice, because he started going on about every law enforcement agent who'd faced aggressive force from a dirty cop, and how she needed to take comfort in the fact it was justified.

Caisey stared at her fingers, clenched together on the desk. Gabe had been carrying her when she came around. She could still feel the rhythm of his steps, just as wet and cold as she had been and he'd still done it. After she freaked out, he'd touched her. So gently she could still see the look of kindness in his eyes. Like she was someone he cared for. Then he'd held her hand while she clung to his warmth until it filled her and she didn't shiver quite so much. He'd never complained, just led her out at the pace she set, content to let her be quiet instead of pestering her with questions about how she was doing.

The young man she'd gone out with all those years ago had grown into a dream of what could have been. The man she was coming to know now was strong and confident. He didn't push, but allowed her to be who she was. It was too bad she would eventually go back to Denver and he'd get on with his life here. She wouldn't have a reason to visit her dad's cabin.

EIGHTEEN

Liam pinched her finger and gave her a look that said, *focus*. Caisey glared, but his attention was on the call. "I'll contact the Medical Examiner and tell him to clear his morning. We'll head out with a search party and locate the sheriff's body first thing."

"Good deal." Someone on Burkot's end said something. The line went quiet, and then he came back on. "Gotta run. Liam get this wrapped up and get back."

Caisey was fine with that. Life could go back to normal instead of her living in this wonky world where nothing made sense. Why else would the Chloroform Killer have left her alive?

Then they'd shown up here right after the sheriff—maybe—killed his niece. The timing had been perfect to help Gabe, so he didn't get arrested for murder. Had God brought them here for exactly that? She'd believe it if the sheriff hadn't tried to kill them too. Had he snapped and suffered a psychotic break? Or had he been cracked before he killed his niece? It would certainly explain why some people killed the ones they were supposed to protect.

What was it the sheriff said right before they went over the edge?

Burkot chimed in again. "Get some rest, Agent Lyons. You're supposed to be on vacation." He hung up.

Liam pushed the phone back into place and eyed her. "We should figure out where we're going to stay tonight. I can have Big Al call the inn and see if there are a couple of rooms, if you want."

A full night of sleep would be good. She set the rest of the burger down, willing to admit there was no way she could possibly finish it all. Her gaze drifted up to Liam. He was staring at her, so she glared right back. Was he trying to read her? He should know by now that didn't work. "What?"

His eyes narrowed. "You want to tell me how you're really doing? You had an ordeal and you spent the whole day with your dream man and you're both still in one piece. Mostly. Talk to me, Case."

She wasn't even on the same planet as being up to firing back over that crack about her dream man. "I'm okay."

Liam threw up his hands.

"I am. It wasn't fun, but I'm here, aren't I? Gabe and I got out of there in one piece, like you said. I could've done without waking up and thinking he was a serial killer for a second. But when I saw the sun and really looked at him, I realized it was Gabe—"

"Sparks—"

"As opposed to being back in that mine? Sure, I'll take that any day of the week, even if romantic relationships aren't exactly my strong suit."

Liam had the good grace to cover his snort.

Caisey folded her arms. "How about you?"

She paused before she snapped at him about his sister, long enough that her brain caught up with her mouth. *Thank you, God.* That wouldn't be something Liam would appreciate, for all the compassion in the intention. If she fluffed up the delivery, it would only make it worse.

"You spent all afternoon and evening with the body of a dead teenage girl. It must have brought up some not so pleasant memories for you. How are you doing?"

His face softened. "I don't think I'll ever see something like that and not remember finding my sister."

Caisey knew how much it took for him to act like he was okay.

What she didn't know was if it was healing or he was still pretending it didn't bother him. Becoming a Christian had smoothed out so much of what set Liam's emotions all over the place and made it easier for him to do his job and be detached. Now all Caisey had to do was figure out how to get her faith to do the same for her, when so much still surfaced.

Being with Gabe sent her back to being captured by the Chloroform Killer, which had in turn jolted her back to being seventeen and being abducted—she hated that word. Just one day she'd like to wake up and not remember any of it. A clean slate. That's what she wanted most of all, to step forward and not have the sum of the past in her head all the time.

"You look like you're drifting off."

"Let's get this wrapped up so we can find beds." Caisey stood and stretched. "My car is still at Gabe's."

"I hope Big Al can find us something, because I really don't want to bunk downstairs in the cells."

She grinned. "It could be fun. Like camping, but for drunks you don't want to drive home."

Liam shook his head. "You've always had a warped sense of humor."

They stepped out of the Sheriff's office into the main room of the station. Uniformed sheriff's deputies stood around with Big Al and Babs, their attention on the two FBI agents who had—in a single day—disrupted their lives and killed their sheriff.

Gabe was dipping French fries into ketchup, his focus solely on his meal, which Caisey was grateful for. She still wanted to ask God why. Why after all these years of being hung up on a guy did she suddenly find him again if she was just going to go back to her life?

What was the point? God wasn't in the business of poking his children like a kid with a stick in an ant hill. If this was her one chance at claiming happiness for herself she was doing a lousy job of it. Serial killers and homicidal cops didn't make for good date material. But she honestly didn't know what did.

Liam nudged her. "You're staring at him."

~

GABE SAW her face and wondered what her partner said to her. He got that their job meant they had a close relationship, and it was clear from the way they interacted that they understood each other well, so what did it mean? If he and Caisey ever came to some kind of understanding, would Gabe always wonder in the back of his mind if something was going on between her and Liam?

He closed the container on the last few fries he didn't need and tossed it in the trash.

Why couldn't he just have a normal relationship where he got to know a woman and gradually fell for her? It had to be better than this paralyzing condition that meant he hadn't been able to get close to anyone in all the years since the date with Caisey. He should probably call Becka tomorrow, or stop by the diner and tell her they should probably call off their date.

Speaking of Becka.

Gabe made his way past officers milling around and through the divide in the counter. Becka was at the front door, wide-eyed at all the activity in the room. He didn't blame her. It was like every sworn-in cop in the county was here.

"Hey."

She gave him a small smile, one that made him inexplicably sad. She was a nice girl, the timing was just bad. Gabe had thought he was free to explore a relationship with a cute, home-town girl who would be enjoyable company.

Concern furrowed her brow. "Are you okay?" She looked tired, probably from being on her feet at the diner all day. And yet she had come here, ostensibly to check on him. "I heard the sheriff brought you in for questioning about Emma's disappearance. Then I heard you were missing."

Gabe touched her arm. "It's been a long day, but I'm all right."

He let his hand drop and she saw it, but he couldn't help that his heart had always been all about Caisey, even if she was probably taken. That one date had been a measuring rod against which he set every woman he saw. And when he looked at Becka, there was nothing there but pleasant feelings. There was just no...*what was that word?* Whatever it was, it was glaringly obvious now that it was missing.

Gabe looked back over his shoulder. Caisey's eyes were on him and Becka, and he thought he saw a flash of something there that made him want to smile.

"Who is that?"

Gabe turned back to Becka. "It's complicated."

"I see that." Becka bit her lip. "When the big-shot FBI agent leaves, why don't you give me a call?"

"Becka—"

"I'm not going to lie and say its fine, Gabe, because it isn't. But I get it."

Gabe opened his big idiot mouth to apologize, but she was halfway out the door. At the last second Becka turned back to give him a sad look. "Maybe I'll see you around."

Big Al shook his head, like Gabe disappointed him, but he didn't understand about Caisey. Gabe didn't even understand it himself; he just knew his heart refused to listen to what his head thought was the most sensible course of action.

Gabe strode to where Caisey and Liam stood talking to a female officer. "Do I need to stay, or is there someone who can give me a ride home?"

Caisey nodded. "You don't have to stay, but—"

"Your cabin was trashed." Agent Conners was taller than Gabe and clean cut. Even though it was late, he still looked like the all-American kid who grew up to be a cop and not a lawyer only because he wanted to carry a gun for a living. "It's not exactly livable, but I can take you to get some stuff if you want to get a room in town."

"And my computer?" Gabe saw the look on the man's face. "Look, Agent Conners—"

"Liam is fine."

"If my computer is gone, there's not much point going back there at all." Gabe blew out a breath. "It's a good thing I back everything up online, or I'd be totally lost."

Caisey moved between them. "Liam, you wanna give me your keys and I'll take Gabe to get a change of clothes?"

Agent Conners frowned. "You sure about that?"

Gabe didn't even want to know what they were talking about, at least not since Caisey immediately lifted her chin and went into a stare-down with her partner. "I'm sure."

Liam sighed and gave her a set of keys from his pocket. "We're still going to have to pick up your car at some point."

"Tomorrow will be fine. I'll go with Gabe now and come straight back, mom."

"Case—"

"It'll be fine. That coffee gave me a second wind and I can grab my duffel while I'm there. Chill, okay? I won't do anything you wouldn't do in my place."

Agent Liam Conners clearly knew something Gabe didn't, since he glanced between Gabe and Caisey. Did he have a problem with them being together? Gabe had figured she was spoken for, but by her partner? He didn't know if the FBI allowed that.

Maybe it was just friendly concern, since Gabe was the unknown component. But whether or not they were, or ever had been, in a relationship that was more than partners and friends, Liam seemed to think he had a say over what she did. That could be good for Gabe, or it could be really bad.

The door flung open and two uniformed Colorado State Patrol officers sauntered in. One was older and his hat was askew, showing off silver hair that matched his handlebar mustache. The other was in his twenties and had a rough beard.

The first one pulled a toothpick from his mouth. "We'll take it from here, folks."

NINETEEN

"You say sheriff Allens is dead?"

Caisey nodded. She was in the front seat of the state patrol car while Gabe rode in the back. "I appreciate you giving Mr. Thompson and I a ride back to his place. I left my car there earlier and after the day I've had I just couldn't face waiting for my partner to sort himself out."

Her leg had started to throb again and her muscles all felt like jelly, but she shot the cop a smile. "You know what I mean?"

He nodded, like she was the little woman he needed to placate. "It's no bother at all, ma'am, just doing my duty for a fellow law officer."

Caisey nodded herself, seizing the opportunity to study the man. "Long drive?"

He shrugged. "Couple hours."

"You like working this region?"

"Sure." He shrugged again, like that was his default response. "I like the mountains."

Except this was Colorado and you didn't need to come west of Denver just to see mountains. He must not have worked for the state patrol long if he didn't even know that. Maybe the younger officer had been with them longer. That guy had stayed behind at the sheriff's office with Liam to get the run down on the case.

On the surface they were doing everything they should be, but still. Caisey couldn't quit the idea that something was...off with these guys. What it was, she couldn't put her finger on.

She glanced back at Gabe in the backseat. "You fall asleep yet?"

A low chuckle emerged from his throat. "Just about. I think I lost my second wind. What time is it, anyway?"

"Almost two."

"Seriously? I don't think I've stayed up this late since college."

Caisey laughed. "Those wild days of youth?"

"More like all-nighters studying."

"Ah, the studious type."

"That's me. Nerd to the core." He paused. "But there was this one time. I had this date that lasted all night." His voice was wistful, now.

Caisey pressed her lips together so she didn't grin like an idiot. He might be a nerd, but he filled out the shoulders of his t-shirt nicely. The glasses he'd been wearing before they jumped in the ravine suited his face. A face that was older now, but what drew her to him was still there. His intelligence made him seem so solid, deep like he saw underneath what was on the surface.

She smiled. Their date-night conversation had covered everything from the views they shared and what they didn't agree on, to their hopes for the future. "Do you have another pair of glasses at home?"

"Somewhere. I can see enough without them, but I shouldn't drive unless I can find my spare." He blew out a breath. "I think I know where I put them."

The State Patrol officer glanced in the rearview. Was he concerned about Gabe?

Caisey studied the officer again. "What did you say your name was?"

"Bill Peters."

"And how long have you been a trooper with this fine state?"

"Eons now, or so it feels."

Caisey smiled. "I know what you mean."

"You've been with the FBI a while?"

She nodded. "Coming up on six years. My dad was an agent too, shot in the line of duty four years ago. The Bureau was everything to him."

It hurt to say, but it was the truth. Her dad had been more concerned about whatever case he was working than anything else. Then when Caisey got hurt, it seemed like he withdrew even more into his job, bound and determined to keep the two separate. Sure, it was an honorable pursuit in life to uphold the law; too bad it seemed to come at the expense of a personal life, and of love. It had cost her a family that was hers alone, as much as she loved the makeshift one she'd built. Belonging to people who loved her without question was everything that made this world worthwhile outside of her faith.

And yet what she really wanted was out of reach, like trying to catch a snowflake.

She focused on the cop again. "That's why I can't stand people who take the responsibility of this job for granted."

"Take a right just up here."

The patrol vehicle made it up the mountain at a caterpillar's crawl. Caisey had never been so relieved to see her car in her life. Home was good; her own pillow, even better. She slammed the door and blew out a breath. The car's headlights lit up the cabin, which looked intact except from the broken front door that had been shattered by the blast of the sheriff's shotgun.

Gabe got out and came to stand beside her. "Are you sure you're okay to drive? We can crash here tonight instead of heading back out, if you want. I'll take the couch...if it's still in one piece."

Caisey squeezed his elbow. "That's sweet."

Gabe gave her a jaunty smile. "That's me, Mr. Sweet."

Caisey chuckled and walked with him to the cabin. Apparently the trooper was going to watch them go inside. She looked back at the vehicle, but couldn't see anything beyond the blinding brightness of his high-beams. Caisey lifted a hand in thanks, stepped over debris and went inside.

"I love what you've done with the place."

Gabe groaned. "I doubt it's even livable now." He flipped on the light. The floor was a smorgasbord of papers, torn up books, and leaves. The computer screen was completely shattered.

He ran his hands through his hair. "This is unbelievable. I get hauled into the sheriff's office for questioning about Emma's disappearance, now she's a murder victim and the sheriff tried to kill us? My home is completely wrecked, and for what? I can't live here now and all my work has been destroyed."

Sure enough, the tower had been shot through. "Do you want the facts, or a consolation speech? You said you backed-up online."

Gabe blinked. "What?"

"Do you want me to tell you the sheriff probably murdered his niece and tried to pin it on you because he doesn't like you, or for whatever other reason? He even tried to make it look like you're the Chloroform Killer. Guess he didn't figure Liam and I would show up ahead of a team of FBI agents and not just take his word for it. So the sheriff has to scrap his plan in favor of a new plan, which happened to involve yet another homicidal episode."

Something niggled at the edge of her thoughts, only she couldn't pin-point what it was. "Or I could tell you that your stuff was an extension of the person you are and you'll need time to honestly grieve its loss. But it's only for a season, until you can rebuild your life."

"What if I don't like either of those?"

"I could just help you clean up."

Gabe smiled. "That would be appreciated. If you didn't look about as good as I feel." He pointed to the couch. "Brush yourself off a seat and I'll get you a blanket."

Caisey started to shake her head. "I really should hop in my car and get back to Liam before I crash completely."

"He's a nice guy, isn't he?"

"I'm kinda partial to him, he's a good partner. He became a Christian a few weeks ago, so he's in that beginning stage where everything's new and exciting."

It took a second, but realization washed over Gabe's face. "You saw my Bible when you were here before?"

Caisey nodded. "And the verse on the sticky note on your bathroom mirror. If any man come to me, and hate not his father, and mother, and wife, and children, and brethren, and sisters, yea, and his own life also, he cannot be my disciple." She blew out a breath. "That's a tough one."

"How about you?"

"Sure, I go to church." Caisey didn't want to get into a deep theological conversation about how she wasn't nearly the Christian she should be. Not just because she was so tired and liable to say too much. She pushed off the wall and walked to the door. "I really should be going."

"So it's goodbye then?"

She shrugged. "I guess. I don't know what else it would be."

Nothing tied them together, not anymore. Caisey needed to get back to work so she could get on with her life. Gabe's presence here was curious, but it made sense her dad hid him somewhere familiar if he thought he couldn't trust anyone else to protect Gabe from his uncle. Caisey needed to get home to Grams, Jenna and Jake where she belonged.

HOLDEN ARTURO CURLED his fingers around the telephone cord and gripped the handset while he was briefed on the situation in Buckshot.

The man said, "What are your orders?"

Holden leaned back in his chair, the leather creaking. "Samuel's daughter is collateral damage. I want my nephew."

"Yes, sir."

"HOLD UP A SECOND." Gabe's hold on her arm was gentle, but that didn't mean she was going anywhere. "Are you sure you're okay?"

She didn't look like she should be driving all the way to Denver. More like taking a twelve hour nap. "It's been a long week."

"So this isn't just about the sheriff, or my uncle?"

She frowned. "Why would it be?"

"I don't know." Gabe crossed his arms. "Maybe because the sheriff said his name right before he tried to kill us?"

Caisey slumped onto the couch and ran her hands down her face. "Okay, I think we need to run this down. My brain isn't firing on all cylinders."

Gabe strode to the kitchen, heated some water and found some black tea at the back of the cupboard. Thankfully his electric kettle hadn't been smashed up like the rest of the house. He didn't know what he was going to do about work. He was going to have to order a new desktop, or make a day trip to a computer store.

All he knew right then was he didn't want Caisey to leave.

LIAM STUDIED the State Patrol officer, trying to figure out where he knew him. The guy was younger, but not by much, and his accent had a twinge of Boston to it. Was he trying to cover it up by softening the sound? Liam ran down the specifics of the case and the state of the investigation into Emma Allens' murder while Officer Maddens looked around the room, checked his phone, and generally acted like he had a million places he'd rather be.

Liam talked through the specific pieces of evidence, rambling on for the sake of drawing out the conversation. While Officer Maddens' eyes were on his phone, Liam made like he was checking the computer file. He pulled up an internet search engine and typed in 'Boston Cop' just on the off-chance his hunch was right.

Bingo.

An article popped up of a disgraced officer facing charges of corruption who'd been acquitted on lack of evidence after the whole case fell apart, making everyone involved look like inept idiots. Liam didn't like it when honest lawmen and women looked bad and a criminal who was a disgrace to the uniform walked. It really ticked him off.

Liam rambled on at length about the backpack and what they knew about that completely generic brand, which could have been bought anywhere, making it sound like key evidence.

What was a disgraced Boston cop doing in Colorado dressed as a State Patrol officer? Whichever way you swung it, this wasn't good. Liam needed to get to Caisey. She had no weapon and Gabe had no training, going up against a fully loaded gun in the hands of...whoever that old guy was.

Liam lifted his chin. "And so you can see, Officer Maddens, clearly this was the work of someone emotionally pre-disposed to violence. More than likely they will strike again."

Unless the dead sheriff was the killer, in which case he wouldn't be doing much of anything ever again.

Liam pushed back from the desk and stood. "I think that covers it. So if you're happy taking it from here, I'll get out of your hair and let you get to work."

Officer Maddens looked up from his phone. "Sure, whatever."

Liam strode through the main office straight to where Officer Kurter was at her desk. He put one palm on the center of the page she was reading and leaned in. "Call the State Patrol. Tell them you have two guys in town impersonating their officers."

Her eyes narrowed. "Already did. Clocked them the minute they came in. State patrol—real ones—are an hour out."

"You did?"

She smirked. "My brother is a Sergeant with Colorado State Patrol down in Colorado Springs. Seriously, these guys didn't hardly even make an effort to be real. It's pathetic really."

"Right then."

"You should probably go check on your partner."

Liam straightened. "You'll hold down the fort here?"

Completely straight face, one of her eyebrows lifted.

"Right. You've got it covered." Liam grabbed a notepad and scribbled the real name of the disgraced Boston Cop.

And then he booked it up the mountain.

He slammed the car door and Gabe came out. As he approached the cabin, Gabe put his finger to his lips.

"What's going on?"

"She fell asleep."

Liam's whole body relaxed. "That's a whole lot better than what I'd imagined." He blew out a breath. "I guess I'm tired and seeing danger where it isn't. I swear I thought that cop who drove you back here was going to try and kill you guys, or something."

But the State Patrol officers weren't cops. They'd been sent there by someone to impersonate them. The question was, who was behind all this? There had to be a bigger plan, since someone had gone to a whole lot of trouble to insert themselves into this scenario.

He followed Gabe inside, where Gabe handed him a steaming cup. "I made this for her, but..."

Liam dumped a spoonful of sugar in to make it more palatable and stirred. While he drank, he studied the man who had put a serious crimp in Caisey's ability to have a romantic relationship.

Gabe leaned his hip against the kitchen counter. "Something you want to say?"

Interesting, most people asked it as a simple question and not one that invited confrontation. Liam shook his head, but it was a lie. He wanted to sit with the man and ask all the questions he had, followed with what his intentions were toward Caisey, and who that other woman was. "Maybe—"

Caisey jumped off the couch, yelling one of Jake's fake curse words. She brushed off her jacket and winced when her hand touched the area where the knife had gone in.

TWENTY

Liam strode over with Gabe right behind him. "You all right?"

Caisey nodded, vigorous like she was trying to convince herself.

"The Chloroform Killer?"

Her eyes were glazed, as though the nightmare was still dissipating. "Then it was my dad, the prison chaplain, and then the sheriff. And he didn't just stab me in the leg."

"Someone stabbed you in the leg?" Gabe grasped her elbow, like she was about to fall over. "Are you okay?"

Caisey set her hand on his forearm. "We need to figure this out. I need it straight so my head can be straight."

Liam nodded. "Sit down." He took a seat on the armchair while Gabe sat with Caisey on the couch and handed her a full cup. "So we show up in town and immediately get on the sheriff's radar. You spring Gabe out of his hands and what either one of us, or both of us, do is enough for the sheriff to come after you and Gabe and try to kill you."

"But this wasn't the Chloroform Killer, any of this."

"Right."

Caisey clutched her mug with both hands. "Are we assuming the sheriff killed Emma?"

Liam shrugged. "That would be my guess. Maybe he was trying to pin it on Gabe, make him look like the Chloroform Killer, or a copycat, but it fell through when you got in the middle of it."

"And that was enough for him to try to kill us?" Caisey squeezed her eyes shut. "It'd make more sense to me if something else pushed the sheriff to come after us. Like Arturo."

Gabe's head whipped around. "He said Arturo before he came at us on the ATV. But what does my uncle have to do with the sheriff? He doesn't even know I'm here."

Liam's brain connected the pieces like a puzzle. "And the two fake cops."

Caisey gaped. "Both of them?"

Liam nodded.

"Then it's all linked." Caisey turned to Gabe. "Think about it, if your uncle wants to get rid of you, what better way than having an officer of the law pin a murder on you? You wind up in jail just like your dad. But Liam and I showed up and screwed up that plan, so he decides to gun us down and just get rid of us once and for all. To earn points with your uncle. Or because Arturo told him to."

CAISEY WAS SUPPOSED to be here to see the cabin, and maybe draw out the killer. Instead she'd walked back into Gabe's world. Which might not be bad, if she hadn't led Gabe's uncle right to him.

Gabe glanced between her and Liam. "What about the two guys pretending to be cops?"

Liam scratched the stubble on his chin. "They arrived too fast to have been brought here by the sheriff. But what if Arturo sent them right after we arrived? Separate, but all tied together."

Caisey nodded. "That makes sense. I'd love to get a look at the sheriff's phone records, see if he called your uncle after we arrived."

Gabe shook his head, like all this was unreal. "If he knew where I was this whole time, why now?"

She strode across the room and set her mug in the sink. "He

might not have." She sat again, her lips pressed together. "What if I led him right to you?"

Gabe's face betrayed nothing. Was he mad at her? She hadn't done it on purpose. "Did you?"

"Your father wrote a letter. The prison chaplain brought it to my house, looking for my dad to pass it on to you."

Gabe's eyes widened, and for a second Caisey saw a hurt little boy in there. "Why would he do that?"

Caisey bit her lip. This wasn't the way she wanted to tell him this. "Your dad has terminal cancer. The prison chaplain said he recently became a believer. Evidently he wants to make amends."

"So that's why you're here? To deliver the letter."

Caisey shook her head. "The letter was stolen from my house during a break-in."

"But you knew I was here? You came to tell me."

"I had no idea you were living in my dad's cabin all this time. Liam came here because of Emma, and I was going to check on the cabin and get some space for a few days while my leg heals." Caisey scratched her hairline. "But if your uncle found out about the letter, maybe he thought I'd know where you were. He could have followed me up here. We might have led him straight to you."

Gabe's jaw flexed. He blew out a breath, took two steps away and then turned back. "So he's still trying to kill me? Even after all these years he hasn't let it go."

Caisey's heart hurt for him. "I'm sorry. But it doesn't explain the Sheriff trying to pin Emma's murder on you, if it really is connected."

Gabe's face softened. He didn't say anything, but she couldn't help thinking it meant he wasn't sorry they got to meet each other. Caisey wanted that to be true, which wasn't good at all. Why did her heart have to be so tied to a man who was virtually a stranger to her? Why couldn't she have moved on?

"I'm sorry, Gabe." She didn't want to do this, but he needed to go if he was going to be safe. "You're going to have to move again."

Gabe turned away and walked down the hall.

Caisey looked at Liam. "I guess he didn't take that too well."

"He'll be okay. And he'll be alive."

Caisey nodded, even though she didn't like it.

"I'm going to head back to the sheriff's office now. See you back in Denver."

"What about the team?" She walked with him to the door. "Will you tell them not to come?"

"I'll call Burkot and let him know it wasn't the Chloroform Killer."

"Will you tell him about Gabe?" Caisey wasn't sure she wanted it to get out. "It'd be pretty easy for word to get out, and then his uncle will know we're involved."

Liam nodded. "I'll let you decide on that one."

"Okay."

He squeezed her elbow. "Take care on the drive back, you look tired."

GABE STUFFED his t-shirts into a duffel bag. His room was a mess, but he picked through the dissonant fragments of what had been his life for years and found what he needed. He was in the bathroom gathering up his razor and toothbrush when Caisey showed up in the doorway.

"You okay?"

Gabe shoved the stuff in his travel kit and zipped it up. What was the point in answering? It was clear his life was done. Again.

"As soon as you're ready, I'll leave too. Liam already went back to town."

"Right." Gabe ran a hand through his hair. "Is this normal for you guys? Because if it is, it's insane. In one day we've been shot at, you killed a man, we were pushed off a ravine into freezing water, practically got hypothermia, and now I find out my uncle is coming for me again."

Caisey's lips twitched. "Not usually all at once, no. I'll give you that. But my job isn't exactly boring."

"Why on earth would you choose to do it?"

"Why do you love historical books?"

Gabe frowned. "I love discovering something new about how people lived hundreds of years ago. It gives us insight into past events and their implications on today."

"It's not that different from what I do. Except I discover things about people who live now, ones who commit crimes. It keeps people safe."

"What about you?" He frowned. "Who keeps you safe?"

"I won't tell you there isn't an element of risk. You were there today. You're not dumb and I'm not going to sugar-coat it. It is what it is."

Gabe sighed. "I just don't get why you would want to."

"What made you testify against your dad?" Her voice was quiet and she shifted, like she didn't know how he might react to the question. Or did she regret putting distance between them? He supposed it was for the best, since they were going their separate ways...again.

"I thought it was the right thing to do, to put away someone who had hurt a lot of people. Turns out he wasn't the real threat."

Caisey squeezed his hand. "It was the right thing to do. You put a criminal away, and that's exactly how I feel about my job. I can't live with any self-respect if I don't do everything I can to protect the people I love."

She moved aside so Gabe could exit the bathroom. He went into his room, but he still had something he wanted to say to her. When he turned back she was leaning against the doorframe looking bone-tired.

"What if the people you love are the ones you need to protect everyone else from? I did the right thing and I thought it would feel different than this. Better. But it doesn't feel good at all that I tore my family apart and had to live the rest of my life in hiding."

"Gabe—"

He shook his head. "Let's just get moving, okay? It's late and we're both too tired for this conversation." Not to mention, did it even matter if they understood each other if there was little chance they were going to see each other again?

Mitch would miss him until he could explain. Would Caisey?

He'd thought he would never get to meet her and now that he had, well...he'd assumed it would go differently. Holding on to the dream, the desire of his heart, for years, he'd prayed that God would someday bring it all together. He'd get the girl, and testifying wouldn't have meant his world was destroyed. There would still be something salvageable.

Work had been enough for a long time. But now he'd seen Caisey's strength, her pure convictions, the sound of her voice, and the way her mouth crept up at one side when she thought something was funny. Despite denying it for so long, Gabe needed to face the fact that he was a romantic. And there was nothing he could do about it, because one day soon his uncle was going to find him again.

Gabe loaded up his Jeep. When he shut the back, Caisey was right there. He didn't want to say goodbye, so instead he said, "What's your phone number?"

~

CAISEY HIT the button for speakerphone and set her cell in her lap. "Okay, I'll admit it. This was a good idea to stay awake."

Highway stretched out in front of her, thick and black, except for the covering of stars overhead. Gabe might be heading in the other direction, but the presence of his voice made it feel like the miles between them weren't multiplying.

"I have them from time to time."

Caisey gripped the steering wheel with one hand. "So tell me something, then. We have to talk if we're going to stay awake."

"True. We wouldn't want to talk about nothing in particular when we could be deep and meaningful at two a.m."

Caisey smiled. She would have laughed, but she was way too tired to worry about anything except getting home and going to bed. After she slept for two days she would figure out what they were going to do about Gabe's uncle. Although, she'd already pretty much decided she was going to call him and set up a meeting. She needed to get to the bottom of what happened with the sheriff and the two guys pretending to be the state police.

The sheriff's death needed to be investigated and she'd have to follow up on the statement she'd given, but the state police could do that through the FBI office in Denver.

There were procedures.

Then there was Gabe.

He was nice, good looking, and seemed like a decent guy instead of any of the parade of losers she'd met who either still lived in their mom's house, or they didn't have a job they could share in polite company. She really didn't want to date someone she'd end up having to arrest.

"Caisey?"

"What?"

"Deep in thought, or asleep?" His voice shook with humor.

Someone who saw the lighter side of life would be good for her, since she was so exposed to the darkness in the world.

"Well?"

She watched a lone trucker pass going the other direction. "Not asleep, just thinking."

"About what?"

Of course he asked that. And what was she going to tell him? He didn't need to know she had already written off their relationship or, at least, the lack of potential for one.

There was no way on earth she could see how they would ever be able to merge their lives. It would take an act of...oh, right.

Okay, God. Here it is. I don't ask for much, it seems like you've given me the skills to take care of whatever gets thrown at me. So how about this? Gabe is it for me, isn't he? It feels like this is my one chance to have everything I want, but it looks impossible. So...how about you take the reins on this one? She sucked in a breath, suddenly incredibly nervous. I'm giving it to you...giving him to you, because this one's too big for me.

"Caisey?"

She needed to say something before Gabe got worried she really had fallen asleep. "I was just thinking about how funny life is. It never really works out the way we think, does it?"

Gabe's voice came back. "Okay, maybe it is too late for deep and meaningful. I'm not sure I can cogitate this right now. But I do know what you mean. It's never sunshine and roses. Why do we think it should be?"

Caisey shifted in her seat, trying to shake some life into her heavy shoulders. "My pastor says it has to do with heaven. We're discontent with what's happening here on earth, because we know we're destined for something better."

"Like how Adam and Eve messed up what was supposed to be the real plan? Perfection, walking with God."

"Yeah," Caisey sighed, glad he was on the page with her. "That's proof right there God desires something better for us. We get little glimpses of it on earth, like a good marriage, and a little kid laughing, and cream-filled chocolate-covered donuts."

TWENTY-ONE

The sound of Gabe's laughter filled the inside of her car and she turned up the volume, smiling.

When he managed to calm down, he said, "You're a typical cop, then?"

"Who doesn't like donuts?"

"They're not exactly nutritional."

"Oh, no." She wanted to roll her eyes. "Don't tell me you're one of *those* people."

"What people?"

Caisey shook her head, even though he couldn't see it. "I saw it in your cabin, but I didn't want to believe it. Green tea. Fish. Whole wheat bread."

"What's wrong with all that?"

She smiled. "Uh...nothing if you're part rabbit, or training for the Olympics or something. You're not are you...training for the Olympics?"

"Not the last time I checked."

"Good. Because I hear it takes up a lot of time and you probably have enough on your plate as it is."

Gabe laughed. "So you're serious about your faith then?"

"Random segue back into talk about religion. Okay. Yes, I'm

serious about it. I don't completely understand everything, but I don't think we ever really get to that point. That's why we have to accept we can't figure it all out and make the choice to just believe anyway. How about you?"

"I never had any connection with God or a church, not growing up. Except for Mitch. He talked to me about his faith, but I just dismissed it. Your dad was actually the one who told me I wasn't ever going to have peace about my life if I didn't know Jesus. He told me to find a church where I felt accepted and make friends. Be part of something, otherwise I was going to live my life disconnected with everything and everyone."

That made sense. Her dad had a passing affiliation with 'church' as an institution, but she'd never seen that it was anything more than that to him. It made sense he would encourage Gabe to find friends and not be a loner forever. But it was certainly not the relationship she had, where she couldn't imagine not going to services, or not have God be present in her life.

Still, there felt like there was something missing in her experience. Like she should know...more. Feel more. A lot of the time she was just too busy to make time for Bible reading and more than a quick prayer, but it seemed like there was so much more to Christianity that she'd so far failed to connect with.

Caisey wanted to know what Gabe had found. "So you discovered something there?"

"It was new people and a new place, a new town and a new life but something about it was like coming home for the first time and I realized that was God. I started to bring Him into every part of my life and suddenly I could rest. I had joy for the first time in...I don't know how long."

Caisey changed lanes. There was something about this guy that she just couldn't walk away from. She couldn't see how she could move on with someone else with Gabe out of her life when she felt like this. God was going to have to make a way, because she sure couldn't see one where his uncle didn't find and kill him because of her.

When his voice came through again, it was heavy with emotion.

"Okay, enough of the heavy stuff. Tell me, crunchy or smooth peanut butter?"

~

GABE'S PHONE BEEPED AGAIN. He pulled it away from his ear and looked at the flashing red light, accepting the inevitable. It was about to die. "Almost out of battery."

"Okay." Caisey's voice sounded disappointed, which actually made him feel better.

"When I get to a store I'll get an untraceable phone and call you."

"Sounds good." She paused. "Take care, okay?"

"You too."

Gabe hung up and looked down at his dash. The gas gauge was low. He'd have to find somewhere to fill up soon. The car slowed. He looked at the rev counter and sure enough, it was dropping off. But his foot was still on the gas pedal. What was going on?

He fought the stiff steering to the side and came to a stop.

Headlights pulled over behind him.

~

CAISEY STRETCHED, her head full of fog and the entirety of her body tight like she'd been holding it tense all night. Her pillow. Her bed. She smiled, rolled to see what time it was and lifted up on her elbows. Ten forty-five and it was light outside.

Time to get up.

She needed a new service weapon. Although, a shower first was probably a good idea, since she stank.

After she blow-dried her hair enough it could dry the rest of the way on its own, she got dressed and grabbed the key for her dad's gun safe. The inside of the safe smelled like her dad. Polish. Oil. Her dad's old hunting rifle was tempting, but could be construed as overkill. And it wouldn't fit in her boot, either. She picked out an old revolver, loaded it and stuck it up on the shelf in the closet safe. Her dad's backup weapon, a .38, was on the highest shelf where she'd put it after they gave it to her along with the stuff he had on him the day he died.

"Hey, you're awake." Caisey spun. Jenna raised both hands, her eyes wide. "Don't shoot."

She didn't dignify that with a response, but grabbed a small caliber gun from the safe and knelt to wrap the holster around her ankle, covering it with the leg of her jeans. Some people might think it was weird to be armed in your own house, but when you got out of the habit that made you liable to forget, and forgetting got you killed.

"Did you sleep okay?"

"I'm thinking that isn't the question you really want to ask me." Caisey remembered the rush of wondering if it was really him or not. "I saw Gabe."

Jenna's jaw dropped.

Caisey grinned and told her the story. "Only he hasn't called yet."

Jenna was still smiling. "He will."

An hour later she set up shop in her dad's old office. In his chair, behind his desk. The whole room was kind of neglected. The print on the wall was still the same guy on a motorcycle riding off to the mountains. It was cool and all, but totally eighties. Jenna clearly dusted the bookshelves and desk, since she used the computer and phone sometimes, so it was clean. But it was still eerie being in here.

It took her two hours while the phone charged to clear out her email and type up her notes about what happened in Buckshot for her boss. She typed a separate statement for the Colorado State Patrol about specifically what happened with the sheriff. Liam had sent an update saying the state police arrived and this morning they were going out with cadaver dogs to locate the sheriff's body.

She texted him and in thirty seconds her phone rang. "Lyons."

"You got home okay?"

"Yeah, thanks. How's it going with the state guys?"

"Can you get a location on my phone?"

"Sure." Caisey tucked her cell between her shoulder and cheek and typed. The webpage loaded. She entered Liam's number and waited for the signal to show up. "What's going on?"

"We're at the location you gave me, but there's no body."

Caisey started. "ATV tracks?"

Wind buffeted the phone line. "Two grooves in the dirt, plain as day. The ATV is even here, so they're looking at that, but there isn't much else to process."

"My gun?"

"Haven't seen it yet, but I'm guessing it's downriver."

Caisey stared at the map image of the ravine and the edge on which she'd stood. She could still feel the warmth of Gabe behind her, and the surge of anger that someone wanted to harm him. "But no sheriff?"

"The dogs have nothing, so there's no body hiding in the brush and he can't have rolled too far."

"Blood?"

"Nothing."

Caisey held her fingers still. She bit her lip. "I shot him."

There was silence on the line. "Not even you would joke about something like that.

But then where is he? Do I need to get the state guys to launch a manhunt?"

"If you do, will you be coming home?"

Liam sighed. "We found the primary crime scene for the niece. A rancher called in a mess of blood in one of his disused barns."

Caisey didn't need that mental picture...but there it was. She blew out a breath and thought of Hawaii. "So it looks like the sheriff killed Emma?"

"That's the theory we're working with."

"Great." Caisey sighed. "If he's alive, he's going to be ticked."

Liam hung up.

Caisey left the office, since it was weird being there. Instead, she wandered the house trying to think of something to do. Her leg hurt, so she just ended up watching a nineties movie she'd seen a bunch of times. The Mummy wasn't even scary anymore, or funny.

At dinner she sat at the head of the table, despite the look Jenna gave her. They hardly ever used the dining room, except for holidays.

Her friend didn't let it go. "What is up with you?"

Caisey's head whipped around. "Nothing's up. I'm wondering what's up with all of you."

Jenna set the steaming dish of lasagna on the table and sighed. "So where's Gabe tonight?"

Caisey shrugged. "How should I know?"

Jenna's face fell. "He didn't call?"

She was trying not to be worried, or—truth be told—a little bit annoyed that he hadn't called yet. He was the one who said he was going to get a new phone and call her. But no, he'd disappeared again. Just like the last time. So, was she supposed to wait another seventeen years until she saw him again?

Jenna swiped off her oven mitts. "Huh...I guess I just thought—"

"I know what you thought."

Grams came in, pulled up short, and eyed both of them like she knew there was tension. But they weren't going to talk about it. Gabe was gone. The end. Jenna could get as excited as she wanted at the idea Caisey had spent days with him, but it was over now. For the sake of keeping them all safe, Gabe was out of her life.

If his uncle came looking she would pull the trigger, knowing it meant the threat to her family was eliminated. But he was just one man and there would always be others. No let up. No break. That was why she was an FBI agent—to be as prepared as possible against the danger.

"Are you okay?"

Caisey blinked and looked at Jenna. She could feel moisture on the back of her neck and her hairline, so she took a sip of ice water and tried to smile. "Sure, I'm fine."

"Look who's here!" Jake strode in, hand in hand with a blonde and slender teen girl who resembled a pixie. "This is—"

"Natalia."

The girl's eyes landed on Caisey and she gasped. "Special Agent Lyons."

Jake pulled up short. "You two know each other?"

Without taking her eyes off Natalia, Caisey nodded. "Yeah, Jake. We've met."

"Well then." Jenna's voice wavered. "Dinner will be all the more enjoyable now we know that some of us have met."

Caisey glanced at her friend. Jenna looked mad. What was that about? Jenna saw the look on Caisey's face, but looked away and smiled and dished out the food like a mom was supposed to. Hopefully the lasagna was good enough to take away the taste of way too many unspoken questions. It was probably some weird 'mom' thing that made her ticked because she didn't know her son's new girl and Caisey did. Why couldn't Jenna say something if it was making her this mad?

The prospect of everything that happened with Natalia becoming their dinner conversation made Caisey's leg twitch. Then, in a few years, Jake would marry Natalia and then every Thanksgiving until her death, Caisey would have to sit across the table from the head of Denver's Russian mafia.

She shoveled in bites of Caesar salad, just so she didn't say something...anything that would make everyone at the table immediately start yelling at her.

Grams turned to Caisey. "How was your trip, Case?" Her fork was trailing the spaghetti and plain tomato sauce Sarah had probably made for her especially, knowing they would sit down to dinner. The home assistant probably coordinated with Jenna just so that Grams could eat the same kind of meal they had.

Caisey nodded around a mouthful of lasagna. Jenna was a good cook, not like frou- frou good which was pointless, but solid. And a whole lot better than Caisey could ever do it.

"It was fine, Grams. Eventful." Caisey smiled. "I probably need another week of vacation."

"You're going back to work? When?"

Why was Jenna so surprised? Jake and Natalia weren't even paying attention. They were busy sending each other moony looks while pretending to eat.

Caisey shrugged. "I should stop by the office tomorrow, just to check in. See if anything came up on any of my cases while I was gone." She looked around the table. They were all silent, staring at her. She set her fork down. "You know what? We forgot to say grace."

There was more than one startled look, but she ignored them and bowed her head.

"Precious Lord, we thank you for the many ways you've blessed each of us. Thank you for bringing us together at the end of this day. I ask for your protection on each of the people at this table. Guide us and give us your wisdom in all things. Amen."

"Amen."

The quiet was only broken by the sound of forks tapping plates and crunching lettuce.

Caisey's phone buzzed. Thank heaven for that. "Excuse me." She stepped away from the table and walked down the hall. "Special Agent Lyons."

"It's Burkot. I've got an update from the State Patrol. They want to bring in Marshals to find the sheriff, since they claim they don't have the manpower."

"Did you get the latest from Conners?"

"I sure did. And isn't that a fine kettle of fish if ever I've heard one. Shoot a guy at point blank and he walks away." Burkot huffed. "Maybe you need to hit the range if your shot's that sideways, Lyons."

"I'll be sure to do that, sir." She was due for some time at the range, anyway. And her quarterly qualifying was coming up. "Was there anything else?"

"Why, you got a hot date?"

"Yeah with a lasagna."

"That's my girl."

Caisey hung up the phone laughing. Burkot hadn't called her that since she was a kid. Those years felt like a lifetime ago, which they were—Jake's. Most everything could be measured pre- and post-Jake, or along with whatever stage of life he'd been at. In two years he'd be out of the house and then what would she do? Caisey would be a thirty-something single federal agent with no prospects except the likelihood of being shot on the job. Like her dad.

Caisey grimaced.

"Something funny?" Jenna leaned against the arch that led to the living room.

"What's funny is that Natalia even thinks she's good enough for Jake."

The minute she said it, Caisey slapped a hand over her mouth. Jake appeared behind Jenna, his eyes hard. "That's your opinion, but it doesn't make a difference to how I feel." He crossed his teenage arms. "Mom likes her."

"Your mom likes the mailman."

Jenna gasped. "Joe is a nice man."

Caisey turned her focus to her friend. "He's creepy and he smells like a hobo."

"Well, maybe you need to pray for more love in your heart, because clearly something happened that made you immediately dislike everyone you don't know. Oh wait...except one guy you met once a billion years ago and decided to fall in love with even though you only went on one date."

"Is that really what you think of me? Do you think I wanted to be unable to fall in love with anyone else for the past seventeen years?"

Jenna crossed her arm. "You forgot cynical."

"That's a good thing. You would invite the Unabomber to dinner because you thought he needed a warm meal after living in a mountain cabin in Montana for so long. Never mind that he killed people." Caisey stepped away, rubbing the spot behind her ear that was pounding again. If something happened to any of them, she didn't know what she would do. When she opened her eyes she looked at the carpet.

"What is up with you?"

Caisey sucked in some deep breaths. "I don't know."

"Well you need to figure it out."

Uh-oh...that was the mom tone.

"And then you need to apologize to Jake."

TWENTY-TWO

Gabe couldn't breathe. He tried to suck in air but all there was, was fire in his chest.

His face didn't feel much better and he couldn't see out of either of his eyes. He thought he heard a door slam.

But there was nothing.

LIAM STRODE through the Denver FBI office, glad to be out of Buckshot and back in the city. Caisey was at her desk, typing so hard it was a wonder the keys on her keyboard weren't flying off. He tossed his backpack down and set the white paper bag in front of her. Then he got a look at her face. "What happened now?"

Whatever it was, she blanked her look and tried to convince him otherwise. "Nothing happened."

"Right—"

"I can't talk, I'm typing up notes. I interviewed the assistant on the Alton case."

"Yeah?"

So she'd used work to keep her mind off whatever happened. That wasn't unusual, since Caisey pretty much saw work as the remedy for everything, stemming the tide of evil in the city and all that. He'd almost laughed the day she explained it. The idea mostly ridiculous, but it helped him understand how she saw the world.

Liam folded his arms. "What did she have to say about the boss maybe, or maybe not, killing his wife?"

"When I'm done, you can read my notes."

He sat and pulled the chair up to his desk. "Why don't you just tell me? Does she think her boss killed the district attorney or not?"

"When I'm done. You. Can. Read. My. Notes. Now hush. I'm trying to think."

Liam pulled a sandwich from the paper bag and grabbed a soda from his desk drawer. He'd learned the hard way he had to hide stuff around here or it disappeared. He'd take room temperature over leaving it in the fridge with his name on it. Stealing apparently wasn't illegal among co-workers.

"So what happened in Buckshot?"

Liam glanced at her. She was still typing, but he could see the wheels turning. The woman couldn't wait five minutes until she asked you to spill. Heaven forbid he ever keep something from her... like the ring burning a hole in his pocket. He needed to call Andrea, make a reservation somewhere with candles. Pick up his dry cleaning, take a shower. Unpack.

Liam sighed. "The State guys have the case for the murder of Emma Allens. The sheriff is the primary suspect and they have a warrant out for his arrest. Are you doing okay?"

She didn't even blink. "Did they say anything about my leaving?"

"They'd like a statement from you in person. The written one will do for now, but if they catch up with the sheriff and he tells a different story they'll need to follow up. Although, since he'll likely be convicted for Emma's murder and you said you shot him but he's not exactly dead...I'm not sure what difference it will make."

"It still doesn't look good, shooting a sheriff. Even if it was self-defense."

"Not if it's the word of an FBI agent in good standing versus a sheriff convicted of murdering his niece."

"Okay, I'll give you that."

Liam smiled. "Well, thanks."

"You're welcome." She hesitated and then said, "Do you think I'm phoning it in?"

"What?"

Finally she looked at him. "My life. Do you think I'm in limbo, like I'm too scared to take a risk and really live?"

She was a grown woman, but there was something in her eyes that he imagined looked very much like the scared little girl who needed to be picked up from that truck stop in Sturgis. Abandoned.

Liam laced his fingers on the desk and leaned in. "There's nothing half about the life you live."

"But you do think I'm scared."

"I think you went through something huge and then huge things keep happening to you, over and over again. Anyone else wouldn't have survived that, but then you actually volunteered to put yourself in harm's way again. Your mom abandoned you, Gabe's uncle had you abducted and beaten to send your dad a message. The Chloroform Killer abducts you and takes you to a mine so he can send us a message. You stumble onto Gabe again after all these years at the worst possible time, and then a homicidal sheriff tries to kill you."

Liam shook his head slowly. "There isn't a person on this earth, man or woman, who could survive the stuff you have and not be freaked out. It's not bad and you have a lot to work through, but who doesn't? Give yourself a break. You can only do the best you can and then pray that God pulls through on the rest."

"But what if He doesn't?"

"You really think there's even a remote possibility of that?"

Caisey's mouth twitched. "So why is it so hard to believe it? I'm supposed to be this long-time solid Christian, but it barely even feels like I'm hanging on by my fingertips."

"Why are you hanging on at all?" Liam tilted his head to the side. "Let go, Caisey.

Don't assume you can do it all, because you won't be able to."

"How do you know all that, anyway? That's deep stuff." "You've been my partner two years."

Caisey frowned. "So?"

"I've been listening."

"Really?"

Liam shook his head. "I think you need coffee if you're this off your game." She blew out a breath. "I think I need to go home."

"That's probably a good thing. We can start fresh in the morning. You want to run tomorrow?"

Caisey nodded. "I should. I've eaten way too much the last few days. I can feel it creeping up on my backside."

Liam winced. "Too much information."

"Conners! Lyons!"

Liam looked over. Burkot was at the door to his office, face red. He strode over. "I need you both in Aurora. Now."

Liam glanced at Caisey. She looked as confused as he was. He turned back to Burkot. "What's going on?"

"There's been another body. It looks like the Chloroform Killer's work."

Caisey was on her feet. "What's the timeline?"

"It's fresh, and Agent Miller says it looks like the real deal." Burkot nodded at Caisey. "You both better get down there and find out what's going on."

Burkot strode away and Liam's phone started ringing. He muted it and slipped it back in his pocket. "I'll call her back later."

"Or I can drive, and you can talk to Andrea."

"I'd rather be making a dinner reservation than going to see another dead body."

"No duh." Caisey snorted. "Let's go. You'll have to propose another night."

Liam started. "How did you know that? I haven't told anyone."

"We've been partners for two years. You think I can't tell?" Caisey rolled her eyes. "Let's swing by your place. You can take a shower and wash off the stink of the countryside before you get more dead-person stink on you."

Liam grabbed his backpack. "Nice."

"That's me. I'm a nice person. And a partner who won't risk you getting lost when you wander off on your own like you usually do.

The search dogs won't be able to find you, you smell so bad. They'll catch the wrong wind and end up chasing a skunk."

~

SIX HOURS later they were back at the office. Another body dumped, and Caisey had even gotten a little sick when she saw what remained of the woman. That hadn't happened in a long time. She couldn't even imagine what it would be like to go through that, and prayed desperately the victim had been dead first.

Doctor Amanda was standing at Caisey's desk, waiting. Caisey pulled up short. This wasn't a good time to get into anything, but Amanda saw her face and motioned with a tilt of her head to the hall at the end of the room.

Liam took her bag and she let him. Caisey didn't look at him, she just followed Amanda again.

Was this her life? People trying to kill her, busting her bum to keep her family safe, trying to get home in time for dinner, keeping a finger on the pulse of how Jake was doing, spending time with Grams. Honestly, it was exhausting. Caisey was bone tired and desperately in need of a vacation that didn't involve seeing a long lost crush and then shooting someone. She wanted her dad so she could ask him how he managed to stay sane when it all got so heavy it was suffocating.

God, I don't even know what to say. I didn't think it would be like this. I thought it would be...easier. Aren't I supposed to have peace, too?

Amanda shut the door to her office.

Caisey slumped on the couch and closed her eyes. "Can I ask you something?"

"That's why we're here."

"What does it mean when you decide you don't like your life? Is there something wrong with me?" She opened her eyes, wanting the truth of Amanda's answer and not just the words.

Her smile was warm. "There is, without a doubt, absolutely

nothing wrong with you. After all, would someone want to kill you if you weren't doing something right?"

Caisey snorted. "That's a great measure of an FBI agent who dies a hero, but does it say much about me as a human being?"

"You have to decide if you're just having a rough few weeks and you need a break, or if you need to decide to change something permanently. But either way, you need to be sure."

Caisey nodded. Her phone rang. The display said, *Jenna Calling*.

TWENTY-THREE

"Grams is throwing up." Jenna's voice was all jittery. "We got her back in bed. Jake is making tea and I need to clean up the bathroom so I can't be long, but I wanted to fill you in."

Caisey sat at her desk. "You think she got a bug or was it something she ate?"

Liam's work focus moved and settled on her. They needed to run down all the evidence they'd collected from the body site, which wasn't much. It never was; which was why they hadn't caught the Chloroform Killer yet. Tomorrow would be about interviewing friends and family so they could get to the bottom of this colossal mess that kept churning out victims.

"I have no idea. But if she's like this into tomorrow morning then she needs someone to take her to the doctor. I'd do it but I have back to back appointments all day."

Caisey quit twirling the pen and tossed it on the desk. "I'm in the middle of something."

"You always are."

"Jenna—"

"It's fine. I'll have Sarah take her."

"Don't be mad. You know I'd do it if I could. It's probably just one of those twenty- four hour things that knocks you out and then it's gone."

"I'm not mad. I just don't like cleaning up puke, especially when Jake had to carry her back to bed."

It wasn't good, if Grams was too weak to walk. And it had to suck for Jenna to see her son be the strong one. But Caisey was glad Jenna was only ticked because she felt helpless, and not because they were butting heads about Caisey's job.

Jenna just needed a distraction.

Caisey probably needed one too. "We should hang out at the weekend."

"Are you asking me out?"

Caisey laughed. "You're cute, but you're not my type."

Jenna laughed back. "Right back at ya, darlin'. Girl time sounds good. Jake's new girlfriend came over again tonight and they watched a movie together, all cuddled up on the couch. I kept finding excuses to walk through the room for a book, or my reading glasses. At one point I interrupted a *look*."

"What?"

"He was looking at her, Case."

"Jake was...looking at his girlfriend?" Caisey frowned. Sometimes she really did not understand the whole 'mom' mentality. "And we don't like that because..."

"I know that look. I've seen that look because I've had it directed at me. Piercing green eyes and that hair?" Jenna groaned. "I nearly swatted him with the newspaper, but what I really wanted to do was curl up on my bed crying, surrounded by the discarded wrappers of an entire bag of peanut butter cups."

"Ah." This was about Nic, which was true of most things about Jenna, even after all these years. It was probably why they were such good friends since they were both hung up on long ago lost forever love. Which showed how screwed up Caisey was, considering she put all the eggs of her romantic future into the basket of a guy who'd disappeared. Again.

"Saturday. We'll get dinner and—" *God, help me.* "Go dancing."

There was silence on the line. "What did you do?"

"What?"

"You're buttering me up. You're apologizing. What did you do? Does it have something to do with Gabe? Did you lie about the dating service? Are you mad I signed you up?"

"This isn't about the dating service. I said I was fine with it." Which didn't actually mean she was going to use it, since she was done with men. Caisey sighed. "I didn't really make a plan with him. I don't know where he went, or if I'll see him again."

"Of course you'll see him again, Case. Don't say that."

"I really don't know, Jenna. It didn't go well and something opened up at work so I'm going to be tied up. I don't know when I'm even going to have time to connect with him. Not to mention I don't have his new number yet."

"Well, fix it. Find him."

Caisey shifted in her seat. Someone across the room burst out laughing, making her jerk around. She looked back at her desk. "It's not that easy."

"You have the resources of the FBI, you can't find one guy?"

"That's not what it's for."

Jenna huffed. "You could find him if you wanted."

Probably, but she wasn't going to tell Jenna that. "Listen, I gotta go."

"Yeah, me too. Puke doesn't clean up itself."

"Holler if you need anything, okay?"

"Sure."

Caisey set the phone down and blew out a breath. Liam opened his mouth, but she beat him to the question and told him what was going on with Grams.

"I'll text Andrea. When she gets up she might be able to switch up some things to be able to take Grams to the doctor."

"Thanks, Liam."

He shrugged. "She's family."

"Grams or Andrea?"

"Both."

Caisey smiled. The weight of the day lay heavy on her. She rolled her shoulders and stood. "I need more coffee."

Liam stopped typing and held up his empty cup. Caisey swiped it up on her way past, giving it extra attitude so he knew she was getting some for him out of protest. She'd figured out quick that male agents started to expect it, if you got them coffee all the time without giving them sass. Liam wasn't part of the old boy's network in the bureau, but if the other guys saw her catering to him they would get ideas.

She pulled up short.

Former congressman Alan Cartwright was in Burkot's office. Jenna's dad leaned forward, elbows on his knees, intently talking. Burkot had a pen in his hand, taking notes. Not a friendly chat then. Business. Information. Cartwright had something to say, so he'd come to the one man at the bureau he knew was solid, her dad's old partner. Someone he would trust with what he was going to say.

Caisey did an about face and strode back to her desk. Liam looked at his mug and frowned. "What happened to the coffee?"

"Get it yourself. I don't want any."

Liam frowned and swiped up his mug. "Don't mind if I do."

Caisey watched him disappear down the hall. If Cartwright was doing the right thing, that was good. But who or what was he into that he felt the sudden need to spill to a senior FBI agent?

Why did everything have to be so difficult? Why couldn't life be easy for once?

Where was Gabe, anyway?

~

GABE FINALLY CAME AROUND ENOUGH to tie two thoughts together.

He tried to breathe again, but it felt like someone had lit a fire in his chest. After all this time, hiding away so his uncle could find him, the inevitable had happened.

How could he have been so stupid? When his car slowed and the other vehicle pulled over behind him, he should've known. Realized it was a trap. Instead, he trusted when he should have been cautious. And after half a lifetime of living with mobsters, what did that say about him?

He tried to shift his position, but his hands were tied behind his back. He was lying on a dank linoleum floor that smelled like dirt, in a trailer that had been decorated like a low budget office. Even after all these years, it still looked the same. Gabe had been here years ago...after he followed his dad one night.

The pretend State Patrol officer with the handlebar moustache strode in, holding the door open for someone else. Gabe's uncle stepped inside the room in a silk suit with his tie loosened and the collar unbuttoned. "Well, well, well."

Gabe didn't move. He would betray how he felt, here at what was likely to be the end of his life. His uncle didn't need to know he had accepted this would be the way his life might go. Surprise wasn't in him, not when he'd had years to mull over all the outcomes. Gabe had long ago acknowledged his uncle would catch up to him. He just hadn't thought it might be Caisey who brought him to Gabe's doorstep.

If any man come to me, and hate not his father, and mother, and wife, and children, and brethren, and sisters, yea, and his own life also, he cannot be my disciple.

Gabe knew what it meant now. Not that he took pleasure in the hatred he felt for this man, but that his faith and following God meant more than pleasing his family.

Gabe looked up at the two men, but kept his mouth shut.

"Nothing to say?" Holden's brow crinkled like paper that had been folded many times and now held a permanent crease. He'd lived another lifetime in the years since Gabe had been gone.

Was he supposed to beg? That wasn't in him either, so he stared the man down with the partial sight he had through his swollen eyes. "I said all I wanted to in the courtroom."

His uncle's lip curled. "You've got a pair, I'll give you that. Testifying against your own father, trying to bring me down. Not many people would have the guts to do that."

"Happy to oblige."

"As am I."

Gabe's stomach churned. It was going to happen now, he was going to die. He might have made peace with it a long time ago, but that didn't mean this was going to be easy. Or pain free.

His uncle turned to the other man. "Make the call."

~

"AGENT LYONS." Jenna's dad's voice was low and scratchy, like he was fighting emotion. Or felt guilty. She remembered him from years ago when she'd hung out at Jenna's house. Strong. In command of himself and even the air around him, but not anymore.

Caisey backed up her chair and stood, but didn't offer her hand. "Congressman."

"I think at this point you can probably call me Alan."

Yep, guilty. Caisey lifted her chin. "Is there something I can help you with, Congressman?"

Liam came back over. She saw his wide eyes trained on her and Jenna's dad and resisted the temptation to glare at the congressman.

The older man's eyes flashed, but he pressed on. "How are they?"

Caisey wanted to roll her eyes, or punch him. What happened to being gracious and forgiving? Faith should have changed her, but sometimes she wondered if she just wasn't made that way.

The congressman really did look guilty...and his suit and hair was all mussed. "I'm leaving my wife."

Caisey nodded. "When you get settled somewhere, give me a call."

"You'll set something up?"

"I'll broach the subject."

Years bled from his face. "Thank you."

"If I was you I wouldn't expect miracles."

"At this point, that's about all I have left."

~

TOBEN CARLEN WALKED the hall to the jingle of his shackles, flanked by armed guards. Not to protect him, but to protect the world from him. Conversation hummed in every corner; the relentless press of humanity that flooded in from every side and never ever receded, not for even one second. The tide of it covered him, suffocating until his soul cried for just one second of peace...even from himself.

A young man in a cheap suit sat behind the table in the small room. Not the one man in the world he actually wanted to see.

"You are not my lawyer." Disappointment likely took precedent on his features, as the guy's brow flickered and Toben would have sworn he detected a flicker of fear. But Toben didn't care. The only thing left that he wanted was to see his son one more time.

God, I'm delighting myself in You. Or, at least, figuring out what that means. Fulfill Your promises...please...before it's too late.

Life had made him hard, through experience and necessity. Over the years that

hardness had been broken, and now water rushed in and revived it.

"Have a seat, Mr. Carlen."

He eased into the aluminum chair. What had started as a come-and-go burn in his chest was now a constant gnawing. He stared until the agent cleared his throat and opened the file in front of him.

He spoke to the page. "If you'll turn your attention to the camera behind me, to my right, you'll note the red light indicating it is functioning is about to turn off."

The light went out.

The man's eyes came up, the eyes of a killer. "We have precisely two minutes. Let's not waste time."

He produced a small TV-looking thing. Toben had seen them on commercials, but he'd never seen a cell phone like that in person.

The man tapped the screen and Gabe's face appeared.

Toben sucked in a breath.

TWENTY-FOUR

Gabe stared at the phone held out in front of him, at his dad's face. Surprise, coupled with what looked like a serious case of yearning for something you thought you could never have. His cheeks were concave where they had been full and pink years ago—when his father had been healthy.

The reality that his father really did have a terminal illness hit Gabe like a punch to the sternum. It knocked the breath out of him and he realized this might be his last chance to apologize.

But he couldn't make a sound.

Instead, Gabe mouthed, *I'm sorry.* His father jerked back and surprise flashed across his features. Gabe tried to breathe, but could only cough up blood.

He'd said it. He had actually done the one thing he didn't want to die without doing.

This was the end.

But why did his dad look like he was about to cry? Did he still love Gabe, even after he'd testified and put him in jail for what was supposed to be years, and would now amount to the rest of his life?

Holding the phone, the fake State Patrol cop started to chuckle. The guy was going to enjoy ending Gabe's life, and no one but his dad and Caisey would know it was all on Holden.

No one would know.

Gabe couldn't let that happen.

The rage in him burned hot and he stoked it, until the heat touched to every part of him. Gabe took a deep breath. He was going to talk, even if it killed him.

~

GABE'S FACE was covered with cuts and bruises and blood was pouring from his nose, a cut on his lip, and his forehead. "Dad."

It was probably just a gut reaction. Toben knew his son hated him enough to testify, but here he was. Or he thought he had, until Gabe mouthed those words. *I'm sorry.* Toben had said that so many times, but never to the one person who needed to hear it. Instead, his son was giving him the apology.

He shook his head. It made no sense. What did Gabe have to be sorry for? Toben thought he saw desperation in his son's eyes.

"Gabe." His voice sounded strangled. Toben cleared his throat, trying to pretend the hatred his son surely felt for him still was mutual. *Don't show them weakness.*

The young man holding the phone smiled. "Holden would like you to know that his debt to you has now been paid."

"Caisey Lyons, Dad! Call Caisey Lyons! Tell her Neveya."

Toben blinked. Holden was going to kill his son.

~

CAISEY ACCEPTED the charges and waited.

"Special Agent Lyons?" The man's voice was older, winded, but still had a familiar quality to it.

"Yes?"

"Thank you, Jesus."

She frowned. When her phone said Florence, she'd assumed it would be the chaplain with another message. "Toben?"

"He has Gabe. Holden has my son."

Caisey jumped up from her desk. "Where?"

"He said Neveya. It was a trucking company Holden and I owned. It was in Lincoln Park—" he sucked in a breath "—but that was nearly twenty years ago."

"Give me the address." She pulled on her jacket and saw Liam do the same. They hit the doors at a run and got in the elevator while Toben rattled off a street address. "Got it." She hung up. "Gabe's in trouble. His uncle is going to kill him." Caisey's fingers curled into fists. "I went to the cabin. I brought his uncle to him."

Twenty minutes later Caisey pulled up outside a compound. The high fence was topped with barbed wire. She swung the car around back and parked.

"There." Liam pointed to a gate that was open, barely.

God, please let us be on time. Don't let him die.

They crept inside, between huge big-rigs, over to a trailer that she prayed housed the office.

Please let him be here.

She didn't want to know what it felt. Not now that she knew he hadn't left her again.

The hood of the Toyota outside was still warm. Caisey nodded to her partner and they crept up the ramp to the front door. Inside she could hear thuds and then a man cried out. She knew what that felt like. Wanting to get this done, she stopped beside the door and nodded to Liam.

He kicked the door in.

Gabe was on the floor with his eyes squeezed shut. The fake State Patrol officer who had brought them back to the cabin stood over him, his foot back to kick Gabe again.

It was on the tip of Caisey's tongue to yell, "FBI!" but they weren't there as agents. Liam planted his feet and trained his backup weapon on the guy. Caisey stuck hers in the back waistband of her jeans and grabbed the guy's arm. His foot swung, missing Gabe, whose eyes were now open.

Caisey swung the fake trooper around, ducked her head and used his momentum to flip him on his back.

He looked up at Liam's gun, and froze. Liam shook his head. "Don't even think about it."

Caisey rushed to Gabe. His face was a mess of bruises. She didn't want to know what was going on internally. "Please don't be dead."

He coughed, which might have been laughter. "Hey."

"Are you okay? Can you walk? Maybe you should stay lying down and I'll call an ambulance."

Liam got her attention and shook his head. Right. No one was supposed to know they were here, that way Gabe's uncle would think—at least for a while—that he was dead.

"I thought I *was* dead." He winced. "I was okay with it."

She'd been about to haul him to his feet, but she froze. "You wanted to die?"

"I'm not saying that." He swiped at the blood on his upper lip with the back of his hand and sat up. "I'm saying I'd accepted it."

"So why'd you change your mind?"

"I couldn't let him get away with it." Gabe's eyes shone with something she couldn't pinpoint. "I didn't want you to have to live with that."

This was about her?

As easily as he seemed to accept death, Caisey could accept a life consumed with getting justice for the senseless murder of someone she cared about. And she did care about Gabe; even if it was in a weird way in which they'd only had one date and not seen each other for seventeen years.

Liam flipped the fake cop onto his stomach and held him down.

Gabe stood and leaned a lot of his weight on her, and Caisey said, "You don't seem surprised we knew where you were."

"I prayed my dad would call you. It seemed like he might not have been hoping for my death all these years. He might actually have changed."

"I hope he has." Then Caisey could go with Gabe to see his father. She could thank him in person for helping her save Gabe. "I can't believe you would have let that guy kill you."

The idea just didn't compute. No one wanted to die, that was ridiculous. Caisey would go out fighting until the bitter end, even if it was the scariest moment of her whole life. She had too much to live for, people to protect and stuff she hadn't done yet. Gabe's nobility didn't make any sense to her whatsoever.

The arm he had around her shoulder squeezed. "I'll explain it to you sometime, when it starts to make sense to me."

She started them walking slowly to the door and nodded to Liam. He had the guy covered. Probably thought he was being arrested.

She wanted to kick that guy, but she had to take care of her guy first.

They turned sideways to squeeze out the door, still connected.

Gabe's chest jerked like he was laughing and he groaned.

"Cracked ribs?"

He nodded and blew out a breath. "I'm still here."

"Because I saved you."

"Yeah, because I told my dad to tell you where to find me."

Caisey shook her head. "And what if I'd been two minutes later, what then?"

"It wasn't a perfect plan, I'll admit, but I had to take the chance. I didn't want to leave you with another cause to champion."

She stopped, two feet from her car and shifted back enough to stare up at him. A cause to champion?

"I'm thinking I shouldn't have said that."

She didn't move, couldn't continue when the words seemed to hang around in the air like a bad smell. "That's what you think of me? That I have to fight everyone's battles?"

"You did allow yourself to get abducted by a serial killer."

She waited for him to say more.

"I knew you wouldn't let me die when there was something you could do about it. I knew you'd swoop in and rescue me like you probably do with everyone you know."

Caisey looked away, across the compound and the road outside where an RV was parked across the street. She could hear cars on a road nearby, the low hum of humanity that meant they weren't the only two people in the world.

"We can talk about it later." Gabe sighed. "I'm kind of bleeding here. At the very least, I'm going to need something to bandage my ribs and half a dozen ice packs."

Caisey set off again and piled Gabe in the front seat. What was wrong with helping people? Even the chaplain had mentioned something to her about fighting everyone's battles. Was it written on her forehead? And what made it so obvious that people she didn't even know, or barely knew in Gabe's case, could see something that was apparently plain as day?

She buckled up and started her car.

"What's going to happen to that guy?" Gabe motioned to the trailer he'd been held in.

Caisey pulled out onto the street and then said, "Liam will make an anonymous tip to the local police. The fake cop will likely not be a problem anymore."

Unlike the vanished sheriff. And the serial killer. And Gabe's uncle.

Baby steps.

"Is this really what your life is like?"

Caisey glanced at him. "When I'm not fighting other people's battles."

Gabe winced and she didn't figure it was because of his injuries. "I'm sorry I said that. I shouldn't judge the way you live your life. It makes you happy to take care of the people you love. Your dad was the same way."

"He was?"

"I spent a lot of time with him before he brought me to Buckshot. We talked a lot. About you, mostly." Gabe sighed. "You remind me of him."

"Fighting a losing battle? My dad might have wanted your uncle off the streets, but he didn't finish what he started."

"And you will?"

"If I can help it." She glanced at him. He really did look like he shouldn't be having this conversation right now. But they needed to make a plan. "What's to stop him from coming after you again? If he wants to kill you, you'll never be safe."

A smile curved the corners of his lips. "Ever eager to get rid of me, aren't you?"

"I just don't see much point in getting attached to each other when you won't be around."

"Because we're not already attached to each other?"

Caisey sighed. "I can deal with longing. I've been doing it for seventeen years."

"I'm just trying to get a handle on where your head is at."

She pulled up outside a chain pharmacy on Colfax, where no one would look twice at them even though Gabe looked like he'd lost a bad fight and it was the middle of the night.

He took her hand, which oddly enough made Caisey feel like crying. "Case..."

She looked up at him.

"I want you to promise me something." He took a shallow breath, full of pain. "I want you to promise me that you'll fight for this the way you fight for everything else in your life."

Caisey squeezed her eyes shut. The adrenaline she'd been coasting on all day had bled away and her body felt like it weighed a thousand pounds.

"Can you do that?"

She nodded.

Gabe squeezed her hand.

"I thought you thought it was a bad thing." She opened her eyes, feeling like a hollow shell of the person she usually was.

Gabe touched her cheek, his eyes were rapidly bruising but he seemed to not care at all. He leaned in and pressed a soft kiss to her lips. "There's been some longing on my end, too." He smiled. "Okay, a lot of longing."

He kissed her again and then leaned back. "Ouch." He touched a finger to his lips. "So, I've decided your fight just might be the only thing that's going to make this work."

"It is?"

"I'm going to trust that if anyone can figure this out, it's you. And I'm going to pray like I've never prayed for anything before that God gives you the answer. Because I've done the only thing I had left to do in my life, so if I'm being given a second chance then this is my new goal."

~

THE CHLOROFORM KILLER gripped the steering wheel and watched them walk into the store. She was touching him again, as though this man was good enough for her.

Why couldn't he get her out of his head?

Caisey Lyons was an anomaly. There was nothing special about her. She was no better than any of the other females he had taken, except the fact that she had chosen it.

She'd chosen him.

TWENTY-FIVE

Two days later Gabe parked his rental car outside the office where his cousin Nic worked. The morning air had a bite to it that ruffled his hair out of place and stung the bruises on his cheekbones. His ribs were wrapped, which mostly just muted the pain. He felt a lot better, unlike the disaster that was the rest of his life.

He paused at the door. Maybe he'd wrecked enough people's lives. He should get back in the car and leave his cousin alone. Holden's son might take one look at him, pull out a gun, and shoot. Gabe might be banking on the close relationship they'd had years ago, but there was no other way to get what he needed to stop his uncle.

That alone made him go inside.

The receptionist looked up. "Help you, hon?" He saw the suspicion in her eyes, and faced the fact he either looked like a thug or a mugging victim.

Gabe nodded to the mature woman in the wool skirt and jacket. She had a flowery scarf tied around her neck. Just the type of grandma secretary he would put in one of his books, except for the fact that she wore rings on every finger and her skirt rode up where she had her legs crossed.

"Nicholas Arturo?"

She gave him a conciliatory smile. "He isn't to be disturbed at the moment."

"Tell him Gabe Carlen is here. If he believes you, he'll want to see me."

The woman's lip curled and she huffed out a breath, muttering something about self- important types and picked up the phone.

Gabe had torn their family apart. Did he even have the right to ask for forgiveness? God had saved him, but there were consequences he still had to live with and God wasn't going to just wash that away so that Gabe could live fun and carefree.

He'd set himself back too much, even in doing the right thing. He'd been obedient to the truth, but what had that ever done for him? Certainly not set him free. That's why he could pray, but Caisey would be the one to find the answer. If anything were to happen between them it would be because God chose to bless Caisey.

The sound of a gunshot blast echoed down the hall.

Gabe flinched, ducking down before the thought registered that no one was shooting at him. Then he ran, hit the door at a dead run and crashed through with the force of his weight. Nic was on the floor behind the desk, a gun discarded like it fell from his hand. The room smelled like someone lit off a firework—smoke and a metallic tang.

Nic's eyes were wide and fixed on the ceiling.

Gabe crouched beside him. "Nic?"

His cousin blinked and focused on his face. "Am I in heaven?"

"You should be so lucky." Gabe grabbed fistfuls of his shirt and hauled him up to sitting. "Were you trying to kill yourself?"

The assistant bustled in. "Should I call an ambulance?"

Gabe glanced back at her and shook his head. "Not right now."

Nic glanced away and muttered, "I can't even do this right." He pointed up and Gabe saw a hole in the wall beside a picture of Nic and his father.

Gabe squeezed the side of his cousin's neck. "Come on."

Nic stumbled to his feet. "You're really here? This isn't a joke?"

"What was it you used to say?" Gabe grinned. "Dost mine eyes deceive me?" Nic laughed and Gabe grabbed his cousin in a hug so tight it was painful to his ribs. He retaliated by slapping his cousin on the back extra hard. "I missed that."

Nic's body shook with laughter that could have been misconstrued as tears. "You'd better have, because no one else seems to think it's a good thing."

"Hey, I run a bookstore."

Nic grinned. "No kidding?"

"First thing I did was order copies of every Shakespeare play." Gabe cleared his throat. "I also write. Carl Gabriel."

"No way. I have all his books...your books." Nic sighed. "I'm happy for you man."

The two of them had been little terrors, cousins the same age who alternately tore up everything fighting and then went off to get up to more trouble together. But that was forever ago. No doubt Gabe missed out on countless things his cousin went through during that time, and likely not all good things considering he had Holden for a dad.

"And you're a...what do you do here?"

Nic shrugged. "Nothing important. Turns out dad wanted the contract for the renovations for city hall, among other things."

"Oh, buddy."

"Yeah, that's what I thought." Nic's eyes roamed over Gabe's face. "I'm guessing he found you. I'm glad you're okay."

"When he realizes I got away, he'll come for me again. That's why I need your help." He pulled Nic up to standing. "Come on. How about a cup of coffee? Though, I'll warn you I don't drink it. I prefer green tea."

Nic's face morphed and Gabe finally saw humor there, with the disgust. Gabe clapped him on the shoulder and led him out. There would be time later to formulate a plan for survival. He wanted to know what had brought Nic to the point that he had a gun in his hand and pulled the trigger, though he had an encyclopedia's worth of ideas. Gabe could only thank God his cousin didn't do himself any permanent damage.

Now there was a chance Gabe might actually be able to do some good in this family, instead of destroying what little bond was left.

~

CAISEY PULLED up a ways back from where Gabe had parked. It wasn't stalking per-se. She just wasn't taking any chances where her family was concerned. Her knowledge of Gabe's uncle had come first-hand from being abducted by the man. It might have been seventeen years ago, but she could still remember the look on his face. Didn't want to get his hands dirty, but had no qualms telling two guys to send a message to Caisey's dad.

She wasn't going to let that happen to anyone else when Holden realized Gabe was still alive and came for him again.

The sign out front of the swanky office building said Nicholas Arturo, LLC. Caisey gripped the steering wheel so hard her fingers hurt. He'd been there that day, working alongside his father like the loving son of a criminal. No matter that he looked like he'd rather be anywhere else. Nic should have sucked it up, pulled out of that family for Jenna. But no, he'd chosen to stick with his dad instead.

She could still feel the impact from every blow. But it got worse when she got home and her dad wouldn't even look her in her good eye. After that, things were never the same. It was like being abandoned by her mom all over again. Her dad pushed harder than ever in the case against Gabe's family and secured his testimony, but it still wasn't enough to bring Holden down. They couldn't even get him for her assault, since her dad had forbidden her to tell anyone, lest it compromise his investigation.

And now Gabe thought she was just like him.

Caisey got out of the car before she even thought about it, and strode on her boot heels down the sidewalk. They walked out together, Gabe's hand on his cousin's shoulder even though he was the injured one. Nic's face was pale and gaunt, and she might have felt sorry for him.

If she hadn't reared back and punched him with every ounce of strength she had.

~

SOMEONE RUSHED past Gabe and all he saw was a blur right before a fist connected with Nic's face. The force of impact knocked Nic back two steps and he grabbed his jaw and hissed.

Caisey hissed too, and flexed her fingers. "Forgot how much that hurts."

"What do you think you're doing? That's my cousin you just punched." Gabe pulled Nic's hand away and winced. He glared at Caisey. "I told you I was coming here."

"You said your cousin. I didn't know you were going to see Nic Arturo, the son of Holden Arturo who is *trying to kill you.* Are you nuts?"

"Why are you shouting at me?"

An older woman strode out. Caisey took one look and thought, *cougar*. "I brought you some ice, hon. Should I call the police?"

"I am the police." Caisey whipped out her black wallet and flipped it open. "FBI."

The cougar put her hands up. Nic's eyes darted to Gabe and he frowned. It didn't look as menacing as it should have, since Nic was holding a towel full of ice to his jaw. "You brought the FBI here?"

"I didn't bring her."

"He's right." Caisey put her badge away. "He didn't. I followed him." She turned to the lady. "Though, maybe you should call the police. I'd like Mr. Arturo arrested for being a class-A jerk."

Nic looked at Gabe. "What is it with you and the FBI?"

And wasn't that a loaded question? Caisey didn't give Gabe time to answer. "I'm not just the FBI, pal. I happen to be the godmother of a sixteen-year-old boy. Jacob Samuel Cartwright."

Nic's eyebrow lifted. "Who?"

There was what could only be described as a loaded silence, wherein Caisey desperately wanted to punch Nic all over again. "Your son. That's who."

Gabe opened his mouth, but all that came out was an unintelligible sound. The look on Nic's face wasn't much better.

"My son?"

Caisey's face morphed into disgust. "It isn't like you didn't know. Don't pretend, just so you don't look like the loser who abandoned his family."

Nic tossed the ice on the ground. "I remember some supposed friend of Jenna Cartwright's calling me to tell me that my girlfriend was better off without me."

"She was."

"Forgot to mention she was pregnant, didn't you Caisey?"

Gabe glanced between them. "What are you guys—?"

Caisey ignored him. "She told you about Jake."

"No, I broke up with her. Not because you told me to. I'd had enough of my dad destroying my life, and I wasn't going to let him do that to Jenna." Nic's face was pale. "She was going to tell me she was pregnant?"

"She didn't tell you?" Caisey blinked. "You didn't know?"

Gabe put his hand on her opposite shoulder so that his forearm crossed her body. "You've said what you had to say. Now you need to leave."

She glared at him. "You're taking his side? This is unbelievable. He's lying. He knew about Jake."

~

"THERE ARE NO SIDES," Gabe said. "If what you're saying is true, this is between Nic and your friend, and the son he never even knew about. We don't get a say."

"Don't get a...are you nuts? He was there. I saw him. He was with them." Her eyes glazed, like she was lost in her memory.

Gabe shifted, wrapped one arm around her waist and touched her neck with his free hand. "Caisey, you need to breathe."

"He was there."

Nic shifted, now behind him. And Gabe heard a whispered, "That was you."

He glanced between them. "One of you needs to tell me what this is."

"I thought it was Jenna at first because she was blonde, but then I realized it couldn't be. They'd brought her in, tied her to a chair, and beat her. I didn't like it, but I couldn't stop them. He said they were making a statement."

Making a statement? Holden making a statement at that time couldn't be about anything but Caisey's dad. *We can get to your daughter*. Because of Gabe's testimony.

He held her gaze. "They did this to you, too?" She didn't move, just held her gaze on his bruised face. "Case." Gabe touched her cheeks, careful to keep his grip soft. "You have to breathe. Everything is okay. No one's going to hurt you."

She huffed through the tears. "It's not me I'm worried about."

Gabe tried to swallow down the lump in his throat. He'd thought he knew the extent of the damage his testimony had caused. But Caisey had been hurt, too.

And Nic was the father of Caisey's best friend's son. He remembered her telling him about Jenna on their date. In a weird way, it made complete sense. Life had tied them together in so many other ways, why not like this, too?

"You want Jenna and her son to be safe from my uncle." Gabe let her go, but stayed close. "You don't think Nic wants that as well?" His cousin would never do anything to harm the people he cared about. Nic was about as different from his dad as it was possible to be.

"You said his name is Jake?"

Gabe nodded. His cousin was holding fast to the need to shake Caisey and tell her everything about the son Nic had never met.

Caisey swallowed. "He's a great kid."

Gabe didn't know whether to push them apart or walk away. "And you kept them from being a family?"

"Nic was the one who chose to stay part of his family instead of being with Jenna."

Nic threw his hands up. "You think he'd ever let me walk away? I didn't know I had a son. You think I wouldn't have moved heaven and earth, done everything I could to keep them, if I'd known?"

"Gabe managed it."

No, Gabe had had every reason not to testify against his father after his date with Caisey. But he couldn't just let things lie. Not when his father was hurting people and that was the only way to make it stop.

TWENTY-SIX

"Caisey." Gabe shook his head. "Does Jenna even know about this?"

Caisey rolled her eyes. "You think I told her that her boyfriend was a spineless jerk who left her high and dry? She had enough of that from her own dad. She didn't need it from Nic."

"What happened with her dad?"

Caisey folded her arms. "Seriously, Nic? Now you decide to care?"

"Tell me what happened."

"Her mom kicked her out. Her dad didn't stick up for her; he just let her walk, like being homeless and pregnant at seventeen was no sweat."

Nic ran a hand down his face. "What happened to her?"

"My dad brought her to my house. She's been living with us ever since."

"And J-Jake?" Nic's voice broke, like just saying the name of his son broke his heart.

"Smart, so smart. For some reason he actually wants to study. It's like everything he reads sticks in his head. It's so full I'm surprised it doesn't explode."

Nic closed his eyes. Gabe laughed and clapped his cousin on the shoulder. "Sounds like genius runs in the family."

Nic shook his head. "It's not genius, just eidetic memory."

"Yeah, that's what the doctor said." Caisey glanced between them and then settled on Nic. "You have it?"

"Yeah, I have it, though it's not common knowledge."

"I'm sure it isn't." Caisey's chin lifted. "No doubt your dad would find some way to exploit a son who could do that. Or a grandson."

Nic ran a hand down his face. "I want to know, but asking would make not seeing them worse. But, I need to...Are they okay? Is Jenna doing okay?"

CAISEY STUDIED him and Gabe prayed with every bit of faith he had that she would answer the question. "She's busy, she loves her work. She loves Jake."

"But..."

"Do you really want to know this?"

Nic was silent, so Gabe said, "Life is way too short. You know that, I know that. We don't want Holden finding out about Jake, but if we do it right he won't ever have to."

Caisey shook her head. "I'm not sure it's worth the risk."

"Case, I get that something horrible happened to you, but that doesn't mean it will happen to Jake."

"It happened to you." Her lips pressed into a fine line. "And what about Jenna, or my Grams?"

"What's the alternative? What if you're hindering something that could be perfect for her?"

Caisey shook her head. "I don't want Jenna anywhere near him."

"Nic or his dad?"

Her face got red. "Either of them."

Nic shook his head. "My dad really did a number on you, didn't he?"

Her head whipped around and her eyes narrowed on Nic. "You don't get to talk about that. And it wasn't just me, he tried to kill Gabe just days ago. Why do you think he looks like that?"

Nic blew out a breath. "I wanted to tell him about Jenna and he dragged me into that room with you. I'm just glad the least of what he made me do was carrying you to the car so they could take you home."

"Take me home?" Caisey laughed, but the sound held no humor. "They pushed me out at an intersection downtown in broad daylight, for everyone to see. Do you have any idea how much it hurt when I hit the pavement?"

Nic flinched. "I didn't know that part."

Gabe wanted to touch her, but she looked like she'd snap. "You need to tell Jenna what you did."

"What I did?" Her eyes were wide, her breath coming fast. "I kept my family safe from him."

Nic's head whipped from side to side. "I'm not the bad guy here."

"Maybe not, but you have a direct line to the one who is."

"What am I supposed to do about that, huh?"

"Oh I don't know." Caisey put her forefinger on her chin. "How about, take your family somewhere else where he won't find you? Live your life. Make them happy. Protect them so I don't have to spend every second of every day and night figuring out ways someone might get to them so I can keep them safe."

"All of a sudden you want to quit?"

"No, Nic. It's my job and I wouldn't have it any other way. But it's supposed to be you doing this. Sucks for them you're too scared."

Nic's hands were fisted by his sides. "My sister Gloria left six months before I met Jenna. She was a few years older than me. You remember her, Gabe?"

He nodded. Gloria had been all smiles and laughter. She made Christmas at their house worth it.

"Gloria disappeared, rumor was she took off with her college boyfriend and got married in Vegas. One day she was having dinner with us and the next day her closet was cleaned out and she was gone."

Caisey huffed. "And you're telling us this fun story because...?"

"Because Gloria's new husband was killed in a random drive-by, gunned down outside his office building and suddenly Gloria was home again. She stayed in her room all the time, crying, while Dad strode around like he was king of the world. She killed herself two weeks later. She didn't want to bring a baby into our family."

Caisey's eyes flashed. "So you went out, armed with this precious knowledge, and got Jenna pregnant?"

"It wasn't supposed to—I didn't even know that happened. She should have told me."

"You broke up with her and she was devastated." Caisey sighed. "I'm so sorry about your sister, that shouldn't have happened. But my only concern is my family." She turned to Gabe. "Nic cannot have contact with them. They either disappear like you did, or he never sees them. And since I doubt Jenna would agree to give up their whole lives that leaves us one option. No contact."

"But he found us." Gabe blew out a breath. "He sent those two guys dressed as cops.

It's not like they'll be safe anywhere else."

"They'll never be safe from Holden, period. And neither will you."

Gabe winced. "But Nic is Jake's father. If it's what he wants, shouldn't Nic have the chance to see what can be between him and Jenna?"

Caisey shook her head. "It's too risky. You shouldn't have come here."

Nic clapped his hand on Gabe's shoulder. "I'd like to say it was good to see you, but— " He tipped his head in Caisey's direction. "As much as I hate to say it, she's right."

~

CAISEY WALKED TO HER CAR, aware Gabe was right behind her.

"You're just going to walk away? You're not going to do anything?"

She spun around. "You already tried to run, and I'm sorry it was my fault he found you in Buckshot. But if my dad couldn't get enough for your uncle to finally be convicted of something, who can?"

"There has to be something we can do."

"There isn't."

"I don't buy that." Gabe's face was flushed.

She understood his anger, she just processed hers differently. Which was why her hand hurt like she'd hit a brick wall. Why did Nic's jaw have to be so hard?

"We have to take him down. We can't live with this over our heads."

Caisey shook her head. "How do you propose we do that? I'm not a miracle worker."

"You're an FBI agent. You can't do anything about this?"

"I can see if anyone has an open investigation. I can put out some feelers and see what I can dig up that might get what we need. But prison won't take away his power."

"Then what's the point of it?"

She folded her arms. "It's justice. That's the point."

"Like condemning my dad?"

Caisey studied him. Did he regret what he did? His dad was a bad guy too, but nowhere near the scale of Gabe's uncle. Which gave her an idea. "What about your dad?"

"My dad?"

"Would he help us solve the problem of your uncle?"

"Like testify?"

Caisey shrugged. "It's been a lot of years. Maybe he really did find God in prison and now that he's dying, maybe he'll be willing to tell us what he knows. Give us something on your uncle's operation that we can corroborate."

Gabe frowned. "Are you always this calculating?"

"I call it problem solving. Some people think it's a good thing." She sighed. "But we'll still have to take steps to stay safe."

"Like warning away your best friend's boyfriend? Maybe you were just freaked out because of what happened to you that you wanted to keep her safe all on your own and wouldn't trust it to anyone else."

Caisey's stomach knotted. "That's not what it was. You make it sound selfish. I loved having them with me and I wouldn't have it any other way, and there is no way on earth I could have known Jenna's family would kick her out. But we made it work."

Gabe's mouth thinned. "Well, now you need to make this work."

"Why is everything my responsibility?"

"Because you're the one who's kept them both safe all these years. Now it's time to give them a future, and in the process give yourself one."

"I can't even think about that now."

"You deserve more than the limbo you've been living in, hiding just like me. You think I don't see it? You guard your heart so fiercely I wonder that it even works at all."

Caisey flinched. He really thought that? Like somehow she was defective because she'd chosen to be an agent and all these years later she was still single? She strode to her car door and opened it, staring at him across the roof. "Thank you very much for your insight, Gabe. I'll take it under advisement."

His face softened. "Case—"

"No. It's fine. You're right. It's time I got on with my life. Clearly the one I'm living isn't good enough for you."

TWENTY-SEVEN

Caisey stepped aside so the rush of agents could pass by her in the hall early the next morning. She knew the surge of adrenaline that made a cop's eyes focus and darken, she'd felt it many times when the rush of the hunt coalesced into action and investigation became arrest. Something was going down this morning, and here she was headed to her desk for more hours of computer searches.

Caisey set the extra-hot vanilla latte in front of Liam and hung her jacket on the back of her desk chair. "Okay, hit me."

His mouth twitched. "They think they finally got a lead on the Chloroform Killer."

No wonder they were in such a hurry. "They've been pulling all-nighters for weeks. I'd be fired up for a takedown too, if it meant being home in time for dinner for once. What'd they get?"

Liam laughed. "Tire tracks on the vehicle used to dump the body in Aurora led to a plumber."

Caisey shook her head. "There's no way he's that stupid."

"Maybe."

"So why didn't you go with them?"

Liam shrugged and picked up his coffee mug. "It's been a crazy few weeks."

"So you're saying that your health and well-being comes before catching the decade's most notorious serial killer?" Caisey grinned even though he wasn't looking at her. "Or were you just not in the mood for a takedown because you're a wee bit tired?"

"You're a pain, you know that?"

Caisey laughed. "Yeah, but you love me anyway."

"Love might be too strong of a word." Liam's gaze settled on his computer screen and he clicked the mouse. "It's possible, anyway, likely even, that all this is connected. Your house was broken into and then the guy impersonating state patrol kidnapped Gabe. I'd like to tread cautiously. The sheriff is still unaccounted for."

"Most of that links back to Gabe's uncle, not the investigation."

"I know. And it depends on what the State guys dig up on the guy they have in Buckshot pretending to be one of their cops. Then they have to co-ordinate with Denver police and the guy they have here."

"They haven't sent you anything yet?"

Liam shook his head. "They're not even done processing evidence on Emma Allens' murder, which I guess means they're no closer to figuring out what the heck happened with the sheriff. And the BOLO hasn't turned up anything yet, so he's still at large."

"Yippee." She blew out a breath.

"Gabe's dad agreed to help?"

Caisey nodded. "So we're not supposed to go after Gabe's uncle now, until Toben coughs up what he knows. And that won't happen until after the agents on the case approach Gabe with the offer. I guess he wants to see Gabe before he dies. Which means I get to sit here until either Holden gets indicted, or he tries to kill Gabe again."

Liam tilted his head to one side. "I wouldn't be worried about sitting here. I'd be worried about going outside."

Caisey rolled her eyes. "Wow, that's super helpful. Thanks."

"You're welcome." Liam leaned back in his chair. "Where is Gabe, anyway?"

"How should I know? He disappeared with Nic."

Liam's lips twitched. "He chose his cousin over you? How dare he?" Caisey glared at her partner.

"And how's Grams?"

"Dehydrated. They admitted her to hospital, but only so they could give her fluids because she can't keep anything down." Caisey shifted in her chair.

"Why don't you go see her?"

"I need to clear out some of my work first. I'll go as soon as I'm done."

Liam nodded. "Let's get to work then."

JENNA STOOD at the window of her spa with her arms folded and one toe tapping on the tile. Her stomach felt like the time she drank orange juice and it was fizzy. She stared across the street where he'd been when she walked from the parking lot to open the spa that morning, carrying her large sugar free, nonfat latte.

That was two hours ago.

He was still there, leaning back against the car that had been her favorite ever since she discovered they existed. Every time traffic passed she wondered if he'd be gone, but he was still there—the arms of his light blue button down shirt folded across his chest. His legs were even crossed at the ankles.

Nic. She couldn't even say his name out loud or she'd likely start crying right here.

She should probably call the cops and have him forcibly removed, but he was across the street and she'd have a hard time explaining exactly what he'd done. Standing there staring at her wasn't exactly illegal. Not to mention that part of her wanted to run across the street and throw herself at him. Except instead of kissing him, she'd more likely burst into tears and end up blubbering on his shoulder.

She was stronger than that...she hoped.

He'd been the one to dump her. Therefore girl-law stated that she had to resist the urge to make the first move. Play it cool and make him come to her, groveling on his knees for leaving her and Jake high and dry. Then she would take pity on him and accept his apology. Then she could throw herself at him and they could make out...you know, after the third date.

But who said that was what he wanted? Maybe he was only here for Jake. Or just to freak her out. That made more sense, being as it had been two hours and he hadn't even moved.

The passenger door opened and another man climbed out—a man with two black eyes, looking more than worse for wear. *Ouch.* It reminded her of when Caisey was beaten up. He said something across the car, but Nic just shook his head. The other man rounded the vehicle and Nic grabbed his arm. They had words, and it was Nic who waited for a break in traffic to cross the street.

Jenna grabbed her phone and sent a quick text. She was going to stand strong, but that didn't mean she couldn't call in reinforcements of her own. She quickly settled behind the counter and perused the schedule to see what needed to be rearranged if she was going to be busy the rest of the day. Plus it had the added bonus of making it look like she hadn't been stressing this whole time.

The door swished open and Jenna saw Pam's eyes go wide. She knew how her receptionist was feeling, since just one of them had enough of a presence to take a girl's breath away. Together they were a double threat, shot-through-the-heart style.

"Jenna?"

She wanted to squeeze her eyes shut. The sound of his voice was like a breath of cool air in summer. Instead, she straightened her spine and looked up. "Hello, Nic."

He swallowed. "How are you?"

She looked instead at the other man.

He strode forward, smiling. "Gabe Carlen."

There was only one man with that name Jenna knew. "Gabe? The Gabe?"

His lips twitched. "Last time I checked."

It was the guy, Caisey's dream man from the date-to-end-all-dates. Jenna's eyes burned, so she blinked.

Nic glanced back and forth between them. "You guys know each other?"

"Uh..." It was Gabe! A million questions flew through her mind. Jenna shook them all out and said, "Does Caisey know you're here?"

He nodded.

Jenna smiled. "That explains why you look like someone beat the crap out of you."

He laughed. "She didn't do this."

Well, that meant Caisey was going to delete her dating profile now and leave Jenna hanging. Jenna felt the smile, so big her cheeks ached. "It's really nice to meet you, Gabe."

"Um...excuse me," Nic said. "I'm here too."

Jenna straightened her spine and looked at him. "Jake and I are well, thank you." She glanced at Gabe, who had a small smile on his face that said he knew how hard this was for her. But he had no idea.

She turned back to Nic. "What do you want?"

It was then she knew that this was make-or-break time for him. The look in his eye was one she'd never seen. The boy she knew had become a man, a serious man.

"I want my life back." He blew out a breath. "If it's okay with you, I'd like to talk. I know we have to go slow with this, but I want to meet Jake when you decide its okay. I've missed a lot...too much. But I'd like to know the two of you."

"And if that isn't something I want?" It broke her heart to say it, but she got the words out. She needed to know where he stood.

"Then I'll walk away. If you don't want me in your life, that's up to you. But I think we'll be missing out on something. But Jake is almost an adult and I am his father. When he turns eighteen I'll be offering him the choice to get to know me."

"Why now?" She said it before she even knew she wanted an answer. "What's changed?"

"That's a fair question, Jenna. But I have one for you." He took a breath. "Why did you never tell me I had a son?"

Jenna's world rocked. "I was going to, but before I could say it you broke up with me. I went to your house and your dad chased me off."

"So why didn't you keep trying?"

"I wrote you a letter."

"I never got it."

She swallowed. "It's plain to see that now."

He looked incredibly disappointed, but what else could Jenna have done? It was right around the time Caisey had been beaten up and they'd both been dealing with everything that was happening. She'd figured if Nic cared, he'd have found her. Besides, who wanted to be with someone who only hung around because they felt obligated? And exposing a helpless baby to a grandfather like that? He'd scared the life out of Jenna.

"Caisey was right when she said I wasn't good enough for you. She was part of what made me realize I'd been too scared before, taking the easy way out."

"When did you see Caisey?"

He ran a finger across a dark mark on his jaw. "Yesterday."

"And she hit you?"

"She had every right to. So do you. I—" Nic sighed. "I can't believe what a mess I made of this."

Jenna came out from behind the desk. Thankfully the lobby was clear of people and Pam had judged the situation well enough she'd made herself scarce. Jenna wanted to run in her office and lock the door, cry it all out, and then come back out and be strong. Caisey would know how to handle this. She would know what to say, but maybe a smart remark wasn't what was needed here.

He was obviously broken. She could see it in the slump of his shoulders and the sheen of tears in his eyes. Could they make something out of this mess? Maybe not the blessed life they were supposed to have had, but some semblance of happiness?

Jenna sucked in a breath and nodded. "We should talk."

CAISEY PULLED into a tight space in front of Jenna's spa and raced inside where her best friend was facing off against Nic and Gabe.

Gabe's face changed when he saw her. "Hey, I was going to call you."

Caisey needed to tell him about the agent's visit to his dad, but couldn't think what he might need to speak to her about. It was clear that the reality had been far off the memory of who he was, but she shouldn't be surprised. He was a regular guy, not a fantasy, and she was here for Jenna anyway. A girl needed her best friend when her kid's dad walked back into her life after nearly two decades.

She brushed past Gabe and got between Nic and Jenna. "Let's go in your office."

Jenna smiled. "It's okay, Case, we agreed to talk."

"Jenna—"

"I've already made the decision. And honestly, this is between me and Nic. I thought I might need you, but I'm doing okay on my own."

"Of course you are, but I don't want you to make the wrong choice."

"And I need you to help me make the right one?"

Caisey flinched. "I didn't mean that. Listen, let's just go in your office and we can figure this out. You shouldn't make a decision on the fly. You need time to think this through."

"You don't get it." Jenna smiled. "I've had years to think it through."

"So you're just going to let him walk all over you again? What if he decides it's not worth it and leaves?"

The smile dropped from her face. "You don't think I'm worth it?"

"No." Caisey shook her head. "That isn't what I meant—"

"But you think he's going to leave me again. Is that why you warned him off me in the first place?" Jenna crossed her arms. "Why don't you tell me about that, Caisey?"

Caisey felt Nic move closer to her back. Did he think he was going to help? "It isn't you, Jenna. There are other factors here you don't know about. It has to do with...with when I was attacked."

"What does that have to do with Nic?" She glanced between them and took a step back at what she saw. "What aren't you telling me?"

"It's complicated. It's—"

"Were you ever going to tell me? I know you were trying to protect me, but I wanted the chance to figure out the relationship myself. I didn't get the chance to tell Nic about the baby and by the time I got to speak to him he'd already taken your advice."

Nic chimed in. "Jenna—"

"No. Both of you are keeping stuff from me. Did you think I couldn't handle it? Because I'm not as weak as y'all think I am." Her eyes narrowed on Caisey. "I'm doing fine. I thought I might need your help, but I don't. Thanks for coming. I know how busy your schedule is."

Actually it was, and Caisey really needed to get back to the office, but she didn't move. "Don't be like this, Jenna. We don't think you're weak."

"Are you or are you not keeping things from me?"

"It wasn't important and at the time I really didn't want to talk about it."

Jenna shook her head. "What does you being attacked have to do with Nic?"

Caisey took a breath.

"It was my dad who did that to Caisey."

Jenna looked at her, and Caisey squeezed her eyes shut.

"She was right not to want that in your life, in Jake's life." Nic's voice wavered when he said his son's name.

Caisey looked at Nic and smiled. "He really does look like you."

"No!" Jenna whirled around. Her face morphed to anger. "You don't get to do that. He doesn't get to have that from anyone except me. You have no right."

"Jenn—"

"No! I don't need your help anymore." Jenna whirled around, raced off to her office and slammed the door.

Caisey winced.

"Come on." Gabe tugged on her arm. "Let's give them some room."

She didn't want to, but the look on Nic's face made her retreat outside with Gabe. "We should be quick. I don't like you being exposed on the street like this."

Jenna was mad at her. Caisey had been trying to do the right thing, but Jenna didn't seem to agree, and she wouldn't even let her explain.

Gabe studied her. "I wasn't trying to insult you yesterday. I just get what you're doing, that's all."

"Fine. You get me. Great."

"Yeah, it is actually." He stepped closer. "Because I'm not leaving. And I'm not going to let your steel reinforced sense of self-preservation push me away. I'm going to break through."

She really didn't like the sound of that. "I'm not some kind of challenge you have to overcome."

Gabe smiled. "Yes, you are. The best kind." Caisey huffed. "I am not—"

Gabe stepped back. "Don't you have to get back to work?"

TWENTY-EIGHT

Gabe was starting to like when she reacted like that. Push a little, and Caisey Lyons' incredulity meter flipped into the red zone. Her face got all flushed and she sputtered, like she couldn't begin to think how to react.

She was so in control when it was anything to do with work. Life or death, firing questions at the sheriff as he came at them on the ATV, swooping in and saving him from the fake trooper like it was no big deal, she impressed him at every turn. And yet Gabe took the most pleasure in throwing her off when she was completely out of her element. Her floundering was incredibly cute.

Gabe decided she'd had enough torture. "So what did you need to tell me?"

She tugged on his arm and they walked to the stoplight. He hit the button for the crosswalk. It would give them some time to talk, going the long way back to his cousin's classic car.

"Just that I talked with a couple of the agents who ran the investigation along with my dad and they say your uncle isn't doing much of anything anymore. When the economy tanked, apparently so did the market for illegal arms. Who knew?" She shrugged. "Anyway, he streamlined his businesses and concentrated on what was doing well, like gambling and drug dealing, until things like construction began to pick back up and he could get back in that game."

"Where does that leave us?"

"Well, officially the FBI considers the death of the undercover agent closed, since your dad was convicted. They are, however, talking to him about Arturo to see if they can finally pin something on your uncle."

Four steps removed was closer than Gabe thought he'd ever be to his father again. "My dad and Arturo might only be brothers-in-law, but they both have the same unbreakable stubborn streak."

Caisey's lips twitched and they set off across the street. "Don't we all?"

"You'll keep me posted?"

"Are you going to try and see him?"

Gabe was curious to know what his father was going to do. Curious enough to stay in Denver and put his life on the line for the sake of getting word that his father wanted to see him.

"I'd like to ask his forgiveness, if I can. Is that nuts?"

She laughed. "You did the right thing, testifying, but if you're carrying guilt it's not going to go away unless you make peace with it. That doesn't mean it has to involve your father, though."

"I've been praying about it for so long it's hard to believe I might actually be able to see him. I'd like the chance to look him in the eye and say more than sorry in the heat of the moment."

He'd also thought he would never get to meet Caisey again and now that he had, well...he'd assumed it would go differently. Holding on to the dream for years, he'd prayed that God would someday bring it all back around—that the time spent wouldn't be wasted, that he'd get the girl, that testifying wouldn't have meant his world was destroyed and there would still be something to salvage. Writing had been enough for a long time, but now he'd seen Caisey's strength, her pure convictions, the sound of her voice and the way her mouth crept up at one side when she thought something was funny he didn't think he could let her go.

A horn blared. Caisey whipped around. An old seventies RV

accelerated toward them. The driver was a man, but not close enough Gabe could make out his features.

Caisey didn't move. He tugged on her arm until she blinked, whipped around and shoved him back, moving with him to get them out of the path of the vehicle. She kept shoving until the back of Gabe's shoes hit the curb and they fell. He locked his arms around her.

They hit the concrete. "Ouch."

She shifted and looked down at him. "I think the word you're looking for is, 'thank you'."

"That's actually two words."

"Whatever. I just saved your hide."

His eyebrows lifted. "Do you want a medal?"

AS SOON AS the car moved past, Jenna sprinted across the street with Nic right behind her. She reached them just as Gabe stood up and brushed off the back of his jeans. Jenna nearly tripped. She'd half expected them to be dead. Not only were they alive, but they looked unharmed.

She pulled up short. Both of them were looking at anything but each other.

"Are you guys okay? What was that?"

Caisey rolled her shoulders. "We're fine."

"That RV just tried to run you over. What is wrong with people?"

Sirens turned the corner and two cop cars with lights flashing pulled up either side of Nic's car.

Caisey frowned. "Who called the police?"

Jenna put her hands on her hips. "I did."

Three uniformed officers climbed out; an older black man with stripes on his sleeves and two younger guys all strode over. Jenna's eyes caught on one and she laughed at the high school flashback. "Bobby Summers?"

The officer grinned. "As I live and breathe, Jenna Cartwright. How are you, girl?"

Jenna shrugged one shoulder. "Can't complain."

Nic reached out his hand. "Summers."

The two men shook and the officer looked to Jenna and then back at Nic. "You two together, just like high school. Am I right?"

Jenna felt her cheeks warm. "We have a son." Bobby Summers didn't need to know Nic hadn't ever met Jake.

"No way! Awesome, dude."

"Officer Summers!" They all turned to look at the guy with the stripe on the sleeves on his dark blue shirt, where he stood to the side with Caisey. "Get started with interviews. I'd rather not be here all day."

"Sure, Sarge."

The old man shook his head and Jenna watched him look at Caisey, who shared a smile with him. Apparently they knew each other. They stepped further away, in their little cop huddle.

"Hey." Nic nudged her elbow. "You okay?"

"I cannot believe she nearly got splatted and she's standing around like it's no big deal."

"They seem fine. Gabe looks windblown, but that's probably just because she shoved him out of the way."

"Yep, that's Caisey. Defender of humankind."

"You don't think she should have?"

Jenna stared at him. "You think she was right, telling you to stay away from me and Jake? I don't think you understand what you missed."

Nic's lips pressed together. "Sixteen years of his life. That's what I missed." And that was her fault?

Jenna ducked between two cars and ran back to her spa. Why couldn't he have stayed away? Everything was fine this morning, and now she knew Caisey lied. Nic showed up, bringing danger. She wanted to believe she could handle it all, but she hadn't ever tried before, content to let Caisey take on the hard decisions. Standing up for herself was harder than she thought.

~

CAISEY SAW Jenna duck back across the street to her spa and shot Nic an inquiring look. He shook his head and made his way over to Gabe.

"That all of it?"

She turned back to Sergeant Tucker. "If I think of anything else, I'll give you a call."

He nodded. "Good deal."

Her phone buzzed. She pulled up the text message that was Liam telling her he was parking around the corner.

A minute later he strode up to her. "You okay?"

"Could have killed me. Didn't."

Liam rubbed his jaw. "I don't like it."

Caisey wanted to brush it off and laugh, but she couldn't.

"I think I have a serial killer stalker."

TWENTY-NINE

Caisey made her way to where Gabe and Nic stood talking to the officers still. "You guys okay?"

The officer stepped back, but Gabe came to her and kept his voice low. "Do you think my uncle just tried to kill us?"

She shook her head. Was she supposed to tell him she thought it was the Chloroform Killer? "The cops will find out for sure, but I think I know who it was. There's not a whole lot we need to do now, unless someone saw the license plate as it was driving away. I'm going back to the office."

"You..." He blinked. "You know who that was?"

"Yes. So you don't need to worry."

Gabe threw his hands up and let them drop back by his sides. "Why would I worry, we only almost nearly died."

"You get used to it."

He blinked.

"Okay. So...I'm going to go now."

Before her burning eyes filled with tears, before she launched herself into Gabe's arms and cried like a baby. She needed to get away, to process the fact that it really was the Chloroform Killer in that RV, and he was watching her. She'd seen it several times now, the same vehicle—in Buckshot, on the highway, and now here.

And it was him, this whole time.

"I'm going to stay with Nic. He's been having a rough time lately."

Caisey latched on to his comment. "Daddy not treating him well?" She pressed her lips together and looked at the sidewalk under her boots. "What do you mean, a hard time?"

"Caisey."

She looked up, trying not to let the look on his face get to her.

"None of this is easy for any of us."

"I know. I just really don't like your uncle. And I don't like that Jake's father has stayed loyal to him all these years." That wasn't all she didn't like, but he didn't need to be dragged into her problems.

"I thought they had you, didn't they?"

Caisey shook her head. "That doesn't mean Jake didn't need a dad. Even though my dad did the best he could, it's not the same. Nic is his father."

"Jenna and Nic just need time to talk it through. Without you punching Nic because you don't like what he did."

Was he going to keep bringing that up?

"And not Nic alone in his office with a handgun."

Caisey's head jerked.

"He was going to hurt himself. I was in the lobby when the gun went off."

She winced. "I'm sorry, Gabe."

"Maybe you should cut Nic some slack."

"Only so long as your uncle doesn't get anywhere near them."

She glanced at Nic then, hands in the pockets of his tailored slacks. Expensive shirt, silk tie. He looked like the son of a rich man, but the businessman thing didn't seem to fit him. Nothing about Nic said he was comfortable with who he was. She could see him needing time to figure out his life. Caisey had done the same thing.

After her dad had handed her the FBI badge that was in her pocket, for the first time at her Quantico graduation, she understood the gravity of being a legacy agent. But she also knew she had to make a mark on her own.

"Caisey!" Jenna stood outside the spa's front door, her cell in her hands. "Grams took a turn for the worse."

~

JENNA SAT on the side of the hospital bed.

"Honestly, you would think I was dying."

Laughter spilled out and Jenna leaned in and kissed Grams on the cheek. "Heaven forbid anyone offer sympathy."

"Sympathy is for sissies."

Jenna sighed.

"What is it, my love?"

Today had been an emotional rollercoaster. Standing on her own two feet was exhausting, but Jenna was glad she'd finally done it. Now she just needed Caisey to actually see that she was doing it. And while it might not be perfect, she was going to make it.

Grams squeezed her hand and Jenna sighed. "Nic wants to talk. He wants to know Jake and be part of our family."

"And how do you feel about it?"

"I just wish I knew what we were aiming for, you know? Then I could work toward that, there would be a plan. But what if we don't feel the same way we did? We're not going to be a real family. We'll be in each other's lives, but not much else. Or what if only one of us falls in love? What if Jake doesn't want to know his dad? How do we see each other and see if we can salvage something if Jake is between us? Maybe there isn't anything to salvage. Or maybe Nic just wants to be friends so he can get to know Jake."

Jenna shook her head. "I shouldn't be laying this all on you. You probably don't feel good and you don't need my drama. Get some rest, okay?"

"Wait a second." Grams tugged on her hand, so Jenna sat back down. "Why wouldn't he want to have a relationship with you? You're a wonderful girl, Jenna Cartwright. Regardless of what that old bag, your mother, said. What does she know?"

Jenna couldn't help it, she smiled.

"You have a lot to offer. And if that boy can't see how incredible you are then he's a bigger idiot than he was when he let you walk away the first time. Is that what you want to hear?"

"What?"

"You should know this already. You shouldn't doubt who you are and what you have to offer. What's wrong with you?"

Jenna's mouth dropped open.

"Close your mouth, dear. You're not a fish." Grams tutted. "You need to move on from what happened. Nothing good is going to come from rehashing the past over and over again. Find out who Nic is, the man he's grown up to be and you show him the woman you are. Get to know each other now, but guard your heart. And Jake is almost grown. He isn't a child who needs you to set the parameters. If he doesn't want to see his father, he doesn't have to, but that doesn't stop you from having a relationship with Nic. You don't have to take on board Jake's feelings. They're his."

Jenna blew out a breath and nodded. "He'll be by later. I don't suppose you could tell him that his dad showed up today and wants to see him?"

Grams eyes narrowed. "Not on your life."

Jenna huffed. "Figures." Grams smiled, but there were dark circles around her eyes. "I'm going to let you rest now."

"Don't tell me, I look old."

"You are old."

Grams shrugged. "You're not wrong."

Jenna kissed her papery cheek again and smiled on her way out, but Grams' eyes were already closed. She closed the door with a quiet click.

"She okay?"

Jenna turned and saw Caisey approach. "She's sleeping now, so we should probably let her rest."

"I'll just peek in on her."

Jenna moved so she was in front of the handle. "Let her sleep."

Caisey frowned, but she was going to have to suck it up. Jenna wasn't going to let her disturb Grams just because she finally cleared her schedule. The sentiment was fine, but it didn't mean she could do whatever she wanted.

"What's up with you?"

Jenna shrugged. "Nothing. I just don't think you should bother her."

"Fine. I'll come back later."

"Okay."

"Good."

Jenna sighed and looked at the ceiling, then back at Caisey. "Look, I don't like this any more than you do. I'm trying to be strong despite the fact you've been keeping all that stuff about Nic from me for years. I might not like it, but it's done and we have to figure out a way past it."

CAISEY CROSSED the width of the hall and sat on the end of a row of four chairs. Jenna sat so there was a chair between them. "You weren't in a position to understand. You'd have told Nic you didn't care about his dad, you'd have pushed him to pull away and be with you and the baby. You would have convinced him it was the right thing."

"Why is that bad? We would have been together."

Caisey shook her head, her eyes on the toes of her boots. "Nic's dad would have destroyed it."

"You don't know that. We might have been okay. Maybe it wouldn't have been perfect, but we would've been a family and there's nothing bad about that."

"Unless you were torn apart for good, then you would have lost everything. Including Jake."

"You don't know that."

"Nic's dad would have pulled you and Nic apart one way or another and he would have taken Jake from you."

"You don't know that."

Caisey turned to her and Jenna saw darkness in her eyes that she'd seen only once. When her best friend was black and blue, bandaged and broken, lying on her bed in a flood of tears she thought she hid from everyone. Caisey had pulled herself out of that, but it was back now and Jenna knew that aching despair. She'd been there too.

Caisey bit her lip. "He told me."

"Nic?"

"His dad."

Jenna scooted to the chair beside Caisey and grabbed her hand. "Tell me."

Caisey sniffed. "I was still tied to the chair, but everyone was gone. My nose had stopped bleeding but my whole head was stopped up like I'd been crying for hours. The door closed and someone came in, but I couldn't see who it was. He crouched beside me and whispered in my ear. He told me he'd taken me to get to my dad, that it was an adult thing I wouldn't understand. Then he told me he knew about you. He knew everything. He said if you ever saw Nic again he would do the same thing to you, to make sure you lost the baby."

Jenna squeezed her eyes shut.

Caisey continued, whispering now, "He said he wouldn't stop until what you had with Nic was destroyed. Because their family didn't suffer mistakes, they cleaned them up. That's why I warned Nic away from you. I didn't tell him what his dad said, either. I didn't need to, because he already knew. I guess he got the same speech."

Jenna looked up at her friend. She wasn't going to bring it up, or acknowledge it, but Caisey had tears in her eyes, something else Jenna hadn't seen in all those years. "Thank you."

"For telling you?"

"Yes. But also for saving my son."

"You don't hate me?"

Jenna rolled her eyes. "Why on earth would I hate you? But if you screw this up for me now, I'll never forgive you."

Caisey grinned. "Check you out, getting all feisty."

"Seriously, I'm going to do this. Nic's dad might still hate us, but I won't let him control our lives. We've missed too much and we can't afford to lose anything else. I have to try. I have to fight for this, or what's the point of anything? I can't believe God would bring us back together now if He isn't going to work it out."

Caisey stood and grabbed Jenna in a hug. "I'll do what I can."

"You can't fix everything."

"I know that."

Jenna studied her friend. "Sometimes things even have to get worse, before they get better."

"I don't see why."

"It's just how it is."

Caisey's lip curled. "Well, I don't have to like it."

Jenna laughed. "And that's why we love you."

THIRTY

Gabe pulled his car over to the side of the street. The drive was a quarter mile long and the house looked like the same two-story, three-wing, million-dollar mansion. He pulled onto the drive. Caisey wasn't the only one who could protect the people she cared about.

Yes, he was really going to do this.

The doorbell echoed through the house, but no one answered. Gabe tried the handle, which opened to the cavernous foyer. His uncle's office hadn't moved, and that was where he found Holden Arturo—alone in his giant house, in the dim light of his office, hunched over his computer.

"Long time no see."

Holden's face jerked up and his eyes narrowed. He whipped open the top drawer of the desk and pulled out a gun.

"You won't kill me."

"After what you've done to this family, I should splatter your brains on the rug. You're supposed to be dead already. I should shoot you right now."

"But who would clean it up?" Gabe had seen the layer of dust on the shelves and guessed that when Nic's mother took her suitcases and her court-appointed assets she'd taken the housekeeper too. But Holden probably didn't care, so long as the outside was up to par.

Gabe folded his arms across his chest and prayed his uncle didn't see the fear coursing through his veins. "It seems imprudent, after all the effort you've gone to, that you would go and ruin the plan now. You'd never get away with it."

Holden's jaw flexed. "I'd like to say I know what you're talking about, but I'm afraid I have no idea. Sounds interesting, though. Perhaps you are confusing circumstances with one of your books."

He said that like it was a foul word. No matter that Gabe had built something for himself through hard work, something that most would consider to be a success. That didn't matter to Holden, who saw only ruthlessness as victory.

Gabe opened his mouth to fire back, but something held his tongue. "What happened to you? I expected the maids and bodyguards you used to have. Where is everyone?"

Holden sniffed. "What, have you been living in the boondocks all these years? The economy tanked. Business dropped off. Layoffs were inevitable."

And instead of consolidating his efforts, Holden had merely clung to the crumbling ashes of his empire. Now he was only left with his pride.

"You know exactly where I've been living. I figured out you had the sheriff try and pin a murder on me." It was a guess, but Gabe figured it was probably accurate.

"So you say." His eyes narrowed. "Wearing a wire, perhaps? Trying to get me to incriminate myself?"

Gabe's cell phone was recording the conversation from his jacket pocket, but he wasn't going to admit that. "I just want to understand why."

"That's why you came? Closure." The older man snorted, his wrinkled face shifting like an accordion being played. "So much psychobabble, like your mother. She always was more concerned with feelings. Your father and I are men of action. But you couldn't be content with the comfortable life we gave you. You had to tear it all apart."

Holden stood, set both of his palms on the desk and leaned forward. "You come to my house and dare ask me to explain myself? You are nothing, Gabriel. We gave you the world and you threw it back in our faces."

Gabe wanted to step back, but he had to hold his ground. The old man would think him weak if he retreated, never mind that stomach acid stung in his throat.

"Leave us alone."

Holden tipped his head back and laughed, but there was no humor in it.

~

NIC PULLED onto the drive with Jenna in the passenger seat. His headlights lit up the back of Gabe's Jeep.

"I was right."

Jenna glanced at him, eyes wide. "He's really here?"

"That's his car." Nic blew out a breath. "What is he doing? This is suicide."

Jenna had already pulled out her phone. "I'm going to call Caisey."

Nic stopped her fingers with his. "That might not be a good idea."

"She's a cop, Nic."

"I know."

"She can keep Gabe safe, and he'll need her if your dad is half as bad as you all say he is. So which is it? Is he homicidal, or just a jerk?"

Nic worked his mouth back and forth. "Okay, call her."

After Jenna hung up, she said, "Should we go inside? She said to wait for her, but maybe Gabe needs strength in numbers."

Halfway to the front door, Nic stopped and turned to her. "You should wait in the car."

"No, that's not going to happen."

"Jenna—" Nic sighed. How did he tell her that things between them were still so delicate that he didn't want anything to crush either of their hopes? They could still have something great, just like he'd known when he walked away. "He'll say stuff to you, horrible things. Trust me, it's what he does. Threats. Belittling. He doesn't mince words. That's never been his style when he could go for the jugular and get faster results."

She nodded, resolute. "I understand." She looked like she was arming herself for battle.

"You'll risk this all, for Gabe?"

"Of course. If he and Caisey are going to work out what's between them they need the time to do that. They don't need your father to destroy their future either."

"Can you let me do this, please?" He held her shoulders. "I'm used to it."

"Why?" Tears filled her eyes. "Why didn't you just walk away?"

Nic held her gaze. He didn't want to, but he had to explain it sometime. Why not now? Caisey was likely speeding across Denver and when she got here, she could use her clout to get Gabe out. Nic wouldn't have to face the old man again.

He took a deep breath and let it out. "He had pictures of you."

"Of me?"

"He knew everything about where you went and who you were friends with. He knew about us from the beginning. He said he let it go, because he assumed it was just some passing phase before I would settle for what he thought was better. But he didn't know what I was feeling. He didn't know I loved you. When I saw what he did to Caisey I knew he brought me there so he could show me what he would do to you. If I didn't walk away. And that was when I didn't even know you were pregnant."

Jenna shut her eyes. "I don't want Jake anywhere near him. Ever. We have to keep him safe."

Nic shook his head. "I don't know how to do that. He's morphed my life into what he wanted to suit his purposes. I didn't have anything else and maybe that made me weak, but I let him. I think I was trying to prove he was right, because admitting the alternative—that I'd made a horrible mistake in letting you go—would have been worse."

Jenna lifted her chin, her eyes blazing with a fire he hadn't seen in years. "We can't let Gabe and Caisey lose what we lost. We have to help them."

Nic wanted to laugh. "I just told you I'm a miserable excuse for a man, and you want my help?"

~

CAISEY PULLED up behind Nic's car and saw him and Jenna in a huddle. She strode over, pulling out her weapon and flipping off the safety as she walked. "Gabe is inside?"

Nic nodded.

She didn't wait to hear what else he had to say, just trotted up the front steps and went inside. The halls were dark, but dim orange light shone in the doorway of the study. She kept her steps quiet on the tile floor. She felt like throwing up at the thought of looking in the eyes of the man who had a teenage girl beaten bloody like it was just another day's work. It would be incredibly satisfying if she were the one who finally got to arrest him. When she got back to the office, she'd have to ask the other agents if they would do her that favor even though she was on desk duty for a while.

Muted voices came from inside the study. Caisey rested her hand on the butt of her gun, still in its holster. She wasn't here officially, so there wasn't a whole lot she could accomplish without cause. She took measured steps to the door and then scanned the room too fast to connect with Holden Arturo's eyes, imagining he was one of those beings that would turn her to stone if she did. Keeping him in view, she let her gaze settle on Gabe.

"Let's go."

"No. I want him to promise he'll stop trying to kill us."

Holden's voice was low and lethal. "You think too much of yourself if you think I'm expending energy crushing a bug that means nothing to me."

"Of course not." Caisey turned her head a fraction toward him. "You have people for that."

"I do?" Holden straightened. "Perhaps this is only due to your...tenacity."

"Yeah, I'm sure."

"So eloquent, Special Agent Lyons. Just like your father."

Fury whipped through her like a match to accelerant and Caisey had to grit her teeth. "Gabe. Let's go."

There was no point in being here. What had Gabe hoped to achieve by coming? They weren't going to get the truth or even a remotely straight answer from a compulsive liar and life-long dealer of destruction. Every word he said sounded like honesty if you took him at face value. He was very convincing. But Caisey didn't believe for one second that Holden didn't know exactly what she was talking about.

Even if he confessed, it still wasn't enough to bring him down. And looking around, he seemed like he'd fallen pretty low already. She almost felt bad for him.

"No? You don't wish to discuss the old man who failed you?"

Caisey's head started to pound. "That was your doing."

"All I have ever done is strive to maintain the integrity of my family." Holden glanced between her and Gabe. "It was the two of you who tore it apart."

"You think you're helping your family? You're the one who destroyed it."

Holden shot to his feet, gesturing with his gun at Gabe. "He destroyed it, when he betrayed us all!"

Caisey aimed. Would it be that bad if she ended this all now? Their troubles would be over, but at what price? "Put your gun down, Holden."

Did he really think he was helping his family? He had destroyed them trying to do everything the wrong way. Even that couldn't be absolved by the best intentions. Love didn't matter if you put it into practice in a way that harmed.

"Both of you get out!"

Gabe backed away toward Caisey, who was closest to the door. When he was behind her, she retreated with him, her weapon aimed at Holden. The world would be a better place if he was gone. Eradicated.

When they stepped out the front door, she rounded on Gabe. "What were you thinking? No. Don't tell me, because you weren't. Not going in there like that, with no clue what you were doing. You could have been *killed*."

"I could have been killed?" He laughed. The sound was an echo of his uncle's voice. Did he even notice? "You don't have the monopoly on protecting the people in this family, Caisey. Some of us can do it too."

"I'm not saying that."

"Right."

She folded her arms. "You could have been hurt."

"And I'm sorry that worried you. But you can't handicap me from doing anything for you, for us, or for anyone else in our family. Because that's what they are...our family."

She knew it was true. She wasn't going to argue. But her heart was about to burst. "Then why would you put yourself at risk like that?"

Jenna rushed over with Nic right behind her. "Can you even hear yourself? Gabe is right. You're not the only one who gets to look out for us. Sometimes we even get to do it ourselves."

"I know that. I—"

"He's my uncle." Gabe folded his arms. "This was my decision."

Jenna huffed. "Funny. I remember someone saying that to me before she got abducted by a serial killer."

Caisey shook her head.

Gabe didn't look all that impressed. "So what do we do now?"

"You don't worry about it. And you try not to get yourself killed, okay?" She took a step back, toward her car. "You guys should take off. I've got this covered."

THIRTY-ONE

Caisey trapsed from the garage to the kitchen in the mood to collapse on the couch with a jumbo bag of chips. Grams had been eating dinner when she stopped by the hospital on her way home. Well, not eating so much as picking at the edges of limp pasta. The chocolate pudding had been completely gone, though. Clearly when Grams had drilled into them the importance of finishing dinner before you had dessert, she didn't mean it to apply to herself.

Caisey stopped by the kitchen table. The murmur of voices was low, like more than one man. *Someone was in her house.* Was it the Chloroform killer? She dropped her backpack and drew her weapon. Agent Stern and Agent Wing both jumped to their feet, halfway to their own weapons before she stood down.

"Guys." Caisey holstered her gun and moved her jacket to cover it. Two agents sat in her living room across from Gabe, who had his elbows on his knees and looked shell- shocked.

"Lyons." The agents both nodded.

Gabe shook off whatever he was feeling and looked at her. "Jenna said it was okay for us to meet here."

"And we're actually done, so we'll be going." Agent Wing turned to Gabe. "You'll let us know?"

Gabe took a breath. "There's no need. The answer is yes."

The female agent nodded. "We'll make the arrangements and be in touch." "Actually, I'm not sure where I'll be. Can you let Caisey know the details?"

The agent turned to her, and she nodded.

"Very well."

They said the perfunctory goodbyes and then it was just Gabe and Caisey alone in her house. Gabe leaned his head back on the couch and closed his eyes.

"You okay?"

He shrugged.

"You wanna talk about it?"

Gabe opened his eyes. "Are you being polite, or do you actually care?"

Caisey sat opposite him. "If I didn't want to know, I'd have to fake it and pretend I do or I'd look like a jerk. So for argument's sake, let's say I care."

Gabe's lips twitched. "You're not like anyone I've ever met."

"Is that even a good thing?"

"Definitely."

"How can you be so sure?"

He leaned forward again and she was held in place by his gaze. At least, that was what it felt like. "Because you're you. Not the FBI thing, or your family, or saving my life when the sheriff or the other guy tried to kill me. It was before then, when you walked in to the cells at the sheriff's office and your eyes were smiling. Like you knew we had a secret no one else was ever going to know. I knew then that you'd felt the same all these years. That you held on to the dream of what could have come after that date just like I did."

Caisey didn't move. She didn't even blink. "Are we crazy?"

Gabe laughed. "Probably, but who cares? It'll be a cool story to tell our grandchildren."

"What makes...I don't..." White spots pricked the edges of her vision.

His lips twitched. "Take a breath, Case."

She sucked in air and the dizziness dissipated. "You really need to stop doing that."

"Why? You react so well. I liked the hyperventilating especially, it was a good touch."

"I'm not sure I like you."

Gabe shrugged, apparently not too bothered by that. "We'll get there. Whatever happens, I want you to know where I stand. This isn't something you have to worry about, or try to figure out. However it happens and however it grows, to the point where I actually get down on one knee and ask you, let's just enjoy the journey."

"What if I'm not as sure as you? I mean...marriage?"

"Don't you wish you could be sure, that just for once you could relax into it and trust it to be what it's going to be without overanalyzing? We discuss things as they come up and take each day as it is, building a foundation for something that, from where I'm sitting, could be pretty awesome."

Caisey liked looking at his face. It was a good face, with strong lines and just enough roughness that it wasn't boyish. It was really tempting to just let go and fall back on the familiarity of being with him. To accept this for what it was, without worrying about how it was going to go wrong.

"Maybe, I could do that. I think." She blew out a breath. It was better than worrying about what the Chloroform Killer was doing. And she'd been talking about him all afternoon, between telling Burkot about the almost hit-and-run and talking to Amanda. Again. "So what do we do now?"

If things went the way he thought they would, where would they live? How would they merge two completely different lives? Provided they could even walk away from this unscathed, and possessing something solid that would last the rest of their lives.

Gabe stood. "Dinner?"

"That's it, just dinner?"

He shrugged and tugged her up by her hand. "I'm hungry." But he didn't let her go, he put enough pressure on her hand that she understood what he wanted and moved to him. Approval shone in his eyes. "Seal the deal."

"What?"

"I know what I want, Caisey. And I don't want to doubt that it's what you want, too. That maybe I just talked you into it. So convince me."

Caisey couldn't say she didn't have doubts but she was more than willing to try. And to face the fact that she'd had all her relationship eggs squarely in the "Gabe" basket for so long it would be criminal not to give it a shot. She would end up regretting it for the rest of her life.

She lifted up on her toes and put her hands on either side of his face. The touch of her lips to his was like lightning that whisked her away from everything and everyone. It was like falling, and being lifted and soaring, all at the same time, existing in a world populated by two heartbeats. It lasted for all of three seconds before Gabe's arms came around her and he lifted her all the way up. Caisey circled his shoulders with her arms and let him take over.

She wasn't sure who pulled back first, but she was suddenly aware of just breathing and looking into his eyes. Her lips tingled and when he set her back on her feet, Caisey touched her lips. "Huh."

Gabe stepped back and ran a hand through his hair. "We should probably be careful with that."

"Because it felt like catching fire?"

A gleam of satisfaction sparked in the curve of his mouth. "Good to know it wasn't just me." He paused. "We should probably go out to eat."

Caisey smiled. "Good plan."

She drove him to a steakhouse that was a hole in the wall, but the steaks melted on your tongue. Neither of them said much until the waitress came and Gabe ordered a salad and minestrone soup.

Caisey gave him a look.

"Vegetarian, remember?"

"Shoot. I'm sorry." It was official, she sucked at this. Maybe, despite the sparks, there wasn't anything else that connected them. What if it was just shallow attraction?

"Are you okay? You look freaked."

Caisey entwined her fingers and rested her head on her hands.

"I'm messing this up. I don't even really know how to do this...whatever *this* is."

Gabe took her hand. "Pray with me."

Caisey nodded and closed her eyes. She soaked in the cadence of his voice and the soft tone of intimacy that said he did this often. Prayer seemed to come naturally to him, where she wasn't sure she could say the same thing. She wanted them to be on an even playing field. Or were they supposed to balance out each other's shortcomings? She didn't even know the answer to that either.

Gabe asked for wisdom and guidance, as well as protection for their hearts and bodies. Caisey couldn't believe this gift that seemed like it had been dropped in her lap. Why would God do this now? She wasn't a particularly good Christian; she knew she was far too willful to be happy with obedience. But that didn't seem to matter, not if you looked at all the good in her life. Grams, her dad's love, Jenna and Jake, Liam's unrelenting friendship—without them her life would be a barren wasteland. And now Gabe?

It just didn't make any sense.

"Amen."

Caisey smiled at him. "Amen." But what she really meant was 'thank you'.

Life wasn't without its hiccups, but seriously, how did she get here?

Then her phone rang.

"PULL OVER." Caisey motioned to the street in front of a drycleaners and Gabe parked the car. If Natalia's grandfather had information that might help bring down Holden Arturo, she had to jump on it.

Gabe shut the car off and frowned. "Isn't the restaurant way up there?"

Caisey turned to the backseat where Jake sat with Natalia. She looked between Jake and Gabe. "You guys stay here. Nat's with me."

"But—"

She stopped Jake's objection with a look. "This is non-negotiable."

He didn't like it, but he would suck it up and he did. Jake gave Natalia a small smile and squeezed her hand before she got out. Caisey opened her door, but Gabe waylaid her with a hand on her arm. "I don't really know what this is, but be careful."

Caisey nodded. "You guys too."

They might only be waiting in the car, but she didn't like anything about this. She'd had enough of messages that were sent to get another person's attention—either being the message, or receiving it. That stripping of power sent her right back to the intersection where she'd lain bleeding on the concrete with the sun bright in her face.

Natalia Silver walked beside her to the restaurant, a teenage girl stuck in the push and pull between the world of math tests, her high school boyfriend, and her family's business. It was highly likely she would never be in direct danger a day in her life, since no one would be stupid enough to cross Lazlo Silver. Walking beside the granddaughter of Denver's Russian mafia boss was probably the safest place in the city to be.

The restaurant was decorated in gold accents and bold red carpet, and smelled like funky sausage. Caisey walked the line of sight from the door to the table where Lazlo held court among his soldiers and two waitresses who were clearly not hired for their brains. The Russian boss was built like a boxer and his biceps bulged from tailored silk shirt sleeves, showcasing his tattoos. His hair was shaved and his eyes were so dark brown they looked black, as though the stains on his soul couldn't be contained.

"Special agent Lyons!" He tugged the napkin from his shirt collar and stood, enveloping her in a cloud of cigar smoke. She stood frozen while he kissed both of her cheeks.

When he pulled back, Caisey saw the smirk on Natalia's face.

The teen girl was practically laughing. "Hi, Papa."

"My darling." Lazlo Silver's love for his granddaughter was rich and genuine, and Natalia seemed to bask in it like treasure as they embraced. Caisey had met the girl's mom, so she knew Natalia saw that rare affection for what it was.

But Caisey wasn't here to chat. "So, what's up? I have to admit I'm curious why you had Natalia bring me here."

Lazlo shrugged and turned his beady eyes to her. "Professional courtesy. Your father was a good man, though we didn't often see eye to eye."

No kidding, since her dad upheld the law and this man looked for ways to break it.

"We were still alike in many ways. Family is everything in this world."

Caisey nodded. Seemed like there was a lot of that going around.

"Drink?"

Caisey folded her arms. "No, thank you."

"Come." He waved her to the table. "It's the least I can do after all you did for my Natalia."

Caisey shook her head.

"Very well. It has come to my attention that your life is in danger."

"That's it?"

Lazlo blinked. "I would think you'd take threats more seriously. Perhaps you are not aware that my son was contracted."

Lazlo's son—not Natalia's dad, since he was dead—was rumored to be a hit man, though no one knew for sure. Whatever this was, it was huge since Lazlo was basically admitting the rumors were true. Caisey wouldn't be able to sit on this information, she'd have to report it and it would be investigated. Apparently Lazlo's professional courtesy meant a lot; especially considering it impacted his own son. Maybe they were at odds, because he either didn't care his son might be convicted, or he didn't think that was likely, or Lazlo wanted his son the hit man on the inside of a jail cell for some reason.

The possibilities made her brain spin.

"Holden Arturo has you and Gabe Carlen at the top of his hit list."

Caisey waited for something she didn't know.

"Agent Lyons, you are in a unique position to solve what has become a problem for me."

"Having trouble with Arturo?"

"You can bring him down."

But for what? She didn't think the statute of limitations on abduction and assault had expired, but could they really pull that move? Could Arturo's pride really be his destruction? Gabe's dad needed to come through with something, or the Denver police department would have to find a link between Holden and the moustache guy impersonating state patrol.

Lazlo handed her two photographs. One of her, and the other of Gabe—who was sitting outside in the car with Jake.

Caisey pressed her lips together, ready to leave. "Thank you."

Lazlo nodded, like some regal king of old bestowing a blessing on a peasant.

She needed to get to them. They were too exposed on the side of the street, even if it was dark. She wasn't going to let anything happen if she could help it. Whether the FBI brought down Arturo or not, her first priority was her family. The agents on the case would get him eventually, especially if Toben testified.

THIRTY-TWO

Gabe let go of the steering wheel and folded his arms. Jake was in the passenger seat beside him, eyes on his phone. "Are you worried about them?"

Jake looked up at him. "Nah, Case will look after Natalia. And Nat's granddad wouldn't let anything happen to her. Not since her mom went mental and tried to burn her with an iron. She said Caisey was the one who sat with her at the hospital."

Gabe swallowed.

"It was totally nuts. Natalia missed, like, weeks of school, and she was all freaked out. But her Granddad was really cool about the whole thing."

"Families can be crazy, in a good way or a bad way. Sometimes both."

"For sure."

Gabe watched a BMW drive past and then looked at Jake again. The kid looked so much like Nic it was eerie, like the past had morphed into the present and he was sitting with his cousin as a teen. "You know, you and I are actually related."

Jake frowned. "Yeah?"

Gabe bit his lip and decided to go for it. "Your dad is my cousin."

"My dad?"

The hunger in his eyes took Gabe's breath away and he knew he'd done the right thing. "His name is Nic."

"My mom told me that. So did you, like, grow up together?"

Gabe nodded. "Nic and I used to ride bikes to the park, or we'd hang out. He was always tinkering with something. His dad's VCR, or a dirt bike he was fixing up. He played baseball and he was good, but he didn't really enjoy it. He just did it because his dad thought it was a good idea. The old man is kind of overbearing. Nic liked old movies, like noir films, you know? We'd go to all-nighters at this movie theatre on Broadway."

"The retro one. I know that place."

Gabe smiled. It'd been old when they went there, now it was retro. "He used to read too, anything he could get his hands on. Books. Manuals. Encyclopedias."

"So he's smart?"

Gabe nodded. "Crazy smart, but he downplays it because he doesn't like attention. He gets enough crap from his dad that he isn't interested in being a spectacle."

Gabe realized he was talking about the Nic he used to know. Not the guy now, the businessman. He barely knew that man.

"What about my mom?"

Gabe nodded. "I left for college before they started dating. But before her, he used to call me every week. Then it was like he dropped off the face of the earth. He came to visit one weekend, stayed in my dorm and all he could talk about was this girl he met."

Jake's lips curved into a smile. "That's cool. I mean, that's like me and Natalia, but it's my mom." The kid chuckled. "It's also kind of gross."

Gabe laughed. "Get used to it kid. From what I saw, they both might actually still feel the same way."

Jake's face fell. "They've seen each other?"

~

CAISEY TURNED TO NATALIA. "Are you going to hang here, or you want to say bye to Jake?"

Lazlo waved. "Go, I have more business. You won't want to be here. It will be boring."

"Okay, Papa." The girl gave her Granddad a kiss on the cheek.

Caisey walked with her to the front of the restaurant. She turned and held the door for the girl to walk through. The rapport of automatic gunfire erupted.

Natalia's body jerked and she fell to the floor.

Caisey dived down beside her. She wrapped her arms around her head as debris rained down. Bullets sprayed tables, chairs. Fabric and white poofs of stuffing flew in the air. The noise of gunfire and breaking glass was deafening.

Caisey shifted enough to get to her phone and speed-dialed Jake.

"Caisey? What's going on? Guys with guns pulled up outside the restaurant."

"Get out of here."

"But—"

"Go!" She hung up.

Gunfire answered; single shots from a handgun and then cries of pain. Heavy feet ran past them amid shouts and crying. Caisey shifted.

Natalia's lifeless eyes stared back at her. The dark spread of blood covered her shirt and her neck. Lazlo knelt and drew his granddaughter into his arms. The tough old man bowed his head and wept into her neck.

Caisey breathed, trying to get her world to trip back from shock into normal function so she could get up and get moving.

Lazlo looked up. "The deal is off. Now I end this my way."

ELENOR LYONS SHIFTED in the hospital bed, drifting in a sea of memories where her Frank turned to her, smiling. Doves called out and swooped in a flock above the cliff edge. Waves crashed on the shore below. Icy waves she'd dipped her fingers in the day before, shaking at the cold amid a rain-soaked afternoon. Elenor had never once missed the British Isles, not when she had Frank and the family they made together.

His uniform made him look so handsome, even despite the shadow of the horrors he had seen darkening his blue eyes.

"Come."

He lifted his hand, palm up. Waiting for her to take it and go with him.

But she couldn't.

"Come."

She didn't know if she could leave Caisey. Her granddaughter might not act like she needed much, but Elenor could clearly see the need in Caisey to be loved and accepted. Jenna was a strong woman who had withstood fire and come out standing, but still seemed to doubt herself. Jake was a wonderful young man who gave love freely, but held so much of himself back, like he was scared to connect.

Elenor didn't want to leave without telling them. Would they even know how she'd felt all these years, how blessed she'd been to be part of their makeshift family?

How could Frank ask her to go now, when Caisey had just reconnected with Gabe and Jenna was talking to Nic again? She wanted to see it through...but was this to be the end? Now?

"Come."

She looked up at him. Saw the wind ruffle his hair and the smile that stretched his face, and her heart swelled the way it had when he first took her hand. It had been too long that she missed him, wanted to touch him one more time. To hear his voice and fall into his embrace.

Had she done enough? Said enough? Loved enough?

Elenor reached out and took her husband's hand as her heart lifted in prayer that her family would be safe. That the children of her heart would know the comfort of the Father.

Her heart beat slowed and time stretched into eternity.

And Elenor Lyons took her last breath.

THIRTY-THREE

Jenna ran her fingers along the bumper of a sixties car, one of the ones you had to climb in the window because the door didn't open. If she'd known she would be spending their date in a dirty car garage, she'd have worn a different dress. But the look on Nic's face when she opened her front door had been worth it.

She looked over at him. "You found a niche. Your niche."

He still carried that air of nervousness in his shoulders since they pulled up outside, but with her words they relaxed a little. "Thanks."

Jenna strode to where she had set her purse and pulled out the thing she'd brought for Nic. His eyes widened when she handed him the recent picture of Jake that Caisey had snapped at Jenna's birthday breakfast. Old t-shirt, head tipped back full-out laughing and eyes shining, like he felt that joy every minute of every day.

Nic's chest shuddered.

"That's for you."

"I should have come to you." Nic ran a hand through his hair, wrecking whatever style he'd been going for. "I told myself it was because I didn't want to let you down, even as I didn't want my dad to get wind of you. I don't want you to ever be leverage in this tug of war he and I play over what my life is going to be. I mean, seriously? Did you ever think I'd be a stuffed-shirt businessman?"

Jenna coughed. "No."

"Are you laughing?"

"Uh..."

Nic put his hands in his pockets, like he was trying to keep from touching her. "I like it here, in the garage. It's so much more peaceful. I don't know why he can't be satisfied with me having the life I want to have."

He'd always been like that, considerate of her and not wanting to rush her. Except when she pushed it...and look what happened then. This time she needed to stand strong and let him lead all the way, instead of as far as he was willing and then take over.

"I want to do what's best for us."

"I don't want what we had before." Jenna didn't realize it until she said the words. "I want something better. If we can have it, if it's still even possible."

"It's not going to be mistake free. We're the same people. We're grown and different, but we're still us." His hand slid behind her ear until his fingers were in her hair. Jenna closed her eyes but he gave her a gentle shake and she opened them again. "I want something better, too."

"There was never anyone else." Jenna sighed. "It's only ever been you."

Something dark flickered in Nic's eyes.

"Nic?"

He stepped back, disconnecting them. That's what it felt like... being unplugged.

"Nic, just say it. How bad can it be?" Although, honestly, Jenna wasn't sure she wanted to know exactly how bad this was. Especially if it was making him shut down like this. "Tell me."

"I was married."

Jenna started for the door, but Nic got in front of her, stalling her progress without touching her. Which hurt worst of all.

"You're right, though. Don't you see? When you said there was no one else but you I realized it was true for me too. I didn't want to believe it. I didn't want to face the fact that I wasted my time and Tammi's."

"Tammi?" The image of a Barbie doll-type girl slammed into Jenna's mind and she shut her eyes. "Just spit it all out so I can deal with it. I don't like hedging. Stop trying to protect my feelings, it's too late for that."

Nic's face paled. "I'm sorry I'm such a failure."

"Nic—"

"No. You're right. Maybe it is too late."

Tears filled Jenna's eyes. She turned away as a surge of something hot and fierce churned in her stomach, filling her until the tips of her fingers burned. She spun back. "You know, I almost believed you were sincere. I was this close—" she held out her fingers, an inch apart, "to introducing you to Jake. I thought, hey, why not let them have a relationship. What can it hurt? Well, let me tell you. It can hurt a lot. Trust me. I know how a father's words can cut you until you don't think anything else can possibly ever hurt that badly."

"Jenna—"

"So maybe we had something good once, but it didn't work. Let's just face the fact that it was messed up and go our separate ways. Because I can't do this, and I won't put Jake in the middle of it."

"Because it got hard? So you're just going to give up? It's going to be hard sometimes."

"I don't want it to be hard!"

Nic took a step toward her, but Jenna backed up. He sighed. "Nothing good is ever easy."

"Yes it is. It can be effortless."

He shook his head. "I don't believe you."

"Me and Jake? Effortless. Love like that, it just is. No thinking about it, or figuring it out, or pushing it to be something. It just is."

"So parenting is all plain sailing?"

"No."

"But under all that, there's love."

Jenna nodded.

Nic smiled. "So let's make this, like that. Not perfect, but great."

A tear ran down her face and Jenna swiped it away. "I don't think it can be."

"We can at least try. Wipe the slate clean, accept the fact that we both made mistakes and not get swallowed up in the guilt. We created something wonderful out of less than perfect circumstances. But that doesn't make him any less wonderful."

Jenna looked at the ceiling. She wanted to believe him, but would it just be her falling for it all over again? "Tell me about your wife."

Nic's hands settled on her shoulders. "Ex-wife. For years now." He huffed. "She always said it was like I wasn't all-in with the relationship. Now I know why."

"Was it good?"

Nic shook his head. "It was pleasant, and polite. Like an arrangement, which she eventually realized wasn't going to be what she dreamed. So she wiped me out and walked away with half of my assets."

Jenna winced.

"Yeah." He stepped closer. "It was empty, Jenna. I thought I needed to be married. Tammi was just there, I didn't really expend any effort and all of a sudden my life was a certain way. Living in a house that was a wedding present from my dad, married to someone who never let me see her with no makeup on."

Jenna bit her lip. "Do you think he orchestrated it?"

"Probably. And I wasn't in a place where I objected to anything. It was just easier not to feel, than to deal with the fact that everything I ever wanted was right here."

"The car garage?"

"No, dummy. You."

Jenna sucked in a breath. "Why don't you come for dinner tomorrow night?"

Nic smiled. Then his whole body jerked and he spun. The front window shattered, the shards falling to the floor as several objects sailed in, bright and sputtering. Jenna heard the smash of each one in succession—four—and she was shoved to the tile floor just as fire burst across the room.

Her mind blanked, eyes fixed on the sea of flames whipping with the breeze from the open window. Alarms blared. Nic moved, his body forcing her to step back until she hit a wall. Then he grabbed her hand and dragged her through a door into a hallway.

Smoke laced the air. Jenna coughed and covered her mouth with the collar of her jacket.

Nic's eyes were dark, his brow furrowed. But he didn't stop. He dragged her to a back door and twisted the handle. Jiggled it and pushed against the door. He stepped back and slammed the door with his shoulder. It didn't open.

He turned to her and shouted over the sound of multiple smoke alarms. "Where's your phone?"

Jenna pointed to the front of the garage, now awash with flames. "Purse." She coughed.

Nic pulled his undershirt up to cover his mouth and nose. He grabbed her hand again and pulled her down the hall to an office. He closed the door and grabbed the phone from the desk. Pressed buttons. Listened. Picked it up and threw it against the wall. He went to the window and tried to open it, but even with all his muscles straining couldn't get it to budge.

They were trapped.

Jenna shifted, her body itching to make a break for the door. They couldn't just sit here and do nothing when the building was in flames. But there was no way out. "Where is your cell?"

He came over and dipped his head low so she could hear. "Car. I didn't want anything to disturb tonight and my dad's been calling me all afternoon." He lifted his shirt collar over his nose again.

"What are we going to do?"

He squeezed her shoulders. "The police and the fire department won't be long. Someone will have seen the flames, or heard the smoke alarms."

He stepped away and got two bottled waters from a fridge in the corner and handed one to her.

They were probably going to burn to death and he was acting like this was no big deal. "You're not mad someone is burning down your garage?"

His head jerked. "You think I'm not mad? I'm mad, Jenna. And I know exactly who I'm mad at, but that's for later. Right now I just want us to be safe until we can get out of here."

Maybe it wasn't the right time, but Jenna thought that was pretty sweet. Not the later, being mad part, but wanting them to be safe. She wanted to be strong, but who said she couldn't do it while he was protecting her? Especially when it seemed so important to him.

Jenna shook her head. The room was cloudy, like blurry contact lenses making her eyes sting. She coughed again and took a sip of the water. Nic pulled her to the corner and they sat side by side on the carpet at the furthest point from the door.

Sirens cut across the blare of smoke alarms. Nic squeezed her hand and drank some of his water. "Help is here."

"You're going to lose everything."

Nic nodded. "I know."

"What will you do?"

"Rebuild? Move on? I don't know. I'll figure it out."

"Who did this?"

Nic shook his head. "Don't worry about that right now."

"You don't have to protect me. If someone is trying to kill me, I need to know."

"No one's trying to kill you. Or me, I don't think. Probably someone just wanted to destroy the garage and we were here. I don't think we were the targets, because if we were then they aren't very good. I think they were just going for vandalism."

"Who would do that to you?"

Jenna studied his face. He didn't answer, but she could see he knew exactly who had done this. His dad was the only person who came to mind. And while Jenna's relationship with her dad wasn't the greatest, she didn't think he would try and destroy her spa. What kind of a person did that to their child? She just didn't understand it. But she did understand that she didn't want Jake anywhere near a man like that.

So how could she make a way for Nic to see his son when it put them all in the line of fire? If Jake wasn't going to be safe, maybe Nic was right to stay away all these years. Especially when stuff like this happened.

"Is this because of us?" Jenna coughed. "Because of me?"

Nic shook his head. "I'd like to think he doesn't know about you, but I'm not going to count on it. But I don't think this is about you. It's about me not towing his line."

"How do you know?"

Nic's lips thinned. "Because he told me if I crossed him, he would destroy my life."

THIRTY-FOUR

Caisey had seen death many times and the shock of it never ceased. One minute there and the next minute, gone. She shook her head to dissipate the image of Natalia's lifeless eyes and surveyed the crowd of local police, FBI agents, ambulance crews and firefighters all busy at work in and around the destroyed restaurant. "Buckshot is starting to look appealing."

Gabe's mouth twitched. "Even with the sheriff still missing, you want to go back there?"

"I can appreciate the peace and quiet."

"Interesting."

She glanced at him. "What?"

Gabe shook his head. "It'll keep. You have bigger stuff to deal with right now." He motioned with his head to where Lazlo stood, talking to Jake. The heartbreak on her godson's face made Caisey want to curl up and weep. Gabe was right. Whatever was happening between them would keep. It wasn't more important than the task given to her. Protecting them meant everything, but even though he was physically safe, Jake had been broken. And boy, did Caisey ever know what that felt like.

Still, Jake shouldn't have been there. Gabe should have taken him away from all this destruction when she'd explicitly called and told them to go.

"Don't think I'm ignoring the fact that I told you guys to leave and you didn't." She narrowed her eyes. "I can't believe you stayed."

"We called 9-1-1."

"You were supposed to get out of here."

"You think I'm going to leave you to get shot at and not make sure you're okay?"

Caisey shook her head. "I called."

"You called Jake, but whatever. It was while you were being shot at. You think that fills me with confidence?"

"I think you should do what the federal agent tells you."

Gabe smiled. "Sometimes. Maybe. But mostly not."

"Are you kidding me?"

"No. I'm just saying you're not the boss."

"When someone is shooting a machine gun, I am."

"Okay, I'll give you that one. There are instances where you clearly have more training."

A knot pressed hard against her chest. "If I tell you to go, you better go."

Gabe pressed his lips to hers. The kiss was quick and then he touched his forehead to hers. "We're all fine."

Caisey sucked in a breath and grabbed his elbows to steady herself. He was right. They were fine. She had to remember that even with all that happened, they hadn't been harmed. Jake wasn't okay. Natalia was gone, but he would survive.

Two firefighters passed them and one clipped the other on the arm. "Hey, did you hear about that blaze over at the custom car shop? I'd much rather be saving those sweet rides than doing cleanup for the Russians."

Caisey trotted up behind them, grabbed the guy with the big mouth's elbow and swung him around. "Are you talking about LoDo Custom Cars?"

Jenna had told her where she would be tonight. It was a standing agreement they had, even if Caisey was working Jenna would have an idea what part of town she'd be in.

The guy shrugged. "What about it? What's your problem, anyway?"

She let him go with a shove. "We don't have long enough for me to explain it to you."

Gabe had his phone out. "Nic?" His body stilled. "Yeah, we heard about that." Gabe paused. "No way. Are you guys okay?"

Caisey wanted to shake him. Or grab the phone and pepper Nic with questions herself.

"Okay, we'll do that." He hung up. "Nic and Jenna were at the garage. They're okay, but EMTs took them to the hospital to get checked out. He said Jenna was coughing pretty badly. We're supposed to meet them there."

"Okay."

"Did you want me to tell them what happened here?"

Caisey shook her head. "I'll do it later, when we know for sure everyone's okay. Smoke inhalation can be pretty nasty."

"You okay?"

Caisey didn't answer Gabe. Instead, she glanced at Jake who was still deep in conversation with the Russian mafia boss. She looked back at Gabe. "Sure. I'm okay. I'll go tell Jake so we can get going. Though, I'm not sure this is exactly how he wanted to meet his dad. Especially not when his girlfriend just got killed."

"I'm sorry about what happened."

Caisey nodded. "Me too. She was a sweet girl who didn't seem to be able to catch a break on anything. Until Jake. He's going to be a mess."

"Should we finesse this so he doesn't have more drama? He needs to be with his mom. Maybe I could take Nic aside so Jake doesn't have to deal with that too, right now."

Caisey smiled, enamored by the layers of Gabe that were peeling open. Jake was wrapping it up with Lazlo, so she motioned to where he was standing. "I'll be back in a sec." She walked to their huddle, flanked by Lazlo's soldiers who hadn't been detained for returning fire. They would all be taken in for questioning before the night was over, but these guys hadn't been arrested.

Caisey got close to Jake, whose eyes were bloodshot and his

cheeks red from wiping away tears. She got in his face and held his eyes. "You okay?"

Jake's eyes flashed. "No. I'm not okay."

"We should go."

"Maybe I'm not done talking."

Caisey sucked in a breath. She didn't want to come down hard on him, not at a time like this. She had to remember he wasn't lashing out at her, this was grief. "We can't stay here all night. It's late and we need to get you to your mom."

He leaned in close to her. "I'm not a child."

His face morphed into a Jake she'd never seen before in the happy kid she knew. "It's not that. It's—"

"Don't tell me what to do. This is all on you. You brought us here and you're supposed to be the big special agent. You're the one who let her get killed." Tears filled his eyes. "You want to go? Then go."

Lazlo had thankfully turned away, though he was right beside them so it wasn't like he couldn't hear everything. Caisey wanted to grab Jake's hand, but she didn't dare reach because he would probably push her away. What was she supposed to have done? There was no way she could've known those men would open fire at that second and Natalia would be killed. A matter of inches and Natalia would've been in the hospital right now with a solid chance of a full recovery. And yet the coroner had removed the body, and all that was left now was emptiness.

"I'm not going anywhere." Caisey gritted her teeth. "Hate me if you want, but I can't control everything." Caisey heard the words as she spoke them, and realized it was true. She tried so hard to take care of them, but she couldn't cover it all. "We really do have to go. Your mom is at Mercy. There was a fire and she's being checked out for smoke inhalation. We're headed over there now."

His eyes flickered. "A fire?"

"She's okay." Caisey nodded. "She was with your dad."

"Arturo." Lazlo said the name like a curse, his voice low and hard.

Caisey turned to him. "We don't know that for sure." She tugged on Jake's arm. "Go wait by Gabe, okay? I need a minute."

He pulled his arm from her grip and shoulders slumped, but he walked to where Gabe stood. When he was out of earshot Caisey turned to Lazlo. "This is where our association ends. You said what you said to Jake when he needed the comfort of his girlfriend's grandfather, but that's it. I'm very sorry for your loss."

"Arturo will pay."

"I'm not sure this was him." Caisey saw movement. Several sets of eyes were on them, no doubt hoping to hear something incriminating come from Lazlo, spurred by a special agent on the job. But she wasn't on the job now. She just wanted to say what she had to say, and get to Jenna.

"Why would Arturo offer your son a job and then target the restaurant? This wasn't a precision attack, it was a rampage. He had no idea you were going to call me, or that I would be here." She motioned to the restaurant's destroyed front windows. "Could your son have done this?"

Lazlo didn't say anything, so Caisey continued, "What happened tonight was terrible, there's no doubt. This had nothing to do with me, and while I'm sorry for what happened to Natalia, I can't be involved any further. This wasn't about Gabe and me. This was about you, and that sweet girl got caught in the crossfire." She pointed to where Gabe and Jake watched them. "I'm sure you can appreciate that I won't let the same thing happen to them."

Lazlo's dark eyes narrowed, but he dipped his head before he walked away.

Caisey watched him go and went to Jake, making a point to ignore the agents who'd been listening. She might not be able to keep them safe from everything, especially not heartbreak, but she was certainly going to try. She led Jake to Gabe's Jeep and sat beside him in the backseat while Gabe drove to the hospital.

She didn't doubt that, as young as he was, Jake would go on to find someone who would fill his life with love and happiness. But this would shape him. A defining moment— much like her attack— one that made her squeeze her eyes shut and pray that the grief wouldn't overwhelm him. She didn't like to admit that her fear of being vulnerable sometimes sucked her under like a tidal wave, or that she would happily work her fingers to the bone if it meant protecting the people she cared for. As much as she didn't wish it were true, that attack had shaped her. It made her the agent she was.

Jake squeezed her hand and pulled her close until her shoulder hit his. "I'm sorry."

She leaned her head down and the wet from her eyes soaked his shirt.

Gabe pulled up at a stoplight and glanced back. The small smile was a comfort, but her pain was so much less than her godson's. Why couldn't they live in a world where death didn't lurk around every corner, waiting to strike? The whole point of being an FBI agent was to keep it at bay and yet here it was...part of Jake's world.

Stopping Holden Arturo wouldn't be enough. It would never be enough, because there would always be a new threat to take the place of whoever she brought down or arrested. It was enough to drive her crazy, trying to figure out how in the world she was going to fix it so they were safe.

"I'm sorry I yelled at you."

Caisey sniffed and lifted her head. "I'm sorry...about Natalia." She could see the shock still in his eyes, like he didn't totally believe that she was gone. "She was a sweet girl."

"Yeah, she was." He turned away and looked out the window. "What do I do now?"

Caisey sighed. "I don't really know. You know how it was when my dad died. Mostly you just keep going, keep moving, and keep getting out of bed even though it's hard. Life goes on and it sucks and it's painful, but there's so much beauty and love still. It's hard to see it in the darkness, but in the light it's easier."

"What if I don't want to see?"

Caisey squeezed his hand. "It might take time, but you will."

He looked at her. "Is my mom really okay?"

"Your dad said she was coughing. She's just getting checked out."

"Is he with her? Can I see him?"

Caisey bit her lip. "Do you want to see him?"

Jake took a deep breath and then nodded. "I think so. I think Natalia would like that I'm going to meet him, even though she isn't here."

Caisey couldn't believe how well he seemed to be doing. Apart from his outburst of blame, Jake seemed almost contemplative. She wanted to believe it was something innate in him, strength he'd gained from life and family. Was it just shock? Maybe he was numb and it would hit him later and lay him flat. This was too much for a teen to deal with. She wanted different than this for him.

She wanted to rail at God and ask why. Why had he given her so much to take care of, when she clearly wasn't cut out to serve and protect?

~

JAKE CONCENTRATED ON JUST BREATHING. In and out. He was finally going to see his dad. Natalia would think that was cool. Her mom—and her dad—hadn't been the greatest, but her grandfather sure loved her. And now she was gone and he'd never see her smile at him when he got to English Lit and she was waiting by the seat she saved.

Caisey grabbed his hand, the way he used to do with her if there were a lot of people in the grocery store. They walked the hospital hallway with Gabe trailing behind them— Jake's uncle, or whatever, he didn't know how that worked. Was Nic like Gabe? Jake wanted to see his mom and all, since she almost got hurt in a fire. But his dad was here. That was so huge Jake wanted to run. And shriek and scream. He didn't know whether he was going to hug the guy or yell at him for abandoning them.

He'd been right when he told his mom that she shouldn't call her dad back. She didn't need that negative crap in her life. His dad had left them high and dry until they had to stay with Sam and Caisey and Grams instead of being a family. Not that anyone had a normal family these days. It seemed like every one of his friends had dysfunctional parents or brothers and sisters who made their lives a misery.

"Your mom's okay."

Jake looked down at Caisey. "I know."

She was shorter than him, but her presence usually made up for her lack of height. And the gun didn't hurt either. It was pretty cool. Jake figured he was going to be some kind of cop after he went to college. That had been a given, since he grew up with Sam Lyons. Now that man had presence. And Jake figured he was pretty lucky to have grown up knowing a man like that. Going to father son church camps and learning how to change oil on a car, or fish socks out of the dryer vent when it got clogged that one time.

"You want to talk about it?"

Jake hit the button for the elevator. "I miss Uncle Sam."

Caisey looked away. "Me too."

Gabe clapped Jake on the shoulder. "He was a good man."

"He told me I could tell him anything." Jake chuckled. "Then everything I'd tell him, he'd say, 'that's cause you're a sinner, kid'. I mean, he wasn't wrong, but still..."

Gabe smiled. "Your dad's a good man too."

"He left us."

The elevator chimed and they got off. Jake looked at Gabe, wanting desperately to understand. To know what made a man leave what was supposed to be the most important thing in life.

"It has to do with your grandfather." Gabe sighed. "It's complicated."

"Adults always say that."

He turned away. If they weren't going to explain it because he couldn't know, then why not just say that? Why did adults always say stuff like "maybe" or "it's complicated" when they didn't want to tell you?

Then Jake saw him. His feet faltered and Caisey bumped into his back. The man was an inch or two taller and their shadows would be identical and he knew, finally, why his eyes were grayer than his mom's blue. He wanted to be mad, to ask why this man had to be a stranger. Then he saw Nic's eyes and the tear traced its way down his face. Jake didn't want to react, but his heart squeezed in his chest until he thought it would burst.

Caisey's fingers laced with his and she squeezed. "Jake, honey, this is your dad."

He looked at her. "I think I just want to see my mom."

THIRTY-FIVE

"It's okay." Nic couldn't move. All he could do was stare at his son and just soak in the fact that Jake was here. Caisey looked ready to argue, but Nic shook his head. He didn't want to know how he looked, given that he stank like smoke and his face was smeared since he tried to wash off the ash. His hair was probably all over the place and at some point he'd wiped his hands on the front of his shirt.

The ER wasn't the place to do this and if the kid needed a break, Nic was going to give him one. On a night his mom could have been killed, he didn't need the added pressure of more emotional upheaval and now that he thought about it, Jake didn't look so good.

"Is everything all right?"

Gabe caught Nic's eye and shook his head.

Nic motioned to the room where Jenna was with a tip of his head. "Come on. I'll show you to your mom."

Nic didn't wait for Jake to answer, he just set off walking. Jake caught up and Nic glanced over. The kid's face was tight like he was holding back a bucket-load of emotion. He wanted to pray that one day they would get to a place where they were tight, but he'd never put much stock in a higher being. Did God still listen, even if you weren't sure you believed in Him?

Jenna sighed, like Jake had been the one in danger and opened her arms. She was sitting up on the edge of the bed, still in her smoky dress and clutching Nic's jacket on her lap. The teenager burrowed into his mom's arms, his face in her neck. His breath hitched.

"I'm okay, honey."

"Mom, Natalia—" Jake sobbed.

"What?" Jenna's gaze darted between them. "What happened?"

Nic got nudged aside and Caisey and Gabe came in the room behind him. Gabe looked him over, so Nic nodded so his cousin would know he was fine. They might not have seen each other in years, but their relationship seemed to have slipped back into place. Then Jenna looked up, her face a question Nic didn't even begin to answer.

Caisey spoke. "Natalia and I went to see her grandfather. He has a restaurant over on Seventeenth. The guys were in the car down the street."

Jake sat beside Jenna on the bed, his hand in hers. She glanced at him and then looked back at Caisey. "What happened?"

"Someone attacked the restaurant. Natalia got caught in the cross-fire."

"Oh, honey." She pulled Jake close. "I'm so sorry, baby."

Caisey looked at her friend. "It happened so fast I didn't even have time to draw my weapon. Gabe said you got caught in a fire, you okay?"

Jenna nodded. "Just a cough. The doctor was coming back with discharge papers so I can go home. But I want to run upstairs and see Grams before we leave."

"Okay." Caisey glanced at Nic.

He scratched his ashy scalp, his hair wiry. "Someone decided tonight would be a good night to vandalize my car garage and burn the place down. I don't think they even knew we were there."

"Your dad?"

One thing Nic was learning about Caisey, she always got right to the point. He nodded. "That's what I'm thinking." Nic sighed. "I just wasn't going to be that man anymore. I don't want to cow-tow to him just because he'll retaliate. It isn't all it's cracked up to be."

And wasn't that the truth. Nic couldn't believe all he'd missed out on. Now that he could see it, right in front of his eyes see the bond between Jenna and Jake. This was what family meant. Not just Jenna and Jake, but Caisey too, and the unspoken stuff that whipped back and forth between them.

Jake's eyes were on him. Did the kid know that Nic had made mistakes but he was ready to try? Would Jake let him in, or never get over all the ways Jake had failed? All Nic could do was give Jake all the information he needed to make the choice and hope like crazy he made the right one. Because Nic wasn't sure he could give up Jenna, not again. Not now he'd seen the woman she had become.

Jenna squeezed her eyes shut and kissed her son on the forehead. "All this in one night? Could it be linked?"

Caisey shrugged. "We could theorize, but I'd have to look into the details to know for sure."

Jenna turned to him. "When you talked to the police, did you tell them you think it was your dad?"

Nic shook his head. "Like Caisey said, no proof. If it was him, it'll be tough to find a link. He isn't going to want anything to get back to him."

A thick knot in his chest crept up and lodged in Nic's throat. He tried to swallow. "I'm really sorry." His eyes strayed to Jake, and then back to Jenna. "I know that barely covers it, but I was a coward. I should've known what I had. I thought I was keeping you safe from my dad, but I didn't realize what I'd be doing to us."

"Your dad really did all this?" There was no judgment in Jake's eyes, only question.

Nic sucked in a breath and nodded. "I don't know about your girlfriend—I'm so sorry about that. But if I had to guess, I'd say yes. My dad probably did this."

"That's why you weren't around?"

Nic nodded. "I didn't want this for your mom."

"Why did you come back now?"

Tears welled up in his eyes. "You could say that Caisey knocked some sense into me." Nic smiled. "Or the change was a long time coming, or Gabe coming back made me realize how important family is. But it was mostly your mom. I was nervous as all get-up. But after I saw her I just couldn't walk away."

Jake shifted and looked at his mom. When he looked back at Nic, a small smile played at the corners of his mouth.

The door opened and a doctor came in, his tired face about a decade younger than Nic's. "Whoa, Grand Central Station much?"

Caisey shifted. "Piccadilly Circus."

Jenna grinned.

The doctor paused, one eyebrow raised. "Piccadilly Circus?"

Caisey nodded. "My Grandmother raised me on British cultural references. Guess some things get lost in translation."

The doctor pointed at Caisey with his pen. "That's funny, because my girlfriend works upstairs and she had an old lady she was taking care of earlier who was British. She passed away, though. Though, if you're gonna go, go in a hospital. Am I right?"

Nic saw it wash over their faces.

Caisey hit the door at a run, Gabe right behind her.

CAISEY PASSED the elevators and made for the stairs, thanking God she'd been here so many times with suspects and victims she knew the hospital layout. She hadn't known that jerk of an intern though, he must be new.

But not for much longer.

She ran up the stairs, two at a time.

Before she was done, that intern was going to know her real well.

The fourth floor door snapped back on its hinges and she heard Gabe grunt, but didn't slow down. Nothing would have made her stop. Not until she knew for sure that idiot wannabe doctor didn't know what he was talking about.

Someone yelled for her to slow down, but she didn't.

Caisey ran to the door to four-sixteen and hit the handle at full speed. The heavy door opened and she saw the empty bed.

"Case." Gabe's voice was behind her.

"Is she Mrs. Lyons' next of kin?" A pause. Then someone in a white coat was beside her. "I'm sorry. It happened fast and we did everything we could to get Elenor back, but there was nothing we could do."

People crowded in behind her. She heard Jake's voice. Jenna started crying. Gabe's hands touched her shoulder, her arms, but she didn't move.

"Breathe."

She couldn't. She didn't know how.

THIRTY-SIX

The blanket was scratchy against her cheek, but she wasn't ever going to move. It smelled like Grams.

"Is she okay?"

"I don't know. I've never seen her like this. I'm really worried."

"Maybe we should call her doctor."

"She doesn't *have* a doctor."

THIRTY-SEVEN

"I'm so sorry for your loss."

A hand grabbed Caisey's and tugged until she was sitting. The wooden bench was so cold it crept into her and froze her spine. Someone sang an old hymn in the clipped way British people pronounce words. Grams had sung those words many times, kneeling in the dirt in their back garden. Pulling weeds and praising God, singing about sin being removed.

A tear snaked down Caisey's cheek, tickling her dry skin. Tissue touched her cheek and she turned her face toward the comfort.

"The Lord gave and the Lord has taken away. Blessed be the name of the Lord."

THIRTY-EIGHT

Caisey ran and ran. Down sidewalks, through alleyways and across parking lots she followed a path that snaked beside a river, the relentless pursuit that followed her mile after mile. She had to get away, but it was everywhere around her.

It was inside her.

Tears streamed down her face. Her hair flew behind her in a stream, sweat dampening the back of her neck. Why hadn't she tied it up?

Her foot clipped the asphalt and her knees slammed the ground.

She heard a groan and a body surrounded hers, gathering her up and in until she felt cocooned in his warmth. But it wasn't Liam, it was Gabe. His face was red and his t-shirt was damp with sweat. How far had they run?

He touched her face. "Hey."

His face washed away in a blur of tears. Caisey dipped her head and squeezed him tighter.

THIRTY-NINE

First she was in a car and then she was carried inside to sit cuddled up on Grams' couch.

"I can't be in here." She pushed and struggled against Gabe's arms. He let her go, but didn't let her get off the couch.

"Just sit, Case. You're pushing the grief away and it's tearing you up. You can't run from this, you have to face it. It's hard because you see the hole where she was, but you have to feel it or it won't ever progress to where you can embrace the memories."

She shook her head. He didn't know what he was talking about. He'd never lost anyone like this. He walked away from his family and she could see he missed them, but he didn't know that it felt like her foundation had been ripped out from under her. First her father. Now Grams.

"Still, Case."

But she was struggling and she didn't think she could stop.

Gabe pulled her onto his lap and wrapped his arms around hers, holding her. "Still."

She squeezed her eyes shut and sucked in slow, deep breaths until the shakes went to jerks and finally the jerking stopped altogether.

"I don't...I can't..."

"I know." His voice rumbled through his chest, under her cheek. "That's why I'm here."

She squeezed her eyes shut. "Gabe."

"You need to get it together. Your family needs you. So take your time, right here with me, and get through it. Because they're seeing you fall apart and it's tearing them up."

Caisey nodded against his shoulder. She could do that. Jake and Jenna were the most important things in the world and she couldn't hurt them, not now.

JENNA PUT her hands on the edge of the kitchen counter and bowed her head. It was like a hole had opened up in her chest and nothing would get rid of it. She didn't want to be strong anymore. This was too hard. Caisey was a mess. Jake had retreated into himself. And she was barely holding it together.

She stared at the coffee maker, trying to dredge up the gumption to make a fresh pot. The whole house was freezing, like Grams took all the warmth and light and happiness with her. Now all that was left was black and way too quiet and empty.

Nic rinsed out the pot and set the coffee to brew. He leaned against the counter next to her, not saying anything. Just being there and making her feel stronger with his presence.

Part of her wished she didn't need him there. She should be able to stand on her own. That was what she wanted. It was better that way, wasn't it? Being independent. Strong. But then, Caisey was the strongest person she knew and her best friend had been a wreck the last few days.

They never had called the doctor, despite Gabe's insistence that it might be necessary. Jenna just couldn't bring herself to do that to her friend, who would've hated it when she found out. Caisey always came off as so tough, like nothing bothered her. Or if it did, she wasn't the kind who talked about it.

God, she's broken. What hope is there if this storm has toppled even Caisey?

Nic grabbed a paper towel and handed it to her. Jenna wiped her cheeks, but more tears kept coming. He pulled her to him and wrapped his arms around her. Jenna sighed into his embrace. Leaning on someone wasn't so bad.

She didn't want to, but she pulled back. "I should check on Jake, make sure he eats something."

"How about you?" Nic squeezed her waist. "Did you eat something?"

"Toast. I'm okay, I just need to make sure he is."

Nic nodded. "I'll go with you."

He followed her up the stairs, holding her hand like he needed the comfort of touch just as much as she did. For years Jenna had missed his presence, and the small ways he let her know he was there for her. Now after almost two decades of famine, she was soaking it up like spring rain in the desert.

Jenna knocked on her son's door and eased it open. "You okay, honey?"

But the bed was empty. And he wasn't at the desk. She turned to Nic, who was frowning. "Did he go downstairs?"

"I'll check."

Nic left and she sat at the computer, waking it out of sleep mode. At her request, he kept her informed of what his password was. When she entered it, a web page came on screen.

"Oh, no."

"He's not downstairs and your car is gone." Nic was out of breath, like he ran back up. "What's wrong?"

Then she knew something bad had happened. Jake wouldn't have taken her car without a fantastically good reason. Did he even know how to drive? What on earth was he doing? She couldn't help thinking the answer was in what he'd been looking at on his computer.

Jenna waved him over. "Check this out."

He came to stand behind her and she scrolled down the page where Jake had searched for Holden Arturo. The articles that came up were from newspapers or blogs and Jake had opened multiple tabs. The police had suspected Holden as being involved in the disappearance of a businessman from New York. It was never proven, but the blogger knew he was involved. The next tab was an article about Gabe's testimony against his dad and the dropped case against Holden, and rumors surrounding Gabe's disappearance immediately following his appearance in court. The third was the obituary for Natalia Silver.

"You don't think he would..." Nic's voice trailed off.

"I don't know what to think. He was doing okay, you know. As well as could be expected, anyway. I didn't know he was up here doing this. I thought he was reading."

"Jenna, you can't control his actions. He has to make decisions for himself."

She shook her head. "But why was he looking at this? What is he going to do? Where did he go?"

Nic thought for a minute. Jenna wanted to scream at him to hurry up, but she waited him out.

"Is he the type of kid to retaliate?"

Jenna bit her lip. "I didn't think so, but I don't know where his head is at right now." "We need to figure out where he went. Then we can sort out his head."

Jenna typed in the web address for her cell service and pulled up the GPS for Jake's phone. The dot flashed along a street in Greenwood Village and stopped halfway down. At a house Jenna had been to before, years ago. Where she'd had the door slammed in her face and been chased to her car by Rottweilers.

"He went to confront my dad."

Jenna was already halfway to the door. "We have to get to him before something happens."

She ran by Caisey's open door and nearly tripped. The door to her closet was open, and so was the gun safe.

"What?"

"Caisey would never have left that open."

"So Jake..."

Jenna looked at him. "Jake took a gun."

They ran down the stairs together just as Caisey and Gabe came in from Grams' side of the house. Caisey frowned and focused on

Jenna's face. Jenna didn't have time to be relieved that her friend was out of the funk she'd been in and back to some semblance of normal.

"Jake went to Nic's dad's house. Your gun safe is open. We think he's going to do something stupid."

Caisey grabbed her keys, turned back around and headed for the door. "Let's go."

Gabe drove and Caisey made a call. Jenna huddled in the back with Nic, holding on for dear life at the thought that they might get there too late.

God, help him.

"Get over to Holden's. Jake went there and we think he took one of my guns." She paused. "I know that." She paused again. "Oh, crap."

Caisey hung up and pulled a gun from the glove box.

"What is it?"

Caisey glanced back at her. "Toben came through on the evidence. He gave his testimony and they're ready to move forward on the arrest.

"So cops are on their way there?"

"They might be there already, they might not move in until tomorrow. It's bureaucracy. Bottom line is, this could all get a lot worse before it gets better. If the FBI strike team shows up and Jake is waving a gun, things could go south. Fast."

Jenna knew that's what she did for a living and Caisey was trained, but this was Jake.

"You're not going to shoot him, are you? Even if he tries to kill Holden?"

"You really want me to answer that question? You think I'd do anything to hurt Jake?" She shook her head. "I know I haven't been much help lately, and I'm sorry for that. You guys needed me."

"You weren't being selfish, you were grieving."

"Even still, I should've been there. But I'm here now and I'm not going to let Jake do anything that will mess up his future or hurt him in any way. Okay? You can trust me. This is what I do. Liam is getting word to the agents on the case to find out when they're going to take Holden down and let them know there might be a minor involved. You guys need to wait outside and I'll go in. When Liam gets there he'll come in too, but you all need to wait for the police."

"I should come with—"

Caisey cut off Nic with a short head shake. "You all stay outside."

They pulled onto a street Jenna usually purposely avoided. Who wanted to be reminded that they weren't good enough? She wasn't itching to relive the day her world came crashing down and she realized that she and her baby would have to rely on Samuel, Grams and Caisey. She had a blessed life, but there had always been something missing. And that something now sat beside her, squeezing her hand and worrying about his son just as much as she was.

But if anything happened to Jake...she wasn't strong enough to even think about that.

FORTY

Jake lifted the gun and saw the old man's eyes flash. Good. He should be scared. Jake wanted to kill him for what he'd done to Natalia, and his mom and dad. Jake's whole life went the way it did because of this guy's selfishness. Standing there in a shirt and slacks and his socks, Holden Arturo didn't look like much. Certainly not the killer everyone said he was.

"You're a monster."

"You don't know me, kid. You can't show up at my door like this and barge in and insult me. Put the gun down before you hurt someone."

"You're wrong. I do know you. Grandpa."

The old man's eyes widened. "No." Then something dawned on him. "Jenna Cartwright. I knew that little—"

"Don't call my mom that!"

"Hmm...you do look a little Cartwright. Though I can see a measure of my son in you. Blood does tell."

"I'm nothing like you! You might be my grandfather, but you're a monster!"

"And that's reason enough to want to end me?" He chuckled, a low dark sound. "Perhaps you do know me after all. Perhaps a little closer than you'd like, eh?"

"This isn't a joke! You killed Natalia Silver. You burned down my dad's car garage and nearly killed him and my mom. Aunty Elenor might have been in the hospital, but you probably had someone kill her too. An old lady who only had a stomach bug, and now she's dead." Jake sucked in a breath. "What did we ever do to you? Well I'm not going to let you do it anymore. Not to us and not to anyone else."

He adjusted his grip on the gun. He knew enough of the basics he'd managed to load it and everyone knew you just pulled back the slide and then you could fire. He was going to do it. He was going to put a bullet in this murderer, just like Caisey would if she could. Take down the bad guy. Protect the family, even if it costs you everything. Jake didn't have anything left, not now that Natalia was gone. The future was black. His mom would be sad, maybe even disappointed or mad at him, but in the end she would see he'd done the right thing.

"So you're going to shoot me in my living room." The old man's eyes were hard. "What will you do with the body?"

"What do you care? You'll be dead."

"True." He sniffed. "And you'll be in jail for the next twenty years, if you don't get the death penalty."

Jake's stomach clenched. He shook his head. "I have no future without Natalia. What do I care what happens to me?"

"You think I destroyed your family? I don't know this Natalie person."

"Her name was Natalia. She was Lazlo Silver's granddaughter and your men shot up his restaurant last week and killed her."

"Ah. You have to know, with men like that it's almost inevitable that an innocent will get caught in the crossfire."

"And Nic's garage?"

"I heard it was vandals who started the fire."

"They could have been killed! They were in there that night. You just don't like the fact that Nic wants to have a life. Just because he won't jump when you tell him to isn't reason to kill him."

Arturo motioned to a cabinet topped with a silver tray, glasses and multiple glass bottles filled with colored liquid. "Do you mind if I pour a drink? Your rambling is making me dizzy."

Jake clenched his teeth together. "Don't move!"

"Honestly, if you were going to shoot me you should have done it already. Stand there long enough and you'll lose your nerve."

"I said don't move!"

"Jake."

It was Caisey.

~

WHEN HE HEARD HER SPEAK, Liam blew out the breath he'd been holding. He turned to Burkot and motioned to his phone, the line open to Caisey's cell. "I've got ears inside the house."

Burkot nodded and trotted across the street to the van. The strike team was in place, ready to take down Holden Arturo, but Caisey had wanted five minutes to try and diffuse the situation first. He hoped she was able, because Jake was a good kid who didn't deserve all the trouble he would surely be in if he did what they thought he was planning to do.

"I don't give a crap what Agent Lyons said."

Liam's head jerked away from the house and he looked at the SWAT team leader. "We've been working this case for months. The bureau has had this guy on radar for years. There's no way we're going to let Arturo be taken out by a kid. She can have two minutes and then we're going in."

~

CAISEY BIT HER LIP. The gun jerked, but Jake kept his aim and didn't look back. Caisey kept her voice soft as she moved to him. "Jake, what are you doing?"

"If you're here to arrest me, don't bother. I'm not done yet."

She came close, but he saw her and stepped back. She halted and raised her hands. "Give me the gun, Jake."

She needed to get closer. He was still nearer to Arturo than her.

Jake shook his head, eyes on his grandfather. "I'm going to kill him."

Arturo didn't look convinced. In fact he looked smug, like things had just taken a turn for the better. Caisey almost wanted to let Jake shoot him, just to prove him wrong.

She looked at Jake. "Why do you want to kill him?"

She knew why, but he needed to talk it out and she needed to get the gun. He needed to be distracted enough she could get close.

"You know why! Grams and Natalia, they're both dead because of him. I'm only doing this because you couldn't. Otherwise, I knew you'd be here. It's what you do. Protect us."

"I don't kill unarmed people. Regardless of what they have done." Caisey sighed. "I can't protect you if you do this. He won't pay. It'll just be over for him and all you've done is destroy yourself. This isn't the way, Jake. It's not the answer."

God, it's not helping. You have to do this. If he kills Arturo I can't protect him.

"I don't care. He'll be dead and that's all that matters!"

Caisey saw his finger flex on the trigger. She rushed at him, the shot went wide and she slammed into Jake. They hit the floor and he brought the gun up again. Straddling her godson, Caisey slammed his wrist with her left hand so he dropped the gun, and punched him in the face.

"FBI!"

"FBI!"

"Freeze! Hands in the air!"

Arturo went for the gun. There was a scramble and she was pulled back up by her jacket.

"Caisey!" Liam's voice came on the heels of the strike team.

Jake was pulled aside and Arturo lifted the gun.

Pointed it at her.

Inches from her chest.

God—

Jake gasped. Arturo's finger twitched and the muzzle flashed. Gunshots filled the air, like bowling pins knocked down by a strike.

Caisey fell backwards.

She hit the floor and all the air in her body rushed out. The room filled with a cloud of gun powder and smoke. Air rushed through her ears and she heard only muffled yelling. Her chest screamed with fire. She gasped for breath and Jake was flipped on the floor beside her, his cheek to the rug. His arms were pulled behind him and he was cuffed by an agent in full body armor. She wanted to stop them, tried to tell them he was her godson. He wasn't a criminal. What were they doing?

"Calm down."

She blinked and black spots peppered the edge of her vision. Liam's face got right in front of her. "Seriously, Case. Take a breath."

She tried to suck air, but only a rasping sound filled her ears. How bad was it? Was she bleeding out? Caisey lifted her hand and ran it over her front. Where was she hit? How long did she have?

She wasn't afraid to die, so long as Jake was going to be released. She tried to say his name.

Liam shook his head. "You need to breathe. You're just winded."

Her vision blurred and she tried to blink.

"Breathe Caisey. You have to breathe."

Darkness descended on her. It wasn't warm or cold, just a thick black she knew was the end. She'd done it. She'd protected her family all the way to the end. Just like her dad.

Dad.

He might not have been perfect, but she missed him like crazy. She didn't want to leave Jake and Jenna...Gabe and even Nic. Liam and Andrea. But they would live without her. Grief hurt, but they would pull through it together and become a new family. They didn't need her.

God, they don't need me. Did they ever? Why did I think I was so irreplaceable, like I was the only one who could take care of them? I'm so stupid. I'm sorry I didn't learn that earlier. I could have spent more time just loving them.

Help them. They'll need each other now. Bind them together and show Jake that the future can be wonderful. I'm so sorry. But I know they'll be fine without me. I trust You.

~

GABE COVERED his mouth and watched them work on Caisey, cutting off her vest with a knife and peeling her shirt back to reveal the red welt in the center of her chest, above her sports bra.

Nic put his hand on Gabe's shoulder and squeezed. Liam sat back on his heels while the EMT did mouth to mouth, leaned down and listened to her chest, and then continued to breathe into her mouth.

Gabe bit his lip. He'd only just found her. He couldn't lose her now.

The agents all crowded around. Jenna stood by Jake, still cuffed and being held onto by a tight-end FBI agent who had a grip on his elbow. Tears streamed down Jake's face and Gabe watched his lips move.

God, we're all crying out on this one. I don't want to lose her now and I don't think her family can afford another loss. We want Your will, even when we don't understand why someone like Grams had to die. Or Natalia. Don't take Caisey. Please.

Gabe's breath hitched.

The EMT sat back. "She's breathing. Let's go." He nodded to his partner and Caisey was loaded onto a stretcher.

Gabe walked beside her to the ambulance. Several of the agents started, but Liam waved them back and nodded to Gabe. "Go. We'll meet you there."

~

NIC HELD on to his son and squeezed his eyes shut.

Jake sobbed. "I'm sorry."

Nic leaned back and looked at him. "We all make mistakes."

"But they killed your dad."

"And he would have killed Caisey if she wasn't wearing a vest."

Jake's face crumpled and he looked like the little boy Nic had missed. "She nearly died and it's all my fault. I shouldn't have come here. I shouldn't have done this."

Nic touched both hands to his son's cheeks. "We all make mistakes. We'll figure this out and we'll go from there. A fresh start, okay?"

The special agent holding on to his son snorted. Nic didn't care if he didn't think that was going to happen. He would do everything in his power to clear this up for Jake. Because that's what fathers did.

"Time to go."

Nic ignored the agent and kept his eyes on his son. "I'll see you soon, okay?"

Jake dipped his head and was led away. Jenna watched him go and Nic went to stand by her. Eyes bright, Jenna blinked and looked at Jake and then the direction the ambulance had gone.

"They'll take care of Caisey. Gabe is with her and Liam will be there too. Focus on Jake and we'll check in on her later. Okay?"

"She nearly died. She couldn't breathe." Tears spilled down her cheeks. Cops walked by them, talking and making like they had super important things to do. Like stuff like this happened every day. Which for them, maybe it did.

Nic pulled Jenna close. "She'll be okay."

"What if she hadn't been wearing a vest?"

"But she was." He rubbed her back. "Let's go. We aren't helping standing here."

Jenna sighed. "I think I need to call my son a lawyer."

"We'll figure it out." He tried to lead her out the door, but she didn't move.

"He nearly got her killed."

Nic nodded. "I know."

"I'm so angry at him right now I don't hardly want to help him out of this. Maybe he should realize how bad that was. Sit in jail for a while and think about what he's done. What was he thinking?"

"I know."

"Is Caisey really going to be okay?"

Nic kissed her forehead. "Let's go see about our son."

FORTY-ONE

A movie film score played in the background. It was small compensation for a job well done. Life was, after all, duty and reward, checks and balances, delayed gratification. All the better to keep away the turning tide of darkness that swelled inside him, ready to break on the shore.

He clicked the mouse on the window open on the left computer screen, bringing up her picture in pristine color in the newspaper article.

She was perfect.

Every composer had a magnum opus. Every artist had a masterpiece. And she would be his.

Such determination. Such strength. She would be his grand finale.

Caisey Ann Lyons.

~

CAISEY DIDN'T FEEL GREAT, but she went to work anyway. She had the all-clear from the doctors under the proviso that she didn't do anything strenuous. But seriously, it hurt to breathe. It wasn't like she was going to join an operation. She was crazy, but not that crazy. People needed to quit giving her that look, like they fully expected her to jump in her rust-bucket car and run off to go skydiving or bungee-jumping when she had a bruise the size of Wyoming on her front that was just now starting to go away.

She headed for her desk. Only two weeks since she got her sternum broken by a point-blank bullet and the whole place looked different. It even smelled different, like a weird mix of leather and coffee and printer toner. There was still a hum of activity. Nothing had changed, but there was this niggling feeling where her stubborn will used to be that didn't feel like it always had when she saw this place.

It was weird, like it wasn't the home- away-from-home it used to be, the sanctuary where she dug in and prepared to do battle. Now it wasn't even the home of a relative you didn't like that much. She probably needed a vacation, even though she'd spent the last week and a half since she got out of hospital supervising the estate sale of Grams' furniture and working out all the details of her will and the life insurance.

She and Jenna hadn't had the heart to do more than slice a chunk off and set it aside for Jake's college fund. Caisey wanted to pay off the house, but she didn't particularly like being there now, so what was the point? Even with Jenna and Jake still there and Gabe hanging around, there were too many memories of the past crowding her so she couldn't sleep for dreaming about Grams and her dad. That led to wondering where her mom was, and all kinds of other rabbit trails that didn't lead anywhere but south.

Caisey slumped into her chair and winced. She was ready to be done with the incessant pain in her chest, but it wasn't going away, especially since she'd confined herself to the minimum dose of regular pain killers. She'd seen too many agents retire early after a bad incident because they got dependent and she wasn't even going to go near that whole thing. She would rather live with this right now than live with that forever.

She looked around, avoiding the winces and pity in the eyes of other agents. There wasn't a lot she needed, but that definitely didn't cover it. None of them bothered to come over and ask her how she was doing. Though, they probably figured she'd just snap like she always did when she was in a bad mood because something was hurting. Why did she have to be like that? Why couldn't she be full of love like she was supposed to be?

A change of scenery was probably in order. Jenna and Jake were moving on with their lives, and Nic was a big part of that. They'd probably hardly notice she was gone if she went on vacation. God would take care of them. She knew that now. Caisey didn't need to be at work for them to be safe. In fact, it didn't matter what she did. They would be safe in His hands, no matter what came at them. Caisey knew that as sure as she knew she had a peace now that she'd never felt before. Peace that reached right down to her soul and spread out like the licking flames of a burning fire, warming her where before there had only been fear.

"You're here."

Caisey blinked and looked up just as Liam sat down. "Hey."

"You okay?"

She shrugged and then remembered something Gabe had told her. She squinted at him. "I know it wasn't you who gave me mouth to mouth."

Liam tipped his head back and laughed.

She frowned. "That wasn't funny. You shouldn't have told me that."

He didn't stop laughing. "You should have seen your face. You wouldn't even look at Andrea, I had to tell her why." He wheezed. "It was priceless."

"Why do I put up with you?"

Liam folded his arms. "Probably because I put up with you."

She glared, but didn't tell him she would concede him that point. "So what's new?"

"Tell me about Jake first. How's he doing?"

Caisey brushed at some crumbs on her desk. Someone had been eating at her desk while she was gone. *Gross.* "He's pretty down, since it hit home what could have happened and he's thanking God it didn't. He's probably going to get probation and it'll go on his juvenile record. But when you have half a dozen FBI agents vouching for you, it says a lot."

Liam shrugged. "Juvie records are sealed anyway. It won't be a big deal since he's not a habitual offender type kid. Who doesn't have a record these days?"

Caisey's eyes widened. "You?"

Liam looked everywhere but at her.

"How could I not have known this? Spill."

His eyes narrowed. "You don't know everything about me."

"Apparently. What else don't I know? What other dark secrets do you have that you're hiding from me?"

Liam laughed. "It's not like that. It was just stupid kid stuff. Boosting cars to get a rise out of my dad. He made sure I got thirty days in juvenile detention and visited me every weekend." He shrugged. "Worked."

Caisey shook her head. "I can't believe you never told me that."

"What about old Gabe? How's he doing?"

"Nice. That was slick. Changing the subject like I'm not going to notice."

Liam smirked. "Andrea seems to think so. We set a date."

"Oh yeah?"

He nodded. "Now tell me about Gabe."

Caisey glanced at her black monitor screen. She should probably turn it on if she was going to be here. She sighed, thinking how much effort it would take to lean down and hit the button.

"Earth to Case."

She shook her head. "Gabe is good. He got tasked with all the hauling of Grams' stuff to the thrift store and he's been sleeping on her couch. I'm not sure what his long term plan is, he probably needs to get back to Buckshot since he has his bookstore. I honestly don't think he expected to live, much less have to deal with going home to get back to his life."

Liam nodded. "Makes sense. How do you feel about him going?"

"I don't know that I've thought about it. But it's been nice him being here. We've talked a lot and um...stuff."

"Like making out?"

She rolled her eyes. "This isn't junior high."

"Yeah, but you really should ask him to the Sadie Hawkins dance."

She laughed, pressed a hand to her chest and groaned.

"Sorry. Probably shouldn't do that."

"No, you shouldn't. But Gabe has been great, you know? Just being there and not pushing. It really is too bad things have to go back to normal eventually."

"Normal? You?" Liam laughed again.

Caisey grabbed a stapler and pretended to throw it at him. He covered his head and laughed harder. She shook hers at his antics and the far wall caught her eye. All the Chloroform Killer stuff was still up.

"What's up with all that? I thought they went to pick him up."

Liam shook his head. "Evaded capture. So now everyone's ticked off and seriously motivated to nail this guy to the wall."

Caisey saw something in his eyes that was more than just what he said. "What happened?"

"They found another body this morning."

Caisey closed her eyes. "They really need to get this guy."

"No kidding."

Caisey glanced at the board. "Just one body?"

"Kills are further apart."

"Something disrupted his pattern?"

"Getting more selective."

Caisey shook her head. She really didn't want to get sucked into this. She needed light, not the mire of darkness that permeated this whole place. For once she wanted to forget that evil existed and bask in the goodness of God that filled His people. Or babies. Babies were good. Which made her think about Gabe, but who knew what the future would bring? She knew what the true desire of her heart was. Would God work that out? She was trying to abide, to stick close to Him, but it wasn't a formula that got you what you wanted. It was life, and life was eminently unpredictable.

She sighed and refocused on Liam. "Anything else happen while I was gone?"

"Sheriff Frank Allens was apprehended in Nebraska a week ago. Marshals brought him back to Colorado to stand trial for the murder of his niece."

"They're sure?"

Liam nodded. "That's where the evidence points. And it's overwhelming, since they found his wife's body too. It was years ago, but the pathologist confirmed the attack was savage. Like he snapped."

She blew out a breath.

"Heard there's a job opening."

"For what?"

Liam gave her a look like she was dense. "For the sheriff of Buckshot."

"Why would you tell me that?"

"I'm sure I don't know, but since you were shot in the vest, I'll give you a break. Maybe you might want to think about it awhile and it'll come to you. What with Gabe going back to his bookstore and your recent injury meaning you might be looking for a change of pace. You did say you liked it there, didn't you?"

Caisey blinked. "I guess. Too bad my dad's old cabin is pretty much uninhabitable now. Gabe will have to totally rebuild, if his bookstore doesn't have an apartment or whatnot above it. I probably should have gone and checked it out while we were there. I would've liked to have seen it."

"You could always visit."

"I guess." She blew out a breath and looked around. They were all safe. The threat was gone and she had what she wanted. She had peace. So why did it feel like something was still missing?

"You okay?" Liam's eyes were soft.

"I don't know."

"Talk it out."

She looked around and then back at Liam. "Is this it? Is this my life?"

"It is for me."

"But you have Andrea. You're getting married."

"Exactly." He nodded. "God knew the kind of job I needed and he brought me here so I could get to know Him through your life. Grams. Jenna. Even Jake. It was undeniable. You're all the reason why I saw for the first time the validity in trusting something more than just myself. There was no escaping it."

Caisey smiled. He'd certainly kicked and screamed against it, until deciding at the last minute when everything was on the line that he was going to trust God at His word."

"But you?" Liam shook his head. "Has this job ever made you truly happy, like down to your bones happy? Or is it just something you thought you were supposed to do?"

"Why does my job have to make me happy? It's just a job. It doesn't have to be some grand calling."

"It doesn't have to slowly kill you either."

"You think...?"

Liam nodded. "This isn't you. Even though you are more than capable of succeeding at this, I just don't think you could do it without it tearing apart who you are. It will rob you of your belief in the innocent. Eventually you'll see evil everywhere, even where it isn't, because I don't think you can do something without giving it everything you've got. It's never going to be just a job. Even if you were a waitress, you'd make it something more. And that's great, Case. It's a good thing to be like that. It's ministry. But if it's not the right thing, I think you'll suffer. Especially when every day is one more killer, one more drug kingpin, or one more crazy person bent on destruction. It'll get to you."

Caisey bit her lips together. "It already did."

The phone rang. Caisey shook her head and reached for it. "Special Agent Lyons."

"Mr. Silver wants to speak to you."

The caller hung up.

Liam motioned to the phone with his chin. "Who was it?"

She told him.

"So, let's go."

"You're coming?"

Liam shrugged. "I'm in the mood for a drive."

"Don't you have open cases? Work to do?"

He met her at the edge of their desks and squeezed her shoulder. "It'll keep."

FORTY-TWO

Nic didn't look happy. "Are you sure you don't want me to come with you?"

His arms were folded across his chest, tucking his winter coat around him. He leaned back against his Triumph on this busy downtown street. Traffic was busy, even though it was two in the afternoon. The air was chilled and the clouds were heavy like it was going to snow.

Jenna shook her head. "I'll be fine."

At least, she hoped she would be. She'd picked a neutral location to meet with her dad. Since it used to be their favorite restaurant she figured that would ease at least some of the tension. What did he want to say that hadn't already been re-hashed fifty million times? Or did he just want to say, 'I told you so', since Jake was currently in police custody?

She looked at Nic. "I will be fine."

"Okay." He sighed.

Their relationship was such a dance right now. Not wanting to step on each other's toes, or push too hard and make the other person back off. Both of them were being so cautious that all the delicate was starting to seriously annoy her.

"Why don't you just say it? Then I'll know what you're thinking and I don't have to guess."

"Right." The corners of his mouth tipped up. "I don't like the idea of you facing him alone. I'm worried what he'll say and I really don't like the idea of him giving you grief over Jake, or the decisions you've made. But I also know it's important to you to stand on your own, and I'm trying to support that. So I'm going to cross the street and get a coffee and I'll wait for your call."

"You don't have stuff to do? Like insurance quotes and rebuilding your garage."

"Is that more important than making sure you're okay when you're done listening to whatever your dad says?" Nic shook his head. "Not really."

"Well...okay then."

He smiled.

"I'll see you in a few."

Nic nodded and set off for the crosswalk. Jenna gave her name to the hostess and was directed to a table with a cloth covering it, and cloth napkins. Her dad stood, smoothing down his tie and smiling like he wasn't sure he was supposed to be happy to see her. Jenna kissed his cheek, because despite all that had happened, he was still her father.

"Hello."

He motioned her to sit. When he didn't say anything, she straightened her knife and fork and waited for him to get to it.

"You look very nice, Jenna."

She glanced up and frowned.

"You look happy."

"I am."

"How's Jake?"

Jenna bit her lip. Here it was. The put down about how she'd raised a criminal son. She took a deep breath. "Why did you ask me to meet you, Dad?"

He looked down at his hands and back up. "I want to apologize. For everything. I've been making some changes, even talking to the

FBI. But being in business with someone I never should have been in business with doesn't even compare to the mistake I made with you. I should have stood up for you, been there for you when you needed me. I put myself first, trying to keep the peace with your mother and I let you down. I don't know how you can ever forgive me, but I have to at least ask. I've been placating your mother for years, but I can't do it anymore. Things have changed and I'm ready to move on."

"What changed?"

"I don't want to go into detail, because I don't want to upset you, but a business associate of mine died recently. I feel like I've been given a new lease on life. A new freedom and I want to grasp this opportunity, not waste it."

"And mom? How does she feel about you meeting me?"

He shook his head. "She doesn't know about this. I suppose eventually I'll have to tell her, but that depends on you. I would like to spend time with you, get to know you. And I'd like to visit with my grandson if that's possible."

"I don't—"

He lifted his hands, palms out. "I'd like you to be there. And I won't expose him to anything that might upset him. I wouldn't ever want to hurt him. Not since I've done enough of that to you." He sucked in a choppy breath. "I saw the papers. I would very much like to know the honorable and loving young man that you have raised."

Jenna blinked away the wetness. "What he did was stupid. It might have been with good intentions, but it was still wrong."

Alan Cartwright sniffed back tears. "Which just proves that you're a better mom to your son than your mother and I ever were with you."

Jenna might be his mom, but Jake soaked up Caisey's guidance and it seemed like he never even listened to her. It was probably because Caisey wasn't his mom, though she wasn't slack with laying down the law to back up Jenna. And now he was in jail. Despite what her father thought, Jenna's mom probably figured it wasn't surprising that she'd raised a son who tried to commit murder. Her mom's litanies replayed in Jenna's head so much she could say with near certainty what bitterness she would spew over this.

"Jenna, will you forgive me for the wrong I've done you?"

She sucked in a breath. "Yes, Dad. I will." It might not happen right away and she certainly didn't feel it when being mad felt so much better. But it was something to work toward. "And I'd like to set up a time when you can come to dinner. Though, I should warn you that Nic will likely be there."

His eyes widened. "Your Nic?"

She nodded. "Is that a problem?"

"Not at all. I'm just surprised, but happy to hear that. For you and for Jake."

"Seems like it's going to be new beginnings all around." Except her mom. "Are you really not going to tell Mother about this?"

Her dad shook his head. "I'd like to get to know you—all of you—before I open us all up to that."

Jenna nodded.

"Actually..." He paused. "I'm having divorce papers drawn up."

Jenna sat there, staring at him with wide eyes while her dad told the waitress they didn't need anything else. "Divorce?"

He looked relieved. "It's been a long time coming. And not an easy decision, but I feel at peace about this move. I can't live anymore with her toxic words. It almost destroyed both of us."

Jenna nodded. "If it's what you want, and there's no hope for reconciliation then I'll stand by you. She wasn't ever easy to live with, so I can't say I don't understand. I take it she isn't interested in changing?"

He shook his head. "That's the worst part. Not that she doesn't want to be different, but that she thinks there's nothing wrong with the way she's always been."

While they ate, Jenna talked a bit about what Jake was like growing up. So much of what was happening now was like the end of an era. She was excited about the future, but couldn't help feeling sad for her mom. Jenna could only pray she would never grow hard to the way she was with her family. The last thing she wanted to do was become the woman her family walked on egg shells around, trying not to set her off. She might resemble her mom physically, but that was where it had to stop. God would help her, but Jenna was the one who had to do it.

She reached across the table and squeezed her dad's hand. "Thank you for inviting me to lunch."

~

THE RESTAURANT where Natalia had died was boarded up. Workmen walked in and out with lumber on one shoulder and tool belts on their waist. Liam followed her inside, where Lazlo Silver stood at the bar with a shorter man in a JC Penney suit and cheap shoes.

"Thank you, Mr. Silver. You won't regret this."

The man collected a stack of papers and shoved them in his briefcase before he shuffled out. On the way past Caisey, he grinned. *I don't even want to know.* She glanced at Liam and saw him smirk. She shook her head and made her way over to Lazlo, careful to sidestep the spot where the blood stain had been cleaned away.

She thought he would be morose, but the old man held his arms out and enveloped her in a hug. Caisey was too shocked to struggle, so she just stood there until he let go, trying to ignore how much it hurt and praying he wasn't stealing her gun so he could shoot her with it. Liam would cover her, hopefully fast enough.

"You look well."

She lifted one shoulder and let it drop. "You rang?"

Lazlo's wrinkled face morphed into incredulity. "So eloquent, Agent Lyons."

Caisey shrugged and ignored Liam's snort. None of them were under any illusions about her, but that was the whole point. She was who she was. "There something you wanted, or is this a social invitation?"

Caisey had been at home and in no condition to go anywhere when Natalia's funeral had been held at the local Greek Orthodox Church. Lazlo looked different now, in the daytime, which she'd never actually seen before. Night covered so much, illuminating hard edges. Looking at him now, he seemed more Grandfather than mobster.

"I have good news. News I thought you might pass on to your fellow civil servants."

"Right."

"I'm retiring."

"Passing the business on to your second in command?"

He shook his head. "Splicing it up and selling everything to the highest bidders, letting go of the restaurants and other...less legitimate businesses. I find I have no heart for it anymore. I wish to retire somewhere quiet and live out my days with peace."

Caisey couldn't imagine he wanted to stick around here either, now that he wouldn't get to see Natalia. And then add to that being constantly reminded she was gone. "I don't blame you."

Lazlo's face softened, which she'd only ever seen him do with Natalia. "That is because you and I are cut from much the same cloth."

Caisey started to object, but he kept talking.

"Your father was the same. Consumed with passion for what you think is the highest good. For me, that would be money. You and your father shared a zeal for justice. But justice comes in many forms and it's easy to lose sight of what is important. I, of all people, know that."

Caisey nodded. "I'm sorry—"

Her voice broke and she cleared her throat. "Thank you, Caisey Lyons."

"We should be getting back to work." She motioned to the door. "I'll pass on your news."

She had no idea who had eyes on Lazlo's empire, but she would put the word out that he was moving on. That would ease a lot of minds, until the new heads started to pop up on the FBI's radar.

Liam led the way out and Caisey glanced up and down the street. Things were calm right now, but life was relentless. Criminals came and went like that arcade game where you hit the critters with a mallet. It wouldn't ever stop. And why did that make her feel old and tired, like she just wanted to curl up with Gabe and nap?

Liam stopped at the car and frowned at her. "All right?"

Caisey shrugged.

"Where to now?"

She grabbed the door handle. "Surprise me."

FORTY-THREE

Gabe pushed out a breath, his hands folded on the table in front of him. His foot tapped a rhythm on the tile floor as he waited.

"What is it you want from this conversation?"

Good question. Gabe glanced at the chaplain, an unassuming man with thinning hair and no observable energy. Had working at a prison for years sapped the life from him? Surely this man had seen good things amongst the bad, testimonies and astounding life-changed God-things. So why didn't he look happy about it? Maybe a neutral expression was how you got by in a place like this.

"I don't really know." Gabe shook his head. "I was the one who put him here. Should I apologize for that? I sort of feel like I should, but I also feel like this is goodbye."

The chaplain nodded slowly. "It likely is, considering his condition."

Gabe didn't want to think about his dad dying in this place. It was justice for the things he'd done for Arturo, but he was still Gabe's dad. You couldn't stop loving someone even when they did wrong. Gabe had righted that wrong, but would his dad respect that?

It seemed like forever before the silence was broken. The door handle rotated and he shot up, the chair sliding back behind him. The chaplain stood also, the slow movement of someone weighted down by life.

Toben Carlen shuffled in. A guard led him to a chair. When he was sitting, he hissed out a breath and looked up. Gabe wanted to close his eyes at this once-vibrant man, now frail and worn. His gray hair was bushy, his face cracked with age. The orange jumpsuit brought out a sallowness in his skin.

Gabe cleared his throat and sat down. His dad wore the same neutral expression as the chaplain. But did he expect a warm reception? Gabe didn't know what he should have expected. Or where to start.

"Gabriel."

He shut his eyes. Since his mom died, his dad was the only one who called him that. "I feel like I should ask for forgiveness."

Shackles clinked and Gabe opened his eyes. His dad was trying to reach for him. Gabe moved his hand so his dad could hold it.

"Son, it's me who needs absolution from you. I'm so glad you're here. Thank you for coming. The fact you're here means everything to an old man with not much time left in this world."

"But I did this to you." Gabe's breath hitched. "I put you here because I couldn't think beyond what you did. I was blinded by a need for justice so I couldn't see what that would do to you."

"And now?"

"Hindsight is a powerful thing."

"You did the right thing, Gabriel. Just like your mom taught you, truth above all else. You should have no regrets over what happened. The only one to blame for this, is me. I broke the law. I did wrong. I hurt people. Justice was served and none of that is on you."

Gabe touched his forehead to the table. His father's hand rested on the back of his head, much like he'd done when Gabe was a kid, sick or scared about something.

"I don't hold you responsible for any of this, Gabriel. And I need your forgiveness. I hurt so many people and I'll never get to ask them, but I can ask you. Jesus has forgiven me, I know that. He died for my sin and it doesn't erase the pain I caused people. But at least now I can spend my last days praying for those I've hurt. Will you forgive me for what I've done?"

Gabe lifted his head. "Sin is sin. None of us can say something is worse than something else. All of it causes pain to someone. We've all done wrong and I can't withhold forgiveness from you, when I've been forgiven so much."

"You believe?"

Gabe nodded. "A few years back I got to the end of myself. I was chewed up inside and I couldn't find peace anywhere, least of all within myself. I decided to give the church thing a try and I found peace that didn't come from me at all."

"That's wonderful."

"It was. I felt free for the first time, like I could face myself in the mirror instead of trying not to think about the kind of person I was. A person who tore apart his family. It might have been right, but it still changed all of us. You were here, Dad. But I was in a prison of my own."

"I believe it, son. I do. You always tried so hard to do right and speak the truth, but you felt everything so deeply. I knew what it was doing to you, to admit what I'd done and speak up about it. You did the right thing, but it cost you your future."

The image of Caisey popped into his head and Gabe felt his lips twitch. "I got it back Dad."

Toben's eyes flickered. "Your future?"

He nodded. "Her name is Caisey. I saw her a long time ago, just once. This is going to sound crazy, it sounds crazy to me and I lived it. But I knew. I saw her once and I just knew she was it for me. It's been nearly twenty years, but I found her again. She just walked in one day and all that knowing rushed back. She's been having a rough time lately, with Arturo, but that's over now. I'm hoping she feels the same. Praying she'll want to make a life with me."

Toben huffed a laugh, his mouth curling up the same way Gabe's did.

"What?"

Toben shook his head. "It was much the same for me, with your mother. One look and I knew she was the woman I was going to spend the rest of my life with. We got married the next day."

Gabe wanted to laugh. "You did?"

His dad nodded, smiling.

"How come I've never heard this?"

"Sounds crazy, just like you said. And your mom said she didn't want you jumping into something without thinking it through. Then as you got older, she realized you had way too much sense to do that. When you'd know, you would be sure and she wasn't going to be able to talk you out of it. You're as stubborn as your old man and she knew that."

Gabe chuckled.

"Somehow you wound up with a streak of honor so strong nothing would break it.Whereas I lost my way."

Gabe studied his dad. They were alike in many ways, they always had been. Which led to butting heads and more shouting than was probably healthy in a father-son relationship. But that was past. The years had taken them on different journeys. Gabe was free to live the rest of his life, with Caisey and the peace he'd found believing in Jesus. His dad had that same faith, but with little time left over.

The guard said, "Five minutes."

Gabe sucked in a breath and squeezed his dad's hand lightly. He didn't feel anything past sympathy for where his dad's choices had brought him. The hurt was gone. Warmth swept through him, and he recognized that peace that surpasses understanding. "I'd like to see you again, if that's okay."

Toben shook his head. "This is it, son. This is goodbye."

"But I want to speak more with you. We've just found each other again." And that's what it felt like, though neither had been lost any way but spiritually. "This can't be it."

"It is, son." Toben labored to his feet. "I love you, Gabriel. Live your life, marry your girl and make the family we never had. Be the honorable man you are, always. God will bless you and He'll keep you and I pray His face will shine on you always."

He shuffled to the door and looked back. "But don't come back."

Gabe stared at the open door.

The chaplain shifted in his chair and Gabe wanted to know what the man thought he was going to achieve by sitting in on this meeting.

"You have to understand—"

Gabe cut him off. "No, I don't."

JENNA UNLOCKED THE FRONT DOOR. Jake brushed past her and raced upstairs. Seconds later she heard his door slam. Nic squeezed her shoulder. "You want me to talk to him?"

She shook her head and set her purse down at the bottom of the stairs. The house was quiet, too quiet. Caisey's dad was gone and now Grams too. Caisey was off, working or whatever. The place was like a mausoleum—if they could be inhabited by surly teenage boys.

"I'll talk to him."

"Okay." Nic motioned toward the kitchen. "You want anything?"

"Coffee would be great."

Jenna made her way upstairs. She knew Jake felt bad about what he'd done. She knew he spent his time in jail upset and trying to be brave, faced with something he'd been certain he would never have to do. Forget being scared straight, her son had never dealt well with doing something wrong. It was like his remorse gene was overdeveloped to where you didn't need to punish him, because he was punishing himself bad enough. Thereafter he would always go overboard to do what was right.

Now she knew Caisey was healing, Jenna settled on being angry at her. She was going to be okay, so Jenna could be mad. Caisey should never have told Jake that protecting your family came above everything, at whatever cost. That line of thinking was what sent a teenage boy, with no experience to fall back on, out in the world to kill a man. Now her son had a juvenile record and was crying in his room.

Jenna stopped outside his door and listened to the coughing

sobs. She waited until he had settled and then got a box of tissues from the bathroom. She set them on his bed and sat beside him. He didn't look up from the pillow.

"Jake, honey."

"Go away, Mom."

"I know you feel bad. That's a good thing. It means you have a heart. But you can't keep beating yourself up about what you did. You answered for it and now you move on."

"How can I do that? Natalia is gone and everyone is going to know I tried to murder someone, Mom. My life is over. I can't go to school. I can't go anywhere. No one is going to want me now."

Jenna wanted to smile at the overblown teenage drama, but he wasn't wrong. Not really. "So we'll move. Start fresh somewhere else. You. Me." She hesitated. "Your father."

Jake turned his head to her. "Dad is coming?"

Jenna shrugged. "We'll ask him. But think about it. His business was destroyed and I'm going to guess he'll want to come with us."

"Really?"

"We'll figure it out, Jake. Just get some rest and when you're ready, come downstairs. The three of us will work this out together, okay?"

He sniffed and nodded. "Yeah, Mom."

Jenna gave his shoulder a squeeze and went downstairs. On the bottom step, her body stilled. Was Nic going to be there when she got to the kitchen? Something dark rushed through her. Maybe he'd decided they were too much to deal with and he'd left.

"You okay?"

Jenna blinked and looked at him. "Uh..."

"You don't look okay." He moved closer and took her arm, leading her into the kitchen. "Sit. I'll pour you a cup. You look like your world is falling apart."

"Well it isn't, because it already did."

"So we put it back together."

She looked up at him. "We?"

Nic pulled a chair out so they were facing each other, almost touching. He grabbed her hand. "I'm in this. All the way. I'm not leaving again. My dad isn't an issue anymore. The road ahead is clear and it lies wherever we want it to lead. And I'm here, so you don't walk this alone. Okay?"

She nodded.

"We do everything together, from now on."

"But I'm supposed to be strong and independent."

Nic cracked a smile, the one she'd fallen for all those years ago. The same smile Jake used to wear so often. Tears filled her eyes.

"Hey." Nic grabbed her hand. "You are strong. It was funny because you don't realize you're already everything you need to be."

"Not for Jake." She sucked in a breath. "What if I can't do this? What if I can't help him get through this?"

"All we can do is give him the tools to move forward. We will get through this and I want to be a part of it."

Jenna bit her lip.

"I can see those wheels turning." He smiled again. "And I'll tell you right now, I intend to marry you."

"Is that really what you want?"

Nic rolled his eyes.

"Don't make like I'm all exasperating, Nicholas Arturo."

He shook his head. "Maybe I'll take your name. I don't want my father there with me, every time I use my name."

Jenna nearly choked on her coffee. "What if I want some time to think about it?"

Nic studied her. "Tell me what you want."

Jenna didn't have to think too hard. "A happy family. A peaceful home."

"That's it?"

She shrugged. "Jake wants out of Denver. Somewhere no one knows who he is."

Nic frowned. "What about your spa?"

"I've had chain spa's approach me about a buy-out before, so that's possible. I could look into that. But if they're going to take all the heart out of my place I'd rather sell it to my assistant manager for a dollar." Jenna smiled at his face. "I'll figure it out, because it's not more important than Jake. It was fun, but it was just a job."

"You blow me away, Jenna." He shook his head, eyes wide. "You're the strongest person I know. How come you didn't see that?"

"I don't feel strong at all."

"But you are. The hits keep coming and you're just rolling with it all. Forgiving your dad and then driving straight to pick up Jake. Bringing your son home and working toward the future." He stood up, pulling her close. "There's nowhere in the world I'd rather be than right here with you, making our family great."

"Do you think it will work?"

Nic smiled. "I think we can try."

"God can work it out." Jenna said it tentatively, not knowing where he stood.

Nic nodded. "You can help me with that too."

FORTY-FOUR

Caisey reached the kitchen and saw Jenna and Nic in passionate lip lock. "Whoa, sorry."

She pulled up short and Gabe slammed into her back.

"What is it...? Oh."

She looked back at him. "Guess we know what they've been doing."

Gabe smiled. "Seems like they've come to terms with some things."

Jenna's face was red. Nic didn't look sorry at all.

Caisey grinned. "We'll leave you two to it."

She strode down the hall and slumped onto Grams' couch. Gabe sat down beside her, his body angled so he could look at her. She glanced at him. "What?"

"You okay?"

Caisey wanted to roll her eyes. "I am happy for them." She paused. "What are your plans? Nic and Jenna look like they know what they want. What about you, Gabe?"

She wasn't sure she even wanted to know. Was she ready to jump into something? It felt natural to be here with him, if she ignored the fact that the walls in here echoed with memories of Grams. Part of her wanted to run outside, just to get away from it.

The rest of her wanted to build a life in this room and never leave. Everything was different. How did she go on from here? Back to a job she didn't particularly enjoy and living in a house that sucked her under every time she walked in the door.

"I should be getting back to Buckshot here pretty soon. I have to open my bookstore or I'll lose all my business for good. If I haven't already. I also have a deadline approaching."

"So you're going back to your life?" Caisey kept still, not wanting to cry all over him and beg him to stay. Why couldn't she be one of those women who did that stuff? She might dislike being all weepy and over-emotional, but it had its advantages.

He nodded, studying her. Was he waiting for her to ask where she fit into that? Because that was a good question.

"Case—" he stopped himself and got up. "Never mind. You have your job. And that's an important thing, being an FBI agent. I should have realized that before. You're not going to want to leave Denver and I can't see myself living in the city after years of boondock neighbors who know your name and ask how you are. And wide open vistas."

He ran his hand through his hair. "I can't ask you to give everything up when you would be completely miserable in my life. Buckshot probably isn't the kind of place you want to live. And you'll be leaving Jenna and Jake...no, I can't ask that of you."

Caisey squeezed her eyes shut. Maybe she wanted that more than anything. Change. A fresh start in a new place that she might not have liked in the first place, but it could grow on her. She could see how friendly neighbors and great views would be a nice life. She would need a job that wasn't pointless or totally boring. That was the one condition. What she spent her days doing was important to her. It had to have value, not like penning her memoirs or something lame like that. Introspection wasn't her thing. She needed to be active.

Like police work.

So long as a town full of people who'd had one sheriff for a decade would swear in the former-FBI agent who was the one who tried to kill their murdering psycho former-sheriff. It made her head spin just thinking about it. But something about it sat right. In her heart. Could she really do it? Quit the FBI and be a small town sheriff.

Days of paperwork interspersed with dishing out speeding tickets and breaking up domestic disturbances. The symptoms were the same, humans being selfish and not caring enough for the people around them. It wasn't different from Denver, just a fresh start somewhere the darkness wouldn't cloud in on her. She would still be able to smell the fresh air.

Where she'd come home to Gabe—if he'd have her.

Build a family of her own.

It was a powerful dream. But one that meant leaving behind everything she had here. Could she do that? Would Jenna and Nic and Jake, especially, be okay with her taking off and having her own life? It wasn't too unexpected. Okay, maybe it was. But she wasn't too old she couldn't make a change. Make life what she wanted it to be.

She could have her dream after all.

Caisey opened her eyes stopped short of speaking to an empty room. Gabe was gone.

She shot up and ran for the front door. She flew outside, leaving the door wide. He was on the street, by his car. His eyes were dark, his shoulders slumped. And Caisey knew then that she would use every bit of what she had inside her so that he never looked that way again. Not if she could help it.

"Gabe!"

His head whipped around. "Case—"

She ran, full speed and saw him brace the last second before she slammed into him. He lifted her and then they were kissing. Caisey wrapped her arms around his neck, her feet off the ground as she was held up by his arms around her waist.

Breathing hard, she pulled back an inch. She wanted to be looking into his eyes when she said this. "I'm coming too."

"What?"

"Not right away. I have stuff to take care of. But I'll be there."

"You can't give up your life."

Caisey shook her head. "I'm not giving it up, just changing it. Hopefully for the better. I don't want to lose this, what we have. What we've always had."

"Neither do I, but—"

"No buts. I'm doing this and you can't stop me."

Gabe chuckled and set her on her feet. "I believe you. But this can't be what you want. What about the FBI, Case?"

"What about it? Liam said it. This job isn't me. I was trying to prove I was better than my dad by taking care of my family. But I'm not the one who holds that job. I don't have to stress, I can let God take care of them and then I just do my part instead of killing myself trying to fix everything."

"That's good, Case. But—"

"Stop saying 'but'!" She laughed. "Are you trying to talk me out of coming with you?"

"No, but—" She smacked his shoulder and he laughed too. "I need to know this is what you want."

"Okay, that's fair." She sucked in a breath and blew it out, trying to collect her thoughts when it felt like the whole world was rushing through her brain. "I'm doing this for you. For us. Not just because I want a change or because I want to be the Buckshot sheriff so bad. It's all of it. I get to have that life and I get to have it with you. And that is what I want. All of it. Not some of what I want. I'm being offered everything I ever dreamed. There's no way I'm walking away from that."

"Well...okay."

Caisey laughed. "That's it?"

"I guess I'll see you in Buckshot, then. We can make a plan. How do you feel about tearing down the cabin and building a house?"

"I'd be okay with that." Caisey smiled wide, thinking that might be a lot of fun. "Is this really happening?"

Gabe smiled. "Seems like it. I'm wondering when I'm going to wake up and find out I'm still living in the cabin and I never ran into you, and this whole thing was a dream."

"I really hope not."

"So you're really coming? Giving up your life for Buckshot?"

"No, for you."

"For real?"

Caisey sucked in a breath. "There's a lot to sort out here. That might take a while, making sure Jake is steady and Jenna and Nic will be fine. But as soon as I can I'll be there." She grinned. "I kind of can't wait."

"Me neither."

Gabe gathered her up in his arms. His lips touched hers and he said, "See you soon."

The movement of his mouth tickled her lips. Caisey smiled and kissed him.

~

"THIS IS REALLY WHAT YOU WANT?"

Caisey stared out the window from inside Burkot's office, but all she could see was Gabe. He was why she was doing this, and she couldn't help but smile at the prospect of what that life would hold. Connection. Marriage—if they could work it out. Being the sheriff of a small town. It was a lot of change all at once, but if she didn't make that move it would be too easy to let what could be slip away.

Now that she'd decided to leave, it was weird being here at the office. Turning in her badge and gun and saying goodbye to everyone. She'd served out her time and now she was ready for a new era. So long as she could smooth the path with her family.

She smiled to the window. "I'm not going to assume you'll understand, but this job just doesn't feel like me anymore."

"Did it ever?"

Caisey turned back, eyes wide.

Burkot gave her a gentle smile. "I won't say I'm happy about this, or that you shouldn't just suck it up and carry on. But it's your choice. I can't force you to stay just because you're one of my best people."

"I am?"

He snorted. "Always fishing for complements. Yes, one of the best, because you have heart, Caisey Lyons. Although it usually takes an act of congress for you to show it."

Caisey laughed. "Yeah, I can see that."

"Your father was the same way." Burkot swallowed. "He was a great agent. Decisive, steady...just like you. He buried that heart the way I've seen you do, too, and thought he shouldn't feel anything, or didn't want to. It's hard in this business to feel too much. It takes its toll. It gets to you and I saw it get to him, regardless of how he pushed it away. I saw the light go out in him." He paused. "I'm glad you're not going to let that happen to you."

"Thank you, sir."

He smiled. "At this point you can probably call me Richard."

Caisey smiled, although there was no way on earth she was going to call him by his given name. Talk about super freaky. Burkot was Burkot, and until three seconds ago, she hadn't even known what his first name was.

Caisey released the clip on her gun holster and laid it on the table. "Why does it feel like I'm not strong enough?"

"Now you want me to talk you into this? You've made this decision already. Are you going to change your mind now?"

Caisey frowned. "No. I just don't want anyone to think I've given up."

"What does it matter what they think?"

"I guess not much."

"You'll be sunning yourself in Tahiti and they'll only be badmouthing you because they didn't have the guts to do it."

Caisey laughed. "I'm going to Buckshot."

"Seriously? No one is even going to believe that. I'll just tell them the Tahiti story."

Caisey took out her badge, sucked in a breath and laid it on the desk between them. "I want to say thank you for everything you've done. You were a great boss. The best."

Burkot pointed at her. "Don't get all weepy on me now, woman. You'll ruin the moment."

Caisey stopped herself before she rolled her eyes. "I'll see you around?"

"That won't do." Burkot rounded the desk, shaking his head and pulled her in to a bone-crushing hug. He slapped her back. "Take care of yourself, Lyons."

"You too, sir."

Caisey walked back to her desk, wincing. Liam smirked, but it fell away quickly. "Everything go okay?"

She stopped before her desk, the last time she would be here. "I guess." Something flickered at the edge of her vision and she looked up. Liam held up a slice of cake on a paper plate, a single lit candle perched on top. "It's not my birthday."

He smiled. "This is 'goodbye' cake. So they got the good kind because, just like every other office in corporate America, we celebrate milestones with a sugar rush from mounds of frosting."

She came around and reached for it. "I could do mounds of frosting."

An hour later, Liam drove her home.

Caisey turned to him, remembering the last time he dropped her here after she'd been abducted. Liam must have read her face, because he said, "Don't get all weepy on me now."

She laughed. "That's funny. Burkot said something similar."

"That's because we are both men. We don't do tears, unless it's our wives."

"You're not married."

"That means I don't have to deal with teary-eyed women at all, until that special day." He smiled. "You'll be back for the wedding?"

"Who else is going to make a spectacle of themselves in front of your Ivy-League family?"

He laughed. "Like I said, it'll be a special day."

"What are you going to do without me?"

"I know. They're going to stick me with the next new guy, fresh off the plane from Quantico and he'll do nothing but complain about how he wanted to be sent to Miami."

Caisey patted his shoulder with zero sympathy. "You can do it. It's all about shaping young minds and hearts into sharp agents for the F-Bee-Eye."

He laughed. "Right."

Liam walked her to her front door and gave her a hug for the first time since they'd known each other. His frame was bigger than Gabe's and he smelled like that fancy Ivy- League cologne he wore. He grinned. "Later."

She leaned back. "Later."

FORTY-FIVE

Liam drove back to work and walked straight into Burkot's office without knocking. "She needs protection."

Burkot looked up. "Everyone is working the case. There's no one to spare to sit on Caisey when she's leaving town anyway."

"He knew she was FBI when he took her. The Chloroform Killer played his game and then he still showed up again here just to taunt her."

His boss leaned back in his chair. "You think he's going to take her again?"

"We can't rule it out." Liam folded his arms. "If you're not going to make it official, I'll protect her myself. Call in some favors, get her covered until she leaves town. If the Chloroform Killer is fixating on her we can't leave her to swing in the wind."

"Agreed," Burkot said. "The team is locating every tan-colored seventies RV in the city. It's a long shot, but at this point it's all we've got."

Liam nodded.

He'd have to call Gabe. The man wasn't trained, but he at least needed to know Caisey could be in danger so he could watch out for her. Liam also needed to put in a call to Deputy Kurter to do the same. His partner hadn't come this far only to lose out now, on the brink of the rest of her life.

"I'll ask around, see who's willing to give up some personal time to keep Caisey safe until she leaves."

Burkot nodded. "I'll take the first shift."

~

THE HOUSE WAS quiet when she let herself in. Caisey pocketed her key and yelled, "Anyone home?"

"In the kitchen!"

Jenna was stirring pink bits of chicken around a pan and she didn't look up. "I thought you'd be gone already."

She was pouting.

"Like I'd leave without saying goodbye? Off to my new life in a new town, with Gabe." "Are you really going to live in that rinky cabin of your dad's?"

"Uh, no, since it got trashed. We're going to build a house on the land."

Jenna nodded to the pan. "Great views."

"So where's Nic? You guys didn't..."

Jenna turned. The first sign of life. "He just went to talk to his insurance adjustor. He's coming back for dinner."

"And you're making him that chicken thing, with the honey?"

Jenna laughed. "Yes, I'm making it."

"Pulling out the big guns. I like it. He'll love it so much he'll probably ask you to marry him by the end of dinner." Jenna's face flickered over to hopeful. "You want him to!" Caisey laughed and hugged her friend. "I'm glad for you."

"You're not the only one with a future to look forward to."

Caisey sobered. "Now all we have to do is convince Jake it's the case for him too."

"Pretty much." Jenna turned back to her chicken. "When are you leaving?"

"I'm not sure. It depends how long it takes for the house to sell. Are you sure you're okay with this?"

Jenna shrugged. "Why wouldn't we be? It's a fresh start for all of us and it's what Jake wants."

"After you're settled wherever, then you can come visit me."

"What if it's longer...than just a visit?"

Caisey frowned. "What do you mean?"

"I mean, what if we moved to Buckshot?"

Caisey stared at her friend. She hadn't wanted to be the one to suggest it, since Jenna might feel obligated to follow her just to keep them all together. She wanted her friend to choose her own life and feel the independence of making and living that choice, since so much had been decided for her.

"If you don't want us to, it's fine. I understand if you want to have your own—"

Caisey covered Jenna's mouth with her hand. Jenna pushed it away.

"I was just saying."

"Well, stop saying. My own life? Is that where you were going?" Caisey rolled her eyes. "Let the record show that I would like nothing more than to have you and Jake and Nic come and live in Buckshot. And since, but for the last week or so, it's been years since Gabe saw his cousin I can safely say Gabe would likely want nothing more either."

"So that's a yes?"

Caisey grinned. "You better believe it!"

Jenna squealed and hugged her.

"Mom?"

Caisey stilled and they both turned to the doorway. Jake's face was pale, his hair matted to his head, and the only color was the purple bruise on his cheek bone. "Yeesh, kid. You look like crap."

"Caisey!"

Jake's mouth flickered. Caisey nearly jumped up and down all over again at another sign of life.

Jenna sighed. "What is it, honey?"

Jake's eyes moved to his mom. "Is it okay if I go out for a while? I want to see Natalia's g-grave."

"I'll drive you." Caisey turned to Jenna. "We'll get something out. Enjoy your dinner with Nic." Jenna blinked. Caisey brushed past Jake and grabbed her car keys. "Come on, Jake. Let's hustle."

He didn't say much while Caisey drove to the cemetery, and she didn't feel the need to say anything that would yank him out of his head. If the kid needed quiet space, she was going to give it to him. She parked the car and pointed the way for him. While Jake wandered over to the headstone, Caisey leaned back against the car.

Twenty minutes later he walked back to her, his cheeks red and his eyes watery.

"Everything copacetic?"

Jake nodded.

"Cheeseburger?"

"Sure."

They climbed in and buckled up. Jake turned to her. "I don't know how to make it stop hurting."

Caisey bit her lip. She couldn't do what she wanted—punch something, or squeeze the breath out of her godson with a hug—she had to hold back her reaction. Despite the fact that he'd seared her to her soul with that one line. She sucked in a choppy breath. "The only thing that will do it is time. Which sounds completely lame, but it's true. For all of us."

Except that Jake had a heap of guilt over what he'd done on top of his grief over Natalia...and Grams.

"Stick close. With the family and with your faith."

"But what if God doesn't want me to get married?"

Sheesh. The kid had years to worry about this. "Natalia was the one?"

Jake nodded; his eyes on the street rushing past out the window. "I thought so. What if there isn't anyone else? Or if I don't want there to be."

"Honestly, Jake, you have a lot of years before you need to worry about that. Let it happen when it's time. Look at your mom and Nic, and Gabe and I. I'm not saying you need to detour the way we all did, but we waited and God brought your mom and I both back around to the people we were always supposed to be with."

"But that was Natalia."

"Or it was always someone else." She squeezed his fist. "And this put you on a journey to *her*."

There was silence for a while, before Jake said, "Are you really leaving?"

Caisey nodded. "Looks like you guys might be coming too."

"Cool."

"Yeah."

Caisey smiled to the road and turned in the direction of home—a journey that would take her to where she was always supposed to have been.

GABE LEANED against his car and sipped bad gas station coffee. He should have been on the road already. He'd have been home by now. Night had fallen and Gabe watched the city lights. He had everything he wanted, but it was here in Denver and not in Buckshot. Not yet, at least.

Caisey had done it. She'd given up her whole life to come to be with him. The whole idea humbled Gabe in a way he hadn't felt ever. No one had ever done something like that for him, it was unreal.

Everything about their relationship was unreal. Seventeen years of longing on the strength of one—albeit fantastic—date and suddenly God throws them on each other's paths again. All so Caisey could get him out from under the threat of his uncle finding him.

And yet what had he done for her? Certainly not quit his job and decide to move to a whole new town. That was for sure. But that was pure Caisey, all in, no holds barred love that was so powerful it took everything she had to give. And Gabe wanted to soak it up.

He pulled out his phone.

It rang twice and then she picked up. "Hey."

He smiled to himself. "How are you?"

"Good. You?"

"Trying to get up the gumption to leave you."

Her soft chuckle warmed his ear. "I'll be there soon. Probably only a couple of days, actually. It didn't take as long as I thought it would to wrap everything up."

Gabe stuck his free hand in his pocket, since it was cold out. "Are you doing okay with all that?"

"Do you want me to have second thoughts?"

He laughed. "Definitely not. But I'd rather you were honest."

"Honestly, I think I'm missing something. Like something should have clicked by now that hasn't."

"About what?"

There was a moment of silence over the line and then she said, "Family. Grams is gone, Jake nearly killed a man, Jenna and Nic are together now and it's all new and when the stress wears off are they going to be solid? And why am I worrying about this anyway, their relationship is none of my business except when Jenna gets mad at Nic and she'll want to unload on me."

His lips twitched, but he needed to know something. "Are you worried about us?"

"No. Of course not, we're like...destined."

Gabe laughed.

"What?"

He laughed harder. "I might go back to Buckshot for a day, get everything I need and come back to help you move."

"I'd like that."

He smiled and glanced at his shoes. "Thank you."

"For what?"

"Everything."

"Oh. You're welcome."

Gabe gripped the phone. "I'll see you soon."

"Bye Gabe."

FORTY-SIX

Caisey set the phone down on the coffee table and picked up the open Bible to see what whoever left it there had been reading.

If anyone comes to me and does not hate father and mother and wife and children and brothers and sisters, yes, and even his own life, he cannot be my disciple.

She tossed the Bible back down. Hate your family? Sometimes the Bible really didn't make sense. She looked again and saw a note penciled in the margin.

Love for Jesus so strong that other loves are hatred in comparison.

Okay, that made more sense. Still, sometimes the faith she was supposed to have asked so much of her. Couldn't she just believe, and that was that? Why did it take so much work to live a certain way and make sure you were in the "right" all the time?

Caisey got up and walked to the front window. Maybe a simpler life was what it took. Small town people, a small town job. Chasing a serial killer had taken its toll, and not just in the scar on her leg. Before she left, she needed to talk with Amanda one more time. Maybe get her email so they could contact each other. The irony of actually wanting to talk with a shrink after being adamantly opposed to the idea wasn't lost on her. But when she could see it help her process the funk her brain was in, she didn't much care what it said about her.

Her family still loved her.

And yet, she was supposed to love Christ so much more. Even when so much of Christianity felt like "supposed to". Maybe she needed to get back to basics. Maybe she and Gabe would have time to talk about all this when she got to Buckshot. In the meantime...Caisey put her forehead against the window and closed her eyes.

God, help me love you more. I'm not sure about the hatred part, but show me what it means. I'd like to love you like that...all consuming, like Liam does. When have I ever felt like that? Show me the way.

She opened her eyes. And saw a familiar car parked across the street.

Burkot was here?

Caisey turned to get her phone and froze. He came at her fast, shoving that chemical- soaked cloth in her face.

She swung her arm back and hit the window with her hand. Thank the Lord for old windows, it broke the glass. She sucked in a breath at the pain.

Then everything went black.

~

BURKOT HIT the front walk and barreled into the house. The alarm blared and he swept through to the living room. Blood ran from the crack in the window.

Footsteps pounded downstairs, but he ignored Caisey's friend and her son and raced for the back door. It was wide open. Burkot's breath came hard and fast as he ran down the backyard to the open gate, past the garage he knew they never used. The street behind the house was empty, but for an RV that sped away. It barreled around the corner.

Burkot pulled out his phone and ran back through the house. "What—"

He hit the kid's open hand with his shoulder and kept going. "Conners."

"She's gone! West toward Highlands, I want everyone with me. Now. Call everyone."

He jumped in his car and hit the gas.

~

AN HOUR OUT OF DENVER, Gabe's phone rang. He didn't recognize the number. "Hello?"

"Turn around."

"Liam?"

"When I get Caisey back, she's going to want you. Turn around."

The line went dead.

~

BURKOT PRESSED the button on his radio. "Suspect is travelling south on Speer."

He pressed the gas, not caring if the guy knew Burkot was on his trail. He couldn't kill Caisey while he was driving.

Ten cars ahead, the Chloroform Killer changed lanes, that ugly RV swinging with the movement like it might topple over at any minute.

"I'm five minutes out." Special Agent Liam Conners voice was full of desperation. Burkot understood that. He didn't want to lose an agent tonight, not this way. The Chloroform Killer needed to be brought down and while he hated that it was going to be because one of his agents had been abducted again, it would be the end.

They were right by Elitch Gardens when a semi changed lanes and Burkot lost sight of the RV. He hit the gas and felt the car strain against the sudden rush of horsepower. He got around the minivan in front of him.

The RV was gone.

Burkot slammed his palm against the steering wheel and cursed.

He snapped up the radio. "All units, I've lost sight of him."

Scanning the area, he saw the RV on Auraria parkway. He radioed it in and raced to the next exit to double back.

~

LIAM WAS at a stoplight on Colfax, making his approach from the south when the RV crossed in front of him.

He swung out of his lane, into oncoming traffic, and straddled the center line until he was close enough to cut between two cars and take the turn.

Horns honked, but Liam didn't take his eyes from the RV.

It pulled off the main street, took two more turns and pulled into the parking lot of a rundown old church.

Liam pulled over on the street. His radio crackled on the seat.

He reported in one last time, and then got out.

~

CAISEY BLINKED, unable to do anything else as he walked over and crouched. His orange beanie was lit up by the glow of the RV's interior lights.

She was lying on a plastic sheet at one end of the vehicle where the interior had been ripped away down to the walls. Opposite her was a shelving unit stacked with folded plastic sheets, carefully labeled with dates.

All those dead women and Caisey hadn't done a thing to help them.

His eyes scanned her face. What should have been a scream emerged from her throat as a low moan, full of desperation. His forehead crinkled with a frown and a wisp of breath escaped from between his lips. "I don't understand."

Caisey didn't either. It wasn't like she'd asked to be the subject of a serial killer's obsession.

"You look nothing like my Amy."

Caisey squeezed her eyes shut. Love got so twisted. This was an extreme example, but all the details of this man's life and how it had unraveled to the point where his choices brought him to this place would no doubt include all the requisite milestones of criminal pathology.

And here she'd been so caught up in the people she loved that she'd lost sight of her faith and the love she should have for God. If only she could have learned it without having to get here, to this point, before she had that realization.

Where are you, Burkot?

He'd been out front, and she prayed he saw her smash the window.

The Chloroform Killer stood. "You are still going to die."

He stepped back, toward the front of the RV where the driver's seat was. The windshield had curtains pulled across. No one knew she was here.

No one would find her.

"Now—"

The door burst open. Caisey saw only Liam's arm before he fired twice into the Chloroform Killer's chest.

Caisey turned to the side and tossed up her dinner. Her hands shook but after Liam made sure the killer was dead, he came over and she had enough presence of mind to be able to speak. "I want Gabe."

LIAM NODDED and then he looked at the Chloroform Killer. "Charles Timson."

Caisey's head whipped around. "Who?"

"The hiker who found Emma's body."

An army of boots crossed the parking lot and the first up the steps into the RV was Burkot, his gun drawn. "Apparently I should have made a point of telling you to wait for the rest of the team."

Liam didn't say anything. It wasn't worth arguing with his boss and getting in even more trouble than he already was.

"Can I go to Buckshot now?"

Burkot's face remained dark, but Liam would have sworn he saw a smile in the man's eyes when he looked at Caisey. His face whipped around to Liam and the light was gone. "Conners. Wrap it up."

"Yes, sir."

EPILOGUE

Six Months Later

The sheriff's uniform was uncomfortable, not to mention it was made for a man, or at least someone with no hips. But to be fair, Caisey figured if that was the worst she had to complain about, small-town life couldn't be that bad.

Was this life going to be like a new car, where it took a whopping three thousand miles before you got used to it? It'd been tempting to put the sheriff's decal on her rust bucket, but she splurged on a brand new Jeep instead. But not black, like Gabe's. She'd picked red, because matchy-matchy couples who dressed alike and drove the same car were just sad.

Maybe when their house was finished and they were done with marriage counseling and finally said 'I do', then she would be able to settle. Living at the bed and breakfast in town was too nomadic for someone who'd spent the majority of their existence in one house. Although, coffee and breakfast already hot when she walked downstairs was pretty good.

Caisey crossed Main Street to Gabe's bookstore. It was sunny out, but still chilly. Or 'nippy' as Grams would have said. Caisey knew in her head that Grams was gone, but it didn't really feel like that when she remembered. She'd expected to get hit with the loss each time, the way Jenna seemed to. But for her, the memories were solace, not pain.

The bell over the door rang. Caisey smiled, seeing Gabe attending to two old ladies who were trying not to make it obvious they were checking him out. He glanced up and relief washed over his face. Caisey strode over.

Gabe tucked her under his arm and gave her a smile. "Hey, stranger."

The old ladies sighed and Caisey glanced at them. "Sorry girls, he's taken."

One gasped and the other started laughing. Caisey chuckled and looked at Gabe. She swallowed the laughter. Evidently, he didn't think it was that funny.

Gabe rang them up, and both of the ladies complemented Caisey on what a cute couple they were before they finally left.

When the door shut, Gabe sighed and came out from behind the counter. Caisey hopped up and sat on the edge, but the detritus on her belt clanked against the surface. This whole "sheriff" thing was a work in progress. Sort of like her.

Gabe put his hands on either side of her and gave her a short kiss. Caisey pouted and he laughed. She grabbed the back of his neck and laid one on him.

When she let go he was still laughing. "You would think I didn't just see you at breakfast."

Caisey smiled. "That was ages ago."

Gabe rubbed his stomach. "Yeah, but those spicy eggs Mavis makes sure stuck around."

She laughed. "Did you hear from Nic?"

"Yeah, they're finally heading up this weekend. We should barbeque or something when they get here."

"Sure, we can haul your grill over to that monstrosity Nic thinks is a house."

"Or..."

Caisey frowned. "What did you do?"

He grinned. "I might have got them a new grill as a wedding-slash-housewarming present. It's cool. It has gas and you can use charcoal if you want and, get this, it has a smoker on the side."

"Good. It'll match the house." She shook her head. "I know he grew up with money, but that thing is ridiculous. I thought our place was going to be too big when I saw the blueprints. We'll be rattling around in there, with all those bedrooms."

"It won't be so empty once it's full of kids."

"Oh, are you going to take care of them while I'm at work?"

He laughed. "I could bring them here. No TV and plenty of stimulation."

Caisey shrugged. "At least the old ladies in town will be coming over for a different reason."

He studied her. She almost squirmed over what was coming, but managed to hold out until he said, "You do want kids, don't you?"

She shrugged. "Sure I do." In theory. She narrowed her eyes at him. "How many?"

"You're the one who has to do that—" he motioned to her stomach, "—stuff. Why don't you tell me?"

Caisey folded her arms. "One."

"Five."

She narrowed her eyes. "Three."

Gabe grinned. "Done."

That was when she knew she'd been played. He'd only wanted three. "Anything else?"

He nodded. "Let's not take forever. I'm not exactly young now, but I don't want to wait a whole lot longer and wind up being ancient by the time they graduate high school and we finally get our quiet space back."

She hadn't even thought of any of that. She just liked the idea of three because two would fight, so they'd need a referee. Although, with three, did one get left out? And when did he figure all this out? Caisey was still reeling from the move.

"You look freaked."

"Me?" She huffed. "I've dealt with way more scary things than tiny people who poop too much and keep you up all night."

He laughed. "Or maybe that's the scariest thing you'll ever do.

Way scarier than being abducted by a serial killer. Uh...twice. But you won't be alone. We're doing this family-thing together."

"Promise?"

Gabe touched his lips to hers. "For always."

"I like that."

"I'm glad."

"Well, gotta run. You know. The sheriff can't be seen necking with the hot-guy bookstore owner when she should be booking old men fishing without a license and the librarian for going thirty-seven in a thirty-five." Gabe's chest rumbled with laughter. She pushed his shoulder aside and jumped down. "I'm on 'til seven. What are your plans for later?"

"I was going to pick up two specials after I close up and see if the sheriff has time to eat dinner with me."

Caisey looked back at him, one hand on the door frame. "I'm pretty sure she'll be available."

ALSO BY LISA PHILLIPS

Other Books in the Denver FBI Series:

Target

Bait

Prey

Available on ALL major eBook platforms!

Also, check out the Last Chance County series of books at
https://lastchancecounty.com

ABOUT THE AUTHOR

If you enjoyed this book, please leave a review at your favorite retailer and be sure to follow me on social media to find out about new releases, updates, and other exciting events!

Visit my Website to sign up for her mailing list to and learn about other books she has written and get FREE books!

https://www.authorlisaphillips.com

Made in the USA
Las Vegas, NV
05 February 2024

85298826R20249